Emile Michel, Elizabeth Lee

Ruben's Life, Work and Time

Vol. 1

Emile Michel, Elizabeth Lee

Ruben's Life, Work and Time
Vol. 1

ISBN/EAN: 9783337226381

Printed in Europe, USA, Canada, Australia, Japan

Cover: Foto ©Raphael Reischuk / pixelio.de

More available books at **www.hansebooks.com**

RUBENS

1

Portrait of Rubens.

(WINDSOR CASTLE.)

RUBENS

His Life, his Work, and his Time

BY

ÉMILE MICHEL
MEMBER OF THE INSTITUTE OF FRANCE
AUTHOR OF "THE LIFE AND WORK OF REMBRANDT"

TRANSLATED BY
ELIZABETH LEE

IN TWO VOLUMES
VOLUME I

*With Forty Coloured Plates, Forty Photogravures
and Two Hundred and Seventy-two Text Illustrations*

LONDON: WILLIAM HEINEMANN

NEW YORK: CHARLES SCRIBNER'S SONS

MDCCCXCIX

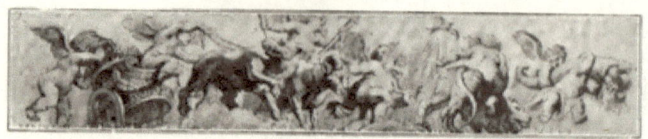

FRIEZE FOR THE DECORATION OF WHITEHALL.
(Engraving by L. Vorstermann after Rubens.)

PREFACE

ENGRAVING FROM THE DRAWING-BOOK.
(Drawing by Pontius after Rubens.)

RUBENS is one of the greatest names in the history of art. His magnificent career, his relations with crowned heads, the events in which he played a part, and far above all these his brilliant genius and the prodigious sum of his works, all combine to give him his high place. But his very fertility and the universality of his gifts have been obstacles to a satisfactory account of his life and his works. Periods of his career, however, and different phases of his inexhaustible activity, form the subject of numerous and valuable monographs. In recent times, the researches of scholars and critics in France, in Germany, and particularly in Belgium, where Rubens has always been held in high honour, have resulted in important discoveries concerning the man and his works. In my attempt to tell the story of his life in these volumes, I have largely availed myself of these scattered publications. The very abundance of the material was to a certain extent a difficulty, because, after I had gathered it together I had to verify it and co-ordinate it before fusing it into the present study.

Rubens's history is well known. His correspondence, although only a portion of it has been preserved, is voluminous, and his contemporaries wrote of him in great detail. We owe much information concerning him to Sandrart, who knew him personally. After his death the facts he had collected were supplemented by the biographical notes furnished to Bellori and De Piles by Philip Rubens, the artist's nephew. But it is only in our own day that these various statements have been properly verified. A Dutch scholar, R. C. Bakhuizen van den Brink, was the first to penetrate the secret of the place of the artist's birth and of the mysterious events that determined it. For the Italian period, M. Armand Baschet's fortunate discoveries in the Archives of Mantua have enlightened us concerning the length of Rubens's visit to Italy, his life at Vincenzo Gonzaga's court, the varied means of instruction he found there and the first pictures he painted. To Cruzada Villaamil and to Justi we owe interesting details of his two missions to Spain, of which M. Gachard has given a careful account in his *Histoire Politique et Diplomatique de Rubens*. Several collections of Rubens's letters have been published, annotated by Em. Gachet, Carpenter, Sainsbury and Ad. Rosenberg. The recent publication of a fine edition of Peiresc's letters, with excellent notes by M. Tamizey de Larroque, throws much new light on Rubens's visits to France and on the friends there with whom he carried on a regular correspondence.

But we owe the most important works on the subject to Rubens's own countrymen, whose efforts to make him better known, best honour his memory. Antwerp has never neglected him, and the third centenary of his birth, celebrated there in 1877, stimulated the production of studies concerning him. Numerous documents dealing with his life were published in that year by M. P. Génard, and two years later appeared the *Histoire de la Gravure dans l'Ecole de Rubens* by M. Henri Hymans, since completed by his remarkable monograph on Lucas Vorstermann (1893). The foundation of the *Bulletin Rubens* in 1882, under the patronage of the town of Antwerp, formed a centre for, and gave a fresh impulse to, the researches of all the great master's admirers, and it was soon followed by the publication of the *Correspondance de Rubens* (1887), under the same patronage, edited by Ch. Ruelens. M. Max Rooses, the distinguished curator of the Plantin Museum, has contributed more than any one to revive research connected with the life and works of his illustrious fellow citizen. In his *Histoire de l'Ecole de Peinture d'Anvers*, M. Rooses naturally gives the largest space to Rubens, the head of the school; he has erected a veritable monument to him in an important work, his *Œuvre de Rubens* (1886-1892), the result of long, conscientious researches in the archives and galleries of Europe. On the death of M. Ruelens, it naturally devolved on M. Rooses to continue the publication of the *Correspondance de Rubens*, the second volume of which has just appeared. Although it seems that a large number of letters written to and by the artist are lost—those of Spinola, for example, of which Rubens himself said that he had "a century"—we may hope that the future has still some interesting discoveries in store for us. Quite recently, access to the papers at the Château of Gaesbeck, which we owe to the kindness of the Marchesa Arconati-Visconti, resulted in the discovery of a complete copy of Rubens's will and of the accounts concerning the liquidation of his property, only extracts from which had hitherto been published.

b 2

There are also numerous critical studies of Rubens's works. In his own time, Sandrart and Huygens, and soon after Roger de Piles and Félibien in France, wrote of him with much penetration. I thought it would be of interest to recall these opinions of a bygone age, and I have sometimes placed beside them those of Eugène Delacroix, a zealous worshipper of the master, and those of Fromentin, whose *Maîtres d'Autrefois* contains many noble passages full of discerning and judicious criticism of Rubens.

As was the case in my book on Rembrandt, it has not been possible to give a complete catalogue of Rubens's works here. Smith was the first to compile a list (1830-1847), which has since been enlarged and corrected by M. Max Rooses. His work has been the most frequent guide of my own researches and I have borrowed freely from him : it is but just that I should here note my grateful sense of obligation to him. I refer those who wish to study all Rubens's productions separately, and to learn the conditions under which they were commissioned or executed, to the five volumes of M. Rooses's work. It will be easily understood that I could not enter into such minute detail; the briefest description of the 1,200 paintings and 400 drawings which form approximately the sum of the master's production, would fill more than the space afforded by these volumes, in which I had to narrate his life and to attempt some criticism of the works that seemed to me most characteristic of the suppleness and vigour of his genius. I have thus restricted myself to the mention at the end of the book of the buildings and the public and private collections which contain his most numerous or most important works.

The greater number of the illustrations in these volumes are reproductions of the painter's pictures or drawings, but I have also included portraits of his masters, pupils, and friends ; views of places in which he lived, and a facsimile of his handwriting. We have relied on photography for the reproductions, as the process best calculated to secure accuracy. Although neither photography, nor any other method of reproduction, can give an idea of the master's colour, it ensures the advantage of a homogeneous and absolutely faithful interpretation. Thirty-seven of the forty engraved plates are due to M. Dujardin, one to Messrs. Braun and Co., and two to Herr Loewy, of Vienna. The other forty full-page plates, the greater number of which are in colour, are facsimiles of the master's drawings, and of a few of his engravings. The photographs which we have used were taken directly from the originals, and are by various hands; we have indicated their authors in the table of contents. A large number are borrowed from the fine collection of Herr Hangstaengel, of Munich; he permitted me, as for my book on Rembrandt, to take what I would, with a generosity for which I cordially express my thanks. I also owe the reproduction of photographs executed specially for them, to the kindness of Baron Alphonse de Rothschild, and Messrs. Léon Bonnat, Stéph. Bourgeois, R. Kann, Le Couteux, and Ch. Sedelmeyer.

In selecting the illustrations, I have tried to include, besides the chief works, which were bound to find a place in a book of the kind, many which give an idea of Rubens's universality by the variety of the subjects. I have sometimes reproduced the sketch made for a picture instead of the definitive painting in which his pupils often had as great a share as himself; in these cases the sketch is superior by the vivacity and spontaneity of its execution, and we are certain that it is wholly by Rubens.

The illustrations have, as far as possible, been arranged to follow the chronological order of the text. But the conditions of Rubens's life have obliged me at times to depart somewhat from this methodical order in the distribution of the engravings. In spite of his precocious talent, the artist did not begin to produce very early, and at the beginning of my work I had to sketch the dramatic events in which his family played a part, then to consider the influence of his different masters on his talent, and to speak at some length of the effect of his eight years' residence in Italy on the development of his genius. Later, his diplomatic missions to Spain and England absorbed a large part of his time. Consequently, while certain periods of Rubens's artistic career are marked by an enormous activity of production, in others his creative activity was reduced, and to some extent paralysed. In order, then, to preserve a certain unity in the form of the volumes, I have been forced to increase the number of illustrations in the chapters that would have been almost deprived of them, and to diminish it in those that would have been overcrowded, distributing them almost uniformly throughout the work. I hope to be pardoned the want of absolute harmony between the text and the illustrations, a harmony to which I would have gladly adhered, but which would have suited neither the economy of the book nor its mode of publication.

My studies on Rubens have occupied me for a long period of time. I made my *début* in art criticism with an article on his pictures in the Munich Gallery, published in the *Revue des Deux-Mondes*, in 1877. But I deemed it necessary to revisit all the galleries of Europe in which his pictures are to be found before undertaking this work, in order to give a right proportion to my criticisms, and to examine difficult questions with all due consideration. It also seemed to me useful to seek out traces of the master in all the places in which he lived, in Italy,—notably at Mantua,—in Spain and Flanders, and above all, at Antwerp, the town he loved so well, where the remains of his house, his most important works, the buildings which contain them, and his tomb, still speak of him to posterity. I have, therefore, lived almost exclusively with Rubens for several years; with the help of his pictures, his correspondence and that of his relatives and friends, and of all the documents concerning him, I have endeavoured to penetrate his mind and heart, to learn his opinions, beliefs, character, manners, and the method in which he employed his time. The two inventories of his collections, that of his property and of the books in his library, furnished me with full information as to his spirit of order, his fortune, his tastes, his reading, his eager desire for knowledge, and his extraordinary energy.

Rubens is a world in himself; it takes time to know such a man thoroughly. To gain some idea of him, he must be carefully studied under the numerous aspects that he presents. If we regard only his exquisite urbanity, the characteristics that are the mark of an aristocratic personality, we should never guess that he loved his home and his work above all things, that he was simple, kindly towards all, helpful and accessible to the most lowly throughout his life. When we consider the claims on his time, and what a variety of occupations filled his days, his extensive correspondence and numerous journeys, it seems scarcely possible that he could have acquitted himself so perfectly of such innumerable tasks. When we think of his diverse gifts, of his taste for science, of his literary culture, of his scholarship, of the political ability that made him the adviser of the archdukes, and the ambassador of Philip IV., we are apt to forget that he was a painter, that he loved his art first, and brought to it all the resources of a wonderful memory, an extraordinary intelligence, a firm will, and unceasing application. I have naturally dwelt most upon Rubens's art; I have extracted his own ideas on it from his writings, and have directed attention to what seem to me

the most brilliant and most characteristic among his innumerable
works.

I shall be satisfied if I have succeeded in preserving a just
proportion between the rich elements of such a noble theme, and
in bringing out the points that constitute the originality of such a
genius.

FRAGMENT OF A DRAWING BY RUBENS.
(Albertina Collection.)

CONTENTS OF VOLUME I

CONTENTS

CHAPTER VI

CHAPTER VII

CHAPTER VIII

CHAPTER IX

CHAPTER X

CHAPTER XI

PHOTOGRAVURES IN VOLUME I

COLOURED PLATES IN VOLUME I

TEXT ILLUSTRATIONS IN VOLUME I

SKETCH FOR THE BATTLE OF TUNIS.
(Berlin Museum.)

CHAPTER I

CONTRADICTORY OPINIONS OF RUBENS'S BIOGRAPHERS CONCERNING HIS BIRTH—
JOHN RUBENS, HIS FATHER, SUSPECTED OF HERESY, IS FORCED TO TAKE REFUGE
AT COLOGNE WITH HIS FAMILY—BIRTH OF P. P. RUBENS AT SIEGEN, JUNE 28, 1577
—RETURN OF JOHN RUBENS'S WIFE TO ANTWERP AFTER THE DEATH OF HER
HUSBAND.

ONE OF RUBENS'S CHILDREN.
(Dresden Print Room.)

THE inscription on the tomb of Rubens's father, who died at Cologne in 1587 and was buried in St. Peter's Church there, states "that he inhabited Cologne for 19 years, and lived for 26 years in closest union with his wife." Save what concerns the length of the union, it must be confessed that the epitaph contains as many inaccuracies as words. The place of Rubens's birth is not more accurately stated in the account which his nephew Philip gives of his uncle—based probably on notes left by Albert Rubens, the great painter's eldest son—an account whence De Piles borrowed the elements of his life of Rubens. According to those writers, Rubens was born at Cologne in 1577. Shortly before De Piles's publication, in some lines placed by C. de Bie under the artist's portrait (1649), the town of Antwerp was designated as the place of his birth ; following De Bie, Bellori, who likewise obtained his information from the Rubens family, Moreri in his great *Dictionnaire Historique* (1674), Sandrart in his *Académie* (1675), and Baldinucci in his *Notizie* (1686) also state that Rubens was a native of Antwerp. The two opposing currents of information have persisted until our own day ; and, in consonance with the mania for absolutely unwarranted legends that prevailed in the art literature of the first half of the present century, writers not only pointed out the house at Cologne in which Rubens was born, but, not satisfied with that, they further imagined that Marie de' Medici ended her life in the same house. At the instigation of those critics, a commemorative tablet was placed on the doubly celebrated dwelling to perpetuate the memory of so remarkable a coincidence.

There is, however, no reason for surprise at so large a number of erroneous statements. They were first disseminated by the persons best placed for knowing the truth. They were made purposely, and the falsehood which was to find credence for so long, and to provoke burning controversies among Rubens's biographers, was inspired by the noblest motives. Like the undiscovered sources of mighty rivers, the beginning of a life that was to run so brilliant and glorious a course, remained veiled in obscurity. His family, instead of throwing light on his origin, purposely took measures to mislead inquirers.

In 1877, when the town of Antwerp was preparing to celebrate the tercentenary of the most illustrious of its sons, and the polemical dispute between Antwerp and Cologne over Rubens's birth was revived in all its vigour, Siegen, a modest town in the Rhenish provinces, interposed with a serious title to the vehemently disputed honour. The moment was ill-chosen for verifying the different claims with the necessary impartiality. The people of Antwerp could not resign themselves to the thought that he whose birth they were about to celebrate with so much solemnity, first saw the light in a foreign land. But however untoward the hypothesis put forward in so inopportune a manner, it was necessary, when the fêtes were over, to examine it, and it was only after defending their ground inch by inch that the Antwerp critics capitulated. Even now, in the presence of what seem to us irrefutable arguments, some of the critics cannot make up their minds to accept conclusions that are generally admitted outside Flanders.

As a matter of fact, the birth of Rubens was accompanied by circumstances more dramatic and romantic than all the inventions of his biographers, circumstances that sufficiently explain the mystery in which the family was careful to envelop it. What interest had his relatives in putting inquirers on the wrong track, and in disseminating as it were, gratuitously, false statements? A simple narrative of the facts to be found in genuine documents exhumed by degrees from the archives will make the reason clear to our readers. The episode in the lives of Rubens's parents initiates us into the manners of a singularly disturbed epoch, and helps us to gain an intimate knowledge of the heroic woman who was the great painter's mother.

Notwithstanding the pretensions to nobility of the immediate descendants of Rubens, the family belonged to the middle class. Instead of the Styrian gentleman who came to Flanders, they declared, in the suite of Charles V., and whom they claimed as ancestor, we find among their progenitors only tanners, or druggists, indeed a series of modest traders long established at Antwerp. Occasionally, a lawyer or a barrister may be found amongst them, and it was probably one of those who, following the custom of the time, fashioned for himself the heraldic device that the great painter, with a few modifications, adopted for his coat of arms. The artist's grandfather, Bartholomew Rubens, was an apothecary. His wife, Barbara Arents, being left a widow, married again; her second husband, a widower, was a grocer named Jan van Lautemeter. Although he already had one daughter, and three children were born of the second marriage, he showed the greatest affection for his stepson, John Rubens, and gave him a careful education. Born on March 13, 1530, at Antwerp he went first to the University of Louvain. His law studies were completed at Padua and at Rome, where, on November, 13, 1554, he received the diploma of doctor *in* _utroque jure._ The young man showed his stepfather the liveliest gratitude, and never ceased to regard him with deep affection. John Rubens returned to Antwerp, and was, in 1562, appointed alderman, an office he exercised for five years. In 1561 he married a young girl named Maria Pypelinx, whose family came originally from the village of Curingen in the Camp-sine; her father, first a tapestry maker and then a merchant, settled at Antwerp, where he enjoyed a modest competency.

CHRIST ON THE CLOUDS.
Albertina Collection: study for the _Trinity_ at Munich.
(From a photograph by Braun, Clément et Cie.)

There seemed no reason why John Rubens should not spend a tranquil and honourable life among his fellow citizens. But at that epoch men whose circumstances appeared most prosperous were exposed to most unforeseen misfortunes. Antwerp was passing through a period of cruel and bloody dissensions. The town, under a rule of absolute religious and commercial liberty, had gradually reached the height of prosperity. The port was the warehouse of the trade of the whole of Northern Europe; every nation had trading houses there, and the relations established between the different elements of so mixed a population naturally created mutual tolerance. In spite of the decrees emanating from the Spanish Court, the Reformation early counted numerous proselytes in Flanders; but, thanks to the secret compliance of the magistracy, who eluded the execution of the rigorous penalties decreed against heresy, they could live there fairly comfortably. John Rubens was himself inclined towards the new doctrines ; but he avoided openly compromising himself. In his quality of alderman, he was more than once charged by the authorities to investigate matters relating to the orthodoxy of suspected persons. Thus in July, 1564, he had to examine the Lutherans, Christopher Fabricius, who eventually paid for his religious opinions with his

PANORAMIC VIEW OF ANTWERP, SEEN FROM THE CATHEDRAL.
Drawing by Boudier. (From a photograph.)

life, and Oliver Bockius, implicated with him in the prosecution. It was indeed a strange epoch, when the magistrate entrusted with such investigations was himself a suspect, and passed for one of the leaders of the Calvinist party. The struggle gradually became more severe ; and controversial pamphlets of an extremely violent tone were issued by both sides. Recognising how greatly it would be to their interest to win over to their ideas so important a centre as Antwerp, Protestant ministers from Germany, Switzer-

land and Holland established themselves there, and found that they
had to contend with adversaries as resolute as themselves.

Closely watched, styled even " the most learned Calvinist," Rubens
tried a devious course ; his courage was not equal to his ardour, and in
order to avoid compromising himself too deeply, he sometimes found
himself compelled to wipe out the effects of his imprudence by capitu-
lations of conscience to which men like him, who wavered and
hesitated between the extreme parties, were exposed. In consequence,
however, of the *Destruction of the Images*, an act that went beyond
his wishes, he consented, at the request of the Prince of Orange, to
serve as intermediary between the magistracy of Antwerp and the
reformers, and with other of his colleagues, he was even set over the
guard of the town gates.

Terrible reprisals were soon to follow. Margaret of Parma,
appointed governor of the Low Countries on August 2, 1567,
demanded of the members of the Corporation an explanation of
their conduct during the disturbances. Delaying their reply, they
were called on to formulate in a written document everything they
could allege in their justification. Thus commanded, the burgomasters
and aldermen set to work to draw up the statement, which was sent
to the Court of Brussels on January 8, 1568. In an exceedingly
voluminous memoir in which John Rubens collaborated, they did
their utmost to exculpate themselves, and to show the efforts made
by them to prevent the propagation of heresy. But on his own
authority the Duke of Alba added cruelties devised by himself to
the rigorous orders he received from the crown, and by the creation
of the *Bloody Tribunal* inaugurated an era of terrible persecution.
To the rebellion of the allied northern provinces for the defence of
their independence, he replied by the execution of Counts Egmont
and Horn in the Grande Place at Brussels on June 5, 1568 ; and on
September 20 of the same year he had Antony von Straelen, the
burgomaster of Antwerp, executed at Vilvorde.

In a dissensious pamphlet circulated at that time, several other
members of the municipality were accused of having compounded
with the rebels, and among them John Rubens was specially de-

II

Children **Carrying** *Fruit.*

nounced. Warned by friends, he determined towards the end of 1568 to quit the country without delay. It was indeed time, for on a proscription list drawn up soon after by the Duke of Alba, Rubens figured as "having already withdrawn to Cologne with his wife, his children, and all his household." As a prudent man, protesting his orthodoxy, Rubens was careful to obtain a certificate from his colleagues on the Town Council of Antwerp, affirming "that in the exercise of his functions as alderman he had always conducted himself in the most honourable manner, and that he deserved a hearty welcome wherever he might present himself." Armed with that testimony, he repaired to Cologne, and asked the municipality for permission to settle there in order to follow pending law-suits, and to attend to various private affairs ; he added that he "left his native land, where he had always conducted himself honourably, neither as an exile nor a fugitive, and without the slightest suspicion of illicit or dishonourable conduct attaching to him."

Among all the towns which at that period received refugees from the Low Countries, Cologne attracted them in the greatest number. Its importance, the tranquillity to be enjoyed there, and the advantages it offered for the education of his children, and for the practice of his profession, determined Rubens's choice. He established himself in a large house in the Weinstrasse, situated between a courtyard and a garden. But if by expatriating himself, he escaped imprisonment or torture, his position was not the less difficult. The property of the exiles was sequestrated, and Rubens, forced amid the new surroundings to earn something to aid in the support of his family, found little opportunity of utilising his knowledge. The Town Council of Cologne, on their part, was not altogether at ease concerning the concourse of strangers who flocked to the town, and who, by their intrigues, might bring it into difficulties with the neighbouring states ; the foreigners were therefore closely watched. John Rubens, pointed out as suspect because he did not go to church, was forced on several occasions to exonerate himself, and to prove the regularity of his conduct and the rectitude of his intentions. Meanwhile, an opportunity presented itself for turning his juridical knowledge to account—an opportunity, however, that was to prove a source of innumerable troubles to himself and his family.

Anne of Saxony, the second wife of William the Silent, the famous Prince of Orange, was then living at Cologne. A portrait of the period engraved without the artist's name, represents her as plain and unattractive, with a high bulging forehead, a flat nose, strange-looking eyes, and a mouth turned up at the corners. The marriage of Anne of Saxony and William was not happy, and in the ill-assorted union the wrongs of the couple were reciprocal. The prince did not pass for a model of conjugal virtue ; his wife, a frivolous and passionate woman, had no more regard for her duty than for her dignity. Her violent reproaches of his infidelities made her insupportable to her husband. William, after the first reverses suffered in his struggle against the Spaniards, begged his wife to join him at the castle of Dillenburg, in Nassau, the cradle of his race, where he himself had been born. He liked to retire to that stronghold, built by his ancestors in a situation which did not permit of sudden attacks, to obtain rest, or to plan new campaigns. He wished Anne to accompany him to the camp, but after delaying her decision for eight months, she refused, saying that she did not possess sufficient courage to face such a life. Settled at Cologne, she endeavoured to obtain the removal of the sequestration placed by the Duke of Alba on the property assigned for the guarantee of her jointure, as well as on that of her husband. She entrusted the defence of her interests to two lawyers, who were, like herself, refugees at Cologne ; John Rubens, and John Bets of Mechlin, a doctor of law, who, compromised by his religious opinions, had been

VIEW OF SIEGEN.
(Fac-simile of an engraving by Merian.)

forced to expatriate himself. In the absence of Bets, who was
defending the cause under his care at foreign courts, Rubens was
left alone with the princess, and as the result of their closer intimacy, criminal relations were established between them. Rubens
often acted as Anne's steward, and accompanied her on her travels.
Finding in 1570 that she was no longer able to keep up the suite she
found necessary at Cologne, she withdrew to the little town of Siegen
which formed part of the domain of Count John of Nassau, brother
of William the Silent, confiding the two children she left at Cologne,

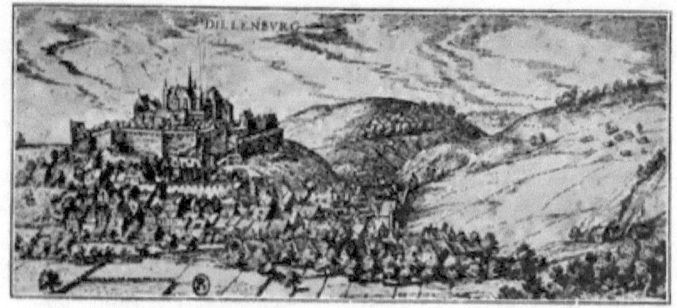

VIEW OF DILLENBURG.
(After an old engraving.)

and the servants who waited on them, to the care of Rubens and
his wife.

Under the pretext of consulting Rubens about her affairs, Anne of
Saxony often invited him to Siegen, and he visited her fairly frequently
at her new abode. As time went on, counting on impunity, they grew
bolder. But the secret gradually leaked out, and rumours of their
relations came to the ears of Count John. One day at the
beginning of March, 1571, as Rubens was on the point of starting
for Siegen to visit the princess, he was seized by Count John's
halberdiers and thrown into prison, first at Siegen, and then in the
Castle of Dillenburg to await the decision of his fate—for according to German law at that time, adultery was a capital crime.
Anne of Saxony was examined, and in reply to questions concerning
her relations with Rubens, gave, at first, a resolute denial. But it is

probable that intercepted letters furnished sufficient proof of her fault, and in face of the fact that the guilty wife was *enceinte*, and gave birth to a daughter in the following August, it would have been difficult to keep up the denial for long. Besides, under the torture, her accomplice made a full confession. Later Rubens tried meanly enough to exculpate himself, and accused Anne of making the first advances. "I should never," he said, "have had the audacity to approach her, if I had feared a rebuff;" and then, believing his end at hand, he demanded death, "so that he might not be made to languish too long." The princess, seeing that it was useless to persist in her denial, determined to avow everything (March 25, 1571), in the hope that Rubens would be allowed to return to his wife and family; for she confessed that "her conscience smote her in no slight degree for having so ill rewarded the unhappy wife for the services she had rendered her."

The secret had been well kept, and Maria Pypelinx's anxiety may be conceived, for not only was she left in ignorance of the cause of her husband's absence, but was without news of him for three weeks. Astonished at receiving no reply after writing to the princess several times, she decided on sending two messengers to try and discover the truth. But on April 1 a letter arrived in which the prisoner informed her both of his fault and of his arrest, and in humble terms asked pardon for his wrongs towards her. The feelings of the unhappy wife may be readily imagined, for with the destruction of her happiness, she foresaw the sad future that awaited her and her family. But stifling the emotions aroused by the double treachery of which she was the victim, she thought only of her husband's wretched situation, and of the dangers that threatened him. She made her decision at once. With all the energy of which she was capable, she determined to make every effort to snatch him from death, and to defend him against those in whose power he was. In order that he should not give himself up for lost, she began by comforting him; she granted him an absolute pardon, and generously desired him not to mention her wrongs.

The sentiment by which she was inspired is so lofty, the terms that she employed are so touching, and breathe so perfect a Christian charity, that it is fitting to let her speak here in her own words. " How could I," she said, " allow my severity to add to your affliction when you are already suffering pains from which I would give my life to deliver you ? Even if a long lasting affection had not preceded these misfortunes, I could never hate you sufficiently to be unable to pardon a fault towards myself. Rest assured that I have entirely forgiven you ; if my pardon was the price that Heaven required for your release, we should be restored to happiness. Alas ! that is not what your letter tells me. I could hardly read it, for it seemed my heart must break. I am so distressed that I do not know what I am writing. If there is no longer any pity in the world, to whom can I apply ? I shall pray to Heaven with infinite tears and lamentations, and I hope that God will hearken, and soften the hearts of your captors that they may spare us and have compassion on us ; otherwise, when they kill you, they kill me." And in order that the guilty husband should never again revert to a subject that must have been painful to him, she added in conclusion, " Never write again ' Your unworthy husband,' for everything is forgotten."[1]

It seemed most likely that the Nassau family, having the author of the offence perpetrated against them in their power, would rid themselves of him with all speed. But a more cautious policy compelled them not to yield to a desire of vengeance. William of Nassau had, by his own conduct, laid himself open to criticism, and, as on the eve of recommencing the struggle against the Spaniards, he had need of all his authority, he felt the evil effects that might result from the divulgation of a scandal which his enemies would not hesitate to use against him. In agreement with his brothers, Counts John, Lewis, and Henry, he determined to keep silence regarding the whole affair, to grant the offender his life, and to give out that his imprisonment was due to political intrigues. Maria Pypelinx's threat to reveal the secret if her husband's life was not spared, helped to save him. So much gained, while waiting until she could obtain his release, she strove to render his imprisonment less trying. In order not to prejudice the Nassaus against her, she promised not to reveal the secret.

[1] Backhuysen van den Brink : *Het Huwelyk van Willem van Oranje met Anna van Saxen.* Amsterdam, 1853 ; 8vo. p. 164.

She preserved a calm exterior, and pretended to be confident of her husband's speedy release. "It is," she wrote, "a continual effort to seem cheerful with death in my heart; but I do my best."

Time passed, and the hope of a speedy liberation, which she had at first been permitted to hold, was not realised. However, she was not discouraged, and thinking that she might plead her cause more effectually in person, she repaired to Siegen, and on April 24 addressed a note to Count John requesting an audience, which he refused. Greatly distressed because for three weeks she had had no news of her husband, fearing either that he was ill or that he was being treated with greater severity, she determined to go to Dillenburg. Immediately on her arrival she asked to be allowed to see and speak to the prisoner, who, informed of his wife's coming, added his entreaties to hers. He observed respectfully to the Count, "that considering how grievously he had offended her, so rare an example deserved pity." He returned to the charge in another letter: "I have deserved my sufferings," he said, "but she is innocent." And he entreated that they might be permitted an interview, if only for a moment, and in presence of any witness appointed by the Count, so that she might at least know "how to reply to those who sought to discover the cause of his detention. And if it is impossible to grant her that favour, let her come outside the walls so that he might see her from his narrow window." The Count remained deaf to their entreaties, and by

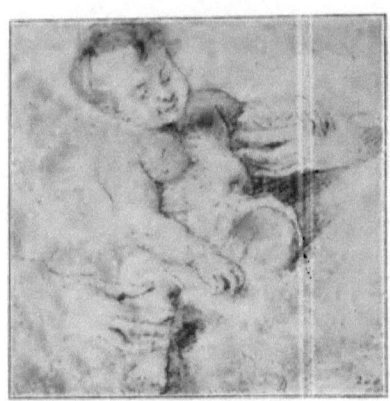

STUDY OF A CHILD
The Louvre
(From a photograph by Braun, Clément et Cie.)

his order, Rubens wrote to his wife not to urge the matter further as her insistance was becoming importunate. There was nothing left for the wife but to resign herself to the inevitable, to return to Cologne, and take up once more her miserable and wretched existence. Nearly two years passed without any important change in the situation and in spite of Maria Pypelinx's efforts, matters did not take a turn for the better until May, 1573. At her instigation an arrange-ment was then made that the prisoner should leave his dungeon on a bail of 6,000 thalers, and, under the express condition of leading a retired life and of surrendering himself prisoner again at the first summons, be permitted to withdraw to Siegen. Maria, having with great difficulty provided the re-quisite sum of money, on Whit Sunday the husband and wife were at length reunited. On that day John Rubens addressed a letter in his affected style to Count John in which, while deprecating any at-

STUDY IN THREE CHALKS.
(Albertina Collection.)

tempt to lend his gratitude "the lustre of ornamental phrases," he paid too high a tribute to the mania that prevailed with some of the men of culture of that period for absurd compliment and fantastic hyperbole.

Once again the Rubenses began a life in common, humble and quiet in accordance with their circumstances, and the pledge Rubens had given not to draw attention to himself. With the greatest difficulty

Head of an Old Woman called " Rubens's Mother."

(THE LOUVRE.)

slanderous denunciations, or what real crimes had once more rendered him liable to suspicion? We do not know; but so implacable a severity left the husband and wife in the utmost distress. Their cup was full. After trying in vain to soften Count John and obtain a reprieve, Maria Pypelinx, driven to extremities by the cruelty of their persecutors, and by the little faith to be put in their promises, reminded them in an eloquent letter, of the terrible sacrifices they had made, of the complete submission and patience of which her husband and herself had given proof, in the face of demands that became more and more unreasonable. Certain that such action was intended to extort more money from her, she threatened to reclaim the bail that she had so uselessly expended, since in spite of formal assurances, her husband's position remained as wretched and precarious as ever. "It is not to be endured," she added, "that after so many trials, and so much mortal anguish, in the decline of life, when our children are grown up and we may reasonably hope for some repose, we should be again overwhelmed, without having given the least pretext for displeasure." And as a suppliant, letting it be clearly seen that her resources were now at an end, she concluded her eloquent petition with an appeal to Count John's mercy and justice.

The firm tone of the letter, which, allowing for some legitimate weariness here and there, contained pathetic notes of pain, did not fail to produce an effect on the minds of the Nassaus. About the middle of October Rubens was granted a reprieve, and after a still more pressing petition, and in consideration of Maria Pypelinx's consent to relinquish part of her claim, the terms of a definitive adjustment were settled. On January 10, 1583, a formal contract assured the Rubenses of their full and entire liberty, without any possible right of action against them. But John Rubens had not much longer to live. His health had been weakened by his distresses; a serious change for the worse set in, and on March 1, 1587, he died at Cologne, at the age of 57. Both he and his wife had, a short time before, returned to the Catholic faith, either from conviction, or because Rubens desired to stand well with the authorities at Cologne. After his death there was no reason why his wife should continue to live abroad, and her interests called her to Antwerp.

Her decision was soon made, and at the end of June of the same
year she returned to her native land, provided with a certificate
from the authorities setting forth that from 1569 to June 7, 1587,

HOLY FAMILY WITH THE CRADLE.
(Pitti Palace.)

the date of the certificate, she had habitually resided with her husband
at Cologne, that she was still living there, and that her conduct and
morals were irreproachable.

PORTRAIT OF A MAN
(Liechtenstein Collection.)

In our exposition of facts gathered from documents in the archives
of the House of Orange, and in those of Antwerp, Cologne, Siegen,
and Idstein, which have gradually come to light, we have spared our
readers the long and violent controversies that have raged over
Rubens's birthplace. With the exception of a few writers, pledged
either by former publications or by patriotic considerations, it is correct
to affirm that critics who have of recent years studied the delicate
problem impartially, have decided in favour of Siegen. As H. Riegel,
who seems to us to have perfectly summed up the question,[1] observes,
the difficulties which surrounded it explain themselves. The family
of Rubens, like that of Nassau, was interested in preserving silence
about the events we have just related. Directly after the doctor's
arrest, the princes tried to hush up the scandal. Policy, and the
desire to maintain the dignity of their race, induced them to conceal
the dishonour. Consequently, all their prescriptions tended to guard
the secret. The guilty persons were imprisoned, and when, later
on, Anne of Saxony was restored to her family, they believed,
or at least pretended to believe, that she was innocent of the crime
imputed to her, since her fault had not been proved by law. If
her accomplice was not immediately put to death, it was in order
to prevent the commotion which his execution would have caused.
After two years of rigorous imprisonment he was sent to Siegen, but
only on the express condition that he was never to show himself in
the town, and that he was at all times carefully to avoid recalling
unpleasant memories.

The Rubenses naturally assented to those wishes. They recognised
how greatly it was to their interest not to rouse the ill-feeling of a
powerful family that had just cause for anger. Maria Pypelinx did not
tell the truth to her nearest relatives ; for them, as for the rest of the
world, her husband was the victim of political intrigues. She
accustomed herself to live in obscurity, and, as she put it, "to bring up
her family without scandal." She carried out her purpose of con-
cealing her unworthy husband's fault with heroic resolution, and kept
the secret to the end. By the one falsehood that may not have

[1] H. Riegel. *Beiträge zur niederländischen Kunstgeschichte. Rubens Geburtsort:*
I. p. 165.

The Small Last Judgment.

(HANNCH GALLERY.)

cost her loyal nature pain, it was she herself who, in the inscription on her husband's tomb in the church of St. Peter, recorded the unclouded happiness that she owed to him. She afterwards upheld the pious subterfuge, and to prevent injury to the honour of her name or to the future of her children, she continued to keep silence about her husband's miserable adventure, and the terrible consequences it brought on her. In order to put ill-natured persons off the scent she invented in all its details the legend of an uninterrupted sojourn at Cologne, of the birth of her children there, and of the tranquil life enjoyed by the family. Her two sons, Philip and Peter Paul, were the only members of it in a position to carry on the legend, for as Veraechter points out in his careful researches,[1] Maria Rubens survived the rest of her children. Three of them, Clara, Henry and Bartholomew, died before the family migrated to Cologne; on November 24, 1581, John, the eldest, had been for more than three and a half years in Italy, and he died in 1600, and in 1606 Blandine, the eldest daughter, followed him to the grave.[2]

But in our opinion neither Philip nor Peter Paul, both born at Siegen, knew the whole truth. The secret was easily kept from them. When the family left Siegen, Philip was only four years old, and Peter Paul not yet one. In consequence then of their age, and of the extremely unsettled existence that both led for a time, nothing was easier for the prudent mother than to allow the impressions that she was anxious to erase from their minds to fade. The family lapse into heresy, the crime and imprisonment of John Rubens, were blots that would compromise their name. During their childhood their mother made them no confidences on those matters; later she did not wish them to blush for their father, and the best, safest, and noblest means of preserving the secret was to keep it to herself. As she was the sole depositary of the facts, she was the better able to conceal them from her sons. When Peter Paul was of an age to question her he was far away in Italy, and he was not to see her again. Thus it was in all sincerity that, in the decline of his life, at the moment when he looked with pleasure on the memories of his youth, the great painter

---

[1] Veraechter. *Généalogie de P. P. Rubens*, Antwerp, 1840.
[2] *Bulletin Rubens*, Vol. I. p. 57.

in a letter addressed to Geldrop, could speak "of the great affection
he had preserved for the town of Cologne where he lived until his
tenth year."

Brought up by such a mother, Rubens owed her much. From
his cradle he had before his eyes an example of devotion to family,
courageous energy, simplicity, perfect tact and temper, and
stoicism under suffering, qualities of which he gave proof during the
whole of his life. But in addition to the qualities he admired in his
mother, qualities which amply justified the ardent affection she inspired
in him, there was, unsuspected by him, a whole past of trials and noble
sacrifice. Even the care which she took to obliterate their traces
testifies to the nobility of her character. Her son knew that she was
admirable, and she was heroic. At length, in spite of the dust
purposely heaped by Maria Pypelinx on the years of exile, and
unspeakable torture, the truth has come to light. It is only just that
some of the glory acquired for her name by the great painter should
devolve on her. She did so much for him in the time of trouble; it
is right that she should share his honour.

COAT OF ARMS OF THE RUBENS FAMILY.

ANTWERP FROM THE SCHELDT.
Drawing by Boudier. (From a photograph.)

CHAPTER II

STUDY OF A CHILD.
Albertina Collection.
(From a photograph by Braun, Clément et Cie.)

WHEN Maria Rubens returned to Antwerp in the middle of 1587 with her three surviving children, she found that many changes had occurred since her departure. During the twenty years of her absence, the unfortunate city had passed through an unbroken period of disturbances and bloody dissensions. In 1576, on the death of Requessens who had succeeded the Duke of Alba, a terrible struggle had taken place between the inhabitants and the Spanish soldiers: the Spaniards pillaged the town, and set fire to the town hall and the adjacent parts of the city. In the midst of such incessant disturbances, the war against the Dutch

rebels continued with alternations of success and defeat, the consequences of which were felt in Flanders. In addition to the general
causes of disturbance, there were accidental risings occasioned by the
ambitions, or the reprisals that such a state of affairs excited. In 1577,
the year of Rubens's birth, the Germans, under the leadership of Colonel
Fugger, directed an attack on the Hansa House, which was successfully
repulsed by the inhabitants. Later in 1583, a rising provoked by
the Duke of Alençon was equally abortive, and his partisans after
attacking the Kipdorp Gate, were pursued through the streets and
thrown into the trenches. Profiting by the discords, Alexander Farnese,
who in September 1578, had replaced his uncle, Don John of Austria,
in the government of the Low Countries, blockaded Antwerp, and
after investing it for a year, forced it to capitulate on November
15, 1585. The Duke of Parma was a clever politician, and knew how
to turn the quarrels of his adversaries to account, and when he died
in 1592, he had succeeded in restoring the authority of Philip II. over
all the Southern part of the Low Countries.

Worn out by incessant struggles, the people of Antwerp were
eager for security and repose. With intelligence and energy they
set to work to repair the ruin and desolation. Religious persecution
had gradually lost its rigour, and by degrees the exiles returned. In
consequence of its exceptional situation the business of the port revived. If there was no longer the activity which, in the middle of the
century, the time of its greatest prosperity, drew to it the trade of
the whole world,—and to such an extent that Guicciardini asserts that
ships had sometimes to wait two or three weeks before they could find
room at the quay of disembarkation—a large number of foreign
trading houses that had been closed at the time of the disturbances,
were re-opened ; and likewise various industries which contributed
not less than trade to the public wealth, such as the weaving of
linen cloth, dye-works, the manufacture of beer, of woollen cloth,
of tapestry, of leather ware and glass, again flourished. The town
hall which had been destroyed during the cruel excesses of the
Spanish Fury, was rebuilt in 1581.

As at Venice and Florence, the more the merchants prospered,
the more did intellectual culture develop among them, and a taste

2

Women and Children in Front of a Fire-place.

(Drawing in Red Chalk.)

(THE LOUVRE.)

for art and literature came to be increasingly honoured at Antwerp. There were three societies of Rhetoric, known by the names of the *Gilliflower* (*de Violière*) the *Pansy* (*de Goudbloem*), and the *Olive Branch* (*de Olyfstack*). They each possessed their armorial device, and held fêtes and meetings to which similar societies from neighbouring towns were invited : on those occasions dramatic representations and allegorical processions, so much in vogue at the time, were organised. Numerous printing-presses spread abroad the works of the most famous ancient and modern authors. The most important and celebrated of those presses was founded by Christopher Plantin, a native of Touraine. A simple workman, Plantin came to Antwerp in 1549, and set up there in 1555 a printing press which through the quality of the work, and the perseverance which was expressed in his motto, *Labore et Constantia*, soon became exceedingly prosperous. In 1576 he located his business if not in the building, at least on the site of the house now known as the Musée Plantin. Carried on after his death by his son-in-law Jan Moretus, about 1500 volumes of a remarkable typographical excellence and often tastefully and lavishly illustrated, were issued from the press. Every subject was comprised in the vast number of publications. Among them were breviaries, polyglot Bibles, works on theology and jurisprudence, geographical atlases by Ortelius and Mercator, and editions of all the classics, carefully revised by distinguished scholars.

In such an atmosphere means of education were not wanting, and at Antwerp, Maria Rubens found all the facilities for her sons' studies that their future careers demanded. Philip, the eldest, before attacking his law studies, perfected himself in literature, a subject for which he always had a strong predilection. Hard working and docile, he would have served at need as an example to his younger brother. But Peter Paul, gifted with exceptional intelligence, early united a love of work with an eager desire for knowledge. He outstripped, and by a long distance, all his school-fellows. Besides a knowledge of French and Flemish, the two languages spoken at Antwerp, and of German which he learned at Cologne, he knew Latin thoroughly, and during the whole of his life he never ceased to read, in the original, the best poets and prose-writers, whole portions of whose works he knew by heart. He was probably initiated into the elements of the Latin language at Cologne, perhaps by the Jesuits, if, as the greater number of his biographers state, he was their pupil. A letter from Balthasar Moretus, published by M. Ruelens,[1] proves that Rubens did not in any case receive instruction from them at Antwerp. Writing to his friend, Philip Rubens, who was at the time in Italy

COURTYARD OF THE MUSÉE PLANTIN, ANTWERP.
Drawing by Boudier. (From a photograph.)

(November 3, 1600), in assuring him of his deep affection he said, "I have known your brother from his childhood at school, and I loved the youth, with his amiable and perfect character." Between July, 1587, and August, 1590, Peter Paul and Moretus, who was three years his senior, attended the same school, and laid the foundation of a friendship which lasted for their lives. In reality, the school was a lay establishment, of which the director, Rombout Verdonck, was, like Rubens himself, buried in the Church of St.

---

[1] *Correspondance de Rubens*, published under the auspices of the town of Antwerp. Vol. I. by Ch. Ruelens, Antwerp, 1887.

Jacques. From the inscription on his tomb, we learn that he was a man as much renowned for his piety as for his knowledge. His school was situated behind the choir of Notre Dame ; Rubens, who then lived in the *Rue du Couvent*, had, on his way to school, to pass Moretus's house, and doubtless often had the company of his young comrade.

It is easy to imagine the affection and interest that such a pupil would inspire in his master. Under his guidance Rubens became a

WORKSHOP OF THE PLANTIN PRINTING ESTABLISHMENT.
Drawing by Boudier. (From a photograph.)

distinguished humanist, but preserved at the same time a large fund of piety. He always remained faithful to the practices of the Catholic Church, and every day, in the early morning, he attended mass before beginning his work. His mother, seconded thus by his teachers, was glad to inculcate in him the religious sentiments which had sustained her during her trials. Those beliefs which, under the influence of so accomplished a mother, took root in the loving heart of the child, were kept alive by the solemnity of the ceremonial of the Catholic worship, held in honour by a people always fond of outward

show. In addition to the ceremonies which appealed to his young
imagination, Rubens gained instruction from the devotional books he
was in the habit of reading, and discovered picturesque episodes in
them, which, consecrated as they were by long tradition, seemed to him
real and vivid. During the journey in Holland with Sandrart in 1627,
Rubens told him that from his earliest youth he took pleasure in copying a large number of the illustrations in a Bible published by Tobias
Stimmer in 1576, which enjoyed a great vogue at that time.[1]
More than once, on days of high festival, Rubens must have contemplated in the great cathedral, or in the streets of the town, the
magnificent progress of imposing pageants and processions—the taste
for them has lingered in Belgium even to our day—the numerous
officiating ministers and the members of the corporations grouped
round them, with their magnificent canopies, their robes of gold
tissue set with precious stones, the varied colours of their rich
costumes, and the tumultuous crowds who assisted at their passage.
In the old church which the pillage of 1566 despoiled of the pictures
that formed part of its decoration, he, who was destined before long
to adorn it with works of a different kind of beauty, felt a vague desire
awake in him to translate by means of pictures, the radiant impressions of light and colour he received there; impressions which,
amid the fumes of the incense, and "the sound of the perfect organs,"
whose harmonies Guicciardini had already described, developed in
Rubens the decorative sense, and the taste for the somewhat theatrical
settings to be seen later in his works. The town itself with its daily
bustle offered at every turn exceedingly picturesque sights. Standing on the other side of the Scheldt, he saw before him the uneven
contours of its pointed gables and numerous buildings, dominated
by the spire of Notre Dame, which greeted from afar sailors returning to their country. Craft of various shapes and colours ploughed
up and down the wide stream of the river, and on the quays near
the cranes which loaded or unloaded merchandise coming from every

---

[1] *Neue Künstliche Figuren biblischer Historien*, Bâle, 1576. Rembrandt must also
have been inspired by Stimmer's religious compositions, and we learn from his inventory
that a History of Flavius Josephus, also illustrated by Stimmer, was one of the volumes
in his library.

IV

*The Virgin and Child in a **Garland of** Flowers.*

(MUNICH GALLERY.)

 Printed by Wittmann Paris (France)

part of the globe, among the heavy drays drawn by the big native horses, an animated crowd presented an ever-changing spectacle of the most diverse types and costumes.

It was indeed a privileged atmosphere for the future painter, and one well calculated to stimulate his precocious talent. But before Rubens was able to devote himself to his vocation, he had to suffer wearying delays. The little family was hampered by poverty; its resources had been exhausted by the sacrifices which Maria Rubens had been forced to make in order to obtain her husband's release. After bringing up her sons, she found herself no longer able to maintain them, and therefore had to separate herself from them. From the will which she made on August 23, 1590, before the marriage of her daughter, Blandine, we learn that they had then both left her in order to try and find for themselves a way out of the difficulty. Philip, who was barely sixteen years old, became secretary to Jean Richardot, then Counsellor of State, and soon to be appointed President of the Privy Council at Brussels. For Peter Paul it had perhaps been a question of devoting himself to the study of law; so at least Sandrart states, according to information derived, doubtless, from Rubens himself [1]; but since his extreme youth did not allow him to obtain employment, he entered the service of a princess of the family of Ligne, the widow of Count Antonie van Lalaing, formerly Governor of Antwerp, as page. The graceful manners and good looks, that judging by the brilliant cavalier he became later, must have already marked the boy, were much in his favour. But finding himself associated with young men destined to wealth and idleness, he soon recognised that he was not intended for a similar life, and unable, as Sandrart also tells us, "to resist the inclination which urged him to painting, he at length obtained from his mother permission to devote himself entirely to it." Recognising her beloved son's enthusiasm and his premature good sense the admirable woman yielded to his desire, happy besides to see him return to her fireside. Although it had not regained its ancient glory, the Flemish school of painting was once more flourishing, and the artistic impulse, formerly spread over Bruges, Ghent, Mechlin, and Brussels, was gradually be-

[1] J. de Sandrart : *Academia nobilissimæ artis pictoriæ.* Nuremburg, 1683, p. 282.

coming concentrated at Antwerp. According to Guicciardini, the art
of painting had for a long while been looked on there as "an
important, useful, and honourable thing," and after mentioning the
masters dead or living who had made the town celebrated, the author
of the *Description of the Low Countries*, added that "nearly all had
been in Italy, some to learn, others to see the antiquities, and to
make the acquaintance of men renowned in their profession; others
again to seek adventures,
and to make themselves
known. And most often,
having fulfilled their desire
in that place, they return
to their own land with
experience, ability, and
honour." Although the
greater number of those
who had formerly given
the artists commissions,
had either left the country,
or suffered losses which
forced them to keep down
their expenses, they found
on the other hand satis-
factory patrons among the
clergy. With the restora-
tion of the Catholic wor-
ship, new churches or

PORTRAIT OF TOBIAS VERHAECHT.
(After the painting by Otto Van Veen.)

chapels were gradually being built. It was necessary to adorn them,
and to restore their former decorations to those which had been
despoiled during the war. Thus with a more stable government,
painters might reasonably hope to derive a sufficient profit from their
work.

Among the painters then settled at Antwerp there were assuredly
many of greater fame than the Tobias Verhaecht to whom the artistic
education of Rubens was first entrusted. But Maria Pypelinx had,
doubtless, little knowledge of the relative merits of the different

artists, and as Verhaecht was her kinsman, she probably thought that he would take a special interest in his pupil, while at the same time he would be likely to render the articles of apprenticeship as little irksome as possible. Born in 1566 at Antwerp, where he died in 1631, Verhaecht in 1590 had just been made free of the guild of St. Luke, of which in 1596 he was appointed dean. Van Mander is contented to mention him as a clever landscape painter, but C. de Bie speaks of him in a more explicit fashion. According to his testimony,

COUNTING HOUSE OF THE PLANTIN PRESS.
Drawing by Boudier. (From a photograph.)

Verhaecht travelled in Italy, and stayed at Florence and Rome, where he painted compositions that were much appreciated "with fine trees, which look natural, and stand out firmly and yet without undue sharpness, against the background." The visits of Rubens to his studio did not leave many traces, for the name of the great artist is not found among the somewhat numerous pupils who studied under him. It is, however, owing to Rubens that the name of Verhaecht has come down to us, for his works would not have been sufficient to rescue him from oblivion. Among those engraved by

Egbert van Panderen and Jan Collaert, we may mention some of the series then greatly in vogue : *The Four Elements, The Four Ages of the Earth, The Four Points of the Day,* with complicated panoramas where the artist accumulates plenty of unexpected objects, mountains, rocks and vast perspectives, peopled with animals and figures, which do not show much study of nature. In the *Night,* which forms part of the *Four Points of the Day,* we notice a fragment of an ancient ruin and a dome vaguely recalling that of St. Peter's, which would seem to confirm the legend of Verhaecht's journey to Italy. Like Lucas van Valkenborch and Peeter Brueghel, he painted a *Tower of Babel,* which was said to be his masterpiece. In the only picture which we know by him, which is in the Brussels Museum, his scanty knowledge is clearly seen in the dull, thin system of colour, in the lack of precision of form, and in the entire absence of character. It is a *Hunting Adventure of the Emperor Maximilian I.,* who, carried away by his ardour in the pursuit of a chamois, advanced to the top of a rock suspended over an abyss, whence he was rescued with great difficulty. Verhaecht did not lose so good an opportunity of recording his early memories of the Tyrol, where the occurrence took place, and the work reveals the poverty of his imagination in as great a degree as the mediocrity of his talent. The picture, signed with his monogram, is, however, dated 1615, that is, more than twenty-five years after Rubens had left his studio, where, in all probability, the young man only stayed a very short time.

He was, on the other hand, to spend four years with Adam van Noort, an artist whose personality has remained somewhat obscure ; and his works, like his life, offer problems which are still far from being solved. Let us state, however, that his life has been unworthily caricatured by fanciful legends which for a long while were complacently echoed by the critics. Some of his biographers represent him as a man of a hard and coarse temperament, addicted to drink, who, if we are to believe them, became brutal after the libations in which he was too fond of indulging. It was, so they say, to escape his bad treatment that Rubens left him. We should remember, however, that Van Mander and De Bie, the first historians to speak of Van Noort, say nothing of his inclination to drunkenness, nor of his difficult temper. The

most recent researches of scholars have done justice to these false imputations by establishing the truth, and the studies of MM. Max Rooses
and Van den Branden permit us now to set down briefly the principal
facts of the life of Rubens's second master. His father, Lambert van
Noort, himself a painter, was born about 1520 in the Low Countries,
and settled at Antwerp, where he spent the rest of his life. Inscribed
on the lists of the Guild of St. Luke in 1549, he received his letters of
citizenship the next year. His *Sybils bearing the instruments of the
Passion*, dated 1565, and other scenes likewise inspired by the narrative
of the Passion—pictures painted for the meeting hall of the guild, and
which are now in the Antwerp Museum—are works of a sufficiently
weak design, of coarse execution, and of somewhat inharmonious
colour. He also worked for the Plantin Press, and the frontispiece
engraved after one of his designs for a *Treatise on Anatomy*, published
in 1566, brought him 3 florins 10 sous.[1] But such works were not
calculated to make their author's fortune, and at the time of his death in
1571, the administrators of the property of the Cathedral, to which
his house belonged, "for the love of God, and by reason of the
great poverty of the defunct," remitted to his children the last year's
rent. Thus his son, Adam, who had adopted the same profession
as his father, was from the age of fourteen forced to earn his living.
It was probably in order to try and improve his position that he went
to Italy, tardily enough, for his name only appears on the lists of the
Guild in 1587. But the previous year he married Elizabeth Neys,
by whom he had two sons and three daughters; the eldest daughter
married in 1616 Jakob Jordaens, Van Noort's pupil. The names of
several notable persons in the Antwerp aristocracy figure in the certificates of baptism of the master's children, a proof of the consideration
he enjoyed, and after taking an active part in the reorganisation of the
Society of Rhetoric, known as *De Violière*, of which he was one of the
most zealous members, he was in 1619 appointed dean. He had,
moreover, acquired a certain competence, for he possessed two houses
in the Rue Everdy, in one of the best parts of the town, of which
one served as a dwelling for his son-in-law, Jordaens, and himself.
They are also both found as witnesses signing death certificates of

[1] *Catalogue of the Musée Plantin*, p. 106.

distinguished citizens with whom they had relations, a fact that demon-
strates the falseness of the accusations levelled against the evil habits
and difficult temper of Van Noort, accusations to which the kind
and placid expression of his honest countenance gives the lie in
Van Dyck's fine etching of him.   Let us recall also, as a further
testimony to the respectability of his long life—he died at the age
of eighty-four in 1641—the excellence of his teaching, and the fact

that, without mentioning
Rubens and Jordaens, Van
Balen, Sebastian Vranex,
and other distinguished
artists were among his
pupils.

If the agreement of so
many moral hypotheses
with positive facts is of
itself conclusive enough
to establish the truth in all
that concerns the artist's
personality, it is unfortunately more difficult to obtain information as to the
value of his talent.   The
only indisputable works
that have been preserved
are unimportant drawings
made for the Plantin Press,
for which he worked like
his father, retaining until

OTTO VAN VEEN.
(After the portrait painted by his daughter Gertrude.)

the end of his life the friendliest relations with the heads of the establishment.   Some of the drawings represent episodes in the *Life of St.
Clara*, which were engraved by A. Collaert ; others are illustrations to
Litanies of the Virgin, executed in collaboration with Pieter Jode for
a collection of prayers published in 1608 ; others, again, to the number
of nine, were engraved in 1630 by Karel von Mallery for the *Sacrum
Oratorium* of Biverus.   In spite of the difference in the dates, the

drawings are insignificant achievements that point to an industrial rather than an artistic end. They are in no way distinguished from the mass of the anonymous publications of the religious picture-trade, of which Antwerp was then the most important centre, publications which spread thence all over Europe, and even into Spanish America. Usually inspired by ecclesiastics, the compositions abound in bad taste and in pretentious subtleties. There is to be found in them the mingling of the sacred and the profane, which, in literature as in art, was so much in vogue at that time. Such subjects, we can understand, were scarcely of a nature to inspire Van Noort : he was content to follow the instructions laid down for him without troubling to be original. Other plates probably executed after drawings of the master, show us his talent in a very different light. A series of the *Five Senses*, also engraved by Adriaen Collaert, reminds us of the familiar subjects treated about this time in Holland by Esaias Van

ADAM VAN NOORT.

(Facsimile of an etching by Van Dyck.)

de Velde or Buytewech. Although Van Noort here showed greater breadth and originality than in his religious compositions, he was far from attaining the force and detailed truth of observation of his Dutch brethren. But in attempting the representation of the nude in the thick set, heavy figures, that without much care for beauty or style, personify the senses, he tried to be original.

There are none of Van Noort's pictures of which the authenticity is certain. The Orphan Asylum, and the Council Chamber of the

Municipal Hospital at Antwerp, possess, it is true, an *Entombment of Christ* and a *St. Jerome* under his name; but it is not possible to legitimise the attribution, either by the origin of the works, or by their execution, which does not sensibly differ from that of the spiritless works of his father, or other mediocre artists of the time. But the case is different in regard to two pictures also attributed to him without more ground, pictures that bear no analogy to the preceding. One of them, a *Jesus in the House of Martha and Mary*, was recently acquired by the Lille Museum, and is a luminous, clever painting, a little hasty in execution, but full of strength and brilliancy. In looking at it, the name of Jordaens naturally rises in the mind, and except for a slight stiffness in the drawing, and a certain hardness in the colouring, it recalls his method of handling in every detail. The figure of Martha, those of the woman entering, and of the grey-haired apostle wearing a whitish cloak, as well as the greyish architecture against which the figures stand out boldly, appear to us characteristic of the manner of Van Noort's pupil. Van Noort has doubtless been suggested as its author on account of its formal resemblance to another and more celebrated picture, likewise fathered on him, which has, however, excited much controversy. We mean the *St. Peter Offering Christ the Tribute Money* in the chapel of the Trinity in the Church of St. Jacques at Antwerp. Perhaps the drapery here is more supple and better modelled, the execution broader and freer, the colour more pleasing than in the Lille picture. We think, however, that the two paintings are by the same hand, but is it the hand of Van Noort? That it seems to us difficult to affirm, and after repeated attempts to solve the irritating problem, we still hesitate to form any conclusion.

Accepting unconditionally the attribution to Van Noort, and regarding the old imputations on the artist's character—now recognised to be false—as true, Fromentin, in a few words, traces a striking but purely imaginary portrait of him.[1] "Van Noort," he writes, "was of the people; he had their brutality, their taste for wine, too, it is said, their loud voice, their coarse, frank speech, their ill-mannered and offensive outspokenness—in a word, everything that was theirs except their good temper. A stranger to society and to academies, he had the culture of

[1] *Les Maîtres d'autrefois*, p. 35.

3

Portrait of a Young Woman.

neither the one nor the other.   He was a painter absolutely by the
qualities of his imagination, by his eye and hand.   Rapid, alert, with a
self-possession that nothing could disturb, he had two motives for
daring much ; he knew that he was capable of doing everything without help from any one, and he suffered from no scruples regarding what
he did not know." Speaking again of his talent, judging from the
Antwerp picture, the only one he knew, and criticising it as " very
characteristic," the author of *Les Maîtres d'autrefois* describes Van
Noort's handling with the fitness and felicity of expression that belong
to him, and deduces naturally the influence that such a painter must
have exercised on Rubens.

M. A. J. Wauters, in his excellent *Histoire de la Peinture Flamande*,[1]
deems it prudent to refrain from affirming what Fromentin affirms.
M. Max Rooses, who, in his turn, attacks the delicate problem, after
setting down all the information that he has been able to gather about
the artist, objects that in the discussion sufficient account has not been
taken of Van Noort's long life ; he may in its latter part have been in
some degree influenced by his two illustrious pupils, Jordaens and
Rubens.   The history of art offers more than one example of such
cross influences in which the master follows the disciple.   According to
that hypothesis, the pictures in the Church of St. Jacques, and the
Lille Museum, might well be by Van Noort ; but instead of leading
to Jordaens, they would have been inspired by him.   The thing is
certainly possible.   It is, however, difficult to answer several of the
objections which present themselves to the mind.   How is it, for
instance, that the drawings of 1630 compared with those of 1608 do not
show the same advance as the paintings ?   If Van Noort painted the
Antwerp *St. Peter*, and the Lille *Christ*, why did he not produce more
works of their value ?   How is it that no intermediate work, marking
the transition between the early manner, so timid and limited, and the
later handling of far greater skill and breadth, is brought forward ?
Since points like those remain undecided, it seems prudent to follow
M. Wauters, and like him, to suspend conclusions that, in the actual
state of our knowledge, do not seem to us to be sufficiently justified.

We are ignorant of the motives that caused Rubens to leave Van

[1] Quantin, p. 196.

Noort's studio for that of the last master from whom he received
instruction, Otto Van Veen, who, following the fashion of the period,
latinised his name into Otto Voenius. But Van Veen besides having
relations with Verhaecht, whose portrait he painted, enjoyed a great
reputation at that time. In contrast to Van Noort, his work and his
life are both well-known, and we borrow from M. Van Lerius[1] the
greater part of our information concerning him.   Born in 1588 at
Leyden, Van Veen was descended from a natural son of John III.,
Duke of Brabant ; his eldest son took great care to have that genealogy
verified and confirmed.   The father of Otto, Cornelis Van Veen,

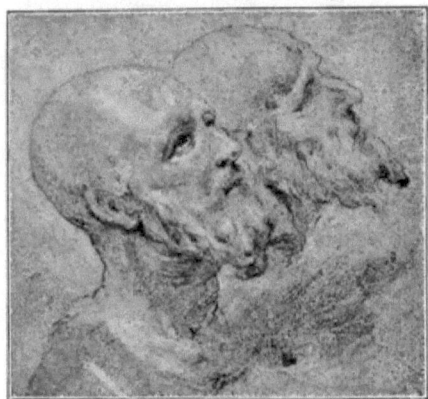

had, on account of his
fidelity to Philip II.,
left his native land,
where his property
was confiscated. Art
and literature were
held in high honour
in his family, and
after a careful educa-
tion, his son, drawn
by an irresistible im-
pulse to painting, be-
came a pupil of Isaac
Klaassen van Swan-
enburch.   The elder
Van Veen settled at

TWO HEADS OF OLD MEN.
Drawing by Rubens.   (Albertina Collection.
(From a photograph by Braun, Clément et Cie.)

Liège, and there Otto was encouraged in his first attempts by Dominic
Lampsonius, the secretary of the Cardinal, the prince bishop of that
town, who, before he put together the information concerning the chief
artists of the north, which he afterwards communicated to Vasari, had
himself been addicted to painting.   Probably by his advice the young
man determined in 1575 to go to Italy, a sojourn beyond the Alps
being then considered the necessary complement of all artistic education.   There he studied under Federigo Zucchero.   On his return to
his native land, Van Veen entered the service of Duke John of

[1] *Catalogue of the Antwerp Museum.*

Bavaria, successor to the Bishop of Liège, as page, and soon inspired in him sufficient confidence to be entrusted with a mission to the Emperor Rudolph II. In August, 1593, we find Otto settled at Antwerp, where he married, probably the following year, Anna Loots, a young girl belonging to a noble family of the town, by whom he had eight children, two sons and six daughters. Gertrude, the second,

born in June, 1602, de-
voted herself to painting,
for she is the author of a
portrait of her father, now
in the Brussels Museum.
There, as in his portrait of
himself, Van Veen appears
as a well-favoured, comely
man.

In fact, he had then
become a personage, and
Alexander Farnese had
attached him to his Court
as military engineer, a circumstance that testifies to
the versatility of his talent.
In 1594 he was admitted
a master of the Guild of
St. Luke, and in 1603-4
held the office of dean.
As he had travelled in
Italy, he was also in 1603
affiliated to the Guild of

INFANT BACCHUS.
Drawing by Rubens. (Albertina Collection.)

the Romanists, founded by the Cathedral in 1572, and there too he performed the duties of dean in 1606. Art did not absorb him to the exclusion of literature. He composed Latin verses, and knowing the classics, he designed illustrations for collections of moral maxims, chosen out of Seneca, Plautus, Juvenal, Valerius Maximus, and others. He also composed *Emblems* for the poems of Horace, with intricate and subtle allegories, calculated to please

the prevailing preciosity, veritable rebuses, fortunately accompanied
by legends, without which it would now be impossible to discover
their meaning. Philosophising on his art, he drew up a *Treatise
on Painting*, of which the manuscript has not been preserved. On the
occasion of the solemn entry of the Archduke Ernest into Antwerp
on June 4, 1594, and a few years later, on September 5, 1599, on
the occasion of the reception of the Archduke Albert and his consort,
Isabella, Van Veen was entrusted with the decoration of the town, and
with designs for decorative paintings, triumphal arches, allegorical
chariots and ships for the same purpose. Later he was appointed
court painter, and enjoyed the honour alone, until Rubens, on his
return from Italy in 1609, obtained the same title. From that moment,
as may be conceived, he was eclipsed by his illustrious pupil, and it
is probably as compensation for the diminution of his importance
that he was made in 1620 director of the Mint at Brussels, an office
which was permitted to descend to his son Ernest. Besides commissions for portraits and pictures from his governors, he received
fairly important commissions from the churches of Alost, of St. Bavon
at Ghent, of St. Andrew, St. Jacques, and the Cathedral at Antwerp.
In that town also the Guild of Mercers commissioned him to paint four
large panels for their Council hall, situated in the Grande Place. Van
Veen acquired a large fortune, and occupied a fine house in the street
which now bears his name, and later, it is believed, a larger one
situated near the Marché St. Jacques. Overwhelmed with favours,
and esteemed by all, he died at Brussels on May 6, 1629, at the
age of seventy-one.

The artist's fertility ran too free a course in the numerous and
somewhat commonplace illustrations that are greatly inferior to his
paintings. The forty plates, inspired by the *History of the Seven
Infants of Lara*, published at Antwerp in 1612, did him no more
credit than the compositions designed the same year for Tacitus's
book on the war of the Romans and Batavians. Notwithstanding
the diversity of the subjects, the drawings derive their absolute
insignificance from the monotony of the artist's work. Van Veen is,
perhaps, even more unattractive, when yielding to his imagination he
contrasts chastity with unchastity, or places opposite Christ's marriage

with the Church, the Devil's marriage with the capital sins. But such violent contrasts, conceived evidently for the purpose of edification, and the affectations and subtleties displayed in them by the artist, were well calculated to delight the cultured minds of the day. Van Veen's early paintings—those, for instance, in the churches of St. Jacques, and St. Andrew, at Antwerp—are not more remarkable. They show a correct, formal talent, but are cold and lifeless. Their stiff style betrays the artist who knew Italy, and had studied and taken pleasure in some of its masters—not always the greatest—and who strove to reproduce in his work the often contradictory qualities of the various painters that attracted him. The involuntary homage rendered by him to those whom he admired, was also shown in reminiscences as frequent as they are little disguised. Thus his compositions lack originality. The invariable purity of the ovals of his heads, and the constant regularity of the features result in insipidity, and the systematic balancing of the groups, the stiffness of the attitudes of the figures, and the too methodical arrangement of the folds of their draperies when confronted with nature savour of the commonplace ; he only succeeded in producing indifferent likenesses, and at a time when the Flemish School included some eminent portrait painters, the coldness and absolute lack of character of his portraits is astonishing. With him we are very far from the force of penetration and the eloquent conciseness with which an Antonio Moro makes the striking figures of a Duke of Alba or of a Mary Tudor live again before our eyes. Commissioned to paint a portrait of Alexander Farnese, Van Veen seems to have mistrusted the result of his work, and to have felt it necessary to have recourse to allegory ; for he represents the Governor of the Low Countries accompanied by Religion, who, club in hand, prepares to fell Heresy to the ground. The large family group in the Louvre, dated 1584, probably executed when on a visit to his relatives at Leyden, reveals his weakness. He could pose his models as he pleased, but the arrangement seems to have been left to chance, and the ill-grouped figures with scarcely defined proportions, completely lack relief and life. Their inert faces, without any individual expression, offer only a vague family likeness. It might be said that Van Veen sometimes tried to compensate for vagueness of form by extravagance of colour. In several of his pictures the colours are variegated and ill-contrasted to excess. In the *Christ bearing the Cross* in the Brussels Museum, the reddish violet cloak worn by the St. Veronica of the foreground, contrasts cruelly with the harsh green of her tunic. Desirous of making some transition between the discordant tones, the painter mingled pink lights with the crude green colour, with the result that while he destroyed the local colour, he rendered the discord of the relationship still more inharmonious. The effect produced by the dark blues and greens of the Triptych of the

MINERVA AND HERCULES DRIVING AWAY MARS.
(The Louvre.)

Calvary in the same gallery is, perhaps, even more disastrous; those colours are accompanied by greenish grey and reddish purple tones that deepen the gloom, and accentuate the earthy, livid appearance of the flesh painting. Although cold, and slightly vitreous, the harmony of an *Adoration of the Shepherds* in the church of Alost is not without delicacy; in that picture Van Veen attains some firmness of drawing with more original composition. The Virgin, with pleasing features, a grave, pure expression, a charmingly frank bearing, differs from the type of conventional nobility, of which the artist has given us too much.

He was intended for such gentle and intimate impressions, and his inability to express action and life is seen in the most unfortunate way in the different episodes borrowed from the *History of Claudius Civilis* in the Ryks Museum of Amsterdam, and in the *Conversion of St. Paul*, in the Marseilles Museum. The *Raising of Lazarus*, in the Church of St. Bavon, at Ghent, seems to us his finest piece of

work, and in emphasising the pathetic side of the scene, he shows more moving accents than usual. As if the beauty of the subject had raised the artist above himself, his colour is more subdued and delicate, and is even more harmonious. If it were not for the violet-purplish tone, of which he was so fond, and which is to be found in nearly all his pictures, the whole painting would be excellent. Certain delightful passages, however, call for admiration ; for instance, the young fair-haired girl, beautifully dressed in a bluish stuff, covered with a gold design, who seems

STUDY OF A YOUNG GIRL.
(The Hermitage.)

uplifted by transports of gratitude at the sight of the miracle, is an exquisite inspiration that reveals what Van Veen would have been capable of, if, instead of persisting in his academic researches, he had been content to pursue the ideal of elegant distinction and quiet charm proper to his temperament.

Rubens remained in Van Veen's studio for four years, but the influence exercised on him by his teacher is perhaps more apparent in the conduct of his life, than in his artistic development. Their two careers, in fact, excepting the splendour of the genius and fame of the pupil, seem traced one over the other: the same culture of mind; the same curiosity; the same versatility of talent; the same knowledge of the world; and a destiny, if not equal, at least similarly favoured, from the point of view of honours and fortune. Accepting the idea which formerly obtained of Van Noort's character and temperament, it was natural to contrast the two masters of Rubens. In that parallel where the unlikenesses which seemed to exist between them were complacently accentuated in order to render the contrast more striking, Van Veen became the counterpart, and, as was said, "the reverse of Van Noort." The one, rough, full of energy, robust even to violence, fond of movement and of life, fearing neither exaggerations nor somewhat coarse familiarities, seemed the very personification of the old Flemish genius. The other, eclectic and cosmopolitan, nourished on the spirit and traditions of antiquity, was a sort of incarnation of the Italianism that was gradually spreading among scholars and artists. If, as far as Van Veen is concerned, the accuracy of the portrait is undeniable, we must, taking into account the little we know of the works of Van Noort, abandon the attractive thesis of a convenient dualism by which an over-rigorous process of deduction seeks to explain the formation of Rubens's talent. In the absence of positive testimony we ought to ignore the influence which Van Noort may have exercised on his illustrious pupil, and while granting him the qualities as a teacher which the names of his pupils sufficiently justify, we must recognise that between the works of Van Balen and those of Jordaens, who both received instruction from him, there exist differences notable enough to render it difficult to fix what each of them learned from their common master. But with regard to Van Veen, it is permissible to believe that Rubens, more matured and more advanced in his art, did come under the influence of a man whose teaching was presented to him with the double authority of a real talent and a great position. Van Veen was regarded as the Apelles of Flanders; he had lived with the great; he knew Italy and never ceased, we are told, to praise its marvels; his trained but somewhat subtle taste delighted in allegories; he had a sense of decoration, a love of fine schemes of arrangement and imposing subjects: in such things lay many attractions for an alert and receptive mind like that of Rubens. Through information derived from the best informed biographers, we may add to those æsthetic affinities the affection that Van Veen had for his pupil, of whom—so Philip Rubens tells us- -" he made his friend, and to whom he unreservedly communicated all he knew—the science of composition and the right distribution of light." Thus before parting from him the pupil had become his equal, and their works showed such resemblances that they were often confused.

It would be interesting to discover some of the works which Rubens painted at this early period. Unfortunately not one can be mentioned which could with certainty be attributed to him. More than once (we know this from the family inventories), he took his mother for model, desirous both to preserve the features of her who had watched over his infancy so tenderly. and to devote to her the first-fruits of his talent. The inventories tell us that at the sale of Rubens's works after his death, his son Albert bought the portraits of his grandfather and grandmother for eighty florins; but no trace of those pictures has been preserved. The Munich Gallery possesses, it is true, the portrait of an old woman who long passed for Maria Pypelinx. It represents a venerable old dame with a ruddy complexion, whose features are to be seen in some of the pictures painted by Rubens between 1615 and 1618, in which he portrayed other members of his family, his first wife and his young children, notably several *Holy Families*, and the *Silenus*, also at Munich. The execution of the *Head of an Old Woman* at Munich certainly belongs to that period, and is rapidly dashed off with the suppleness and sureness of handling then characteristic of the artist.

Made free of the Guild of St. Luke in 1598, Rubens settled at Antwerp, where he began to make himself an honourable position. But he was stirred by a growing desire to see Italy, which exercised an increasing attraction on Flemish painters. Not only had his three masters yielded to it, but also the greater number of his most famous contemporaries, such as Wenzel Coeberger, who, apart from his talent as a painter, was a distinguished archæologist, Abraham

Janssens, and many others.   Rubens was influenced by the Italian
paintings he had seen, and by what his friends, especially Van Veen,
had told him.   But the thought of his mother held him back ; it
would be necessary to leave her when old age made her desire more
than ever to keep with her the son of whom she was so proud.   But
what we know of her authorises us to believe, that with the self-denial
of which she had already given so many proofs, she resigned herself
to the fresh sacrifice.   On May 8, 1600, Rubens received a passport
from the municipality of Antwerp, in which the burgomasters and
aldermen of the town testified that the bearer was not suffering from
any contagious disease.   The next day he set out for Italy.

HEAD OF AN OLD MAN.
(Albertina Collection.)
(From a photograph by Braun, Clément et Cie.)

THE OLD CASTLE, MANTUA.
Drawing by Boudier. (From a photograph.)

CHAPTER III

ARRIVAL OF RUBENS AT VENICE—HE ENTERS THE SERVICE OF DUKE VINCENZO GONZAGA—VINCENZO'S FAMILY, EDUCATION AND CHARACTER—THE PALACE AT MANTUA—THE NUMEROUS WORKS OF ART THERE: THEIR IMPORTANCE IN RUBENS'S EDUCATION—FIRST VISIT TO ROME (1601-1602)—THE PICTURE PAINTED FOR THE CHURCH OF THE SANTA CROCE DI GERUSALEMME.

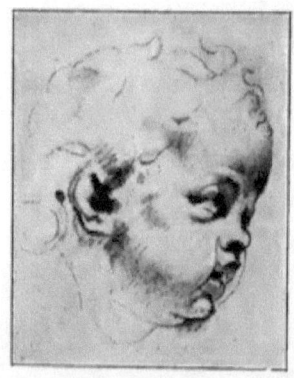

HEAD OF A CHILD.
(The Louvre.)

IN the beginning of his journey Rubens was probably accompanied by sad thoughts. Accustomed to his mother's loving affection, he would have felt more acutely the isolation to which his new life condemned him; he was, however, far from thinking that he was never to see her again. For the first time he was free; in his pockets he had a little money saved with great difficulty, and full of the tales that had been told him and trusting in his star, he went on towards the land which contained so many precious resources for satisfying his ardent desire for knowledge. Perhaps he had some travelling companion, one of the Italian merchants or bankers who

had their offices at Antwerp, or Deodato del Monte, a somewhat
mediocre artist, with whom he was always on intimate terms ; in an
eulogistic testimonial which he presented to him long afterwards
(August 19, 1628), Peter Paul described him as honest, truthful, active,
zealous in the study of painting and the fine arts, upright, honourable and benevolent, "and certified that he accompanied him on his
travels" in various countries, and particularly in Italy.

What route did Rubens take ? That of the Rhine and Switzerland, the usual road taken by his countrymen, or did he go by
France, as Michel states in the biography (to be used with caution,
be it said) which he has left us of the master, but without indicating
whence he derived the information. In any case, the journey made
on horseback, and in short daily stages, must have been long. But
the sights, so new to him, which presented themselves to his view,
the towns and the countries through which he passed, above all
the imposing grandeur of the Alps, were well calculated to interest
him. Yet he was eager to reach his destination, Venice, whither
he felt himself more particularly drawn. Judging by what we learn
from other travellers of the period, it probably took Rubens a
month to reach Venice, and it is certain that more than any
of them, he desired to economise both his time and his money.
Whatever pleasures he enjoyed during the journey, the city of
canals must have especially excited his enthusiasm, with the splendid
decoration of its palaces and churches, and the happy concord of
the works of its painters with the nature that inspired them. The
varied buildings, whose bold contours stand out so exquisitely
against the sky, their bases kissed by the sea, the enjoyable
brilliance of the light, the richness and seriousness of the compositions of Titian, the breadth and expressive beauty of his portraits,
the boldness and spirited eloquence of the large canvases animated
with the powerful inspiration of Tintoretto, the triumphant charm of
the ceilings of Veronese, formed irresistible attractions that capti-
vated the young painter in turn. But he was not the man to
live idle amid such splendours. Active as he was, he not only
desired to see much, but to study much, to get nearer the splendid
models, to surprise the secret of their charm or their strength. The

great colourists, the painters privileged as regards light and life, were artists after his own heart; in contact with them many aspirations, until then confused, again awoke in him, and took a more precise shape.

The drawings or copies which he made after the Italian masters, and the numerous reminiscences of them to be found in his works, testify to the influence which they exercised on Rubens, and to the profit he derived from communion with them. His days passed pleasantly in assiduous study of them, and the work would doubtless have absorbed him for a long period, had not an unexpected meeting changed his plans and procured him a post, which, keeping him in Italy, prolonged his sojourn there far beyond his intention. Vincenzo Gonzaga, Duke of Mantua, chanced to pass through Venice; he remained only a few days, arriving a little before July 15, 1600, and leaving soon after the 22nd of the same month. In the interval, Rubens, having made the acquaintance of a gentleman of the prince's household, happened to show him some of his pictures, either those he had brought with him from Antwerp, or those painted since he had been at Venice. Struck by their talent, the gentleman spoke of them to his master, who, attracted by the young artist's ability, and by his charm of manner, took him into his service. As Rubens was attached to his court for nearly eight years, it is necessary to make a closer acquaintance with the duke's strange personality.

Born on September 2, 1562, Vincenzo I. was now twenty-eight years old. After his divorce from Margaret Farnese, he had, in 1584, married as his second wife, Leonora, daughter of Duke Francesco de' Medici, a woman of distinction, whose patient gentleness and dignity were often subjected to rude trials by her ardent and capricious husband. Three years later, in 1587, Vincenzo succeeded Guglielmo Gongaza, his father, and scarcely was he in power, before he gave himself up without restraint to all the impulses of his wild nature. Impetuous, changing his caprices at every instant, he combined the practises of an extreme devotion with the excesses of a most irregular life. Patron of scholars, writers and artists, he was at the same time in love with every beautiful woman he saw. An immoderate gambler, equally proud of his horses, his hounds and his comedians, he was incapable of resisting any of his passions.

His receptive mind, the care that had been bestowed on his education, and the qualities he showed in youth, had promised a better employment of his life. Faithful at first to the traditions of his ancestors, it seemed that he desired to maintain the rank and splendid reputation of his family. Examples were not wanting, for the little Court of Mantua held one of the first places among the principalities of Italy, rivalling its neighbours in elegance and distinction. The

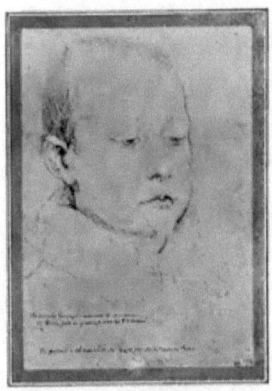

PORTRAIT OF FERDINANDO GONZAGA, SON OF DUKE VINCENZO.
Drawing by Rubens. (Stockholm Museum.)

names of Lodovico III. and his intelligent consort Barbe de Brandenburg, and of Isabella d'Este, the wife of Giovanni Francesco II., were associated with the early period and the full maturity of the Renaissance. By their generous initiative the Mantuan princes had counted among their dependants or their friends, authors such as Ariosto and B. Castiglione ; artists like Pisanello, L. Battista, Alberti, Donatello, Perugino, Leonardo, Correggio, and Lorenzo Costa. After Mantegna, who spent the last forty-six years of his life at Mantua, and produced many of his best works there, Giulio Romano, at the invitation of Federigo Gonzaga, settled there when he was twenty-five years of age, and until his death in 1546 multiplied evidences of his activity as engineer, architect, decorator and painter.

Before coming to power, Vincenzo appeared to model himself on the memorable examples of his predecessors. In 1586, when he was still only hereditary prince, he joined his efforts to those of his mother, Leonora of Austria, to obtain the release of Tasso, then shut up in a lunatic asylum. In 1601, about the time when he took Rubens into his service, he engaged Claudio Monteverde, the celebrated musician, as chief organist. Anxious to show his military skill, he took part three times in expeditions against the Turks, and if his success was not commensurate with his enterprise, he, at least, bore himself bravely. At last, in 1604, he tried to induce Galileo to take up his residence at his court. But apart from his irregular conduct, and the large sums he spent at play, or on his mistresses, the retinue of his household and his equipages, his sumptuous fêtes, his magnificent presents, the maintenance of his troop of comedians, his passion for building, his frequent and extravagant journeys, his incessant purchases of works of art and curiosities of all sorts, were out of all proportion to the resources of a state like his, and must in a short time have exhausted his treasury. Annibale Chieppio, his secretary, a man of proved uprightness and devotion, tried in vain to bring some order into his affairs, but the timid remonstrances on which he occasionally ventured had not the slightest effect. Thus all payments stood over, and the salaries of his dependants were very much in arrears. In this incorrigible spendthrift, Rubens first made acquaintance with the disorder and poverty that he so often encountered in the future among the needy sovereigns with whom he was brought into contact through his work.

DRAWING BY RUBENS AFTER A PORTRAIT OF TITIAN BY HIMSELF.
(The Louvre.)

The preceding year, in 1599, Vincenzo, whose health was somewhat impaired by the fatigues of his campaign in Hungary, and also by his excesses, went to Spa by the advice of his physicians to take the waters. After his cure, he spent a few days at Antwerp, and there entered into relations with Frans Pourbus, the talented portrait painter,

and took him into his service. But although nearly a year had gone by
since then, Pourbus had not yet arrived at Mantua; whether he
had to finish some work commenced in Flanders, or whether he did
not care to make the journey alone, he delayed his departure until he
found a travelling companion in the person of an ensign sent by the
Duke to take the Prince of Orange some horses bred in his master's
stables. It may be asked why Vincenzo, having already attached
Pourbus to his Court, desired to have Rubens there also. Was it a
fresh proof of the Prince's heedlessness or of his versatility? or did
he reckon on giving his two painters enough work to occupy them
both? The last hypothesis seems to us the most probable, for he
was pursuing with great ardour at that moment two very different
projects; he desired to hang in his gallery copies of the most celebrated madonnas, and portraits "of the most beautiful women in
the world, princesses or ordinary individuals." Of the two projects
he doubtless had the latter most at heart.

On his return from Venice the duke merely passed through Mantua,
for he was summoned with the least possible delay to Florence, which
he reached on October 2, to the wedding of his sister-in-law Marie
de' Medici, who in marrying Henry IV. became Queen of France.
Great fêtes were being prepared in the town, and Vincenzo took care
not to lose so excellent an opportunity for displaying his magnificence.
He took Rubens with him, and as Pourbus was just then in Florence,
their master probably intended to make use of them both to transfer
the magnificent receptions and ceremonials in which he was taking
part to canvas.

When the fêtes were over, the duke paid a somewhat long visit
to Genoa, and Rubens doubtless accompanied him. Returning to
Mantua with the prince about Christmas time, the young painter
spent over six months there, and no surroundings more interesting,
or more favourable for the advancement of his knowledge could be
imagined. The position of the little residency and the level marshy
country surrounding it, are in no way picturesque. The variety and
style to be found in many less important centres of the district is
sought in vain in the public buildings. Everywhere, in the big empty

Antique Vase and Coat of Mail.

(THE LOUVRE.)

piazzas or in the dark winding streets, the aspect is gloomy and monotonous. But the palace, now dilapidated and deserted, showing
everywhere traces of the pillage it underwent in 1630, and the damages
that it has since suffered, presented at the beginning of the seventeenth century an imposing aggregation of all sorts of buildings, and
the collections which it contained passed for the most remarkable in
Italy. The dukes who had inhabited and enriched it, had successively added new buildings without troubling to make them harmonise
with those that already existed. Thus round the original edifice, a
massive fortress with grim brick walls flanked by four square towers,
ornamented with machicolations, arose by degrees buildings of different
epochs, joined together by colonnades. The enclosure included large
courtyards, gardens on different levels, a riding-school, a ground for
tournaments, and even trenches, in which, by means of an arrangement
for pumping water into them, nautical jousts could be organised.

Notwithstanding its dilapidated condition, the Palace of Mantua
preserves traces of its ancient splendour, and gives even now the
highest idea of the artists who, in turn, exercised their talent on it,
and of the princes who employed them. The decorations of the greater
part of the rooms have a definite stamp of sobriety and elegance,
notably the smaller apartments, with a view of the lake and the distant
mountains, rooms which Isabella d'Este arranged for her own use.

By an accurate feeling for proportion, by a happy choice of motives
and their intelligent use, the smallest details of the charming retreat
record the fine taste of the princess for whom it was destined. In the
vigorous and supple curves of the scrolls of the ceilings; in the
ingenious arabesques which are interlaced round her initials, or her
melancholy motto, *Nec spe, nec metu* ; in the exquisite medallions in
which the sculptor, Cristoforo Romano, chiselled with so firm a hand
charming figures that personify learning, and the different arts—everything speaks of the distinguished woman's noble recreations, of her
culture and her taste. In the room called *delle Virtù* she gave freer
play to her fancy : its vast dimensions and fine proportions admitted
of a rich scheme of decoration which is broadly treated, yet always
kept within bounds. As it was a state apartment, intended for the

glorification of the Gonzaga family, everything about it expressed strength and magnificence: the busts of ancestors, for example, who brought honour to their race, are conspicuous there with symbolical statues that record their great qualities, or their fame. With more robust forms the reliefs are more accentuated, and the principal lines of the building stand out with greater force. A gilded ceiling, with thick ribs and widely spread rosettes, superbly completes the general harmony.

But the most splendid of the decorations of the ducal palace was

DECORATION OF A CEILING IN THE 'PARADISO' OF ISABELLA D'ESTE.
(Palace of Mantua.)

certainly the famous *Camera degli Sposi* in the *Castello di Corte*,[1] painted in fresco by Mantegna at the age of forty-three, in his full maturity, one of his most perfect works. In the hospitable home to which the great artist had been welcomed fourteen years before, his rugged and powerful genius had unbent, and softened by the affectionate sympathy with which he was treated, he abandoned himself to the charm of his pleasant surroundings and of the life there offered him. His compositions are less severe, less grim. With a

[1] Now in the *Archivio notarile.*

delightful naturalness he grouped round the patriarchal family numerous children, servants, and even favourite animals, and in the portraits lies a sort of hidden tenderness, where, without losing anything of his force of penetration and of the incisive sharpness of drawing of which he possessed the secret, he mingles a trace of emotion from his grateful heart. With the recollections of the antique—effigies of emperors,

episodes from legends, temples, theatres, aqueducts, and statues—that he brings round the patrons who had become his friends, he desired to associate representations of the things they best loved to look on, the familiar outlines of their castles, the green hills of their domains with their varied patches of cultivation, the festoons of delicious fruits which their gardens produced, all the delights, all the perfumes of nature. As if conscious that he had put the best of himself into this

DECORATION OF THE SALA DELLE VIRTÙ, PALACE OF MANTUA.
Drawing by Boudier. (From a photograph.)

work, he painted in the centre beautiful Cupids with variegated butterflies' wings, holding in their little hands an inscription in which, with touching simplicity, he dedicates to Lodovico II., "the excellent prince," and to "the illustrious Barbe, his incomparable wife, the glory of her sex, this modest work executed in their honour."

But at the beginning of the seventeenth century the precursors of the Renaissance found little favour among artists. Repelled by the timid clumsiness or the powerful severity of their style, they did not appreciate the qualities of expression we now praise in them.

Rubens shared the opinion of his time. Neither Masaccio, nor Perugino, nor Ghirlandaio, nor Signorelli appear to have attracted his attention. In the many copies he made after the Italian masters, only Mantegna among the early painters found favour in his eyes, and it was doubtless the young artist's passion for the antique, and his desire to know it better, that drew him to Mantegna. Intelligent as he was, Rubens could not fail to be struck by the penetrating intuition of the past, which, based on a somewhat slender amount of information, permitted his famous forerunner to reproduce the costumes, the scenes, and even the life of antiquity with astonishing success. It was not, however, in Italy, but much later, during his sojourn in England, that Rubens copied the fragments of the *Triumph of Julius Cæsar* painted by Mantegna for the Palace of St. Sebastian at Mantua.

But if Rubens felt little drawn to the early masters, everything attracted him to another artist who, towards the decline of the Renaissance, also held an important place at the Court of the Gonzagas. Giulio Romano was summoned to Mantua at the age of twenty-five, and spent the rest of his life there. The works of all kinds over which he presided were so considerable that the Marquis Federigo, who, through the intervention of B. Castiglione, had attached him to his service, went so far as to say that "Giulio was even more the master (*padrone*) of the city than he was himself." The draining of the land, the construction of dykes, palaces, churches, and buildings of every kind, of which the decoration was also entrusted to him, the training of the numerous collaborators whose aid was necessary to the accomplishment of so many undertakings, were the tasks demanded of his energy. Such manifold talents, and fertility of invention, were of a nature to command the admiration of Rubens, and to exercise on him the greater influence, in that his own temperament, it must be recognised, carried him towards an art so abundant and splendid, fuller of brilliance and strength than of proportion and perfection. It was not only the affinity of their natures, and the prestige of his well-filled life that made of Giulio Romano a model whose steps Rubens aspired to follow. Peter Paul also found in Raphael's disciple many tastes similar to his own, especially the passion for the antique, by which he was himself animated, and which exercised a real fascination on his mind. His residence at Mantua developed the taste still more. The collection of statues, busts, bas-reliefs, and engraved marbles which the Gonzagas had from early times striven to bring together, was enlarged by the purchases that the sculptor Cristoforo Romano had made for Isabella d'Este, and further increased by the collection which Mantegna had formed himself; at his death his sons were forced to dispose of it in order to meet the expenses of the chapel, erected by them in the church of St. Andrew to the memory of their father. The ducal palace contained a large number of beautiful works, and in spite of the dispersion of its rich possessions at the pillage of 1630, the town of Mantua has preserved something from the wreck of the precious collection even to our time. Walking through the two rooms of the *Museo Civico* where they are exhibited, we may recognise several antiques, sarcophagi, altars, bas-reliefs and even figures, by which the Flemish master, following the examples of Mantegna and Giulio Romano, was later inspired. In spite of his modest resources, Rubens also began to purchase for himself busts, gems, and medals, the first nucleus of a collection to which he continued to add, and which in time became his joy and pride.

The collection of paintings in the ducal palace was not less celebrated than that of the sculptures. Without reckoning a fair number of celebrated canvases now scattered through the galleries of Europe, some of the paintings in the Louvre, which were then at Mantua, were directly commissioned from the artists by Isabella d'Este.[1] The amiable and intelligent princess whom Ariosto represents to us as loving all noble studies, *di bei studi amica*, suggested the idea for several of the pictures, among others Perugino's *Conflict between Cupid and Chastity*. By the side of the *Mount Parnassus*, and *The Vices Banished by Wisdom*, now in the Louvre, was a fine tempera painting by Correggio on the same subject, which formed then, as it does now, a pendant to the same painter's *Sensual*

---

[1] *Cf.* on this subject the careful and interesting studies published by M. Ch. Yriart in the *Gazette des Beaux-Arts* from 1895 to 1898.

Man. Other famous canvases of Titian, Lorenzo Costa, Veronese,
together with the more recent productions of Caracci, Albano, and
the pupils of Giulio Romano, also demanded attention. The splendour
of the hangings and furniture was in keeping, and ancient tapestries
from local factories, valuable arms, precious vases of gold and silver,
a great profusion of objects in rock crystal, pottery from Urbino, and

GROUP FROM THE BATTLE OF ANGHIARI. COPY AFTER LEONARDO DA VINCI.
(Berlin Print Room.)

porcelain from China, carefully selected by Duke Vincenzo, were
employed in the decoration of the apartments.

Without maintaining the level of distinction and high culture which
had formerly made its reputation, the Court of Mantua, even at that
period presented interesting and varied objects of study for an artist
so desirous of knowledge as Rubens. Less intellectual distractions
were also to be enjoyed there. Fond of magnificence and pleasure,
Duke Vincenzo often received the visits of neighbouring princes;
on such occasions fêtes, spectacles, concerts and magnificent receptions were given in honour of the passing guests. His company

of actors was the most
celebrated of the time;
and as he himself was
devoted to music, he kept
the most talented virtuosi
in his pay. He sought
out also the best musical
instruments, the admirable
lutes and violins, which
were then made at Cre-
mona. He delighted in
the works of the French
composer, S. Guédron,
and we mentioned that he
had taken into his service
as chief organist, Claudio
Monteverde, the restorer
of Italian opera. Was
Rubens indifferent to the
delights of music? We
do not know, but neither
in his correspondence nor
in his works have we
found any trace of the
pleasure which nearly all
the great painters, and
especially the great colourists Giorgione, Titian,
Veronese, derived from
that art. But Rubens
delighted in conversation,
and with his wide know-
ledge, receptive mind
and pleasing manners he

DRAWING BY RUBENS AFTER CORREGGIO.
(The Louvre.)

was certain to distinguish himself therein. "As he had been

well brought up," Félibien tells us, "he knew how to live with persons
of rank." But if he could hold his own everywhere, he would certainly have preferred the conversation of authors, scholars, and
the excellent connoisseurs of art then numerous in Italy, to the
frivolity and gossip of courtiers.

Adroit, supple and agile, Vincenzo Gonzaga excelled in all physical
exercises ; riding and the chase were his favourite pastimes. After
praising the grandeur and magnificence of his palace, which, in addition
to the numerous apartments reserved for the prince and his family,
contained "many other sets of rooms ready for the reception of
sovereigns and ambassadors," a French traveller who visited Mantua
some years later,[1] mentions the splendour of the stables, which contained
" more than 150 horses of all sorts, Turkish, Spanish, Barbary, Frisian,
&c." It was a family tradition with the Gonzagas, and the race of
horses bred in their stables was much esteemed throughout Europe. In
one of the great halls of the Palazzo del Te, painted in the time of Giulio
Romano, there may be seen faithful portraits of some of the choicest
types of the breed, which presented a mixture of beauty and vigour
then much sought after. Rubens, who preserved a taste for riding
throughout his life, found many facilities at Mantua not only for becoming a good horseman, but for making himself familiar, as a painter,
with the proportions and characteristics of the horse. Doubtless he
took pleasure also in attending the hunts organised at La Favorite,
at Marmirolo, at Bosco della Fontana, and at the different country
residences of a prince whose horses and hounds were maintained on a
very grand scale. The splendid cavalcades, the animation, and the
incidents of the chase suited the young artist's temperament, and
the skill which he manifested later in painting those sorts of subjects,
betrays an intimate acquaintance with that aristocratic pastime. Perhaps, too, it was at Mantua that Rubens began to study from life
lions, tigers, and exotic animals, camels, crocodiles, hippopotamuses
and serpents, whose strange forms and ferocious beauty he so
ably reproduced. The menagerie of the Gonzagas was another of
their hobbies, and it is probably in that which they maintained in

[1] In 1611 ; the manuscript is in the National Library, Paris. MS. no. 19013, p. 99.

VI

Portrait of Jan Vermoelen.

(LIECHTENSTEIN COLLECTION.)

the time of Mantegna that the master had drawn from life the
elephants which he introduced into the *Triumph of Cæsar*. A little
later, in any case, Giulio Romano found in the places specially arranged
in the south of the Palazzo del Te, in the *Virgiliana*, the models for
the elephants of which he made sketches, and for the camels and
giraffes which figure in many of his compositions.

The wealth of resource available at Mantua, evidently made
the residency a privileged place, and as we imagine that the duties
of Rubens—under a master whose inconstancy caused him inces-
santly to change his mind—occupied only a small part of his time,
he had something wherewith to fill his leisure. We cannot say what
were the works on which the duke employed him during his earliest
sojourn at Mantua. The palace has preserved some of its decorations, and I have wandered in vain through its innumerable rooms in
quest of some work from his hand. In one of them, the ceiling of
which is decorated with the ducal arms—golden staves alternating
with flames,—the execution of a frieze of a blackish aspect, on which
are depicted a series of compositions inspired by the history of Judith,
is, as one of the keepers told me, attributed to the painter, *al fiammingo*; in a room of the *corte ducale*, among a quantity of exceedingly
mediocre canvases, I discovered a Venus surrounded by Cupids in the
forge of Vulcan, where the flesh painting, with its warm lights and
cold shadows, the somewhat coarse types, and the bluish backgrounds,
vaguely recalls the artist's early work.

But the canvases are so damaged that it is not possible to pronounce
any verdict on their composition, nor, for the same reason, on their
author. We do not know in what part of the palace Rubens was
lodged. We may still see in the labyrinth of edifices a detached building,
reserved for the occupation of the dwarfs kept at the Mantuan Court,
with cells befitting their stature, a miniature refectory, and a chapel
suitable for their use. But, excepting the apartments allotted to them,
and those that Isabella d'Este arranged for herself, the rooms are so
altered by pillage or fire, that it is difficult to discover their former use.

The archives are equally silent regarding the beginnings of
Rubens's residence at Mantua, and the first document in which he is

mentioned bears the date July 8, 1601.   He was then on the point
of setting out for Rome, in order to make copies or paint pictures for
his master, who was preparing to take part in one of Rudolph II.'s
expeditions against the Turks.   The duke gave Rubens a letter
of introduction to Cardinal Montalto.   He begged him to grant
" to Peter Paul, the Fleming, his painter, the protection of his high
office in everything that he might demand for his business."   The

"ECCE HOMO."
Painted for the Santa Croce di Gerusalemme. (?)
(Municipal Hospital, Grasse.)

Cardinal, an influential
personage at the papal
court, was charged, to-
gether with Aldobrandini,
the Pope's nephew, with
the direction of the political business of the Holy
See.   A scholar, and a
patron of the arts, he had
a large retinue of dependants, and could, by reason
of his exalted station, be
very useful to Rubens.   On
receipt of the letter of introduction, the Cardinal
wrote to the duke to in-
form him that " he had
seen the bearer with
pleasure, and that not
only did he place himself entirely at his service, but that he begged
him to inform him immediately of all that he might need for his
highness's business."

From the date of the letter, August 15, 1601, Rubens had
reached Rome a few days previously, and he probably at last
could enjoy the marvels he had so often heard praised.   We can

---

[1] This and the two following engravings executed after very defective reproductions are placed here in order to give some idea of three of the early works
of Rubens.

imagine his emotion, and the ardour with which he sought to satisfy his impatient curiosity. Under the burning summer sun, in the midst of the silence and desertion of the Forum, he might have been seen traversing its scattered ruins, stopping here and there to sketch a temple, a colonnade, or a triumphal arch. As De Piles[1] says, "he turned to account the things he liked, sometimes by copying them, sometimes by making notes, accompanied usually by a slight pen and ink drawing, invariably carrying with him a blank note book for that purpose." What objects for study or admiration were revealed to him! How all the past, which in his reading he had endeavoured to call up, now appeared before his artist's eyes, illuminated by the brilliant light, beautifully framed by the soft colouring and harmonious lines of the mountains of Albano! The masterpieces of modern art afforded him equal pleasure, and

THE RAISING OF THE CROSS.
Painted for the Santa Croce di Gerusalemme.
(Municipal Hospital, Grasse.)

the numerous drawings that he made at the Vatican show us who were his favourite masters. Michael Angelo and Raphael attracted him in turn, but he especially favoured the first. The lofty bearing and expressive gestures of the imposing figures which adorn the ceiling of the Sistine, were exactly of the nature to attract him. In future visits that he paid to Rome, he must have contemplated them many times, and in spite of the difficulty and fatigue of such a work, he copied them

[1] *Abrégé de la vie des Peintres*, Paris, 1699.

faithfully. In the Louvre are careful drawings by him, after six
of the eight *Prophets*, and two of the *Sibyls*, as well as a study in
red chalk of the *Creation of Man*. If no copy of the *Last
Judgment* by his hand is known, his impression of it was both
profound and lasting, for nearly fifteen years afterwards, when he was
in the full maturity of his talent, Michael Angelo's fresco inspired
him with a series of analogous compositions. At Rome, as at
Mantua, he was indifferent to the works of the early masters. The
beauty or the severe charm which Botticelli, Perugino, Ghirlandaio,
Signorelli, and Pinturrichio displayed on the walls of the Sistine
Chapel touched him no more than the pathos and candour which
a short step from these might have moved him in Fra Angelico's
frescoes in the Chapel of Nicholas V. Even in Raphael he
sought chiefly movement and action, and if he was too intelligent
not to enjoy the fine schemes of arrangement, and the calm
majesty of the *School of Athens*, or of the *Disputa*, it is to the more
animated episodes of the *Heliodorus scourged with Rods*, of the *Fire in
the Borgo*, and the *Battle of Constantine*, that he specially turned his
attention. The imitations and reminiscences of Raphael in his drawings and pictures, are either pathetic or forcible figures, such as the
Vision of Ezekiel, *Elymas struck blind*, *Ananias struck dead*, the
kneeling woman in the foreground of the *Transfiguration*, and her
son, the maniac boy, who, beside himself, throws himself down by
her in convulsions.

Through the works of those masters Rubens learned to know the
radiant maturity of the Renaissance. But although much deteriorated,
Italy had not ceased to be the privileged land of the arts, and among
the painters nearer to him, the young Fleming derived instruction
from the colourists towards whom his temperament led him. Perhaps
Rubens stopped at Parma on his way to Rome, as Van Veen, who
had been in the service of the ducal court of that town, advised him.
In any case, then or later he stayed there long enough to make some
drawings from the pictures, or the great decorative paintings of
Correggio. Formed in Correggio's school, Baroccio, then an old
man, still enjoyed a great reputation, and Rubens found in him,

the principal qualities of Van Veen more brilliantly displayed. If he was scarcely sensible of the laboured grace of his forms, or of the affectations of his methods of expression, he was more alive to the charm of his colour, and for some time Rubens borrowed Baroccio's somewhat artificial colouring of draperies, the local colour of which, scarcely visible in the light, is very strong in the shadows. But another contemporary of Rubens, Caravaggio, exercised a more marked influence on him, and developed his sense of picturesque effects in accentuating the excessive contrasts of light and shadow that occur in the paintings executed several years after his return from Italy. At a time when insipidity and artificiality tended more and more to develop in art, the fame acquired by Caravaggio can be understood. Gifted with a penetrating observation of nature, and a very real knowledge, he introduced, or rather he caused to predominate in his works, a new element of interest, *chiaroscuro*. The powerful relief produced by this mode of lighting gave his pictures an unexpected value as regards strength and brilliancy, which gained for him numerous imitators, not only among his countrymen, but among foreign artists settled either temporarily or for good in Italy, like Ribera, the French painter Valentin, and among the Dutch, G. Van Honthorst, Pinas, and Lastman, Rembrandt's master. Rubens himself was to follow that current, and Sandrart states, " that he first devoted himself to attaining the powerful colour of Caravaggio, whom he studied by preference; but recognising the difficulty and the tedium of such a proceeding, he afterwards adopted a simpler and more expeditious method of execution."

Among the young men whom Caravaggio's style also attracted, we ought to mention the painter Elsheimer; he had come from Frankfort to Rome a year before Rubens, and contracted a close friendship with him. Of nearly the same age—Elsheimer was born in 1578 —they had the same passion for the antique, and as the young German was of a very amiable disposition, not only did he place his experience of Roman life at the service of his new comrade, but he also initiated him into the processes of engraving, an art which he practised himself. Moreover, to bring him into relations with the artists

of the foreign colony, Rubens found another Fleming, the landscape
painter, Paulus Bril, who, like himself, came from Antwerp, and had
been long settled at Rome, where his reputation stood high.   They
probably became acquainted through Cardinal Montalto, because Bril
had executed important works for him, and had decorated one of the
rooms of his palace.   At the Cardinal's house Rubens met scholars,

amateurs, and archæolo-
gists, and doubtless in
that select society he
neglected no opportunity
of gaining knowledge
about the many subjects
that interested him.

Thus he spent his time,
occupied in the studies he
made for himself, and the
copies he executed for his
master.   A skilful and
rapid worker, he could in
a short time satisfactorily
accomplish the tasks en-
trusted to him, and as his
salary was of the most
modest description, he
was forced to seek means
for his support elsewhere.

ST. HELENA.

Painted for the Santa Croce di Gerusalemme.
(Municipal Hospital, Grasse.)

The only trace of a pay-
ment made to the Duke of Mantua's dependant to be found in
the papers of the Gonzagas, is the   notice transmitted on
September 14, 1601, to Chieppio, by Lelio Arrigoni, the duke's
agent at Rome, of the disbursement of a sum of " 50 crowns on
account of the 100 which, in accordance with the orders of His Highness, he was enjoined to give to the Flemish painter."   Although he
was very economical, such slender resources must have made it difficult
for Rubens to regulate his affairs.   However the period fixed for the

duration of his residence at Rome was drawing to a close, but, at the moment when he was arranging to return to Mantua, he received a commission for a work, not very lucrative, it is true, but of some importance.

Before his marriage with his cousin, the Infanta Isabella Clara Eugenia, daughter of Philip II., and his consequent appointment to the regency of Flanders, the Archduke Albert had taken orders, and had even been promoted to the dignity of cardinal, taking his title

WILD BULL HUNT.
(Berlin Print Room.)

from the Santa Croce di Gerusalemme, an old and somewhat dilapidated church, close against the walls of Rome near the Porto San Giovanni. On abandoning the ecclesiastical profession, the archduke promised to contribute to the restoration and decoration of the church. He was the more anxious to do so since his efforts for pacifying the Low Countries by conciliatory measures were not well regarded at the Papal Court, which accused him of want of zeal in the repression of heresy. Entering into the views of the archduke, Jean Richardot, son of the president of the Privy Council at Brussels, his agent at Rome, proposed to him to have an altar piece painted for the Chapel

of St. Helena in the Santa Croce, of which he reckoned the price
might be fixed at one or two hundred crowns. It is probable that
Richardot, in making the proposal to the prince, had already come to
some understanding in the matter with Rubens, in whom he had some
reason to be interested, because Philip, the painter's brother, had been
secretary to the president, before becoming tutor to one of his sons.
The archduke accepted the conditions offered him, and on June 30,
Richardot informed his father that he was arranging the matter.
Rubens set to work as soon as he received the commission ; but,
pressed for time, he could only finish one of the three pictures
destined for the decoration of the chapel, that of the central altar.
January 12, 1602, the date fixed for the departure of the artist, being
at hand, Lelio Arrigoni, informed of the archduke's desire by his
agent, asked Chieppio for a respite, and a few days later, on January·
25, Richardot wrote himself directly to Duke Vincenzo to prefer the
request. One of the pictures, it is true, was finished, but it was to be
accompanied by two other smaller ones, "otherwise the work would
remain imperfect and deprived of its complete decorative effect." He
hoped then that Rubens might be allowed to remain a little longer at
Rome, for, "the short time he would need to finish his task could
not in any way be injurious to the important and magnificent works
which his Highness, so it was said, had commenced at Mantua."

The permission was doubtless granted, since the three pictures
which adorned the altar of St. Helena, in the Church of Santa Croce
di Gerusalemme, are now all together in the chapel of the Municipal
Hospital at Grasse. The first time I saw them I was struck
by their numerous defects : their coarsenesss, the want of proportion
in some of the figures, the banality of most of the others, inspired
me, I confess, with a very natural distrust of their attribution to
Rubens. Having read the documents relating to them, I returned to
Grasse to study them more closely, and a careful examination,
which in no way modified my views as to their value, obliged me
to recognise the authenticity of the attribution, justified, indeed,
not only by decisive testimony, but by the character of the com
position and the arrangement, which agree in every point with
those of other works of the same period. Placed in the Church of

5

The Creation of Woman.

(Drawing in Red Chalk after Michael Angelo.)

(THE LOUVRE.)

Santa Croce di Gerusalemme, the three pictures are mentioned in 1642 in a publication by G. Baglione,[1] and are there very accurately described. M. Max Rooses, who has followed up their history, tells us that in 1763 the central painting, *St. Helena*, having suffered greatly from damp, was placed in the library of the Cistercians, attached to the church. The other two remained in the chapel. Later, all three were carried to England, sold there by auction in 1812, then bought from their various owners by M. Perrole, a wealthy tradesman of Grasse, who in 1827 bequeathed them to his native town. These peregrinations and the unfavourable conditions to which they were originally exposed, have seriously damaged the pictures. They bear marks of numerous repaintings ; the panels of two of them, the *St. Helena* and the *Ecce Homo*, came apart, and were very awkwardly repaired. Besides, at the height, and in the light where they now hang, it is difficult to see them properly.

But none the less, the historical importance of the pictures, is great: they are, in fact, the first original works of Rubens that we know, and for that reason deserve attention. Of the three paintings, the *St. Helena* is the most brilliant, and the most simply conceived. In the *Ecce Homo*, the mass and incoherence of the details at once strike the eye, and the dissemination of the light, as well as the excessive contrasts of colour, exaggerate those defects. But the figure of Christ deserves praise for the nobility of the features, and the pathetic expression of sadness and resignation. Tintoretto seems to have supplied Rubens with the principal idea for the *Raising of the Cross*. The same defects of hardness in the colour, opaqueness in the shadows, excessive use of red in the flesh tints, mar the work, and the want of proportion is even more glaring than in the two others. The Christ is a broadly built athletic Colossus, surpassing in stature and solidity the figures near him ; the fainting Virgin in the foreground and the women who attend her are extraordinarily slender.

Those curious, and it must be confessed mediocre works, are likely to disconcert admirers of Rubens. Hidden in a museum,

---

[1] *Le vite die pittori, scultori, ed architetti dal pontificato di Gregorio XIII., del 1572, in fino a tembi di Papa Urbano VIII., nel 1642*, by Giovanni Baglione. 4to. Rome. 1642.

there is nothing in them to arrest attention. We must be forewarned, and in order to recognise the hand of the master in them, must remember the haste with which they were painted, the price that was paid for them, and the damage that they have suffered. And in spite of their weak points, certain individual and characteristic qualities may be found in them: for example, the comprehension of decorative effect, the sense of life and movement, the delight in tumultuous action which brings all the emotions and passions into play. Moreover, the best proof of the value placed by Rubens on those youthful productions, is that in the *Raising of the Cross* he painted himself towards the centre, with his high forehead, pointed beard, and delicate profile; and after his return to Antwerp, having to paint the same subject for the church of St. Walburga, he retained not only several figures of the earlier composition, but the general arrangement itself, and the significant diagonal formed by the livid body of Christ which crosses the canvas like a cry of pain.

All through his life, indeed, Rubens improved on himself, and in treating, as he does so often, similar episodes, he corrected a defective work by a better work. If the Grasse pictures excite but slight esteem for the talent of the beginner, it is not useless in watching his progress, to remember his humble commencements. Before he was conscious of his power and had confidence in his genius, we find many equivocal productions that seem scarcely worthy of his name. The paintings made for Santa Croce di Gerusalemme permit us by their very mediocrity to estimate the distance he traversed, and to appreciate more thoroughly the progress due to constant effort and a firm will.

MEDALLION FROM A CEILING BY MANTEGNA.
(In the ' Camera degli Sposi' at Mantua.)

PATIO OF THE PALACE OF VALLADOLID.
Drawing by Boudier. (From a photograph.)

CHAPTER IV

RETURN OF RUBENS TO MANTUA—HIS BROTHER PHILIP VISITS HIM IN ITALY—
PETER PAUL'S EMBASSY TO SPAIN—INCIDENTS OF THE JOURNEY—DELIVERY OF
THE PRESENTS SENT TO PHILIP III. AND THE DUKE OF LERMA—CORRESPONDENCE
OF RUBENS WITH CHIEPPIO, DUKE GONZAGA'S SECRETARY—PAINTINGS AND POR-
TRAITS EXECUTED IN SPAIN—RETURN TO MANTUA.

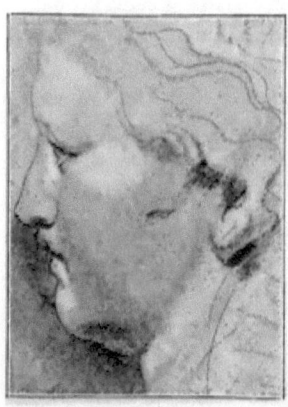

FRAGMENT OF A DRAWING.
(Albertina Collection.)

AFTER finishing the pictures destined for the church of Santa Croce di Gerusalemme, Rubens returned to Mantua. We know that he was settled there again before April 20, 1602, because on that date, Lelio Arrigoni, the agent at Rome, in reply to a question addressed to him by Chieppio, duke Vincenzo's secretary, wrote: "that he would do his best to find young men of talent, capable of painting all the pictures his highness could desire. He would take care that the copies should be made after famous originals, in such fashion, however, that the expense should not exceed the sum of fifteen or eighteen florins, which had been set apart for the commission. But in order to make sure of carrying

out his highness's wishes in every detail, it seemed to him wise
to consult his painter, *the Fleming*, in order to learn which were
the finest and most valuable works he had seen. In specifying
in a precise manner the pictures to be copied, and the places
where they were to be found, it would be easier to satisfy his
highness's taste, and to avoid mistakes." From this letter the value
set on Rubens's judgment may be seen, the choice of the works to
be reproduced being left to his discretion. There is thus reason for
surprise that the duke should have recalled his painter to Mantua,
since he might have employed him on the copies. He purposed
doubtless to entrust him with some important work, such as Richardot
had mentioned in his letter to Vincenzo Gonzaga, but, as we remarked
before, no trace of works painted by *the Fleming* at that time has
been found.

With the exception of a few absences of brief duration, Rubens
spent a whole year at Mantua. Now that the first fever of his
curiosity was satisfied, he was able quietly to test and classify the
impressions that he had received at Rome, and to appreciate her
masterpieces better at a distance. The difficulties encountered in his
first works, and the imperfections he had been obliged to leave in
them, made him feel deeply the necessity of gaining a greater knowledge of the resources of his art, and he attempted to do so with
renewed vigour.

Notwithstanding his energy, he must have often suffered from lone-
liness in a country where he had neither relative nor friend. He had
never known much of the pleasures of home life, and after a joyless
childhood, he had been forced to leave his mother in order to earn
his living. Could he but have received frequent letters from the
loving mother, who with her good sense and her loyalty would have
known so well how to comfort him ! But Antwerp was far off, and the
opportunities of sending letters to Mantua somewhat rare. In any
case no letter from her has been preserved. But we possess three
written to Rubens by his brother Philip, for whom he had a strong
affection. Unfortunately the information they afford us is vague, and
of little interest.

Philip Rubens, forced in early life to make a position for himself, had, as we have seen, while still young, been entrusted with the education of the two sons of President Richardot. He was at first established at Louvain, near Justus Lipsius, who thought very highly of him, and under whose guidance he could carry on his own literary studies even while occupied with his pupils. The first letter he wrote to Peter Paul is dated from Louvain, May 21, 1601, but it is useless to seek in it for family details. A year had passed since he left his brother, and it would seem that he must have had many things to tell him of himself, of their mother, and of their near connections. But Philip was a fine wit, brought up in the worship of classical antiquity, and following the example of a great number of scholars of that period, his letter is a literary composition intended for publication, and entirely lacking in brotherly intimacy. With every elegance of phrase and expression of which he was capable, he deplores a separation, of which he depicts the sorrows in language of glacial prolixity, full of long tirades on friendship, its necessary qualities, its obligations, and its pleasures and pains. Not a word about his mother, his own occupations, his plans, but only laborious metaphors, involved similes, all the empty apparatus of a meaningless and bombastic rhetoric. It is impossible to be more insignificant or futile. On December 13, 1601, another letter was sent by Philip from Padua to his brother, whom he knew to be at Rome, written in Latin, like the former one, but much shorter, and rather more explicit. Philip had arrived a fortnight before with his young pupil, Guillaume Richardot, whom he had accompanied to Italy, where he intended to perfect himself in the study of the law. " My chief wishes were," he said, " to see Italy and you, my dear brother. One of those wishes is accomplished ; I hope to realise the other. What indeed is easier ? The distance between Padua and Mantua is so short. It is only an excursion to be made at one stretch, and when the season permits, we will think of it." He was intending to go with his pupil to Venice about Christmas time, but only for two or three days. " How I should like," he added, " to hear your impressions of that town, and of the various cities of Italy that you have already visited ! Especially of Rome, which you must soon leave, if, as I hope, the duke of Mantua has returned home safe and sound. . . . What, I ask you, is Pourbus doing ? Does he still live and breathe ?

I have heard nothing of our mother since my departure. She has not been able to write to me. Where could she have sent her letters? I hope she maintains her health. Keep well, my dearest brother, and expect more detailed news when I hear where you are."

When Peter Paul returned to Mantua, the proximity of the two brothers permitted them to meet, and in a letter written on June 26,

STUDY FOR AN ADORATION OF THE SHEPHERDS.
Albertina Collection.
(From a photograph by Braun, Clément et Cie.)

1602, to one of their common friends, Jan van den Wouwere, who had come from Spain, Philip, speaking of the pleasure it will be to see him soon at Bologna, adds : " But first we will go to Verona in order that we may thence go together to Mantua," and in concluding, sends him affectionate remembrances from his brother, who was doubtless with him at the time. All three met later at Verona, as the Latin inscription of an engraving, *Judith Holding the Head of Holofernes*, by Cornelis Galle proves: "the first

plate, executed after a work of Rubens, and dedicated by him to the honourable gentleman, Jan van den Wouwere, according to the promise which he remembered to have made him at Verona." Another work by Rubens was to consecrate more especially the memory of that meeting: it is the picture in the Pitti, known as the *Philosophers*, which represents the three friends[1] grouped round a table, in the company and under the presidency of Justus

[1] It is, in fact, Van den Wouwere (Wouverius) and not De Groot (Grotius), as is too often said, who figures there.

Lipsius, with whom they were acquainted, and who inspired them with similar feelings of affection and respect. The work is of importance, executed *con amore*, and interesting both on account of its artistic value, and of the persons it represents. But although it is generally considered to have been painted at that date, we think with Dr. Bode that the character of the composition, and various other indications to which we shall have to return, show it to be later by some years, and that when it was painted neither Justus Lipsius nor Philip Rubens were any longer living.

SKETCH FROM LIFE.
(Albertina Collection.)

Did Peter Paul pass through Padua after his brief visit to Verona in order to accompany his brother? We do not know; but we learn from Peter Paul himself that Philip, thanks to the recommendations of Justus Lipsius and President Richardot, had made friends among the scholars of the town. However, neither he nor Guillaume Richardot, his pupil, attended the University lectures. In their opinion they had teachers of superior merit in Flanders, and as Philip wrote (May 30, 1602) to a scholar, Ericius Pateanus, whom he had known at Milan: "When you have drunk nectar from Justus Lipsius, the weak, sour wine of Padua is not likely to please." Galileo, however, was then lecturing at Padua, and although Philip Rubens does not mention his name, it is certain that Peter Paul, if he did not meet him then, became acquainted with him a little later at Mantua. In any case Peiresc, in one of his letters to the celebrated astronomer, mentions

the interest that Rubens had always taken in his researches, and the
estimation in which he held his knowledge.   Probably, Philip
afterwards visited his brother at Mantua.   Such seems to be the fact
from a letter which he wrote on his return to Padua (July 15, 1602).
Amid the subtleties and affected insipidities with which as always
it abounds, one passage deserves to be quoted because it shows
a really prophetic foresight.   " Take care," said Philip to his
brother, " that the duration of your engagement (in the Duke of
Mantua's service) is not prolonged ; I entreat you in the name of
our mutual affection, I implore you by all you hold sacred, by
your talent itself.   Indeed, I know how much I have reason to fear,
knowing your easy temper, and knowing also how difficult it is
to refuse such a prince when he makes urgent demands.   But remain
firm, and carefully preserve your liberty in a court whence it is almost
vanished.   That is your right : use it with courage.   You will perhaps
say that these recommendations are vain, and that I always sing the
same tune.   It is true, and I intend to fall into the same fault over and
over again, for real love knows no moderation."   We cannot tell from
the letter if Philip merely imagined such a state of things, or whether
his own observation of his brother's position at the Mantuan Court,
showed him the dangers to which his " easy temper" exposed him.
Philip's fear had some foundation, and if, as we have seen, his other
letters are not always remarkable for precision, in this one at least
he betrayed wise judgment.   His clear-sighted affection showed
him that there was reason for anxiety, and that it was as well to
draw the attention of the young painter to the annoyances to which
he might in time be exposed.   Was the advice taken in good
part ?   M. Ruelens is inclined to think that the interference of
his elder brother in his affairs induced some coldness on the part
of Peter Paul ; but this notion, based on the complete cessation
of correspondence between the two brothers, does not seem
to us conclusive, since their letters have probably been lost
or destroyed, with all the others that the painter wrote to his
family.

From the passage quoted above, it is certain in any case that
the duke was anxious to keep Rubens at Mantua, and that he had

VII

The Communion of St. Francis.

(ANTWERP MUSEUM)

(From a photograph by Braun, Clément et Cie.)

made him earnest solicitations on the subject. As time went on, his value was perceived, and Chieppio, Duke Vincenzo's secretary, who, by his office, was brought into direct contact with the painter, was able to appreciate not only his talent, but also his uprightness and intelligence. The isolation in which the young man lived excited Chieppio's sympathy, perhaps, because he himself was not always satisfied with his surroundings. He had often been exposed to the denunciations and calumnies of courtiers who, annoyed by his honesty, wished to bring him under his master's suspicion. That being so, Rubens's loyalty and discretion were well calculated to please him, and an opportunity soon presented itself for utilising those valuable qualities in a somewhat delicate mission, in the course of which the young Fleming showed himself at every point worthy of the confidence reposed in him.

Surrounded by powerful neighbours and too weak to hold his own, the Duke of Mantua was obliged to finesse and manœuvre prudently among them in order to neutralise the greed of one for his possessions by that of another. At that time, when violence and cunning ruled the policies of the different Italian courts, it was difficult to keep on good terms with rivals whose interests were very often opposed. In rendering too marked services to one, or too openly taking his side, there was risk of offending the others. Until then, however, Vincenzo Gonzaga had succeeded in keeping his domains intact, and for the moment was justified in believing himself safe. He had gained a right to the good will of the Pope and the Emperor by taking part twice in expeditions against the Turks ; the Duke of Tuscany was his uncle, and Henry IV., the king of France, had become his brother-in-law, and was on the most cordial terms with him. There remained, however, the king of Spain, who might be tempted to increase his territory at the duke's expense, his possessions in Italy being contiguous to the principality of Mantua. Fortunately for Vincenzo, Philip III. had neither the great ambitions nor the resources of his predecessors. Ruling in his name, his favourite, the Duke of Lerma, kept the sovereign amused, so as to take his attention from matters of state, while he ruined the country through his mistakes and exactions. But the recent memory of Spain's prosperity, and of the

disdainful arrogance of her rulers, still threw illusion over the weakness of a nation that was fast declining. It was necessary for
Duke Vincenzo to secure himself from possible surprises on that
side. For some time his instinct of self-preservation had opened
his eyes to the danger, and he sought to avert it. He was anxious
to know the plans of the Spanish court, and to secure certain
information on the subject. The state of his finances scarcely
permitted him to spend large sums in bribing the high personages
whose co-operation was likely to be useful, but he obtained information
from Iberti, his resident minister in Spain, as to the courtiers or

THE STORM.
Albertina Collection.
(From a photograph by Braun, Clément et Cie.)

ministers among whom it
would be advisable to dis-
tribute gifts, and also as
to the kind of bribe to
which each would be most
accessible, in order that
he might send them suit-
able presents. As the king
could not be left out, and
as riding and the chase
were his favourite amuse-
ments, he was to receive,
together with valuable
arms, some choice horses
from the famous Gonzaga

stables. But the favour of the Duke of Lerma was of even
greater importance. He was known to be a lover of art, and
Duke Vincenzo in August, 1602, had the most celebrated pictures
of Raphael copied for him by Pietro Facchetti, a Mantuan painter
living at Rome. Relics, and other objects connected with religion,
were to be presented to the Countess of Lemos, the Duke of
Lerma's sister, celebrated for her piety, and Pietro Franchezza, one
of Lerma's creatures, was to have some rich tapestries and other gifts
of less value.

To take charge of and deliver the gifts a devoted and trustworthy
man was required, who, if not capable of negotiating (that duty would

fall on the resident minister, Annibale Iberti), would at least be able to ascertain the sentiments of the various persons, and to render them favourable to Duke Vincenzo's cause. Without an official mandate the envoy would have no other credit than that accruing from his personal qualities. Chieppio thought of Rubens. At all times painters have been suitable emissaries, by reason of the facilities of access to princes procured them by their art. By the side of professional diplomatists, the intervention of such semi-official agents offers

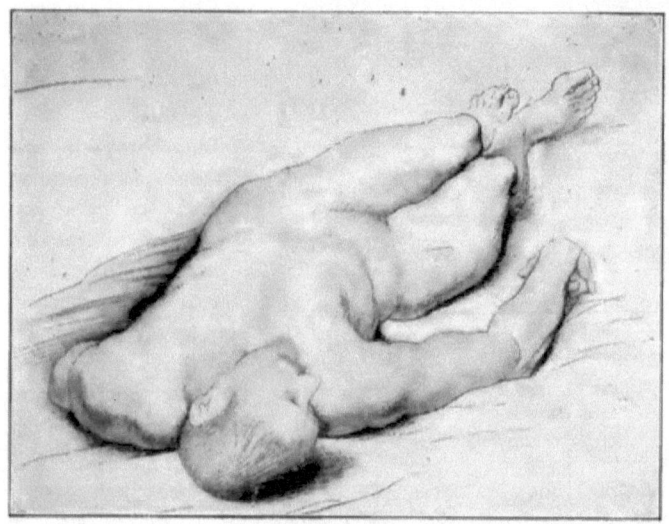

STUDY FROM A MODEL.
(The Louvre.)

a further advantage, that according to the favourable or unfavourable issue of their proceedings, their employer may at his pleasure profit by their services, or disclaim any concern in them. Doubtless in such ill-defined conditions, the position of Rubens was delicate enough ; but trusting in his star, he perceived that here was an opportunity of advancing himself while serving his master.

On March 5, 1603, Vincenzo Gonzaga wrote to Iberti " that he had at length got together the paintings and other presents which were to be distributed in Spain. In forwarding to him the letters to the

different persons for whom they were destined, he charged him to
insist particularly on his desire to please them, a feeling that greatly
exceeded the value of the gifts. He informed him at the same time
of the departure of "Peter Paul, the Fleming, his painter, who was
taking charge of them, and who would give all the necessary explan-
ations about the pictures, and the manufacture of the arquebuses
carefully made of fine steel, and of beautiful workmanship ; "the articles
were to be delivered by Iberti in person, but in the presence and with
the assistance of Peter Paul, who, added the duke, "is by our desire
to be introduced as the envoy expressly sent from here with the
articles. .... And as the said Peter Paul is most successful in painting
portraits, we desire, if there are any other ladies of quality besides
those whose features Count Vincenzo (Iberti's predecessor) had had
reproduced, you may have recourse to his talent to send me portraits
which at a small expense will have even greater merit. If Peter Paul
needs money for his return, you must furnish him with it, and inform us
of the sum, that we may remit it to you by way of Genoa." And with
the ducal letter was enclosed a list enumerating the different presents.

The journey was fated to be long and marked by all sorts of
accidents. Rubens was provided with passports, but at the very
beginning, while following the itinerary laid down for him, he missed
his way ; thereby the journey was lengthened and the expense increased.
Instead of going direct to Genoa, he passed through Ferrara and
Bologna, crossed the Apennines, and having left Mantua on March 5,
did not reach Florence until ten days afterwards. In order to avoid
further delays he left the coach behind him

On his arrival, with the purpose of sheltering himself from respon-
sibility, he hastened to inform Chieppio of his difficulties and of the
unforeseen expenses he had already incurred, which had greatly
encroached on his resources. "In fact if his highness distrusted him,
he had given him too much money ; but too little if he had confidence
in him. . . . It is certain that there would have been no harm in
giving him more than he needed, since he should submit his accounts
to the most minute examination, and as he had only to pay his actual
expenses, the surplus, whatever it might be, would go back to the
treasury. In case of lack of money, on the other hand, what a loss of

advantage and of time !"   He leaves to Chieppio the care of arranging everything, and begs him " to supplement his inexperience."   Written in an Italian of irreproachable accuracy, the letter is a model of frankness and also of dexterity.   Rubens well knew the financial embarrassments of the court of Mantua, and as from his first connection with it he had suffered from the irregular and niggardly payments made to him, he was anxious to establish his position clearly.   With legitimate care for his dignity, he determined that no one should suspect his honour.

After many mishaps, Rubens embarked at Leghorn in the beginning of April, and seventeen or eighteen days later landed at Alicante, where fresh difficulties awaited him.   The court was no longer at Madrid but at Valladolid, a circumstance that considerably lengthened the journey by difficult and little frequented roads.   In order not to delay his progress, Rubens was obliged to leave his heavy baggage behind him.   At length, on May 13, he reached Valladolid, and on the 16th, the agent Iberti informed the duke that " the Fleming had arrived with the case of crystals, and that the horses were in such splendid condition that it did not seem possible they could have had so long a journey."   The rest of the baggage would arrive shortly, before the court, which had set out from Aranjuez for Burgos, returned.   The next day Rubens himself confirmed to Duke Vincenzo the news sent by Iberti, to whom he delivered the articles, and the horses, "which are plump and superb, exactly as they left his highness's stables."   Everything else would speedily follow, and it seemed as if the mission was to be concluded under the happiest auspices.

But Iberti did not regard the new comer with much favour. Knowing the want of means with which his master had always to contend, he was not without anxiety in regard to the increase of expense caused by the slowness of the journey, and the advances which, in consequence, he had been obliged to make for housing the horses and the servants who brought them, and for "giving money to the Fleming in order that he might purchase new clothes."   He also experienced some jealousy in regard to Rubens, at the thought that he must introduce him to the court, and have him by his side to assist in delivering the presents.   His temper and his proceedings soon showed signs of this feeling.

Thus Rubens was not at the end of his troubles, and a new accident, absolutely unexpected, was now added to those which had already marked his mission. The rest of the baggage, of which he announced the speedy arrival, at length reached him, and the coach, the arquebuses, and the crystals were found in perfect condition ; but in spite of all imaginable precautions, the paintings, which at the time of the

JULIUS CÆSAR. DRAWING FROM AN ANTIQUE BUST.
(The Louvre.)

customs examination at Alicante were perfectly intact, had suffered serious damage ; doubtless, in consequence of twenty-five days incessant rain, which, penetrating the cases, had spoiled the canvases. Iberti, in informing the duke and Chieppio (letters of May 24) of the damage, considered it irreparable, and proposed to compensate the loss by half a dozen pictures that the Fleming could paint before the Duke of Lerma's arrival, with the help, at need, of some young Spanish artist whom he would undertake to find.

Rubens, who in no way relished the plan, wrote himself to Chieppio the same day to point out the state of the damage which he would do his best to repair. As to Iberti's proposal, while holding himself ready to obey any orders that might be given him, he protested eagerly against such a plan. In Spain, "in regard to contemporary artists, there were none of worth. . . . The vanity and idleness of the painters were inconceivable, and besides, their style differed completely from his." Also the fraud of such an association could not fail to be discovered ; he had too much care for his dignity to compromise his talent by tasks that he considered beneath him. He asked to be judged by his own works "without being confused with any one else, however great he might be ; and such mingling of the labour of this one or that one would tarnish, by means of an inferior work, the reputation of a name which was not altogether unknown, even in Spain."

The letter, which furnishes a fresh proof of Rubens's practical good sense and tact, informs us also of the route which he followed in his journey from Alicante to Valladolid. It tells us, indeed, that in passing through Madrid, he stayed there long enough to contemplate the " marvellous productions of Titian, Raphael, and other great masters in the king's palace, in the Escorial, and other places, and that the quality and numbers of the pictures filled him with admiration." We can understand the delight and the instruction that the many splendid works

A LADY-IN-WAITING TO THE INFANTA.

Albertina Collection.

(From a photograph by Braun, Clément et Cie.)

which are now the glory of the Prado, afforded him, and we can also imagine that in their presence he would show some contempt for the Spanish artists of the period. The Italian *pasticci* to which they applied themselves were scarcely likely to please him, neither were their rare attempts at originality to his taste ; those of El Greco, for instance, whose long, emaciated and bloodless figures accorded so ill with the aspirations of his healthy and robust nature.

Fortunately Iberti, like Rubens himself, had in the first wave of feeling somewhat exaggerated the damage which the pictures, sent

from Mantua, had received during the journey. After drying them
and carefully washing them with warm water, both recognised that
the damage could be repaired by repainting them in places. On
June 14, Iberti informed Duke Vincenzo that "the Fleming was getting
on with the work of restoring the pictures ; thanks to his industry,
they were in a fair way to be finished, and there were only two which
were absolutely destroyed beyond recovery. In order to compensate
for that, and in some degree to set off the gift, I will take care," he
added, "that if time permits, he shall do something by his own
hand." The death of the Duchess of Lerma having again delayed
the arrival of the Court, a short respite was left to the artist, and on
July 6, Iberti at length informed the duke of the arrival of the king
and his suite, and Chieppio of the completion of the work. "Instead
of a *Head of St. John* by Raphael, and a small *Madonna*, the Fleming
has painted a picture of *Democritus and Heraclitus*, which is considered very good." According to Iberti it would seem that the
composition brought the two philosophers together on one canvas,
but there were actually two paintings which, after forming part of the
Duke of Lerma's collection, became the property of the King of
Spain, and are now in the Prado. In spite of Iberti's eulogistic
appreciation, they do Rubens no great credit. The figures
are commonplace, and the flesh-tints of an exaggerated brown.
The expression of sadness in Heraclitus, as well as the smile and
gaiety of Democritus, are equally commonplace, and verge on carica-
ture. Although the latter figure is a little better than the other, they
are, in fact, mere academic studies, painted without models, and their
hurried execution betrays the haste with which the artist worked.

The court was now installed at Valladolid, where for two years
the king had taken up his residence in the new palace, which had
been richly decorated, with vast galleries and a *patio* of elegant
simplicity, surrounded by a colonnade, and ornamented with busts of
Roman emperors, executed in demi-relief by Berruguete.

On the day appointed, July 11, the coach and the beautifully
equipped horses were, at the instance of Iberti, brought to a garden a
short distance from the town, and he presented them to the king and
queen. They both repeatedly expressed their delight ; and their alacrity

6

Drawing after Raphael's " Transfiguration."

in using the carriage and horses on the following days testified to the sincerity of their satisfaction. The next day, as Iberti wrote, Rubens set out the pictures "with great art" in one of the Duke of Lerma's apartments. He, entering it alone, in his dressing-gown, looked at them attentively one by one, and was greatly struck by the perfection of the work. Indeed, he took the copies retouched by the painter for originals, and much admired the two canvases that he had added to them. The Fleming received his share of praise, and the duke was so delighted with him, that he asked Iberti if it would not be possible to take him into his service. Although he declined that proposal, the envoy assured the Duke of Lerma that as long as the artist remained in Spain he would be at his entire disposal.

According to his custom, Rubens had also, on his part, informed his master and Chieppio of these events, briefly, and with a respectful deference towards the first, and in a free and explicit fashion when writing to the secretary.[1] He referred him to Iberti for the complete narration of all that had taken place. "It was not from idleness that he refrained in that matter ; but by pure discretion, because, except in the case of absolute necessity, he did not like to encroach on the territory of others." Whatever may have been his reserve, he could not refrain from showing his surprise that, in spite of the express recommendation of the Duke of Mantua, Iberti had not thought of presenting him to the king. "I do not mention this," he added, " by way of complaint, from a cavilling temper, or from vanity." He merely stated the facts as they had occurred, without wishing to accuse Iberti, who had evidently acted with the best intentions, and who, at the moment perhaps, forgot what had been decided, although the remembrance of it must have been somewhat fresh. "He had not, however, given any reason, nor made any excuse for not carrying out the programme arranged between them scarcely half an hour before, and although he had had ample opportunity, he had not breathed a word on the subject." Even through the moderation of his language, it is clear that Rubens felt the slight to his merit and dignity, and the need of expressing what was in his mind. Another passage in the letter concerning the pictures is not less significant. "The Duke of Lerma,"

[1] Letters of July 17, 1603.

said the artist, "showed himself entirely satisfied with the excellence, and the number of the pictures, which, thanks to skilful repainting, had acquired, through the damage they had suffered, the appearance of old works, so that they were in a great measure accepted as originals without any mistrust of their authenticity, although on our side we said nothing to foster such a belief. The king and queen, a large number of nobles, and a few painters also saw and admired them." The detail

ST. PETER.
(The Prado.)

is characteristic. Rubens did nothing to mislead those noble personages : but he did nothing to disabuse them of their error, thinking that the value of the gift would thereby be heightened. The proceeding was not perhaps absolutely correct, but it is explained and at need excused by Rubens's desire to serve his master's cause in the best possible way, and also by Iberti's disregard of his presence.

As soon as that part of his mission was concluded, the artist prepared to paint the portraits which had been commissioned from him by Duke Vincenzo. He hoped to accomplish the task unless prevented by some caprice of the king, or of the Duke of Lerma. On that point he should obey Iberti's instructions : then he should be ready to set out for France, and begged "that he might be informed in one way or another of what decision had been come to in that respect." But Rubens's visit was to be prolonged far beyond the time that he foresaw, and the promise given by the Duke of Lerma of employing him on "a picture of which he had an idea," remained for a long while without effect. The duke had just lost his wife (June 2, 1603), and, deeply absorbed in grief, he did not trouble himself about Rubens. The days passed for the painter in an inaction which, with his love of work, he found particularly disagreeable. If only he had been at Madrid, he could have studied at his ease the masterpieces of the Italian painters, that he had only just been able to glance at, and these would have furnished him with the instruction he was so eager to gain.

But the artistic resources of Valladolid were restricted, he dared not go away, and was obliged to hold himself at the Duke of Lerma's disposal, ready to respond to his call when it should please him to employ him. He lived in almost complete isolation, and the proximity of Iberti was not of great assistance. The resident minister was extremely anxious to be repaid the sums of money he had advanced, but in spite of the repeated demands he

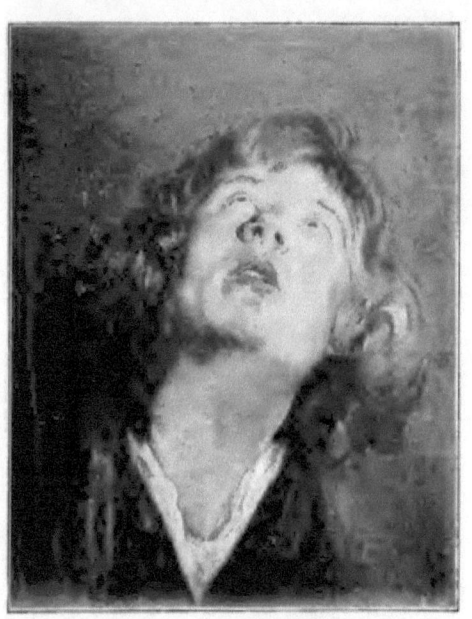

STUDY FOR A HEAD OF ST. JOHN.
(The Louvre : Lacaze Gallery.)

addressed to Mantua, received no reply. He carried on by himself the negotiations with which he was entrusted, keeping Rubens in the background, and, as the tone of his correspondence shows, even regarding him with some suspicion. Isolated, condemned to idleness, the Fleming might, it is true, have occupied himself with the portraits of celebrated beauties with which he was to provide Vincenzo Gonzaga's gallery. But it was only with reluctance that he had accepted a task he considered unworthy of him, and chafing with impatience, he awaited an opportunity of proving the extent of his talent. None of the portraits, in any case, if he did paint them, have

come down to us, whether because, according to M. Ruelens, the Duke
of Gonzaga's descendants took no care to preserve such witnesses to
his gallantry, or because the pictures were dispersed or destroyed in
1630 at the time of the sack of Mantua by the Imperialist
troops.

The reputation acquired by Rubens as a portrait painter procured
him some commissions which, in filling up his leisure, permitted him
to earn a little money, a matter of some importance, considering
the destitution in which his master left him. A portrait of a woman
which figured in the Madrid Exhibition of 1892 [1] appears to us
to have been painted in Spain about that date, and as it belonged
formerly to the family of the dukes of l'Infantado, it represents, in all
probability, a member of that family, with whom Iberti was on friendly
terms. The work is remarkable for its brilliance and good preservation. Seen almost full face, the young woman is dressed in a rich and
elegant costume : she wears a gown of vermilion red silk, embroidered
with gold, with white satin sleeves slashed with red, and round her
neck two rows of big pearls. The red hair is turned up from the
forehead, and sets off the extreme freshness of the flesh tints, which
are heightened still more by the amber tint of the Cordova
leather hangings that form the background of the portrait. The
ingenuous expression, and the candour of the physiognomy are very
pleasing, and the aristocratic delicacy of the slim hands complete the
characterisation of the charming figure. Her reserved and modest
mien absolutely forbids the thought that we are here in the presence
of one of the compliant beauties whose portraits the Duke of Mantua
loved to collect. The execution is remarkably skilful. The face,
somewhat hastily modelled, is most luminous in colour, with light
diaphanous shadows, and the brush-work, although very broad, is
little apparent. Here and there in the hair are found those discreetly
loaded touches which, applied with decision, are in conformity
with the habitual practice of the Flemish school. Rubens always
remained faithful to this method, which allowed him to finish his
pictures with little trouble and without over-elaboration. Thanks

---

[1] Room XXII., No. 215 in the Catalogue. It was exhibited by E. Gomez, and
was formerly in the Palace of Guadajara, where it was then attributed to Rubens.

to the precision of these high lights, the handling, although very
expeditious, presents an aspect of most delicate finish.

M. Hymans found at Madrid, in the Duke of Alba's oratory, a
work of another kind, the *Supper at Emmäus*, which he thinks was also
painted at this time, and which, in any case, belongs to the artist's
youth. But it seems to us difficult to decide whether it was painted
in Spain or a short time after Rubens's return to Antwerp. As
M. Hymans says, the somewhat commonplace composition recalls the Bolognese school, and "its sombre tones give but a
distant hint of the brilliant Antwerp colourist."[1]   At the bottom
of W. Swanenburch's plate bearing the date 1611—the earliest of
the dated engravings after Rubens—is an inscription, according
to which the picture belonged at that time to a Dutch amateur,
a fact which weakens the hypothesis that it was painted in
Spain.   But the mediocrity of the work makes the question of
little interest.   Of superior merit and importance, the three large
pictures from the Church of the Franciscans of Fuensaldaña, now
in the Valladolid Museum, the *Assumption, St. Anthony of Padua
with the Infant Jesus*, and *St. Francis of Assisi receiving the
Stigmata*, present a more delicate problem. M. Max Rooses, who
does not think they are by Rubens, attributes them to a Flemish
contemporary of the master, who had lived in Spain, but whose
works are not otherwise known. Neither does M. Hymans, though
he recognises some merit in the last two pictures, think that
they are by Rubens.   Justi, on the contrary, is of opinion that
the pictures deserve very careful examination, and that, judging by
the similarities they possess to other works of Rubens's youth,
their authenticity is probable.   The reproduction of the best of the
canvases, *St. Francis receiving the Stigmata*, which we give to our
readers, will permit them to judge if the analogies are sufficiently
numerous, and if the animation and expression of the principal
figure, if the form of his hands, and the decorative breadth of the
composition, are in themselves enough to justify its attribution to
Rubens; on the other hand, the type of the saint, the somewhat

[1] *Notes sur quelques œuvres d'art conservées en Espagne*, by Henri Hymans. *Gazette
des Beaux-Arts*, August 1, 1894, p. 162.

angular precision of his features, and the character and composition
of the landscape are not found in the works painted by the Fleming
at that time.

Although positively noted in Iberti's letters, no trace so far of
another large canvas painted by Rubens for the Duke of Lerma, who

at length determined to
employ the artist, has been
found. But after the death
of his wife, the tastes of
Philip III.'s minister
changed. Instead of pro-
fane subjects, the *fêtes
galantes* and love scenes
which formerly pleased
him, he now cared only
for religious pictures.
While his friends were
thinking of a second mar-
riage for him, he was
contemplating retirement
from the world, and he
succeeded a short time
after in obtaining a Car-
dinal's hat. Notwithstanding his altered frame of
mind, Lerma, as if wish-
ing to mingle with the
memories of his political
greatness some unsus-
pected aspirations after
military glory, asked

ST. FRANCIS RECEIVING THE STIGMATA.
(Valladolid Museum.)

Rubens to paint him on horseback and in armour. The artist set
bravely to work. But in consequence of the numerous interruptions to
which his many duties subjected his sitter, the portrait begun at Valladolid made little progress. The duke had even been obliged to leave
that town for Ventosilla, one of his estates about fifteen leagues dis-

tant, where he was visited by the Dukes of Savoy, and where the
king and queen also made a brief sojourn. Iberti was asked to send
Rubens there in order to finish the portrait, and in a letter written
by the envoy to the Duke of Mantua, October 19, 1603, he informed

PORTRAIT OF A SPANISH LADY.
(Madrid Exhibition. 1892.)

him "that in the opinion of all, the portrait, as far as it had gone, was
a distinct success." A little more than a month later (November 23)
he informed his master that the work being finished "it gave the
Duke of Lerma the greatest pleasure, and that he was repeatedly

charged to bear witness to the satisfaction for which the duke was
indebted to his highness." We have every reason to suppose that
the portrait, for which we have searched in vain, still exists in Spain,
probably in some palace of the Dukes of Denia, descendants of the
family of Lerma.[1] But even at Ventosilla the work must have been
interrupted by the goings and comings of the sitter, who was obliged
to accompany the king to the Escorial.

It was doubtless to fill his leisure hours that Rubens, shut up in
the country, also painted for the Duke of Lerma (as he tells us himself
in a letter to Sir Dudley Carleton in 1618) a series of Christ and the
twelve Apostles, now in the Prado. He preserved the pen-and-ink
drawings relieved by red chalk, which form part of the Albertina
collection, and after which, not only the engravings of N. Ryckemans,
but the copies which are now in the Rospigliosi Palace at Rome,
were executed later. These copies are superior to the originals
in their breadth of handling and brilliancy of colouring, for they were
painted under the supervision of the master, and re-touched by him
when he was in the full maturity of his genius ten years afterwards.[2]
The Prado pictures, painted evidently as an academic exercise and
without any regard to nature, are entirely lacking in character. In the
figures with their eyes raised to heaven and their studied gestures we
trace too evidently the efforts of an artist, who, in his attempt to vary
as much as possible the poses and types of his personages, has not
succeeded in endowing them with individuality ; he contrives to show the
signification of each of them by the accessories that he puts into their
hands : a book, a staff, keys, a cross, &c. The heavy, somewhat tame
composition betrays the constraint of a young man who, having to
deal with an unpromising task, does not possess the flexibility of
talent nor the trained resources which would help him to accomplish
it satisfactorily.

[1] Such is also the opinion of M. Cruzada Villaamil, who says that after the confis-
cation of the property of the Duke of Lerma, the great portrait formed for a brief period
part of the royal collections of the Ribera Palace at Valladolid, before its return to the
family by the order of Philip IV. in 1635. It is mentioned in any case in an inventory
of the furniture of that palace drawn up in 1621.

[2] The Christ is wanting to the series in the Prado, but it occurs in that of the
Rospigliosi Palace.

VIII

Portraits of the Earl and Countess of Arundel.

(MUNICH GALLERY.)

Printed by Wittmann, Paris (France).

Meanwhile Iberti, who had asked and obtained his recall, was replaced in Spain by a new envoy, Bonatti, with whom Iberti remained for some time in order to acquaint him with affairs. Before his departure on September 15, Iberti wrote to Chieppio that "he would examine the Fleming's accounts, feeling sure that they would be correct, for he thought him an honest man." By the same messenger Rubens also wrote to Chieppio, telling him "that he had neither merits to insist on, nor faults to acknowledge either in extravagant expenses during the journey, or on any other occasion." He feared no suspicion of carelessness or deceit, opposing to such accusations their experience of his services, and of his irreproachable honesty. As to his return he had personally no knowledge on the subject, and was ignorant of what had been decided. He would do his best to serve his master, and he would act in the same way in France, if he was to pass through that country as he had formerly been commanded to do ; since he had been in Spain he had received no fresh instructions. He would then await orders, and would carry them out as soon as they were communicated to him, "without having on his own account any desire, any plan, so deeply was he *incarnated* in the interests of his master." After many delays, Rubens at length saw the glimpse of a possibility of quitting Spain ; but in spite of his assurances he much hoped that he would not be obliged to travel by way of France. He knew that Duke Vincenzo still held to his idea of obtaining portraits of celebrated beauties for his gallery, and consequently of enriching it by those of the prettiest women at the court of his brother-in-law, Henry IV., whom he knew to be a connoisseur in such matters. This was a task which, as we have seen, Rubens considered unworthy of him, and he was terrified at the thought of finding at the Court of France the inaction and vexations from which he had suffered in Spain. In another letter, also to Chieppio, probably in November, 1603, he tried to ward off the danger which threatened him, and cleverly insisted on the reasons that seemed to him most likely to bring about his desire.

Rubens gained his cause ; we are not able to fix the exact date of his return—for there is a somewhat long gap in the corre-spondence at this period—but he left Spain for Mantua. He had

been away nearly a year. If a year spent thus, in restoring a
few damaged pictures, or in the hasty execution of works of little
value, was almost lost for the development of his talent, it had,
on the other hand, contributed in a most efficient manner to
the formation of his character. Although he was often again to experience the vexations, he had learned once for all the vanity of
court life, and had witnessed its dishonourable intrigues. Disheartened
by the trifling away of days he could so well have filled, days which
passed for him in vain attempts or idle conversation, he was now
anxious to devote himself entirely to his art, and eager to find an
outlet for his energy and opportunities for instruction at Mantua.

THE INFANT JESUS AND ST. JOHN THE BAPTIST.
Fac-simile of an engraving by C. Jegher, after Rubens

CHAPTER V

RUBENS REMAINS AT MANTUA FOR TWO YEARS (1604–1605)—PICTURES PAINTED
FOR THE CHURCH OF THE JESUITS: THE 'TRINITY,' THE 'BAPTISM OF CHRIST,'
AND THE 'TRANSFIGURATION'—THE 'DRUNKENNESS OF HERCULES,' AND THE
'VICTORY CROWNING A HERO'—COPIES AFTER THE ITALIAN MASTERS—SOJOURN OF
RUBENS AT ROME WITH HIS BROTHER (1606)—STUDY OF THE ANTIQUE—THE
'ST. GREGORY' PAINTED FOR THE CHIESA NUOVA—RUBENS IS RECALLED TO
MANTUA (1607)—VISIT TO GENOA—RETURN TO ROME AND THE WORKS PAINTED
THERE—DEPARTURE FOR ANTWERP, WHITHER HE IS RECALLED BY THE HOPELESS
CONDITION OF HIS MOTHER.

ANTIQUE BUST.
Drawing by Rubens. (The Louvre.)

IN all probability Rubens only returned
to Mantua in the beginning of 1604.
So, at least, it would seem from
a mediocre set of Latin verses: *Ad
Petrum Paulum Rubenium Navigantem*,
addressed to him about February, 1604, on
the subject of his journey, by his brother
Philip, probably from Rome, where he
then was. Exact information is sought in
vain in the epistle, which abounds in bombastic apostrophes, digressions, and affected
rhetoric. Since his former visit to Italy,
Philip, uncertain what career he desired
to follow, had led a somewhat wandering existence. He was
then at Rome, and probably saw his brother at Mantua before
returning to Flanders, whither Justus Lipsius urged him to go to be
installed as his successor in his chair at Louvain University. After

Philip's departure Peter Paul resumed with zeal his life of work and
study at Mantua, where he remained for two years. He found there
Chieppio, whose kind offices had been so helpful during his visit to
Spain. The accounts of the money expended during the journey
having been verified, Chieppio, full of sympathy for the faithful servant's
amiable and loyal nature, doubtless commended the devotion and
intelligence with which Rubens had accomplished his mission to his
master. In any case, on June 2, 1604, Duke Vincenzo Gonzaga,
desirous to attach him more closely to his person, renewed the contract
by which he had engaged him, and granted "to Peter Paul, painter, a
provision of 400 ducatoons a year, payable every three months, from
May 24." At that time, also, as if zealous to surround himself with
the most illustrious men of the time, the duke tried to attach Galileo
to his court, and he had twice come to Mantua to discuss the arrangements. But whether Galileo had already the idea of returning to
Florence, or whether the duke considered his demands too high, the
negotiations failed.

Led by his capricious temper, and by his love of pleasure, Vincenzo
Gonzaga had returned to his life of dissipation, when the death of his
mother (August 15, 1604) gave a new turn to his thoughts, and provided Rubens with the long-awaited opportunity of worthily employing
his talent. Eleonora of Austria was greatly loved by her people ;
filial piety and the unanimous regret at her death led the Duke
of Mantua to assign her as a burying place the Church of
the Trinity, belonging to the Order of the Jesuits, situated in
the centre of the town near the market place. A manuscript
chronicle drawn up by Father Gorzoni[1] tells us under what
conditions the commission of decorating the chapel was given
to the Fleming. Speaking of the administration of the Superior,
Father Caprara, in 1605, Gorzoni expresses himself in these terms :
" His directorship was marked by the precious gift, one that will
become more and more valuable as time goes on, of three large
pictures that his Serene Highness, Duke Vincenzo, destined to adorn
in perpetuity, the large chapel which he had perfectly restored, in honour
both of our Order and of the ashes of her most Serene Highness his

---

[1] It is in the Library of Mantua.

mother, by whom a humble sepulchre was here chosen. The three pictures, composed and executed by the famous Rubens, represent, first, the one which faces you, the *Mystery of the Most Holy Trinity*, to which the church is dedicated, the portraits painted from life of all the members of the Gonzaga family then ruling, that is to say, Duke Vincenzo himself and his wife, and their Serene Highnesses his father and mother, with their sons and daughters; second, on the side where the Gospel is read: *The Baptism of the Saviour by St. John the Baptist*; and lastly, the third, on the side where the Epistle is read, the *Mystery of the Transfiguration*. That work is now world famous, and all strangers to it who are good judges, and who see it, are struck dumb with admiration. If report does not lie, the three pictures cost his Serene Highness 1,300 doubloons, but the value of one of them would now be much more than that price."

The three pictures, now scattered, underwent cruel vicissitudes. In 1797, at the time of the occupation of Mantua, the church of the Trinity was used as a forage-store, and an army commissary had the vandalism to have the central picture cut in pieces that it might be more easily transported to France. Measures taken in time by the Municipality prevented its departure, and two fragments that have been found are now placed together in the Mantua Museum. The lower portion shows us on the left Duke Vincenzo and his father Duke Guglielmo; on the right his mother Eleonora of Austria, and his wife Eleonora de' Medici; all four kneeling near a balustrade, under a portico ornamented with twisted columns. Here and there curtains, added afterwards to hide the rents, fill the place of the portraits of the sons and daughters of Duke Vincenzo which have disappeared, and of a soldier of the guards, in which costume, it is said, Rubens represented himself; near him is a tall greyhound, a favourite beast of the duke. Their eyes raised to heaven, the four persons address their prayers to the Trinity, represented in the fragment which occupies the upper part of the composition. Angels placed at the top hold up, or draw aside, the loose parts of a rich drapery which frames the apparition.

The upper part is more careless in treatment; perhaps it has suffered more than the rest; perhaps also Rubens, as he often did,

bestowed greater care on the lower part of the composition, because it was nearer the spectator. The Christ, with His beard, His
long hair, and regular features, has already the expression of strength
and tenderness that he possesses in all the master's works. The
figure of God the Father, the left hand resting on a globe, and a
sceptre in the other, is absolutely lacking in character. Round them
are angels very boldly foreshortened; their attitudes, and the effect
of the white drapery and the flesh-tints relieved against a dark
blue sky, seem to have been inspired by the Venetians, especially
by Tintoretto; but the features of the angels are commonplace, the
flesh too ruddy, and the forms over-soft and ungraceful. Of larger

THE TRINITY.
Upper part of the original picture. (Mantua Museum.)

dimensions, the persons of the lower part are of a broader and more
skilful execution. There, also, are reminiscences of the Venetian
masters, particularly of Veronese. But the decorative sense, the
ease and precision of the brush-work, are already those of Rubens,
and if we find here the twisted columns and the somewhat slender
balustrade which figured before in the Grasse *Raising of the Cross*,
the general aspect has greatly gained in breadth. With a masterly
sureness and decision the artist has characterised the individuality of
the princes of the Gonzaga family, dressed in brilliant costumes, and
arranged symmetrically before their prayer desks; Duke Vincenzo's
bald forehead, proudly turned-up moustaches, and foppish air, cor-
respond perfectly with our idea of that personage.

The two canvases, hung as pendants on each side of the central panel, differ but very slightly in size.[1] Perhaps their original proportions were modified, for both underwent a lamentable fate. They were removed from the Church of the Trinity in 1797 ; the *Baptism of Christ*, after numerous wanderings, found a resting-place in 1876, in the Antwerp Museum. It is disfigured by damages and repaintings, which hardly permit us to judge what it was formerly like. The contrasts are violent, the shadows hard and abrupt, the colour, faded in places, is in others of an extreme crudity, principally in the flesh, the redness of which is most displeasing.

THE TRANSFIGURATION
(Nancy Museum.)

Evidently Rubens was not responsible for all these defects. To be just we should confine ourselves to an examination of the composition of the vast canvas. The artist made a study for it in a drawing which is in the Louvre, and which, contrary to the opinion of M. Max Rooses, we think is by the hand of the master. The traces it bears of having been squared for enlargement, the changes introduced in the picture, and its execution, very like that of other drawings of the period, seem to us fully to confirm

[1] The *Baptism of Christ* is 21 ft. 3·90 in. wide by 15 ft. 9·76 in. ; and the *Transfiguration*, 22 ft. 1·74 ft. by 13 ft. 8·17 in.

the attribution. In the general arrangement it resembles the same
episode in Raphael's *Loggia*, while the figures on the right are
directly inspired by the group of soldiers undressing in Michael
Angelo's cartoon of the *Battle of Cascina*, a group that Rubens had
copied. We must add that the different elements of the composition are insufficiently connected, and the tree planted in the centre
of the canvas, cuts it, in two nearly equal parts, in a most awkward
fashion. When these criticisms have been made, it is only just to
recognise the individual qualities that give a value to the work ; such as
the pictorial comprehension of the subject, the imposing appearance
of the figures, the skill with which the light is distributed, the happy
contrasts it sets up between the different planes, and the accuracy with
which they are determined. We must also note the expression of some
of the figures, those of St. John and of Christ, for instance, and the
knowledge of the nude revealed in the young man leaning against the
central tree, a figure we shall meet again, with an almost identical pose,
in a work painted a short time after, the *St. Sebastian* of the Corsini
Palace.

The last of the three pictures which formed the decoration of the
church of the Trinity, the *Transfiguration*, is in the Nancy Museum,
to which it was presented in 1801. Indeed, many of the masterpieces
accumulated in the Louvre during the conquests of the Empire found
their way into the provincial collections. Although it has suffered
some damage, the Nancy picture is the least spoiled of the three, and
it thus affords a very fair opportunity of appreciating the talent of
Rubens at that period of his career. Of the three, also, it contains the
most numerous and the least dissimulated borrowings made by him
from the Italian masters. The scene itself, and some of the figures introduced into it—for instance, Christ, several of the Apostles, the episode
of the madman, and the woman, in the foreground, who throws herself
violently backward—are taken from Raphael's *Transfiguration*, several
portions of which Rubens had carefully copied. Michael Angelo,
Titian, and the Bolognese painters might with equal justice claim the
paternity of other figures in this cento of scarcely disguised reminiscences. It is all transposed into Flemish with somewhat coarse types,
exuberant masses of flesh, exaggerated gesticulations, and muscularities,

7

Study in Three Chalks

(THE LOUVRE.)

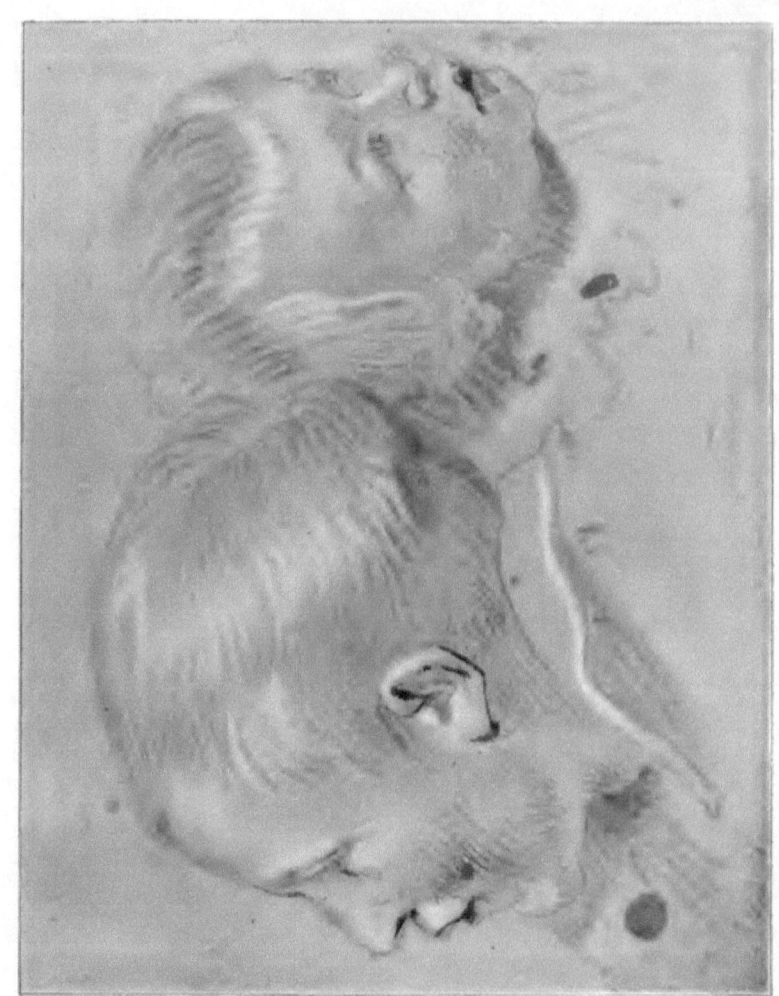

bright red or tawny flesh-tints, and faces streaked with vermilion. The chiaroscuro, directly derived from that of Caravaggio, still further accentuates these contrasts. Even in the centre of his work Rubens places the strongest shadow side by side with the most brilliant light, and has made no transition between the two extreme values. His shadows are opaque, rather black, his contours are strongly defined, and, following Baroccio's example, without more respect for truth than for harmony, he annihilates or perverts the local colour in the high lights, while he magnifies it in the shadows. But notwithstanding its plagiarisms and violent contrasts, the work possesses unity, inspiration, and poetical characteristics that emanate from a powerful sense of life, animation and expression. With an ease that never fails for a single instant, with the joyous confidence of youthful ardour, his brush glides over the canvas, and if sometimes he presses rather heavily on it, if he has for a moment more strength than grace or suppleness, he invariably shows that delight in his work which marks the good workman. His method of painting, based on the traditions of his country, is as expeditious as wise ; it rests on the methodical use of a medium tone, modified according to the needs of the modelling by deeper tones in the bolder parts, and somewhat marked impasto in the high lights. With a firm and vigorous stroke he thoroughly understands when to break the folds of a stuff, to make the gold of an embroidery, or the burnished steel of a cuirass stand out : and how to reproduce the reflected lights of glossy hair, or the pearly moistness of flesh. ' He always says clearly what he wants to say, without hesitation, and without affectation, and the diversity of his work enables him to give the illusion of most elaborate finish at small expense.

The mourning of the court had for some time put an end to the worldly distractions of Duke Vincenzo, and he had thus an opportunity of occupying himself with his painter, and of making use of him. He doubtless turned the talent he recognised in him as a portrait painter to good account, although the inventories of the Palace of Mantua only mention sketches of two heads, and one portrait, *Madame Eleonora Gonzaga*, doubtless a study for the picture of the *Trinity*. Perhaps it was in view of portraits to be painted that Rubens made the drawings in black and red chalk which are in

the Stockholm Museum,[1] and which represent Vincenzo Gonzaga's
two sons, the young princes Franceso and Ferdinando, sketches
hastily dashed off with a few strokes of the brush, but which
accurately reproduce their physiognomies. Of pictures by Rubens
the inventories drawn up in 1627 and in 1665 mention only an *Ecce
Homo*, and three small paintings which have disappeared. But
although they are not mentioned, two other very important works, now
in the Dresden Gallery, were painted by the artist at that period. They

CEILING OF THE CHAPEL OF NOTRE DAME.
In the ancient church of the Jesuits at Antwerp.
Drawing by Rubens.   (Albertina Collection.)

came direct from Mantua, and their dimensions are almost similar.[2]
As they are in excellent preservation, they permit us to appreciate
better than we have hitherto been able to do, what the work of the
master in the early period of his youth was like. *The Drunken
Hercules*, of which the Cassel Museum possesses a replica of reduced
size, presents a symbolic image of man, given up to his senses,

---

[1] They were formerly in the Crozat collection, and both bear these words written in
his own hand : *Fatti in presenza di S. A. da P. P. Rubens.*
[2] 6 ft. 7·92 in. by 7 ft. 3·40 in. ; and 6 ft. 8·31 in. by 6 ft. 8·31 in.

degraded at once by drink and sensual pleasure. Hercules, with the repulsive features of a fat, drunken boor, walks with uncertain steps, haggard eye, and besotted expression, escorted by the companions of his debauchery. The figure of Hercules with its massive forms and its roughly modelled, ruddy, exuberant flesh, is of an extreme vulgarity, and the female form who supports him, equally lacks distinction. It must also be confessed that the right side of the picture is enveloped in blackish shadow, and altogether wanting in trans-

THE DRUNKEN HERCULES ACCOMPANIED BY SATYRS.
(Cassel Museum.)

parency. But the group is well arranged, and is happily finished by the charming silhouette of a bacchante with dishevelled hair and flowing tunic. The low horizon permits the whole figure of the bacchante to be seen against the sky; the grey-blue colour of the sky, and the delicious blues of the distances co-operate with the olive-green tones of the foreground to set off the flesh-tints. The simplicity and boldness of his method characterise Rubens's originality in masterly fashion. If, at that period, reminiscences of Titian and Giulio Romano haunted his mind, in this composition, at least, so freely con-

ceived, and so broadly carried out, he dared to be himself; there for
the first time he hinted at those *Triumphs of the Flesh*, which later
on filled so large a place in his work:

The pendant, the *Victory crowning a Hero*, also painted for Duke
Gonzaga, is likewise an allegory, and symbolises the triumph of man
over his passions. Clad in armour, and setting his foot on the neck of
Silenus with his bestial face, the hero draws Victory, who holds a wreath
of laurels suspended over his head, towards him. On the left, a little
apart, Venus, disconcerted at being forsaken, looks angrily at her
contemner, and near her Cupid, vexed at the impotence of his darts,
peevishly weeps. Above, Envy, his head encircled with serpents,
vainly pours forth his rage. There is nothing remarkable in the
execution, which is slightly flat and weak. The influence of Caravaggio
is apparent in the hard outlines and the violent contrasts of light and
shadow. Later on, by the beneficent introduction of half tones
Rubens obtained stronger effects with less effort.

The figure of Venus, and especially that of Victory, shadows forth
the painter of female nudity, and more than once in his compositions,
notably in the *Venus and Adonis* of the Hermitage, he again used the
undulating line of the Victory, so charming and exquisite in its freedom.
In representing Duke Vincenzo laying hold of the physically seductive
goddess, Rubens unintentionally showed himself a faithful interpreter of
the truth, for in the frivolous and dissipated life of his hero, history
would record more amorous weaknesses than great military deeds.

In addition to these paintings, Rubens did not fail to carry on
his own instruction by making copies of the works that interested
him, either for the duke or for himself. It was in order to preserve
them during the whole of his life that he painted the two copies
of Titian's portraits of Isabella d'Este, which occur in the inventory
of his studio. Only one of them has come down to us, and is
now in the Vienna Gallery. It is a careful study; but although
the slightest details are most scrupulously reproduced, the pearly
freshness of the flesh-tints is obtained by the contrast of brilliant tones
and bluish shadows so characteristic of the Flemish master. Another
copy from Titian, that of the portrait of the beautiful Lavinia,[1] is also

[1] Now in the Dresden Gallery.

in the Vienna Gallery, and it was at Ferrara, where the portrait then was, that Rubens doubtless found an opportunity of copying it. It tempted him, it is clear, on account of the instruction to be obtained from it. No other painting could, in any case, teach him so well to clear his palette of those opaque shadows in which he followed the unfortunate example of Caravaggio. More brilliant flesh-tints, a more decided modelling, more transparent penumbra cannot be imagined. But even here, notwithstanding the copyist's fidelity to his original, his individual temperament is revealed in his manner of spreading the paint over the canvas and handling the brush; he also endows his model with a certain air of Flemish beauty, which renders his copy less delicate and more vermilion, more luxurious, and more artless than the original.

It is not the only copy that the artist had the opportunity of making in the neighbourhood of Mantua, and a drawing after Leonardo's *Last Supper* proves that he went to Milan. The study of the same master's *Battle of Anghiari* must have been made after one of the reproductions preserved either at Florence or Paris, since the original cartoon was at that time already destroyed. The talent of Rubens as a copyist procured him a great reputation; a painter in the service of the Emperor Rudolph II., Johann von Aachen of Cologne, who, about the end of 1603, saw some of the copies at Mantua, praised them so highly to his sovereign, that in March, 1605, he begged Duke Vincenzo's envoy to convey to his master his desire of obtaining reproductions of the pictures of Correggio which were at Mantua. Rubens, authorised by Vincenzo Gonzaga, set to work, and as he professed a vast admiration for Correggio's talent, he doubtless accomplished his task with success; in any case, on the reception of the copies at Prague, the Emperor expressed to the duke his perfect satisfaction. From the inventory of the Palace of Mantua, drawn up in 1627, we learn that there were then three Correggios at Mantua : the *Ecce Homo*, the *Education of Cupid*,[1] and the *St. Jerome Meditating*; but it is not known what has become of the copies in question.

The archives furnish no document relating to Rubens until about

---

[1] The two pictures are now in the National Gallery.

the middle of 1606. The Duke of Mantua was then absorbed in
other cares, and was occupied in the settlement of his children. He
solicited a cardinal's hat for his second son, Ferdinando, and from 1602
hoped to marry his eldest son, Duke Francesco, to a princess of the
House of Savoy. Although the project was several times thrown
aside and taken up again, he had it very much at heart, and, for an
instant, he also conceived the hope of marrying his daughter
Margarita to the Emperor Rudolph, who, in January, 1605, asked
that her portrait might be sent to him " with the measurements of her

stature and body." Pourbus was entrusted with the portrait, as also with
two other portraits of the Infantas of
Savoy that he went to Turin to paint,
with the recommendation to surpass
himself, "but without inventing anything
on his own account, and giving the
exact likeness of his sitters." Moreover,
Henry IV. invited his sister-in-law, the
Duchess Eleonora, to be godmother to
his son. The baptism was to take place
on September 14, 1606, and the duchess
was then making preparations for her
departure for Fontainebleau, where she
was to be joined by Pourbus, because
Marie de' Medici had begged her sister
to leave him for some months at the
French court. Amid all these plans and occupations, Rubens
was naturally somewhat forgotten. Not eager to dispute with
Pourbus the office of errant portrait painter, a vocation that was
not at all to his taste, he had doubtless done nothing to bring
himself into notice. He always felt drawn to Rome, where he had
at that time the prospect of meeting his brother. Philip had
sought a post at Rome, perhaps on account of his great love for
Italy, or because he was not satisfied with the reversion of Justus
Lipsius's Louvain professorship. Hearing that the Cardinal Ascanio
Colonna was occupied in forming a large library, Justus Lipsius

warmly recommended his pupil, who, by the extent of his knowledge, and the reliability of his character, was the scholar best fitted, not only to second his views, but also to serve him as secretary. Another cardinal, Serafino Olivieri, also solicited by Justus Lipsius, interested himself on Philip's behalf, and he obtained the post. Consequently about August, 1605, Philip left Louvain for Rome, and Peter Paul, who had obtained permission to join him, probably arrived there at the end of November. After the trial of a somewhat long separation, they enjoyed the pleasure of being at last together, and of living under the same roof, for a power of attorney given by them to their mother on August 4, 1606, informs us that they were living together in the Via della Croce, near the Piazza d'Espagna. The delight afforded by this life in common to the two brothers, who had great affection for each other, may be readily imagined. They had the same tastes, and already possessed acquaintances in Roman society, among scholars, artists, and

THE ENTOMBMENT.
Copy after Caravaggio, by Rubens. (Liechtenstein Collection.)

princes of the Church. Among the subjects that interested them, archæology filled a large place, and Rome afforded splendid opportunities for that study. In visiting the collections of the chief amateurs, they could exchange their views, and mutually derive information. Peter Paul assisted his brother by numerous drawings of the buildings, statues, and antiquities, and when, a few years later, Philip returned to Antwerp, and published at the Plantin Press the result of his researches on the dress and customs of the ancients, he was able to include, by way of a useful commentary, plates for which the artist furnished the models. In inserting in the volume the elegy in Latin verse of which we have already spoken, *ad Petrum Paulum navigantem*, the author was well justified in adding that it was a testimony of affection and gratitude to " the brother, whose skilful hand and excellent and accurate judgment had been so great a help to him in this work."

Besides the keen intelligence, the literary culture, and the excellent memory which aided him in those studies, Rubens derived a great advantage from his talent as a draughtsman. He could accurately fix in his mind the forms of the ancient buildings he examined, and compare them in order to determine their importance and style with greater certainty. By that means he developed his faculty of observation, and, as his brother said, " a refinement of taste and an accuracy of judgment" which were in the end to make him an expert connoisseur. The Louvre possesses the greater number of the drawings made at Rome after the marbles and medallions in the celebrated collections of that time. The conscientiousness of their execution verges on timidity. All bear the names of their owners written in Rubens's own hand. At Fulvio Orsini's he made drawings from the marble busts of Sophocles, Euripides, Aristotle, Menander, Herodotus and Plato, and the medallions of Archytas, Homer, and Alexander. Other busts, those of Lysias and Servilius Attala, were at Horatio Vittorio's and Cardinal Farnese's. At the British Museum are several drawings made by him from antique cameos. Not content with the copies alone, he took advantage of every opportunity that offered or purchasing examples at moderate prices. Thus he became the owner of engraved stones, and of marble busts of Cicero, Chrysippus and Seneca, which formed the first nucleus of his collection. He frequently used them later, notably the bust of Seneca, which he introduced into several of his pictures.

But Rubens's circumstances were too modest, and he brought into the conduct of his life too careful a spirit of order, to allow himself to give free rein to his fancies. Besides, in July, 1606, he suffered from a somewhat serious illness; he was attended by a German phy-

IX

The Boar Hunt.

(DRESDEN GALLERY.)

sician living in Italy, Dr. Johann Faber, a native of Bamberg. In his collected works published at Rome in 1651 the physician relates "that with the aid of God he cured P. P. Rubens of a severe attack of pleurisy, and that he, out of gratitude, not only painted his portrait, but gave him a picture representing a cock with the following humorous inscription, ' But erewhile condemned, now recovered, I fulfil my vow in dedicating this work to Johann Faber, my Æsculapius.'" The portrait has disappeared ; but the picture of the *Cock and the Pearl*, mentioned by Mariette, is now in the Suermondt Museum at Aix-la-Chapelle. Although the animal, seen in profile, is painted with a certain power, the interest of the work lies rather in the singularity than in the merit of the subject. The artist evidently attached no great importance to it, and it was as a kind of pleasantry that he offered his saviour the image of a bird sacred to Æsculapius. The letters written by Philip Rubens at that period often allude to the illness which probably somewhat diminished the budget of the community—a budget the more modest, since, in accordance with the parsimonious habits of the Court of Mantua, the slender salary of the painter was most irregularly paid. Already, on February 11, 1606, Giovanni Magno, Duke Vincenzo's agent at Rome, wrote to Chieppio to beg him to settle the method of payment of the twenty-five crowns forming the monthly salary of " M. Peter Paul, the Fleming," and to complain of the annoyance he had already suffered in the matter. On July 29 following, Rubens was himself obliged to apply to Chieppio ; they were four months in arrear with the salary which was so necessary to him, " if the Duke wished him to continue his studies without recourse to others for those means which, indeed, he would find no difficulty in obtaining at Rome." It was probably after fresh delays that the painter sought work, which permitted him to fill his leisure, and to provide for his support. Two drawings in the Louvre which we reproduce here furnish a proof of those attempts. Both were formerly in Mariette's collection, and are executed in pen and ink, slightly heightened with washes of Indian ink. The first represents, placed side by side on the same sheet, and distinguished by numbers (1) Abraham preparing to sacrifice Isaac, (2) Isaac blind, "as he was in his old age," (3) Jacob seeing the miraculous ladder in

his dream. In the second, King David, kneeling, plays on the harp,
while angels in Heaven sing praises to the Lord. These lightly touched
compositions do not possess much originality, and derive their
interest from the inscriptions that Rubens placed on them. Besides
the names of the subjects represented, we read on the second the
following note: "It is well to observe that these sketches, hastily

dashed off at a sitting,
give a very insufficient
idea of what the pictures
will be like. They are a
mere indication of the
thought; the cartoons to
be made afterwards, and
the pictures themselves,
will be executed with all
possible care and ele-
gance." The proposition
made by Rubens was
doubtless not accepted,
for neither pictures nor
engravings after the
sketches are known.

But the artist was soon
to be employed in a very
important work which he
was commissioned to
execute under most flat-
tering conditions. On

ABRAHAM, ISAAC, AND JACOB.
Pen-and-ink drawing. (The Louvre.)

the site of an ancient chapel that had been granted to him
St. Philip Neri, the founder of the Order of the Oratory, built
a magnificent church dedicated to the Nativity of the Virgin, and
known by the names of Chiesa Nuova, or of Santa Maria in Valti-
cella. He had placed there the relics of the martyrs Papias and
Maurus, and those of other saints whose remains had been discovered
at the same time, as well as the body of the virgin, Maria Domitilla.
After his death (1595) the work had been fairly actively carried on,

so that the church was consecrated in 1599, and the most famous artists of the time: Guido Reni, Caravaggio, Pietro di Cortona, Barroccio, and Giuseppino, eagerly sought for the honour of assisting in its decoration. Although Rubens was known and well thought of, his reputation at that period was scarcely sufficient to determine the prelates who directed the affair to choose him for the work; probably the painter's acquaintances in aristocratic society, and the kindly intervention of Cardinal Cesi, an intimate friend of Justus Lipsius, and that of Cardinal Borghese, the official representative of Germany and Belgium, were of much service to him. A sum of 800 crowns was allotted to him for painting a large composition for the high altar, in which he was to represent St. Gregory surrounded by the other saints, whose relics were buried there. The composition was to be placed

KING DAVID.
Pen-and-ink drawing. (The Louvre.)

below an ancient and greatly venerated image of the Virgin, which was only uncovered on certain solemn occasions.

Anxious to make a worthy response to the honour conferred on him, the artist was about to set to work and to devote himself entirely to his task, when he was suddenly recalled to Mantua. In a letter to Chieppio, December 2, 1606, Rubens gave his patron what he considered decisive reasons for granting him a respite. "After spending the whole summer in art studies he was bound to confess that with the 140 crowns, all that he had received from Mantua since his departure, he was absolutely unable to provide adequately for the support of his house and the two servants who looked after it during the years he had spent at Rome." By a most flattering choice he had just been entrusted with the decoration of the high altar of the church of the priests of the Oratory, the most celebrated and frequented of all the churches in Rome. He should certainly offend the high personages who had intervened in his favour, if he now alleged some obstacle in the way of accomplishing so honourable a task. He was assured that his patrons, among others Cardinal Borghese, would at need intercede for him with his master, in order to obtain a respite, by representing to him that he ought to be much pleased at the estimation in which his servant was held.

In a letter of December 13, 1606, the duke informed Chieppio that he complied with Rubens's request, and that wishing to be agreeable to him, and "rather to exceed than to come short of his desires," he would permit him to remain at Rome till Easter. During that interval, Vincenzo Gonzaga had frequent occasion to have recourse to his painter, and to consult him about the prospective purchase of works of art. It was by Rubens's advice, and after negotiations that necessitated a busy correspondence (from February 17 to April 28, 1607), that he decided to buy, for the very moderate price of 220 silver crowns, an important picture by Caravaggio, perhaps his best work, the *Death of the Virgin*, which after passing from the Mantua collection into those of Charles I. and of Jabach, is now in the Louvre. Another time Vincenzo Gonzaga, seeking at Rome a suitable residence for his son Ferdinando, who had just received a cardinal's hat, thought of the Palazzo Capodiferro, situated near the Piazza Farnese. The Duke consulted Rubens regarding the artistic value of the paintings, and of the works in stucco with which the palace was adorned, and it was probably by his advice that the purchase was not concluded.

Meanwhile about April 1607, Philip left his brother to return to Flanders, where he was summoned by the state of his mother's health, who had for some time desired his presence. After a severe attack of asthma on December 18, 1606, she felt her life seriously threatened, and expressed a very natural wish to have at least one of her sons with her. Philip had for some time been thinking of leaving Italy: his friends were employed in obtaining for him an honourable post at Antwerp, that of municipal secretary, and he approved of the prospect. His nomination seemed certain: he immediately took steps regarding the act of naturalisation, of *Brabantisation*, as it was then called, which, in consequence of his birth in a foreign land, was necessary for the exercise of his duties.

After his brother's departure, Rubens set to work with renewed zeal on the picture for the Chiesa Nuova which, through circumstances over which he had no control, had been somewhat delayed. The term of Easter assigned for his residence at Rome was past; but as Mantua did not seem anxious for his return, he thought that he would have plenty of time to finish his work, when he was again suddenly recalled. He was informed that the duke intended to drink the waters at Spa, and proposed to take Rubens with him; he must, therefore, rejoin him at once. Rubens wrote to Chieppio on June 9, 1607, to inform him that his picture was on the point of being finished, but that it would probably be necessary to touch it up after it was hung in its place. He would arrange to leave Rome three days afterwards, and put himself at his master's disposal. He hoped, however, that on his return from Flanders he might be permitted to go to Rome for a month, to finish his work and put his affairs in order, a thing that his sudden departure prevented him from doing.

When Rubens reached Mantua the duke, with his customary caprice, had changed his mind. He had abandoned his plan of a journey to Spa, and had decided to spend the summer at San Pietro d'Arena, a suburb of Genoa, where his friend, the son of Antonio Spinola, offered him the Palazzo Grimaldi for his residence. He installed himself there at the beginning of July, and the numerous suite by which he was accompanied—his gentlemen, his painter, and his troop of musicians—occupied two neighbouring houses. During the two months that he spent at Genoa the duke led a gay life. He found many companions there, men of pleasure like himself, and not to mention gambling—his ruling passion—the days

passed in concerts, comedies, dances, and other amusements.
That kind of existence was not suited to Rubens. Extremely
anxious about his mother's health, he had given up the journey
to Flanders, which would have permitted him to see her, with great
regret. However, amid the round of fêtes and amusements that
filled the duke's time, the artist enjoyed some leisure and he

PORTRAIT OF A MAN DRAWING ON HIS GLOVES.
(Dresden Gallery.)

devoted it to work. He
became acquainted with
several families of the
Genoese nobility, and
they gave him a few com-
missions, among others
that of the large picture
of the *Circumcision*, which
he painted for the Mar-
chese Niccolo Pallavicini ;
it adorns the high altar of
the church of Sant' Am-
brogio, to which the Mar-
chese presented it. It is
a vertical composition, a
little incoherent and spoiled
by the faults of proportion
and hardness of colouring
found in the greater part
of the works of that period.
Certain figures like those
of the high-priest, and the
woman standing beside him, and several of the angels hovering in the
sky, appear to be reminiscences of Correggio. The features of the
Virgin are a little vulgar, her pose is mannered, and the affectation
with which she turns her head aside so as not to see the child
suffer, is scarcely in harmony with what befits the subject. Other
persons, however, are already of a purely Rubens type ; for instance,
the woman standing, who raises her eyes to heaven, and the little

fair-haired, rosy angels, whose delicately modelled forms are relieved against the blue of the sky, inaugurate the fresh and delightful harmonies which were more and more to lend vivacity to the painter's works. During his visit to Genoa, Rubens painted several portraits for the nobles of the town, notably those of the Marchesa Brigitta Spinola, and of the Marchesa Maria Grimaldi (now

in the possession of Mr. Bankes, of Kingston Lacy), both in elegant toilettes; and also two boldly dashed off studies of men's heads, now in the Palazzo Durazzo. At that time, also, thanks to the facilities afforded him by the presence of his master, he was able to make drawings and plans of some of the palaces; he was so greatly struck by the robust and splendid architecture, that later he made it the subject of a publication, to which we shall have occasion to return.[1]

PORTRAIT OF AN OLD LADY.
(Liechtenstein Collection.)

But in spite of the interest these works afforded him, the artist was eager to return to Rome, where he found more abundant sources of instruction, and he was also anxious to finish the paintings for the Chiesa Nuova that his departure had not allowed him to complete. As soon as the necessary permission was obtained, and Rubens was once more settled at Rome, Duke Vincenzo, who had returned to

[1] *Palazzi di Genova.* Antwerp, 1622.

Mantua, received a letter from the Archduke Albert, about the
middle of September, 1606, dated Brussels, August 5, in which he
begged him to grant his painter, at the request of his family, permission to return to Flanders in order "to attend to some business
which concerned him, and which, in his absence, could not be properly
settled by a third person." As the artist was the archduke's subject,
he hoped that Vincenzo Gonzaga would grant him leave of absence in
order that he might fulfil his obligations. Perhaps Rubens had himself suggested this step on the part of his relatives, when telling them
of his disappointment at the failure of the plan of the journey to
Flanders ; perhaps his mother's state of health becoming worse, she
expressed a strong desire to see her son. But although the archduke
was technically correct in referring to his position as the sovereign
of his subject, the painter, he seemed to demand the favour he asked
as a right. The Duke of Mantua was offended at the proceedings,
and the two extant rough drafts, with variants, of his reply [1]
testify to his annoyance. Rubens having set out for Rome,
the duke could, in all sincerity, speak as he did in the first of the
drafts, "of the entire satisfaction that his painter, like himself, found
in the contract that united them. I cannot believe," he added, "that
he thinks of quitting my service, to which he shows himself so much
attached. There can be no question of deferring to the wishes of his
family, who have sought the assistance of the authority of the archduke to recall him to his country. Quite otherwise is the desire of
Peter Paul, who wants to stay, as much as I desire to keep him."
Although less drily expressed in the second draft, the refusal was not
less decisive, and it was not possible to insist in the face of such
clearly expressed wishes. Did the duke really consult Rubens, and
had he shown his positive intention of remaining at Rome ? We
do not know. In any case the question was settled, and whatever
were his plans for the future, the painter for the moment had only to
fulfil his engagements with the Fathers of the Oratory, and to complete the picture for the high altar of the Chiesa Nuova as soon as
possible. Assured of a respite on the part of Mantua, he set to work

---

[1] They were written at three days' interval, September 13 and 16, 1607.

8

The *"Baptism of Christ."*

(Study for the picture in the Antwerp Museum.)

(THE LOUVRE.)

once more ; but in a letter to Chieppio, dated February 2, 1608, he expressed the vexation that the matter caused him.

When the picture was finished, the Fathers, amateurs, and artists, who saw it in Rubens's studio, declared themselves quite satisfied. But when it was put in its place, it did not produce the expected effect. The light in which it was hung was absolutely insufficient, and the reflections of the varnish on the canvas, added to the defects of the unfortunate mode of exhibition. The picture could not possibly be left where it was. The Fathers determined to substitute a copy made on a dull surface, such as slate, that absorbed colour and prevented reflections. The original work was therefore on the painter's hands ; the artist thought it might suit "the duke and duchess who had formerly expressed a desire to have one of his pictures for their gallery. It would give him great pleasure if their highnesses would take a work to which he had devoted so much care, and which was certainly, so far, the best of his productions, for he should not easily bring himself to make such an effort again and produce a work into which he had put his whole self. Even if he wished to do so, he might not entirely succeed." The price was fixed at 800 crowns, and Rubens left it entirely to his highness's discretion ; if Chieppio would present this request and support it, "he would by that favour crown the infinite obligations that the artist already owed him."

The same post carried to Mantua a letter written to Chieppio on February 2, by the envoy Magno, in support of Peter Paul's request. On February 15, Chieppio informed Magno that while professing a great esteem for Rubens's talent, the duke was not disposed to buy the picture. "At this time," he said, "an extreme caution is observed in the matter of expense." In speaking thus, the good Chieppio's wishes were father to his statements, for excusing himself for the brevity of his letter, he added : "We are here in the midst of the carnival, and of the bustle caused by the departure of his Highness for Turin, with the most splendid and numerous escort of cavaliers ever seen." The cost of such a *cortège* can easily be imagined, as well as that of the fêtes in celebration of the marriage of Vincenzo Gonzaga's eldest son, with Margaret of Savoy ; but,

in spite of the lack of money, the refusal to purchase the Chiesa
Nuova picture was somewhat humiliating to Rubens, for at that moment
a case full of portraits of pretty women, painted at Naples, by
Pourbus, for the duke's Chamber of Beauty, was sent from Rome to
Mantua, and the duchess, who was treating for the purchase of an
important canvas, by Il Pomarancio,[1] asked Magno to apply to the
Fleming himself to carry out the negotiation, and appraise the work.

MARTYRDOM OF ST. SEBASTIAN.
(Corsini Palace.)

Rubens had too much
dignity to show the least
resentment, but in a letter
written to Chieppio on
February 23, 1608, while
thanking him for his in-
tervention as warmly as if
he had brought about a
favourable issue, he could
not refrain from referring
indirectly to the manner
in which he had been
treated. In order to put
Chieppio more at ease,
Rubens affected only to
be embarrassed concern-
ing the placing of his
picture. "It has been
exhibited for some days
in a better light, and

seen by all the connoisseurs of Rome, and has received the most
flattering approval." He ironically expressed satisfaction that his
proposal was not accepted by the duke, for, in consequence of
the expenses occasioned by the wedding, real difficulty would
have been created for the treasury of Mantua if it had had
to pay for it; "such difficulties will be great enough when it is a

[1] Cristoforo Roncalli, called Il Pomarancio, was then one of the best known artists at
Rome; he had also worked at the decoration of the Chiesa Nuova.

question of paying him his salary, so long in arrears." But if he put up with the delays for himself, he nevertheless considered it needful that an immediate settlement should be made with Il Pomarancio for the purchase of his picture. The purchase had been made by the express order of the duchess, and he had directly intervened in the matter: it was due to his representations that the affair had been so quickly concluded, although the artist was just then very busy. The price of 500 crowns, first asked of her most serene highness, seemed to her exorbitant, for in the habit of ne-gotiating according to the customs of Mantua, she did not know the methods of procedure of the great Roman artists. If the payment was in the least delayed, he would not again risk accepting simi-lar commissions, for after being repeatedly solicited by her highness, and ob-taining an "entire success,[1] he was alarmed to see so much indifference about discharging the debt." Beneath the moderation

ENGRAVING FOR THE LIFE OF ST. IGNATIUS LOYOLA.
(With the correction indicated by Rubens on the margin.)

of its form, the lesson is complete, and in demanding correct methods of procedure for one of his colleagues, Rubens indi-cated clearly enough the manner in which he desired to be treated.

The situation exposed by the letter, and the legitimate griev-ances that are hinted at, explain perhaps the absolute silence which henceforth surrounds Rubens. During the next eight months,

[1] Thanks to the intervention of Rubens, Il Pomarancio reduced the price of the picture to 400 crowns.

in fact, and until the end of his residence in Italy, the archives
of Mantua afford us no information. But from that moment Rubens
had the fixed intention, if not of quitting Duke Vincenzo's service,
at least of going to Antwerp to see his mother, whose health became
more and more uncertain. The intention is clearly revealed in a
letter addressed some time before (March 1, 1607) by his brother
Philip to one of his friends, Luigi Beccatelli, who was then at Rome,
and in which he promises to send him a portrait of Justus Lipsius, as
soon as Peter Paul shall be with him. "My brother," he says, in
his usual affected style, "thinks of flying, to return to his country;
already he spreads his wings, in order soon to be reunited to his
own." But before arranging his departure, Rubens had to fulfil
his obligations to the Fathers of the Oratory, and to paint
a copy of the Chiesa Nuova picture for them. We shall
speak later of this picture, now in the Grenoble Museum. The
artist did not succeed in selling it in Italy, since he brought
it from Rome to Antwerp, where he almost entirely repainted it.
In consequence of the very dark place in which it was to hang,
the copy cost Rubens little trouble. As far as the scanty light
permits us to judge, the execution appears to be rather summary,
and the harshness is further increased by the rigidity of the
slate. While almost preserving the arrangement of the original
work, the young master profited by the freedom granted him to
spread the elements of the composition, before concentrated on one
canvas, over three panels. The hasty execution of the paintings could
not have cost Rubens much time, and his energy certainly enabled
him to paint several other works during his sojourn at Rome. Among
those is the *St. Francis at Prayer*, of the Pitti Palace, a subject to
which he afterwards often returned. The hands pressed against his
breast, the saint kneels before a crucifix, beside which lie the
scourge for his flagellations, and a skull. The figure expresses
the joy and fervour of ecstasy ; the brown, almost monochrome tonality
of the picture naturally concentrates attention on the pale, eager face
of the saint, radiant with divine love.

Although we find in it direct reminiscences of Correggio, and the same faults of proportion that we have had already too often to note in the works of this period, the *St. Sebastian* of the Corsini Palace is of superior merit. With its expression of suffering and serenity, his handsome head inclining slightly towards the shoulder, and his vigorous young body, the dying youth resembles a beautiful lily bending languidly on its stalk. Angels desirous of rendering him help, flock around him with reverent care. If their want of beauty, and the evident lack of skill with which they have been repainted, betray the hand of an incompetent restorer, the martyr's body, on the contrary, is broadly painted with more transparent shadows, and stands out with wonderful clearness against the grey sky, the brown earth and vegetation, and the soft blue of the distance.

While Rubens was painting pictures that more and more showed his individual talent, as if he foresaw that he should never revisit Italy, he continued to take advantage of his residence at Rome, to gain as much knowledge as possible of the antique. Anxious to make his compositions that were inspired by fable or history more exact and realistic, he filled his portfolios with numerous drawings of the buildings, furniture and costumes of the ancients. With equal ardour he was never tired of studying the best works of the masters in the Roman collections, and especially those towards whom his particular temperament drew him. Of all of them Titian attracted him more and more, and it was at that time that he made copies, which are now in the Stockholm Museum, of two of his most celebrated pictures. The *Offering to Venus*, and the *Bacchanal*, painted for Duke Alfonso of Ferrara in 1518 and 1519, by the original sense of picturesque beauty which they reveal, mark in the artistic career of the painter of Cadore, the perfect blossoming of his genius. When the Pope took possession of the duchy of Ferrara, Cardinal Aldobrandini secretly secured the two works, and in 1598 had them transported to his palace at Rome, where they excited the unanimous admiration of connoisseurs.[1] Incapable

---

[1] In 1638 Titian's two pictures were offered to Philip IV. by the Count of Monterey, viceroy of Spain in Italy, and they are now in the Prado. The copies, bought at the death of Rubens by Philip IV., were taken to Sweden at the beginning of the present century by Bernadotte, and presented by his son to the Stockholm Museum.

of tying himself down to an absolute exactness, Rubens insists in his copies on the decorative sides of the episode, and of the happy part played in them by the landscape. In Titian the forms are more choice, the colouring warmer and more concentrated, the handling more delicate, better blended and more compact. In Rubens with clearer, more cheerful, more silvery colouring, the action is more animated, more attractive; the types are modified, and the beautiful figure of the nymph sketched in the foreground of the *Bacchanal*, becomes a Fleming with plump, full contours.

Between whiles, and doubtless to supplement somewhat the insufficiency of the modest salary allotted to him, the payment of which he had so much difficulty in obtaining, Rubens neglected no opportunity of turning his talent to account. We have a fresh proof of his energy and of his spirit of order in the part he then took in a publication which is described in Basan's Catalogue.[1] The publication, which appeared at Rome in 1609 without the publisher's name, consists of a series of seventy-nine small plates preceded by a frontispiece, under the title: *Vita beati P. Ignatii Loyolæ, societatis Jesu fondatoris.*

As M. Hymans[2] justly observes, in spite of the designation of Rome as the place of publication, the character of the greater number of the engravings denotes an entirely Flemish origin. It is probable that, prepared for the occasion of the beatification of St. Ignatius in 1607, the publication was undertaken by some Antwerp publisher,[3] who, after getting together the greater number of the very feeble illustrations which formed the series, had them engraved. Having some acquaintance with his compatriot Rubens, he doubtless asked him to complete the work by undertaking not only to furnish the few drawings that were wanting, but to see the plates executed, and to indicate on the most defective the corrections that seemed to him indispensable. Such are, at least, the details transmitted to us by a valuable autograph of Mariette which, in the print-room of the National Library at Paris, precedes the perfect and unique copy,

---

[1] *Catalogue des Estampes gravées d'après Rubens*, p. 206.
[2] *La Gravure dans l'école de Rubens*, p. 15 *et seq.*
[3] That town was then, as is well known, the chief centre of the religious picture-trade.

formerly in the possession of Mariette himself. Several of the
leaves, in fact, have marginal notes in Flemish, as well as corrections
made by Rubens for the original plates. The changes suggested by
the artist only concern the most glaring inaccuracies in the proportions, the attitudes, the contours of the feet, hands, and draperies.
But what is more interesting to us are the few plates due to Rubens
himself, on which the original owner had marked those that seemed to
be from the master's hand by the letters *Rub.* While insisting on his

predecessor's facilities for
possessing accurate information on this head, Mariette
did not unhesitatingly accept all the plates thus
marked ; but in several of
them he thinks it justifiable
to recognise the hand of
the great artist. Among
those, that of the *Beatification of St. Ignatius*, of
which the Paris Collection
of Prints possesses the only
proof known, is by far the
most remarkable. The
place left for the title is
empty, and the very superior
workmanship of the engraving to that of the other

BEATIFICATION OF ST. IGNATIUS LOYOLA.
(Engraving after a drawing by Rubens.)

plates, shows the importance attached to it by the publisher.
Besides, the aspect of the scene has so remarkable a character
of reality, that it seems to be drawn from life. To reproduce it with
so much exactness, Rubens was probably an eye-witness of it. The
effect is in any case striking, and the magnificence of the grand
religious ceremonies as they were then organised at Rome, the
stately bearing of the dignitaries of the Church, the animation
of the populace whom the guards hem in, or drive back with
their halberds, are rendered with as much truth as art. At that

date with its qualities of composition, the work is significant, and deserves attention.

Weeks and months passed for Rubens amid this active life, without any sign of his recall to Mantua. Duke Vincenzo had, on June 18, set out with a suite of more than thirty cavaliers by way of Switzerland for Nancy, where he stayed with his daughter Margaret, who had married the Duke of Lorraine ; then, after visiting Spa, he arrived on August 29, at Brussels, and went afterwards to Antwerp, where fêtes were held in his honour. Just at the time of the duke's visit, Rubens was about to be summoned thither on account of the alarming news he received on October 26, about his mother's health. He was informed that an exceedingly severe attack of asthma, " to which was added the weight of her seventy-two years, had placed her in a situation in which there was nothing more to be expected than the end common to all human beings." The painter hastily put his most pressing business in order. It seems as if he had some presentiment of his near departure, for, the day before he was informed of his mother's hopeless condition, he had made arrangements regarding the payment for the three pictures painted for the choir of the Chiesa Nuova. Two days later, October 28, he informed Chieppio that he was forced to leave Rome suddenly, without waiting for his master's permission. He would endeavour, he said, to meet him on the way, and according to the information he should gather on that subject, he would choose the route by which he might rejoin him. Instead of returning to Mantua, he would take the most direct road, and his absence would not be of long duration.[1] Although the pictures for the Chiesa Nuova were not yet exhibited to the public, they were finished, so that on his return he should go direct to Mantua to be at his master's disposal, "the will of the latter being always and everywhere to be obeyed by him as an inviolable law." And in the margin at the end of the letter, to show the haste he was in, he added : " On the point of mounting my horse (*salendo a cavallo*)." Notwithstanding his haste, he was not to see his mother. When he received the news of her hopeless condition, she had been dead five days.

[1] Sandrart says that Rubens reached Antwerp by way of Venice ; if that is so, it would not have been out of his way to pass through Mantua.

Rubens was, undoubtedly, sincere in his intention of returning to Italy, and of remaining in the Duke of Mantua's service; but the bonds that attached him to the duke had, for a long time, been somewhat relaxed, and during the last years had become still more loosened. Without having any fixed plans for his future, it is probable that the artist had no very great desire to remain at Mantua. He was conscious of his worth, and the time had come for him to appear on a larger stage. He had now assimilated all the teaching he could obtain from others. Perhaps, with his receptive mind, he had yielded too much to the ardent curiosity which urged him to a somewhat indiscriminate study of the masters. The most dissimilar had in turn solicited his attention: Mantegna, Leonardo da Vinci, Michael Angelo, Raphael, Titian, Tintoretto, Correggio, Paolo Veronese, Giulio Romano, Caravaggio, Baroccio, Domenichino, the Carracci, and many others. And now, in spite of his precocious talent, he was approaching middle age without having shown what he could do. For some years still the reminiscences of the works of the past which floated in his memory or filled his portfolios were, unconsciously, to weigh on him, and prevent the free expansion of his genius. It was time to correct this, and to provide an outlet for the generous enthusiasms that were simmering within him. His long residence in Italy, however, had taught him many things. He had cultivated his mind, lived in varied society, associated with men eminent by their birth, position, or talents. If he had had enough for ever of court frivolities and intrigues, and of the waste of time from which he, with his serious tastes and his love of work, suffered more than other men, his knowledge of the world had widened, and in the dependent position he was obliged to accept, he had, with perfect tact, invariably shown a keen perception of his own dignity. He also learned to understand better the wealth of an art of which he was himself to extend the domain. His disinterested studies strengthened his talents. Familiarised with the forms of the human body, he especially excelled in rendering the lustre and brilliancy of flesh, and his skill in that respect was such that Guido Reni, already very famous, said of him that "he surely mingled blood with his colours." He also acquired more breadth and variety in his compositions, an easier and surer power of drawing, a more perfect understanding of chiaroscuro, a deeper knowledge of all the resources of painting. Whatever were his predilections for the masters who attracted him, even in the copies he made from them, he preserved something of his early origin and education, something of the Flemish method of expeditious and yet steady execution, that suited his nature so well, and through it all he showed his own strong individuality. However exuberant his temperament, his mind was thoughtful, methodical, filled with a sense of order and proportion. After many salutary restraints and delays, the artist, now himself, gradually set aside foreign influences, or, rather, assimilated the many elements that, until then, had been stirring confusedly within him; he welded them together, fused them in the powerful unity of his genius, and, at length, manifested himself in creations that were entirely original.

PORTRAIT OF A MAN.
(Lichtenstein Collection.)

THE ARCHDUKE ALBERT.

(The Prado.)

CHAPTER VI

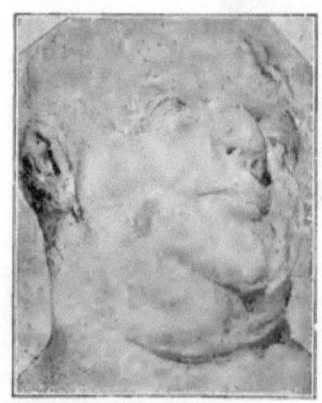

DRAWING FROM A BUST OF VITELLIUS.

(Albertina Collection.)

ALTHOUGH the news received by Rubens at Rome left little ground for hope, his grief may be imagined when, after the difficulties of the journey to Antwerp, he found his mother no longer living. The thought that she died before he could see her again, and that so long a period had elapsed since he had left her, gave him cruel pain. Several of his biographers assert that, absorbed in grief, he lived for several months shut up in the Abbey of St. Michael in lonely retreat. No document authorises this hypothesis, which is scarcely in keeping with Rubens's affection for his brother, or with those habits of work which could alone alleviate such a trial. Perhaps the proximity

of the Abbey of St. Michael to the house in which his mother, and
probably also his brother, lived, lent some credibility to the statement.
The house was situated in the Kloosterstraat, close to the Abbey,
where she had long been accustomed to perform her devotions, and
where she had desired to be buried. Rubens took up his residence
in the Kloosterstraat house, where the memory of his heroic mother
was ever present to him. Everything in the modest dwelling spoke
of her, of her simple and well-ordered life. It was with natural
emotion that he heard from his brother Philip of the strength of mind
shown by her in her last days. Quite infirm, feeling death at hand,
she herself made the arrangements for her funeral, and, as a good
Christian, prescribed the modest sums to be deducted from her little
property for charitable institutions and for the poor. The two
brothers, now become the natural guardians of the children left by
their sister Blandine, occupied themselves, with their strong love of
justice, in the division of their inheritance; but the final settlement was
not made until two years later, on September 17, 1610.[1] They
erected a marble tomb to their mother's memory, with a Latin inscription honouring "the very prudent and excellent lady Maria
Pypelinx, who was united in matrimony to John Rubens, Juris-consult
of Antwerp, and sacredly cherished his memory during her twenty-
two years of widowhood. . . . Philip and Peter Paul Rubens, and the
children of their sister Blandine, have erected this monument to the
pious memory of their mother."

To mark in a more individual fashion the intensity of his grief,
Rubens determined to devote to his beloved mother the first-fruits of
his talent, and to place one of his most important works in the chapel
where she was buried.

During the first period of his residence at Antwerp, Rubens was
occupied with these various cares; but time was passing, and it was
necessary for him to come to some decision about his future. Should
he, as he had stated it to be his intention in his letter to Chieppio,
return to Mantua, or should he remain in Flanders? Prompted by
affection, his brother made every effort to keep Rubens at Antwerp.

---

[1] P. Génard: *P. P. Rubens; Anteekeningen over den grooten meester.* Antwerp, 1897,
4to., p. 436.

Philip Rubens had just settled there, for, yielding to the wishes of the friends, who had solicited for him the post of municipal secretary of Antwerp, he had, in May, 1607, left Italy, and come to Antwerp. The following year he published at the Plantin Press his work, *Electorum libri duo*. At his request, Peter Paul supplied several drawings made at Rome of statues or bas-reliefs representing details of costume, or of furniture mentioned in the text. A short time after Peter Paul's arrival, Jan Boghe, one of the municipal secretaries of Antwerp, died, and by the unanimous vote of the magistracy Philip was, on January 14, 1609, chosen to succeed him. Nominated burgher of Antwerp the same day, he received on January 29 letters of *Brabantisation*, granted him by the Archduke Albert, to enable him to perform the functions to which he had just been appointed. Holder of so honourable an office, the newly elected secretary was in a position to realise a long cherished plan for his establishment. An intimate friend and now the colleague of Henry de Moy, one of the four secretaries, he married, on March 20, 1609, Moy's daughter Clara at the church of Notre Dame.

Philip's example and persuasions acted powerfully on Peter Paul's mind, and greatly influenced him to remain at Antwerp. We have seen how Philip's foresight long predicted the vexations to which Peter Paul was subjected at the Mantuan court. Events had amply justified his prophecies: Vincenzo Gonzaga's caprices and financial embarrassments more and more proved how right he had been. Peter Paul recognised the slight security of his position with the duke. One time or another a separation would be inevitable, and perhaps under more disagreeable conditions; thus instead of facing the almost certain difficulties that would arise from a return to Mantua, he had now an excellent opportunity for quietly breaking the connection. He could allege legitimate reasons for remaining with his relatives, such as attention to his affairs, and anxiety for his future. The general condition of Italy, the disturbances which tore her in pieces, the ever present possibility of an outbreak among so many rival States, scarcely helped to reassure him. The condition of Flanders, while not exactly brilliant, was less gloomy. Under the rule of the archdukes and the toleration it brought with it, the unfortunate country began to recover from its trials. Everybody ardently desired a period of tranquillity, and the calming down of men's minds foreshadowed the truce which was concluded with the United Provinces in 1609. The age of persecution was past, and besides the archdukes who had a taste for art, the clergy gave important commissions to the painters for the decoration of the churches and chapels that were being built on all sides. Considerable works were projected at Antwerp. The citizens were anxious to repair the ruin caused by the sack of the town, and the terrible destruction of the images. They were occupied in embellishing their town-hall, and for that purpose had just bought from Jan Brueghel, a Christ in bronze by Giovanni da Bologna : Abraham Janssens was commissioned to paint a large allegorical picture, *Antwerp and the Scheldt*, for 750 florins ;[1] and Antonio de Succa to paint the portraits of the ancient sovereigns of the city.

Philip was on good terms with many of the most important men in Antwerp, and through him, his brother could reckon on the patronage of Richardot, and on that of the most influential of the clergy. The two burgomasters, Halmale and Nicholas Rockox, were his friends, and on occasion the Town Council would have afforded him useful support. The time was singularly favourable for an artist of talent. Not that distinguished painters, however, were lacking at Antwerp. Several among them, Jan Snellinck, W. Coerberger, Jan Brueghel, and Otto van Veen, Rubens's master, were in the service of the archdukes. Rubens would have become acquainted with Sebastia Vrancx, and Hendrick van Balen in Van Noort's studio.

But none of those artists, esteemed as they were, had acquired any marked superiority over their colleagues. Peter Paul came among them with the two-fold prestige of a long residence in Italy, and of the reputation his talent had already brought him. He could not fail to find opportunities of making himself known, and of showing what he could do ; and without presumption, he had every right to hope that he would soon make a position for himself. Instead of the isolation and vexations that awaited him at Mantua, he found at Antwerp

[1] Now in the Antwerp Museum.

affectionate relatives, an entire liberty, and the prospect that he would be entrusted with the execution of great works. It is clear, then, that both his interests and his ambition counselled him to shake off a dependence which would in time more heavily oppress him.

Rubens's intelligence enabled him to grasp the situation, and his decision once made, he, in all probability, informed the duke and Chieppio, and thanked the latter for the numerous kindnesses he had received from him. It does not appear that the Duke of Mantua

THE TOWN HALL, ANTWERP.
Drawing by Boudier. (From a photograph.)

made any attempt to combat the artist's resolve; at least the local archives contain no trace of letters or papers relating to the matter. Ten years later the name of Rubens may occasionally be found in the despatches of the Gonzagas' agent at Paris, when Rubens went to France to paint the pictures for the Medici Gallery. But the artist always preserved a pleasant remembrance of his residence in Italy, and more than twenty years afterwards, when he was informed, in August, 1630, of the taking and sack of Mantua, Rubens wrote to his friend Peiresc: "We have received very bad news from Italy; on

July 22, the Imperialists took Mantua, and put to death the greater
number of the inhabitants. I am extremely grieved, for I spent
many years in the service of the house of Gonzaga, and in my youth
enjoyed a delightful sojourn in Italy. *Sic erat in fatis!*"

With his passion for work, Rubens could not long remain idle.
Having settled himself as comfortably as he could in the Kloosterstraat house, he doubtless took up his brushes again. Several of his
biographers, among others, J. F. Michel, state that one of the first
works executed by him after his return from Italy was commissioned
from him by the association of scholars known as the *Sodalité*; it was
directed by the Jesuits of Antwerp, and placed under the protection
of the Visitation of the Virgin. The artist chose that subject for the
picture painted by him for the high altar of the society in the place that
it originally occupied.[1] The Virgin is represented kneeling, surprised
during her prayer by the angel, who, kneeling in front of her, announces
her mission. In spite of a certain stiffness, the work interests from its
inwardness. The broad unobtrusive handling, the amplitude of
the draperies, the green and the neutral violet of the angel's robe, the
foreshortening, and the types of the cherubs who hover round in the
upper part of the picture, are characteristic of the period.

The affectionate relations that Rubens already possessed, and that
he always preserved with the Jesuits, doubtless procured him the commission. The Order, then very powerful at Antwerp, soon followed
it by others of greater importance. But it was probably due to the
intervention of his brother, and of his friends among the members
of the Town Council, that Rubens was at that time commissioned
to execute a painting for the State chamber of the Town Hall;
it was an *Adoration of the Magi*, for which he received the
relatively considerable sum of 1,800 florins, disbursed in two payments, on April 19 and August 4, 1610. It was finished the year
before, since the painter-gilder, David Remeeus, was paid for the
frame in 1609. The large canvas,[2] somewhat crowded with persons,
animals, and details of all sorts, shows us gathered together under

---

[1] Later, after 1620, when the Society had built another edifice, the picture was
removed to it, and after the suppression of the order of the Jesuits in Belgium, it was, in
1776, bought for 2,000 florins by the Austrian Court. It is now in the Vienna Gallery.

[2] It measures no less than 16 ft. 0·12 in. high by 11 ft. 4·22 in. broad.

9

Charles V. on Horseback.

(Pen and Ink Drawing.)

(THE LOUVRE.)

Printed by Draeger, Paris.

a shed with a thatched roof, the Virgin standing, with the Infant Jesus in her arms, behind them St. Joseph, and round them the Magi, accompanied by cavaliers and servants bearing gifts, with the camels and horses that brought them at the side. The most varied types, negroes, elegant pages, warriors in armour, naked slaves loaded with valuables, white-bearded old men, elbow one another in the strange composition which abounds in Italian reminiscences mingled with the artist's individual invention. In one of the cavaliers of the escort, seen from the back with his pleasant face half turned towards the spectator, he represented himself. Fresh-coloured or tawny, the flesh-tints of the figures are as varied as their costumes; the purple cloaks glittering with precious stones, the satin robes and bright coloured gowns, the turbans ornamented with aigrettes, and the burnished armour rival in brilliance the vases, censers, gold boxes and coffers, which shine brightly on all sides. The lighting of the scene adds force to the motley confusion of forms and colours. Judging by the lighted torches that are to be seen here and there, by the stars shining in the heavens, and the hard outlines and shadows, Rubens intended to paint night, but the colours, instead of being softened, stand out in their full strength as if in daylight. With little care for harmony, every shade of red is contrasted with the most daring blues. But as if there had not been enough of the tumultuous contrast of entangled lines and discordant tones in the original work, the painter, probably discontented with its aspect, when he saw it again in 1628, during his second visit to Spain, emphasised the incongruities by repaintings that heightened both the gaudiness and the hardness. But notwithstanding its many defects, the arrangement of the composition is masterly, and the planning of the scene, the part played by the architecture and the background, and the effect of the iron-gray tones successfully blended with the bright colours, testify to the painter's decorative instinct. In any case, at that time, Rubens alone was capable of giving such powerful inspiration and animation to a painting of that description. His success was indubitable; from the very first he justified his friends' expectations, and was placed at the head of his rivals without opposition. The fate of the *Adoration of the Magi* sufficiently proves the effect it produced. Painted for the Town

Hall of Antwerp, it did not long remain there. Three years later, when
the Count d'Oliva, Don Roderigo Calderon, was sent as ambassador
extraordinary from the King of Spain, the magistracy, in acknowledg-
ment of the services he had already rendered to Antwerp, the city of
his birth, and in the hope of assuring his favours in the future, proposed
to the Great Council on August 31, 1612, to present him with the
picture. The majority agreed to the proposal, but the members of

ABRAHAM AND MELCHIZEDEK.
Albertina Collection.
(From a photograph by Braun, Clément et Cie.)

the Guild of Mercers, anxious to keep so fine a work in the city,
opposed it. The next day, however, the protest was ignored, and on
Calderon's departure, Van Weerdt, the chief magistrate, presented him
with the large canvas "as the rarest and most valuable gift in the
possession of the magistracy." [1]

[1] Involved later in the disgrace of the Duke of Lerma, Calderon was beheaded on
October 21, 1621, and his property being confiscated, the *Adoration of the Magi* became
the property of Philip IV. It was in the palace of that king that Rubens found it in
1628 ; it is now in the Prado.

We must also refer to this period the execution of the *Dispute of the Holy Sacrament* in the church of St. Paul at Antwerp, the ancient church of the Dominicans, for which it was painted, for it is mentioned in 1616 in an inventory of the Chapel of the Holy Sacrament situated in that church. It is less incoherent than the *Adoration of the Magi*, but presents as many reminiscences and faults of proportion: the composition is visibly inspired by Raphael's on the same subject, and the St. Jerome is a faithful reproduction of that saint in the celebrated *Communion* of Domenichino. Other figures, however, are entirely of Rubens's invention, among them those of several bishops, and notably that of the Cardinal on the left, whom he introduced again in the *Coronation of Marie de' Medici.*

While he was painting the *Dispute of the Holy Sacrament*, the artist certainly had by him the picture originally intended for the high altar of the

ST. GREGORY.
(Grenoble Museum.)

Chiesa Nuova; leaving aside the formal resemblances in the handling of the two works, the splendid cope of the bishop who occupies the right of the foreground, exactly resembles that of St. Gregory. It has been stated that after vainly offering the work to the Duke of Mantua, Rubens had kept it himself, and had had it sent to Antwerp. It may be that the painting, moved before it was dry, suffered damage in the transit, or that when the artist saw it again he felt dissatisfied with the effect it produced ; but, whatever the cause, he determined to repaint it. While leaving the general arrangement as it was, and even several of the faults of proportion, such as the disproportionate size of St. Domitilla's arm, he greatly modified its aspect. The composition brings together on one canvas the figures dispersed over the three panels of the Chiesa Nuova painting, and is as simple as it is picturesque. As Rubens had written to Chieppio on February 2, 1608, he had taken the utmost trouble over it, and in a black and red chalk drawing—which with the painting is now in the Grenoble Museum—we find a charming study for the angels who surround the miraculous image of the Virgin which occupies the upper part, a study, however, which the artist modified when he used it. The reproduction which accompanies these words relieves us of the necessity of describing the composition in detail. The brilliant figures of St. Gregory and St. Domitilla, placed in the centre in bright light, are enhanced by the dark tints of the costumes of the saints who stand on either side of them. In such a setting the lights of the picture, most skilfully distributed and harmonised, are arranged in an undulating line ; the St. Gregory—an old man, wearing a cope of white silk damask adorned with gold embroidery and ornaments—with his fine, venerable head, and his faith-inspired gestures, forms the happiest contrast to the St. Domitilla standing in front of him, a young girl with regular features, a type that in some degree recalls the St. Helena of the Grasse picture. Her costume is as rich as that of St. Gregory, and consists of a red bodice with blue sleeves, and a violet cloak faced with yellow, whose ample folds she lifts with a modest gesture of grace and distinction. The reddish gray of the marble portico, and the blue-gray of the sky seen through the arch, sustain and give value to the bright colour which lights up the centre of the picture. The whole, at once brilliant and soft, is executed in a superb manner, and presents a more harmonious aspect than any of the painter's previous works.

Several other pictures painted by Rubens at this period are only known to us through reproductions. According to information supplied by M. Hymans,[1] J. Matham's plate representing *Samson and Delilah*

---

[1] *La Gravure dans l'École de Rubens.* 4to. 1878, p. 39.

must have been engraved about 1615, after a painting of Rubens, which then belonged to Nicholas Rockox, "knight, several times burgomaster of Antwerp, supreme judge of all the arts." The somewhat commonplace composition is illuminated by the light carried by an old woman, who figures in several of the works of that period, among others in a *Judith and Holofernes*, in which, in the Judith, we find the type of the Grenoble St. Domitilla with her abundant hair and her costume. The subject is conceived by the artist in most revolting fashion ; while the heroine of Bethulia with one hand stifles the cries of Holofernes who writhes on his couch, with the other, in brutal indifference, she calmly cuts off her victim's head. The blood gushes forth on all sides, and three tiny streams trickle over the young woman's arms. Angels with variegated wings, recalling those of the *St. Sebastian* of the Corsini Palace, watch over the accomplishment of the murder, seemingly to assure its impunity, and the moon is seen through an opening contrived in the top of the tent. The brutality of the scene, the profusion of blood, and other coarse details unnecessary to specify, give the episode a repugnant aspect. But such scenes suited the prevailing taste, and many of them occur in Rubens's work, for instead of toning down their unpleasantness, he seemed to take pleasure in them, and omitted none of the coarse details that belong to such subjects. Several copies, one in the possession of Madame Brun of Nice, and another that came to light in a sale at Rheims in 1883, give an idea of the stiff and hard execution of the original which is now lost. According to a letter dated March 18, 1621, from T. Locke to Sir Dudley Carleton, it then belonged to Charles, Prince of Wales. Rubens was not altogether satisfied to be represented in the Prince's collection by so little notable a specimen of his talent, "executed in my youth," as he himself put it when proposing to an agent of the prince the acquisition of another of his works, "greatly superior in technique to the Holofernes."[1] A Latin inscription placed under the engraving by Cornelis Galle, the elder, reminds us that it was in memory of a promise made in Italy to Jan van den Wouwere (*Wowerius*) that the plate, "the first engraved on copper

[1] Letter to William Trumbull, September 13, 1621.

after one of his paintings, is dedicated by Rubens to his illustrious friend."

The diversity of the subjects treated by Rubens clearly testifies to the versatility of his talent. Meanwhile, his reputation was increasing, and the commissions entrusted to him became more and more numerous. The archdukes had been among the first to recognise his merit. Biographers tell us that he painted for them a *Virgin with the Infant Jesus*, and that he was also asked to paint their portraits. The last are known to us only through the engravings executed in 1615 by Jan Muller, and the copies in the possession of the Guild of Fencers of Ghent. During the sittings, the governors doubtless learned to appreciate the artist's distinction, and the charm of his manners and conversation. To testify their satisfaction, on August 8, 1609, they ordered for him of their goldsmith, Robert Staes,

VENUS AND CUPIDS.

Facsimile of an engraving by C. Galle, after Rubens.

for a sum of 300 florins, a gold chain with a medallion of their effigies, a prelude to a greater distinction conferred on him on the following 23rd September. After vainly trying to keep him at Brussels, the archdukes appointed Rubens court painter, with permission to reside at Antwerp, and an annual salary of 500 Flemish pounds. The honour carried with it other privileges, such as exemption from taxation, and permission to inscribe his pupils on the lists of the Guild of St. Luke.

As time progressed, Rubens became more and more attached to

the town of Antwerp, where he enjoyed a discriminating patronage and a liberty of action that the restraints, suffered by him in the beginning of his career, made the more precious. In that year, too, (1609), he was admitted into the Guild of the Romanists, which included all the artists and scholars who had resided in Italy. Founded in 1574, and placed under the protection of St. Peter and St. Paul, it was in 1609 presided over by Jan Brueghel, who, in his office of dean, received the new member. There Rubens could discuss his favourite subjects with his col- leagues, and with the scholars who belonged to the Guild. He was specially fond of his brother's house, which was not only the rendezvous of the most eminent men of the city, but an example of domestic happiness well calculated to attract the artist's affectionate and loving nature. His posi- tion now assured him an honourable career and re- sources more than suffi- cient to set up a home ;

FAUN AND SATYR.
(Munich Gallery.)

his name was already well-known, and with his good looks and pre- possessing manners, he might aspire to a brilliant match. He had not far to seek for a companion to his taste ; he found in one of his brother's nieces all the qualities needed to make him a perfect wife. Isabella Brant, the daughter of Jan Brant, the City registrar, and of Clara de Moy, the eldest sister of Philip's wife, Maria, was eighteen years old, and in addition to her outward charms, possessed a gentle, loving, and loyal nature. The young people had

ample opportunity of meeting, and as both families desired the union,
directly the matter was broached, consent was given. The marriage
was celebrated on October 3, 1609,[1] at the abbey church of St. Michael,
and, in the sacred edifice full of memories of his mother, and where her
remains rested, Peter Paul, calling to mind her beloved memory,
was able to associate her with the most important act of his life.
Philip, we may be sure, did not neglect so excellent an opportunity of
displaying his learning, and he composed a Latin epithalamium in
honour of the couple. The verses, though in doubtful taste, are
instructive, and the grossly coarse expressions give an idea of the
freedom of language usual at the time among even the best conducted
of the middle class. Amid the risky equivocations and allusions in a
Latin, of which the words somewhat offend propriety, a happily
turned line may, with difficulty, be discovered here and there, for
example, that in which Philip addresses the newly-married wife :

" Sola manes, nova nupta, tuo cum conjuge, sola."

A new life opened for Rubens, and the affection and devotion
of his faithful companion secured him, as long as she lived, the
moral tranquillity necessary for the production of the great works
that made his name illustrious. The charming picture, now in the
Munich Gallery, painted in the early days of his marriage, is a
delightful testimony to his happiness. The artist himself is there
represented in an elegant costume—a yellowish-brown coat and orange-
coloured silk stockings—sitting on a slightly raised seat ; his young wife
is at his feet, and wears, like him, a high-crowned hat ;[2] she is richly
dressed in a gown with a violet skirt, and a velvet bodice opening
over a white embroidered vest. Her only jewels are a pair of bracelets
of antique stones, probably bought by Rubens in Italy, and carefully
selected to form a tasteful ornament. Isabella's right hand rests
on that of her husband, and her face is turned towards the spectator
in a natural, unconstrained attitude. Her ingenuous countenance

---

[1] The date is fixed by a letter from Balthasar Moretus, recently published in the
Correspondance de Rubens. Vol. II. p. 16.

[2] Unfortunately a strip of the canvas has been cut away from the upper part, so
that scarcely more than the brim of Rubens's hat is to be seen ; the mutilation causes
the figure to seem rather short.

XI

The Philosophers.

(THE PITTS.)

beams with happiness, and in the slightly roguish expression of the
eyes, may be read a certain pride at winning the heart of the great
painter, who has chosen her for his life's partner. Rubens's face is
full of serenity, and, confident about the future, he gives himself up
to the joy of being loved. Everything smiles around them, and
Nature, in holiday mood, seems to share the sentiments that fill their
hearts. The picture, valuable both as regards its merit and its date,
was probably painted during the spring that followed the marriage ;
for the honeysuckle, against which the two figures stand out in light,
is covered with fresh blooms, and here and there in the green turf are
scattered tufts of fern, and freshly-budded violets. The painting,
limpid and frank, accords in every detail with the character of the
scene, and in the more exquisite harmony of his tonality, and the
enhanced delicacy of the flesh tones in strong light, in the freer, more
supple, and more loving touch, the artist shows the inward satisfaction
he felt in tracing the early days of their happy union.

Detained at Antwerp by his work, Rubens put off the formality
" of the oath pertaining to the court painter of their serene highnesses "
until 1610 ; it was administered to him on January 9 by Ferdinand de
Salinas, councillor and master of requests of the privy council.
Notification of the formality was then sent to the magistracy of
Antwerp, who were thus informed of the privileges conferred on
Rubens by virtue of his office of court painter. It does not seem that
any objection was raised, but when at the request of Jan Brueghel, who
was already exempted from certain municipal taxes, the archdukes on
two occasions (October 1609, and March 13, 1610), asked on his
behalf for an extension of those privileges, the Town Council grew
restive, and objected that the immunities already granted to Otto van
Veen, and more recently to P. P. Rubens, were quite sufficient. They
entreated " in all humility that the town should not be compelled to
extend the exemption from excise taxes further, and that their refusal
regarding Brueghel now, and others in the future, might be accepted
in good part."

It may readily be imagined that Rubens's visit to Brussels was not
of long duration. He was anxious to be at home and at work.

Already regarded with favour, opportunities of displaying his talent followed speedily one after the other. He received that year an important commission for a church at Antwerp, that of St. Walburga, now destroyed. In May, 1610, the vicar and churchwardens raised a subscription for obtaining the funds necessary for the execution of a great picture to adorn the high altar. From the account books of the church we learn that, soon after, a sum of nine florins was expended at the *Petite Zélande* tavern where the contract for the painting was signed by the artist, the vicar, and the churchwardens. Cornelis van der Geest, a distinguished amateur of Antwerp, acted as intermediary; the dedication of Witdoeck's engraving of the subject chosen, the *Raising of the Cross*, specifies Van der Geest as "chief author and promoter of the work." The price arranged, 2,000 florins, a considerable sum for that time, was paid to the artist in instalments until October 1, 1613. Rubens began his task on June 10, and profiting by his experience at the Chiesa Nuova, in order to make sure from the first of the light in which the picture would hang, he worked in the choir of the church itself. The precaution was the more necessary as the triptych was to be shown under quite special conditions, a street of old Antwerp running below the altar over which it was to hang. The Admiralty lent a large sail to protect the artist from draughts, and from the gaze of the curious.

Besides the three panels now in Antwerp Cathedral, the work originally included a fourth above the triptych, representing *God the Father* with two angels, and three predelle below; the central one, which was arched and rather smaller than the other two, represented the *Crucifixion*, and those on either side, the *Translation of the Body of St. Catherine by Angels*, and the *Miracle of St. Walburga*. But all of them, although several times referred to at sales during the last century, have disappeared. We need only mention in passing the figures painted on the outside of the shutters, on one side St. Eligius and St. Walburga, and on the other, St. Catherine and St. Amand. The artist did not bestow much pains on them; for in those most seen, the St. Eligius and St. Catherine, he was satisfied to reproduce the types and costumes of the Chiesa Nuova, St. Gregory and St. Domitilla.

But to the *Raising of the Cross*, which occupies the central panel and the inside of the shutters, and measures 21 feet 0·36 inches by 15 feet 1·88 in., Rubens gave his whole care. In it he found a subject that from its variety of episode and contrast of emotions, admirably suited his genius. A fine drawing in the Louvre, full of fire and animation, and an excellent sketch in the possession of Captain Holford,[1] testify to

THE RAISING OF THE CROSS.
Study for the Triptych in Antwerp Cathedral.
The Louvre.
(From a photograph by Braun, Clément et Cie.)

the importance attached by Rubens to the work. But it cannot be said to be free from reminiscences. The general arrangement of the bold diagonal of the cross traversing the composition, is inspired by

[1] Witdoeck's engraving was probably made after that sketch, from which it presents but slight variations. The composition is more spread out, and the principal episode becomes more conspicuous from the greater space and tranquillity around it.

Tintoretto's great picture in the Scuola di San Rocco; it also contains
some well-known figures, notably, that of the terrified woman throwing
herself on the ground, taken by Rubens from Raphael, a figure he
had used already in the *Transfiguration* of the Nancy Museum.   But
the artist borrowed some of the elements of his work from himself; its
prototype is to be found in the poor composition of the *Raising of the
Cross*, whose defects we have already described, painted in 1602 for
the Santa Croce di Gerusalemme at the beginning of his sojourn
in Italy.   Nearly all the figures of the principal group, the soldier in
armour, the man who pulls at the cross with a rope, another who
strives to place it upright, and lastly, the man who, almost crushed by
its weight, uses all his strength to avoid being thrown down, appear
in the St. Walburga picture.   But, whereas in the earlier work they
are spread about in extreme confusion, and with a most unpleasing
want of proportion, when Rubens turned his attention to them again
after a lapse of eight years, he profited by the experience he had acquired,
and turned them to masterly account.   Reminiscences are indeed
scarcely apparent.   With such a splendid memory, Rubens could
hardly forget the masterpieces he admired, but he was not possessed
by them to a point which trammelled his originality or paralysed his
ideas.   He had now assimilated all he desired to retain of the teaching
of others; the time of *pasticci* was over.   He had a clear vision of what
he wished to paint, and his imagination helped him to see into the heart
of his subject; he understood it, and gave expression to its poetry and
its picturesque resources.   His dominant idea prevails over the
arrangement, and he combines the details with a view to the general
effect he desires to produce.   He divided the composition into three
distinct groups, giving each an importance of its own, but subordinating
them to the unity of the work.   In the centre is the drama itself, and
on either side the accessory episodes, which serve to bring the
striking horror of the scene into full relief.   On the right are the
executioners and the thieves, who have just been brought up, one of
them being already nailed to the cross; on the left are the holy
women entirely abandoned to their despair.   But let Fromentin speak
here, and without attempting to translate into other words the things

he has said so admirably, let us be content to give our readers his eloquent description of the picture.

" Pity, affection, mother, friends are far away. In the pity or despair revealed in the attitudes of the group of suffering women on the left shutter, the painter has depicted every expression of heartfelt grief. On the right shutter are two guards on horseback, and here there is no mercy. In the centre men shout, blaspheme, jeer, trample under foot. With brute effort, executioners of butcher-like appearance raise the gibbet, and endeavour to place it straight on the canvas. Arms contract, cords are stretched, the cross oscillates, having reached only half the distance it has to go. Death is certain. A man nailed to the cross by hands and feet, suffers, expires, pardons. Nothing of him is any longer free, nothing is any longer his ; a merciless fatality is in possession of his body : but the upturned glance, which, leaving earth, seeks relief from doubt elsewhere, and goes straight to heaven, shows us that his soul escapes. The painter brings out every note of the rage for killing and of promptitude in executing the murderous deed that human fury can conceive, and he does it as a man who understands the effects of anger, and knows the working of brute passions. Examine with even greater attention how the artist expresses the humility, the joy of sacrifice which accompanies a martyr's death." [1]

We have seen the care with which Rubens prepared himself for his work. By considering beforehand the best means for producing the result he proposed to himself, he inaugurated a new method. His quick intelligence taught him that the more complicated the subject, the more necessary was such preparation. He turned his attention successively to every possible problem, in order not to be forced to solve them all at the same time. After thinking his composition well out, he perceived its bold outlines and the general arrangement of its masses. The most striking parts of the subject show, at first view, their relative importance, their contrasts, and inevitably rivet attention on " the grand white figure, bright against the darkness, motionless and yet in motion, thrown by a mechanical impulse diagonally across

[1] Fromentin : *Les Maîtres d'autrefois*, p. 89.

the canvas, with pierced hands, arms oblique, and that magnificent gesture of clemency which preserves their equilibrium, wide opened on the blind, dark, and miserable world." [1]   But to counterbalance the struggling and pushing of the heavy, livid, oscillating mass, the artist places on the ground, in a compact group, the despairing women, seized with pity or terror ; while at the other extremity of the canvas he allows the figures more play, and there is a greater repose round the central episode.

The effect adds to the pathos of the scene.   The faces, the flesh, the armour and the draperies stand out in unrelenting clearness against the dark blue sky, and its sombre accompaniment of brown rocks, deep shadows, and olive - green vegetation. [2] In spite of brilliant colour and sharply indicated contours, the unity of the composition is perfect, and the relief of each of the groups, and the distances that separate them, are accurately rendered.   The exact determination of relative prominence in his pictures is one of the qualities peculiar to Rubens ; according to Eugène Delacroix, " his skill in handling the planes raises him above the

PORTRAIT OF A FRANCISCAN.
(Munich Gallery.)

[1] *Les Maîtres d'autrefois*, p. 92.

[2] Certain portions are, however, painted with more suppleness ; for instance, the group of horsemen on the right, the chief and his fine grey horse with its long mane, and the two thieves at the side.   The transparency and masterly boldness noticeable here would be inexplicable at that date ; but we learn from the account registers of St. Walburga, that much later, in 1627, after the picture had been cleaned by J. B. Bruno, Rubens partly repainted and altered it.

pretensions of all other draughtsmen; if they are successful in the management of them, it seems a stroke of good luck, but Rubens, in his highest flights, never fails in it." We shall find frequent proof of this in succeeding pictures, but even at that time his excellence in this respect was manifest.

The handling received special benefit from the carefully thought out division of the work. The ease, freedom, and animation that characterised Rubens's execution was derived from his method of

THE DEAD CHRIST, MOURNED BY THE HOLY WOMEN AND ST. JOHN.
(Antwerp Museum.)

dividing up his task. Always in the right condition for work, he never wasted his powers, but, directing each of his successive efforts towards a determined end, he only emphasised where needful, and to the right extent. We might, doubtless, blame many useless extravagances, eccentric gestures, over-insistent muscularities; but such criticism of details never occurs to us. We are struck and subjugated by the immense eloquence : we recognise that the artist's enthusiasm and powerful emotion were admissible in such a subject, and that never before in the history of art had a painter possessed the power of communicating to his creations the breathing life that animates, supports, and binds together all the varied elements of his great work. We have no longer before us a legendary act, coldly reproduced according to received traditions ; the actual drama in all its reality is played out before us, and as if to concentrate all the poetry of his subject in the one pathetic and truly inspired figure, the master makes the divine man crucified the vital point, the soul of his composition. He contrasts the beauty of the victim's body with the brutal cruelty of the executioners ; in spite of the nails that hold and torture him, the sufferer turns towards heaven with a sublime gesture, and in the ideal expression of gentleness in his face, the artist represents sadness and suffering, and serene and ineffable goodness.

So far Rubens had been undecided, timid, attempting to give expression to thoughts that were still confused, in a style likewise confused, and also harsh, full of weaknesses, rashness, and inaccuracy. Here for the first time he dared to be himself, and is simple, clear, and natural even in his exaggerations. Very soon after his marriage, in the possession of the happiness and moral tranquillity assured to his domestic life by a loved companion, he was able to obey the inward promptings of his genius, and without affectation or the parade of an empty virtuosity, with an intelligence equal to his talent, he painted his first masterpiece.

Thus, at the very moment when the political separation of the United Provinces and Flanders was consummated by the truce of 1609, Rubens, as if to compensate the city for the loss of her commercial supremacy, inaugurated at Antwerp the brilliant dawn of an art of which he was the most glorious incarnation. An era of peace suc-ceeded the terrible convulsions that had so cruelly shaken the country, and the government of the archdukes, with its programme of relative tolerance and of conciliation, accorded with the pacific aspirations of all. Their programme found powerful support even with the clergy. Among the Jesuits, whose influence was becoming more felt, there was a determination to postpone irritating questions to a future period.

The Virgin, St. Elizabeth, the Infant Jesus, and St. John.

(Drawing in Red Chalk.)

(THE LOUVRE.)

Printed by Berger, Paris.

Their Order boldly placed itself at the head of the revival of the classics promoted by the humanists, and their schools competed with the universities recently established in Holland. An intellectual aristocracy gradually arose, and a high state of culture permitted the conciliation of contradictory ideas. The mixture of sacred and profane—David and the Sibyls, Noah and Hercules, the Styx and Hell, Olympus and Heaven, etc.—which the Church had already admitted into its liturgical chants, appeared also in the sermons from the pulpit, and in the controversies of scholars; insensibly, equally unconscious confusions entered into outward forms as well as into men's minds. The celebration of divine worship and the ceremonials of the Church became more and more magnificent. While they lacked style, the newly built churches presented great richness of material and workmanship; precious marbles, heavily gilded garlands, over-elaborate sculptures, abounded everywhere. If the exuberant ornamentation did not exactly show a pure taste, the cheerful, roomy interiors of the buildings offered to painters large and well-lighted spaces, demanding a decoration that in the free development of the forms, and the brilliancy of the colouring, suited the taste of the time. Vainly had Rubens's predecessors attempted such flights: their works were cold, hard, and forced, lacking both character and life. They had lost the sense of their national traditions, without having succeeded in appropriating the abundant facility and elegance of the Italians. But Rubens, by his inborn qualities as by his education, was wonderfully prepared for the task in which they failed. He had a natural leaning towards light, movement, and life, and possessed both the flexibility and vigour required for the expression of the most varied emotions. He was prepared to treat every sort of subject in clearly defined compositions, rendered more significant by the vivacity and harmony of his colour, and always striking from a distance. His residence beyond the Alps had developed his inborn decorative sense. It had, it is true, taken some time for gifts so dissimilar, and aptitudes so irreconcilable, to manifest themselves in their attractive complexity. The elements that entered into the composition of that precious alloy were too

varied for the fusion to be quickly complete, or to permit the speedy
acquirement of the qualities of cohesion, force and brilliance that were
to assure its value.   But on his return to Antwerp, the artist once
again came into contact with the old Flemish spirit, and upheld by
the liberal encouragement he received, his genius developed freely.
Spontaneous and thoughtful, he was able to attract the multitude
and also to please the cultured few.   Sovereigns and members of
the higher clergy welcomed in him an ally fit to second their views,
and furnished him with opportunities for giving free scope to his
genius.

YOUNG GIRL CARRYING A EWER.
Albertina Collection.
(From a photograph by Braun, Clément et Cie.)

CONSECRATION OF A BISHOP.
(The Louvre.)

CHAPTER VII

HEAD OF A FAUN.
(Drawing in the Louvre.)

RUBENS was now able to lead the kind of life he delighted in, a life divided between his art and his family affections. He lived for some time in his father-in-law's house, and found that cultivated home in every way suited to his taste. His wife did all that was possible to secure him the tranquillity necessary for his work. In the enjoyment of a married life that did not separate her from her family, she was proud of her husband's ever increasing reputation, and of the proofs of sympathy that he received. In 1610, the magistracy of Antwerp presented the artist with a silver cup in recognition of services rendered by him to the municipality; what those services were we do not know, but we learn from the municipal accounts that a sum of £82 18s. was paid for the cup to a skilled chaser named Abraham Lissau. A letter written by Rubens on May 11, 1610, to the engraver Jacob de Bye, affords us a still more decisive proof of the privileged position the artist had then attained. Rubens had been asked by De Bye to take as a pupil a young man in whom he was interested. In his reply, Rubens apologised for his inability to do so : his studio, he said, was so much sought after, that he could not possibly take all who desired to enter it. He had been forced to refuse a hundred persons, who had been obliged to go to other painters, among them, to the dissatisfaction of his relatives, several that had been recommended by his family or by friends, notably by his patron, the burgomaster Rockox.

In the postscript to the letter, Rubens, in obedience to the spirit of order that always ruled his conduct, informed De Bye that, as there had been some delay in the purchase of the picture *Argus and Juno,* offered by him to the Duke of Aerschot, he was now treating with another purchaser ; but before concluding the transaction, he desired to warn him of it. In negotiations of the kind, "he liked to be absolutely straightforward, and to give his friends satisfaction ; but he did not find it always possible to testify his good will to princes." Not only did the matter stay there, but no painting by Rubens figures in the inventory drawn up on the Duke of Aerschot's death. The work in question was very mediocre, and Burger, who saw it at the Manchester Exhibition, to which it was lent by its owner, Mr. Yates, found "the composition no better than the execution."

Thanks to the fertility of his invention, and to the increasingly high prices paid for his pictures, Rubens's circumstances went on improving, and he found the apartments he occupied in his father-in-law's house too cramped for his needs. It is not surprising that his love of family life led him to desire a dwelling in which he might definitely settle himself. He required roomy accommodation for himself and his family, suitable apartments for the display of his collections to which he was always adding, a studio of sufficient size for the large canvases commissioned from him, and rooms for his numerous pupils, from whom he now began to select collaborators. The opportunity offered of acquiring a considerable property situated on the Wapper in the very centre of the town. On January 4, 1611, Rubens purchased it of Dr. Andrew Backaert and his wife, Madeleine Thys, for the sum of 7,600 florins. The deed of sale tells us that it was "a house with a large door, a courtyard, a gallery, kitchen, rooms, land and dependencies, with a bleaching ground adjoining the east side of the Company of Arquebusiers." The bleaching ground had formerly served as a drying ground for the fullers. Specified dates were stipulated for the annual payments of the price of the property which were faithfully adhered to.

The spirit of order which, as we have just shown, was paramount in Rubens, caused him and his wife to make a will in favour of the children who might be born of the marriage : but we know nothing of the deed executed on February 11, 1611, in the presence of the notary, Leonard van Halle, whose papers are all lost. A month later, on March 21, 1611, Isabella gave birth to a daughter, who was baptised by the name of Clara at the Church of St. Andrew ; the grandmother, Clara de Moy, was godmother, and Philip, Rubens's brother, godfather. Peter Paul had performed a like office for Philip's daughter, also named Clara, the year before, on August 4, 1610. The brothers in their faithful and enduring affection neglected no opportunity of associating themselves together in their joys as in their griefs, but an unexpected blow destroyed the happiness of their closely united lives. On August 28, 1611, after a short illness, Philip was taken from his affectionate family ; he was not thirty-eight years old. The funeral was of great magnificence, and while the accounts of the expenses testify to the position held by the family, they throw a curious light on the customs of the time. A sum of 133 florins 12 stuivers was expended on the meals given to the relations, friends and colleagues of the deceased on the day of the funeral. To appreciate the enormous quantity of " viands, hams, pastry, dairy produce and wine " that was consumed, it is sufficient, says M. Génard, to note that the table expenses of Philip's household for six months, for the board

of himself and his wife, the two children and the servants, did not
exceed 200 florins.[1] Peter Paul's portrait of his beloved brother was
placed above his tomb erected in the Church of St. Michael near that
of their mother; a Latin epitaph, engraved in gold letters on the
marble, briefly recounts the principal offices filled by Philip, and the
faithful memory his friends would ever retain of his virtues and learning.

Abiit non obiit, virtute et scriptis sibi superstes, ran the epitaph,

and the most celebrated
scholars of the time did
not fail to pay to the dead
man's memory the tribute
of their dithyrambic eulogies, in which a sincere
esteem and affection pene-
trated through the usual
bombast and affectations
of such compositions. The
verses together with a
funeral oration addressed
to Peter Paul, by way of
consolation, by Jan van
den Wouwere, were col-
lected in a volume dedi-
cated to the magistracy of
Antwerp, and printed in
1615 by Martin Plantin

PORTRAIT OF A YOUNG MAN.
(Cassel Museum.)

and his sons. Jan Brant, who superintended the publication,
included in it a selection from the best of Philip's own compositions,
translations, poems, panegyrics, etc. ; the portrait that forms the
frontispiece is by his brother.

Shortly before the publication of the book, Rubens, as in the
case of his mother, consecrated Philip's memory in a work which
better testifies to the depth of his sorrow, and to which he brought all
his talent. We refer to the fine picture in the Pitti, known as the

[1] P. Génard : *Anteekeningen over P. P. Rubens,* p. 455.

Philosophers. Rubens there represents, assembled round a table covered with books, Justus Lipsius and his two favourite pupils, Philip Rubens and Jan van den Wouwere; with serious mien the master comments on some passage of an ancient author.
Near his brother, yet at a
discreet distance, we have
the attractive countenance
and refined, distinguished
features of the painter.
The two pupils, attentive
to the master's lesson,
listen to his words, and
seem to approve his com-
ments. Above them, a
bust of Seneca,[1] of whose
works Justus Lipsius pub-
lished a scholarly edition,
presides over their learned
discussions ; in front of
the bust in a small crystal
vase filled with clear water,
are four bright-coloured
tulips, which seem the
expression of the homage
of the philosopher's four
admirers. As if to char-
acterise better the com-
munity of their tastes,
through a partly drawn
curtain is seen a glimpse

STUDY OF A NUDE WOMAN.
(The Louvre.)

of the Roman Campagna with walls and ruins, and on the

---

[1] The bust, then believed to be that of Seneca, is really that of Philetas of Cos. It probably belonged to Rubens, who brought from Italy a so-called bust of Seneca, mentioned in the preface to the *Seneca* of Justus Lipsius, published in 1615.

horizon the vague outline of the Italian mountains. The view is
full of frankness and light. Perhaps the blue of the upper part of
the sky, and the red of the hangings are a little strong; but with
this trifling exception, the harmony is at once vigorous and
delicate, and the extremely frank colour is discreetly distributed.
Save for the bright tones of the Turkey carpet, of the red curtain, and
of the tawny fur of Justus Lipsius's robe, the scheme of colour is
reduced to the golden greys of the architecture, the blacks of the dresses,
and the whites of the collars. The whole is admirably arranged to
bring out the lustre of the flesh painting, in which cold and pearly tones
are contrasted with luminous tints. The skilful management of the
paint, the precision and singular accuracy with which the high lights are
applied, the intelligent moderation of the work where, at a small cost,
the illusion of the most careful finish is given, indeed, everything
in this fine painting tells against the generally adopted date of
1602. After carefully and repeatedly examining the picture, we think
we are right in referring it to 1612—1614, a conclusion reached,
unknown to us, by Dr. Bode.[1]

In the beginning of his residence in Italy Rubens could not
have had any exact material for painting a portrait of Justus Lipsius.
In a letter dated from Antwerp, March 1, 1608, to Luigi Becatelli, then
at Rome,[2] Philip, in mentioning the recent death of his master,
deplores the lack of portraits. "It is not fitting," he wrote, "that his
portrait should be painted by the first comer to bring him before
the eyes of the Romans," and he adds that he hopes to get a portrait
from the hands of his brother, whose return he shortly expects. But it
was only later, and at Antwerp, that Rubens was able to obtain the
requisite information. A cursory examination of the picture makes
it clear that neither Justus Lipsius nor Philip was painted from life.
In the somewhat uncertain modelling of the figures, and in the
indecision of the features, there is none of the penetrating vivacity of
observation, and the firmness of touch, which, face to face with life
the artist would have given them. The contrast of their inert and

[1] J. Burkhardt and W. Bode. *Der Cicerone.* 6th ed. Vol. III. p. 813.
[2] Ruelens. *Correspondance de Rubens.* Vol. I. p. 420.

XII

The Descent from the Cross.

(From a photograph by Braun, Clément et Cie.)

indistinct physiognomies with the living countenances of Van den Wouwere and of the painter himself is most striking. The apparent age of the two latter still further confirms our hypothesis : both have passed their youth, they are of ripe years, and the type of the artist with his mature appearance and slightly bald forehead, is very like that which we find in other works of the period. It is the same with Van den Wouwere, who, two years younger than Philip, was a year older than his brother. Early intimate with the two Rubens, he possessed similar tastes, and the same veneration for Justus Lipsius. The death of Philip, for whom he had great affection, brought him still nearer to Peter Paul ; he could discuss with him not only Italy, where they had been together, but Spain, which they had also visited. As we have shown, he poured forth his grief for the loss of his friend in a literary composition : *De Consolatione apud P. P. Rubenium Liber*, which was inserted in the volume published in Philip's honour. Acquaintances from their youth, the painter and the scholar were never to be separated again, and with an almost equal duration their lives[1] progressed on parallel lines with nearly the same fate and the same honours. Here are then affinities enough to explain Van den Wouwere's presence by the side of the two brothers and of Justus Lipsius.[2] Everything therefore coincides to show us that it is probably correct to see in the picture of the *Philosophers*, not a mere collection of portraits, but rather a composition destined to perpetuate Philip's memory. In the supreme homage thus rendered him, the artist endeavoured to recall all that made the happiness of their closely united lives : Italy, where they had known the delights of a common residence ; their love of the antique and of the classics ; and the deep affection, so honourable to both, which had united them. Even the dog in the foreground probably had its significance, a symbol of the fidelity with which the survivors desired to preserve memories which would always be dear to them.

[1] Van den Wouwere died September 23, 1639, less than a year before Rubens.

[2] Rubens painted two other portraits of Van den Wouwere, of smaller dimensions, of which one in the Aremberg collection is of a remarkable finish and preservation ; the other is in the Kums collection at Antwerp, but the landscape background, absolutely identical with that of the *Philosophers*, seems to be from the brush of Jan Brueghel.

The death of his elder brother imposed on Rubens obligations which his natural kindness of heart made him earnestly desire to fulfil to the best of his ability.   He was now the head of the family, and had not only to replace his brother in the guardianship of their sister Blandine's children, but he had, with the assistance of Jan Brant, his father-in-law, to watch over the interests of the minors left by Philip himself, and of the son to whom his sister-in-law gave birth a few days after her husband's death.   The burgomaster, Nicholas Rockox, from a sentiment of touching sympathy, accepted the office of god-father to the child, who was baptised on September 13, 1611, in the cathedral, and received the name of Philip, in memory of his father.

PORTRAIT OF JAN BRUEGHEL.
Facsimile of an etching by Vandyke.

At the same time as he invariably showed the greatest solicitude for the welfare of his family, Rubens practised the greatest kindness towards other painters.   He was always ready to do them a service, to give them the benefit of his advice, or to further their interests with his own patrons.   At that period the greater number of his colleagues were much attached to him; with Jan Brueghel, for instance, he was on the most affectionate terms during the whole of his life.   Rubens held his father, Peeter Brueghel the elder, in particular esteem, and not only did he seek out his pictures—of which he had a dozen in his collection at his death—but he had several of them reproduced by skilful engravers. Although Jan Brueghel's elaborate and somewhat thin execution seemed hardly calculated to please him, he appreciated both his works and his person. With him he could evoke memories of Italy, where Brueghel had spent three years ; he preserved excellent relations with the friends he had made there, notably with his patron, Cardinal Borromeo. The latter, who had become Archbishop of Milan, continued to entrust him with numerous commissions, very often with the purchase of works of art in Flanders. They carried on a regular correspondence in this connection ; but Brueghel, who was more familiar with the brush than the pen, found it a fatigue and a trial to write a letter. His inelegant and involved style, the laboured turn of his phrases, clearly show the difficulty he had in expressing his ideas, and in consequence

PORTRAIT OF A MAN.
(Brunswick Museum.)

of his eccentricity of spelling, more in accordance with pronunciation than with the rules of grammar, it is often somewhat difficult to decipher his meaning. Nevertheless, the correspondence had lasted fourteen years, when, on October 7, 1610, there appears in the collection of the letters a missive which, by the elegance of the handwriting as well as by the clearness and correctness of the language, forms a contrast to the preceding ones.[1] On that occasion Rubens took up the pen for his friend, and henceforward often acted as his secretary, at first preserving his anonymity, then gradually intervening in the correspondence in his own person. Soon we shall see him associate his work with that of Brueghel, and paint charming figures in his landscapes in which he will do his best to bring his touch into unison, and make his colouring harmonise with that of his colleague.

Both had frequent opportunities of meeting at Brussels at the Court of the Archdukes, who sought to attract them thither. Brueghel in painting his favourite subjects for them : the *Four Elements*, the *Four Seasons*, the *Five Senses*, the *Creation*, the *Tower of Babel*, etc., found in the palaces of the princes models for the innumerable details—arms, books, pictures, flowers, all kinds of animals—that he introduced into his paintings, objects which permitted him to display the suppleness and marvellous finish of his execution. Old plans of the *Court of Brabant* show us the imposing mass of buildings which then formed the ducal palace, a confused heap of edifices in the most varied styles, occupying a picturesque site in the highest part of the town. A French traveller, Pierre Bergeron, who visited Brussels in 1612, notes the splendour of the apartments filled with works of art, the crowd of courtiers and servants, the richness of the equipages and stables, the beauty of the gardens and the park, for which that very year Salomon de Caus had designed a labyrinth. Accessible to all, the Archdukes, in spite of the austerity of their personal religion, practised a tolerance which corresponded with a wise perception of the state of the country, a tolerance which they would have practised even more widely if their ideas of conciliation had not so often met with vigorous opposition at Rome and Madrid, where the concessions to which they were inclined, were condemned as weakness. They liked to assist at the popular fêtes ; a picture by Antonie Sallaert in the Brussels Gallery shows us the Infanta Isabella in the midst of a great concourse of admiring spectators, taking part, on May 15, 1615, in the shooting feast of

---

[1] The correspondence is the subject of a pleasant volume by Signor Giovanni Crivelli. *Giovanni Brueghel, pittor fiammingo.* 8vo. Milan. 1868.

the *Grand Serment* in the Place du Sablon, when she shot a bird
at the height of the steeple.

The genuine benevolence which Albert and Isabella showed their
subjects was even more actively practised towards artists, and the
princes frequently stood godfather or godmother to their children,
and gave them marked proof of their sympathy. Their regard for
Rubens can readily be imagined. When he went to Brussels by their
request, he was doubtless lodged in the palace, and his talent and his
distinguished intellect marked him out for their favour. Coming
gradually to recognise his unerring judgment, they liked to discuss
matters of state with him. He deserved their confidence by reason
both of his frankness and his discretion. But far from seeking to
advance himself and push his own fortunes, he acted with the moderation and tact that stood him in such good stead throughout his career.
He knew the value of independence too well to remain long away from
his beloved home, and without ever neglecting the obligations of his
office, he was glad to get back to Antwerp, and resume his quiet life
and habits of regular work.

An important commission, however, was now to keep him at home,
and to absorb his energy for a long while. He owed it, probably,
to the kindly intervention of Rockox, who was president of the Guild
of Arquebusiers when they commissioned Rubens to paint them a
large triptych for their altar in Antwerp Cathedral. In contrast to the military associations of Holland, which had gradually
assumed a purely civic character, the companies of archers or arquebusiers in Flanders preserved their religious ties, and, faithful to
early traditions, remained veritable brotherhoods. Placed under the
protection of St. Christopher, the arquebusiers of Antwerp suggested
to Rubens that he should take from the legend of the saint the
episodes that seemed to him most suitable for representation. But
finding, doubtless, that the episodes did not offer sufficient interest,
the artist asked and received permission not to restrict himself
to the suggested limits. Enlarging the subject, Rubens, by a
somewhat subtle extension of the Greek name Christophoros (Christ-
bearer), determined to introduce into his picture all the persons who

had borne Christ during the course of his earthly existence. Without
troubling to supply a direct link between the different compositions,
he represents the Virgin during her pregnancy visiting St. Elizabeth ;
the old man Simeon receiving the Infant Jesus in his arms; St.
Christopher himself carrying Him on his shoulders, and lastly, as the
central episode, the dead Christ, descended from the Cross, borne by
reverent hands. The plan with the modifications was accepted, and

on September 7, 1611, the
agreement was concluded
in the presence of Rockox,
the commissaries of the
Guild of Arquebusiers, and
Rubens, who was allotted
a sum of 2,800 florins for
the work.

The accounts of the
Guild permit us to follow
the various phases of the
execution of the triptych
of Notre Dame, and, at
the same time, furnish
some curious information
about the native customs
of that period. As pru-
dent men, a little mis-
trustful, the deans paid
three visits to the

THE VISITATION.
(Borghese Palace.)

painter's studio, not only to see the progress the work was making,
but also to satisfy themselves of the quality of the panels employed,
to make sure that the wood was quite "sound and free from
sap." Each time, according to custom, they took wine, and bestowed a gratuity on the servants. On September 12, 1612, the large
panel of the *Descent from the Cross* was removed from the studio
and placed above the altar in the right transept of the Cathedral, not
far from its present position, and in 1614 the shutters were successively

transported there, one on February 18 and the other on March 6. According to custom, the Guild presented Isabella Brant with a pair of gloves, which cost them the sum of eight florins ten stuivers.   The

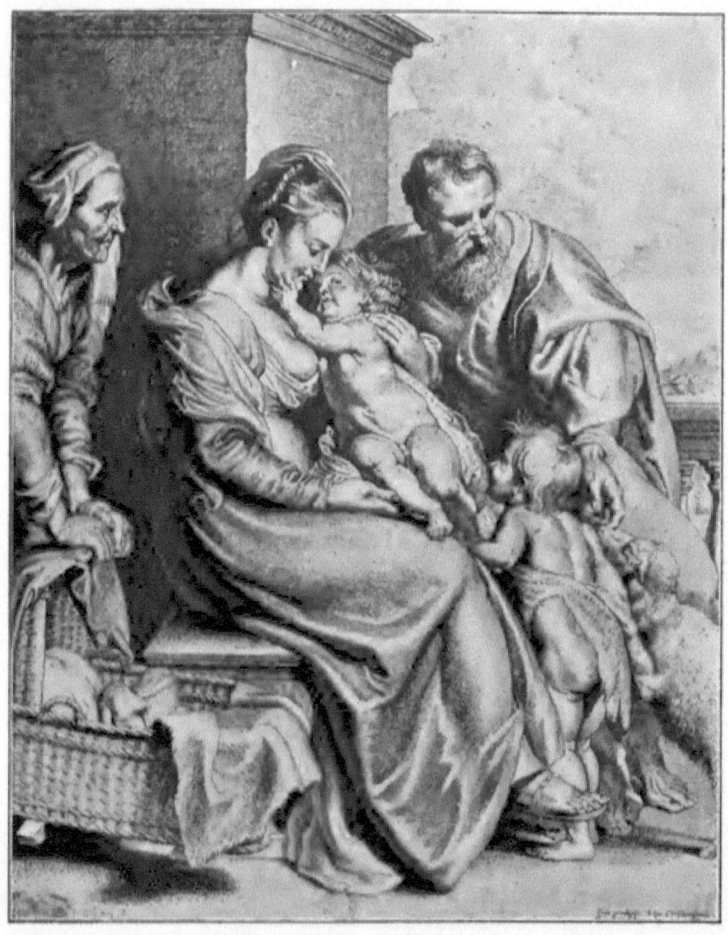

THE HOLY FAMILY.
Facsimile of an engraving by Vorsterman.

altar being at length arranged—doubtless according to designs furnished by Rubens himself—the ceremony of consecration took place on St. Magdalen's Day, July 22, 1614.   Three days before, when the clergy were settling the details of the ceremony, they desired the figure

of St. Christopher to be repainted, because its nudity seemed to them
indecent ; and also that advantage should be taken of the opportunity
" to cover up a woman's bosom " in a picture by W. Coeberger, and
" other things if need be."

Although the shutters of the triptych are, as we have seen, later in
execution than the central panel, they need not detain us long. The
arrangement of the *Visitation,* undoubtedly inspired by Titian's
Presentation (Accademia delle Belle Arti, Venice), presents a similar
plan, with the staircase which the Virgin ascends, and the portico
under which the other personages stand. But instead of spreading
out the composition in width, it is contracted into a narrow space, and
the homely conception of the scene gives it the appearance of a
Flemish translation of the master of Cadore's picture. The Virgin, a
matron of Antwerp, with features vaguely recalling those of Isabella,
advances, modestly lowering her eyes, to meet Elizabeth, who with a
naïve and somewhat coarse gesture indicates with her finger her
cousin's condition, affirming her right to figure among the *Christo-
phores.* The close contact of the unalloyed red and blue of the
Virgin's-robes is not, perhaps, a happy combination ; but the boldness
with which the architecture and the figures stand out against the bluish
background, denotes a masterly comprehension of decorative effect.
Rubens had already appropriated the subject in a painting probably
executed during his residence in Italy, and now in the Borghese
Palace. It is a curious piece of work of almost trivial reality ;
the arrangement is almost identical, but the figures are more thick set
and common, especially that of a strapping wench who ascends the
stairs with a parcel of linen. The handling is in keeping, easy and
swift, rather coarse, and without any other merit than decision. In
view of its slight interest we should not, perhaps, have mentioned this
early conception of the *Visitation,* had we not found, for the first time,
in the St. Elizabeth an old woman with features of a kindly and
benevolent expression who appears frequently later ; we have already
spoken of the portrait of her in the Munich Gallery, which, for a long
time, passed for that of Rubens's mother. Is it really, as M. Rosenberg
thinks, a portrait of Maria Pypelinx,[1] painted by her son from memory,

[1] *Zeitschrift für bildende Kunst,* July, 1894, p. 231.

Study of a Naked Woman.

(THE LOUVRE.)

(From a photograph by Braun, Clément et Cie.)

and introduced by him successively into several *Holy Families* painted shortly after? Is it not rather that of Isabella's mother? for there frequently appears by her side, in the figure of St. Joseph, a man with a long beard, of robust aspect, with a sympathetic countenance, perhaps Jan Brant, the artist's father-in-law. These are only conjectures; but it is advisable to note the persistence of the same types in the productions of that time, for, in all probability, the models were drawn from Rubens's immediate connections.

The sketches, very slightly modified, made for the *Visitation* and the *Presentation in the Temple*, which forms its pendant, are in the collection of Prince Giovanelli at Venice. The *Presentation* shows more distinction in the bearing of the personages, and a richer and more harmonious colouring. The gratitude and respect with which Simeon presses the little Jesus to his breast, the maternal solicitude of the Virgin, who, with a gesture as touching as it is natural, spreads her hands below the child so as to catch him should he fall from the old man's arms, the reverent admiration of the prophetess Anne, indeed, all the impressions of a scene of so penetrating an inwardness, are represented with both charm and truth. It is full of gaiety and brightness; it seems as if the painter desired to associate all the delights of colour with the hymn of joy breathed from their glad hearts. With M. Max Rooses,[1] we think we can recognise Nicholas Rockox among the bystanders, for, by a very natural feeling of gratitude, Rubens was anxious to introduce the portrait of the devoted friend who had so efficiently assisted to procure him the commission into the picture.

In the St. Christopher the artist followed at every point the traditions observed in the representation of a subject so frequently treated before him by the masters of the northern schools. He shows us, as usual, the hermit standing on one of the banks of the stream which St. Christopher is crossing, and throwing the light of his lantern on to the giant who bears the Infant Jesus on his shoulders. The Child, smiling roguishly, leans all his weight on the kindly giant, a sort of Christian Hercules, who, in spite of his strong muscles, sinks beneath his pleasing burden. The water is sullen, of a dark green

---

[1] *L'Œuvre de Rubens.* Vol. II. p. 111.

colour, mysterious, treacherous. The sky is dimly lighted at the horizon
by the last rays of the setting sun. Amid the foreboding darkness,
the young, supple body of the Child stands out, modelled in full light.
The beautiful sketch in the Munich Gallery, in which the compositions of the two shutters of the Cathedral triptych are united in one
panel, is more brilliant and in better preservation than the two
originals for which it formed a study ; although the contrasts are
less marked, the effect of night is more concentrated and more
striking.

The *Descent from the Cross* might also have been inspired by
many remarkable works painted by his forerunners, for, in the early
days of the Flemish school of painting, the fine subject tempted some
of its most illustrious masters : notably Van der Weyden in the
admirable composition in the possession of the Chapter of the Escorial,
and later, Van Orley in the great picture now in the Hermitage. But
notwithstanding the fine qualities of the two paintings, the arrangement of both is defective in according almost equal importance to the
two episodes that demand the spectator's attention : on one side,
Christ descended from the Cross, on the other, the holy women
crowding round the fainting Virgin. Thus conceived, the two works
lack the strong unity that so moving a scene demands. Likewise
lacking in unity, the celebrated fresco of Daniele da Volterra[1] in the
S. Trinità de' Monti at Rome, was certainly in Rubens's mind. But
in consequence of the exigencies of the brilliance he brought into his
art, Rubens knew how to avoid the mistakes of his predecessors.
As we have seen, he never hesitated to take his advantage wherever
he found it. In borrowing without scruple, however, the whole of
the upper part from Daniele da Volterra, Rubens was careful not to
break up the effect as Daniele does, and so to diminish the impression
that ought to dominate the composition. It is the *Descent from the
Cross* and not the *Fainting of the Virgin* that he intended to paint,
and he excelled his predecessors in the use of the expressive and
picturesque resources of dramatic action ; he alone understood how to
concentrate them, and subordinate them to the emotion he desired to

---

[1] Michael Angelo is supposed to have furnished the design to his pupil, who may also
have been inspired by Marc Antonio's engraving after a drawing by Raphael.

call forth. Let Fromentin again describe the force and originality with which Rubens accomplished this.

"All is over. It is night; at least the horizon is of leaden blackness. All are silent, all weep, all receive the august remains, and give them pathetic care. At most they seem to exchange the words which form themselves on the lips after the death of our loved ones. The mother, the friends are there, and foremost of all the weakest and most loving of women, she in whose frailty, grace, and repentance, are incarnated all the sins of the earth, pardoned, expiated, and now redeemed. Living flesh is contrasted with the pallor of death. There is even a charm in death. Christ reminds us of a beautiful flower cut from its stalk. As he no longer hears those who curse him, he no longer hears those who weep over him. He belongs no more to men, to time, to anger, or to pity; he is beyond everything, even death." [1]

PORTRAIT OF A MAN.
(Dresden Gallery.)

Rubens has evoked in marvellous fashion all the emotions that such a spectacle could arouse in those who were present, all that it ought now to suggest to us. As in the *Raising of the Cross* the scene was complicated, tumultuous, full of agitations and contrasts, so here everything is simple, touching, silent, strong only by its eloquence. However great the part due to art in this work of the imagination, its aspect is so striking that it seems to be copied from life. The

[1] *Les Maîtres d'autrefois*, p. 89.

inspiration, apparently so spontaneous, is based on an exact observation of realities, and to conceive with so powerful an emotion a scene
so fine but so difficult to treat, demanded the co-operation of a
tender heart, a singularly fertile imagination, and a well-balanced,
clear-sighted mind. The perfect rhythm of the masses, the way in
which their contours are united and bound together, bring the composition into entire harmony with the scene. Analyse in your mind the
construction of the picture, try to penetrate its hidden mechanism,
and you will see how solidly it is built up, how skilfully and
naturally the figures are distributed in the various planes, and how
they balance and echo each other. Above are the two workmen,
almost nude, rough and indifferent, yet unconsciously affected by the
solemnity of the act, by the reverence those around them show for the
victim. They have carefully unfastened his arms from the Cross,
and let the corpse glide down the length of the shroud. Below,
stepping aside to give it space, Joseph of Arimathea and Nicodemus
half efface themselves, ready to aid if need be. Below again the
Virgin and St. John standing, keep closer, the beloved disciple
especially, for, delivered from his torpor, he feels driven to do
something, to bear almost alone the whole weight of his Master's
body. Lower still, kneeling on the ground, Mary Magdalene and
Mary the wife of Cleophas cling to each other, bracing themselves, as
it were, to arrest the fall, and to support at their point of meeting the
thrust of those downward lines which abut and press upon them.
Lastly, in the centre is the corpse abandoned to itself, and outstretched
hands, distressful and pitying countenances, form, as it were, an aureole
of love and tender reverence around it.

As in the *Raising of the Cross*, the poor lifeless body is the
central point of the picture ; drooping, inert and bent as it is, the
body retains in the passive yet delicately curving attitude something of the litheness of life. In the former painting the tortured body
is, at the moment of being raised on the fatal wood, still beautiful, and
seems to ascend gloriously to Heaven with the principal lines of the
picture. Here, on the contrary, the livid corpse, all that remains of
Him, inclines downwards, and glides towards the earth. Until the end
of His slow martyrdom He was left alone, abandoned without mercy to

the bitterness of His thoughts, to the terrors of His agony ; now when His sufferings are ended, those whom He loved return, and crowd around Him powerless. He is still here, and although He is no longer theirs, His friends are prodigal of their last caresses. They feel that soon He will be taken from them, and they surround Him with vain solicitude. What diversity, what sincerity of emotion breathes from these superbly inspired and original figures ! How can we describe the supreme distress and pity of the Virgin's sorrowing countenance, or the mechanical gesture of the arms as she tries to guide her son's oscillating body through space, just as if she still feared for Him, as if she desired to save Him from the pain He no longer feels. With what an ardent and fixed gaze Mary Magdalene follows the corpse that is slowly lowered towards her, of which " one livid and stigmatised foot, with almost imperceptible contact, lightly touches her bare shoulder."[1] Unable to separate herself from the object of her love, she tries to discover what He has experienced, to understand what He has now become. She watches the decomposed features for some glimmer of intelligence ; she waits for some sign in the breast of the beating of the heart that is motionless for ever. In reply to her feverish interrogations, she finds only the icy coldness of death. For the first time Rubens gives us the poetical type of the sinner, a type that he henceforth makes his own, and to which he never tires of returning in order gradually to transform it, to invest it with more charm, tenderness and youth, to lend a more graceful suppleness to its attitudes, and to leave some remnant of involuntary coquetry in their ease and freedom. Her form here is still somewhat too thick and sturdy, and her features have no great distinction. But Rubens never expressed her despair with more pathos, or showed by simpler means the stupor and contrition of the soul when overwhelmed by grief. " And in the fine head of Christ Himself, inspired and suffering, virile and tender, the hair clinging to His temples, His tortures, His ardours, His pain, His ecstasy, the eyes shining with celestial light, what true painter of the best Italian period would not have been struck by the capabilities of expressive force raised to such a height, and would not have recognised here an entirely new dramatic power ? "[2]

---

[1] *Les Maitres d'autrefois*, p. 81.   [2] *Ibid.*, p. 91.

The composition, compact, condensed, compressed with difficulty within the limits accorded to the painter, leaves no empty spaces round it. There is no landscape; the horizon is very low, with a scrap of dark brown vegetation; the sky is a blackish mass. Thus isolated, lost in the darkness that surrounds it on all sides, the group stands out from the gloom in full light, and alone occupies our attention. In the violence of this effect, in the blackish shadows, in the too strongly defined contours, in the sudden contact of certain tones of colour placed side by side without the necessary gradations, the persistent influence of Caravaggio may be recognised. But in the diffused light that strikes the corpse, in the supple modelling of the head and torso, in the delicately mobile arabesque of the outline, we have evidence that such a perfect possession of chiaroscuro, which he so admirably turns to account, is a recent acquisition of the young master. The execution, although still somewhat heavy and laboured, is more personal. Careful, restrained, and firm, it has neither the charm nor the ease that Rubens shows later. It marks the salutary effort of an artist who applied himself to his work, and restrained his impulse in order to treat the subject that tempted him with the necessary reverence. In his manner of colouring, which is fuller, more severe and less superficial, we see the refinement of his mind, the scruples of his genius. In his indifference for the local colour in painting certain textures, for instance, in Mary Magdalene's dress, where the green, bold enough in the shadows and half tints, disappears completely in the high lights, and gives place to a meaningless yellow, we may trace signs of his Italian preoccupations. The greater part of the tonalities are, it is true, more exactly observed, and although most delicately shaded, the red drapery which clothes St. John never loses its particular quality. We may also note some successful and new ventures in the warm transparency of the shadows of the flesh tints, and especially in the boldness of the reflections to which Rubens resorts more and more in order to harmonise colours that it might be dangerous to bring together, and to derive harmonies, as varied as they are unexpected, from the contact. Face to face with so complex an art, we are struck by the clearness of the great mind which, in the sacred poem of the Passion, in subjects so closely allied as the *Raising of the Cross* and the *Descent from the Cross*, selects and brings into play the most striking picturesque elements in each of them ; and then succeeds in producing two equally dramatic creations, but so dissimilar, that instead of repeating and injuring each other, one composition completes and gives value to the other. So great was the success of the *Descent from the Cross* that Rubens had almost directly to paint variants for other churches of the district. Although

it has not the same importance as the Antwerp picture, the *Descent from the Cross* in the Cathedral of St. Omer is a well-arranged composition, but the attitude of the body of Christ, which is held up by passing the shroud under His chest, is somewhat awkward. It is, moreover, difficult to judge of the original state of the canvas, for it is much injured by alterations and repaintings. Another variant, now in the Hermitage, resembles the Antwerp picture in the types of the persons and

PORTRAIT OF A WOMAN.
(Dresden Gallery.)

the brilliancy of the colouring; it was painted much about the same time for the Capuchins of Lierre, and presents a modified arrangement in which the body of Christ is rigid and almost vertical. Arras possesses two *Descents from the Cross* by Rubens; one, in the Cathedral, differs little from the Hermitage picture ; it was probably only touched up by the master, and is, in any case, much damaged ; the other, in the Church of St. John the Baptist, was formerly in

the Abbey of St. Vaast, and is later by some years. Less elongated
in form, it has but four figures round the very low Cross :
above, Joseph of Arimathea and St. John ; below, the Virgin
standing, and Mary Magdalene kneeling, her hair dishevelled,
stretching out her arms with a passionate gesture towards the precious
corpse. In the copy in the Valenciennes Museum, formerly in the
Church of Notre Dame de la Chaussée of that town, the artist, in
accordance with the space assigned him, had to compress his composition vertically. The body of Christ is still fastened to the Cross by His
left arm, and a man, half leaning on the horizontal bar of the Cross, tears
out the nail that retains it. The Virgin, despairing yet struggling
against her grief, prepares to receive the corpse with a superb gesture,
while Mary Magdalene, crouching down, reverently kisses the legs. A
man's head, foreshortened, with upturned eyes, a painting dashed off
in masterly fashion, which served as a study for the St. John of
this picture, is now in the Lacaze Gallery ; its broader handling, more
liquid impasto, and less sharply defined contours, permit us to fix the
date about 1615—1617. To that period also is to be assigned the
best, in our opinion, of the variants of the *Descent from the Cross.*
After adorning the high altar of the Capuchin Church of Lille, it
is now in the museum of that town ; beside it hangs a charming sketch,
purchased at the Hamilton sale, and it is interesting to compare it with
the original. While the composition is less grand than that of
Antwerp, it is of a more pathetic inwardness. There is more of
the unexpected in the arrangement, and the harmony is quieter and
more expressive. The indistinct green of St. John's tunic, the violet
grey of Joseph of Arimathea's gown, the purplish or bluish greys
of the costumes of the other figures, set off the brilliancy of the corpse,
and of the white shroud painted in full light. The yellow cloak faced
with pale pink worn by Mary Magdalene, the soft carnations of
her charming countenance, and the gold of her dishevelled hair,
add a tender note to the general severity of the colour. The broad
painting of the textures contrasts with the extremely delicate brush-work
of the flesh tones, especially those of the noble figure of Christ, which
with its fine head bent towards His mother, the beautiful curve of the

body, and the languor of the limbs, is one of the master's most exquisite creations.

The resources of so richly endowed a nature are more easily understood when we find the artist drawing such numerous and varied inspirations from the same episode. Rubens employs neither elaboration nor effort in his repetitions of the great subject. His clear good sense suffices for the task; he never exhausts himself in vain researches, and succeeds through the means of expression which he employs. Where others become subtle or confused, or spoil their work by timidity, and by too complicated exigencies, he goes straight on with the confidence of a man who knows the right road. As Delacroix says, " He is in the position of an artisan who does the work he knows how to do without endless seeking after perfection. He produces with what he knows, and consequently has nothing to hinder his thought. . . . He translates his sublime ideas into forms that superficial persons blame for their monotony, not to mention other of their grievances. To the man who has probed the secrets of art the monotony is not displeasing. The return to the same forms is the stamp of a great master, and the result of the irresistible force of a learned and practised hand. Hence follows an impression of the facility with which the works have been produced, a sentiment which adds to their power. . . . In any attempt to chasten the form, the artist would lose the impulse and freedom which make for unity and action." [1]

But while employing somewhat massive forms and not seeking to improve them, he does not repeat himself. He modifies his composition according to the conditions laid down for him, according to the dimensions imposed on him, or according to what is to be the destination of his work. Restraints, instead of making obstacles for him, offer further stimulus. His repetitions will never become dull and tiresome; he will put into each enough that is new to give him an interest in his work, and the changes that he introduces are not merely picturesque: they spring from the particular conception which commended itself to his thought. Following the clearly designed programme that he set himself, he amplifies, exalts, puts this side in

[1] *Journal d'Eugène Delacroix.* Vol. III. Plon. 1893.

shadow and the other in light, and carries on his task to the end with as much freshness of impression and pleasure in painting as if he were dealing with an entirely new work.

It must be acknowledged that Rubens has made the great subject of the *Descent from the Cross* his own by his representation of it. It is from his pictures that we always imagine it, and of the different conceptions, that of Antwerp, historically the first, has perhaps, not quite justly, supplanted all the others in public favour. It has special qualities of its own, and has been the most conspicuous, for, with the exception of the years 1794 to 1815, when it was in the Louvre, it has never left the old Cathedral for which it was painted.

STUDY OF A BLIND MAN.
For the Miracle of St. Francis.
Albertina Collection.
(From a photograph by Braun, Clément et Cie.)

XIII

The Virgin and the Holy Innocents.

(THE LOUVRE.)

Printed by Gény-Gros, Paris (France)

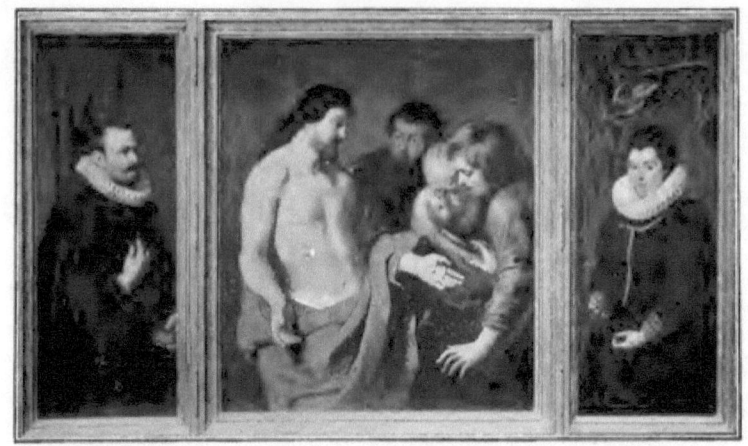

THE DOUBTING THOMAS.
With the portraits of the Burgomaster Rockox and his wife.
(Triptych : Antwerp Museum.)

CHAPTER VIII

RUBENS'S PRACTICAL MIND—HIS POSITION AT THE COURT OF THE ARCHDUKES AND HIS REPUTATION—VERSATILITY OF HIS TALENT—WORKS EXECUTED FOR THE PLANTIN PRESS—TRIPTYCH COMMISSIONED BY NICOLAS ROCKOX—MYTHOLOGICAL AND RELIGIOUS PICTURES (1614—1615)—'PERSEUS AND ANDROMEDA'—'NEPTUNE AND AMPHITRITE'—'STUDIES OF WILD BEASTS AND HUNTING PIECES'—'THE FALL OF THE DAMNED' AND THE 'SMALL LAST JUDGMENT'—'THE VIRGIN WITH THE INNOCENTS' IN THE LOUVRE.

FRAGMENT OF A DRAWING.
(The Louvre.)

THE numerous variants of the *Descent from the Cross* that Rubens painted for the churches of the district, afford ample testimony of the favour with which the clergy regarded him. With his practical mind, the artist could not bear to see things drag along slowly, still less to lose the profit of his work. He expected to find in others the punctuality with which he fulfilled his engagements. If there was delay in deciding, or in carrying out promises made to him, he put pressure on the persons concerned, and if he did not obtain satisfaction, he asked distinguished persons to intervene on his behalf. A letter that he wrote to the Archduke Albert on March 19, 1614, affords a decisive testimony of the fact, and well brings out this side of the master's character. At the request of Maes, Bishop of Ghent, Rubens had undertaken the decoration of the high altar of the Cathedral of that town. In importance and beauty the work was to surpass everything that had yet been done in the country. The bishop dying, the work was suspended, although the chapter had approved of the commission, and the plans furnished by Rubens not only for the pictures, but also for the construction of the altar, were left unrecompensed. He hoped, however, that the new bishop, Frans van der Burch, in taking possession of his predecessor's see, would desire to carry out the projected work. But Van der Burch only desired to erect a marble altar with a statue of St. Bavon. Rubens then invoked the assistance of the Archduke, who had seen and approved his plans. Consequently the artist begged the prince to intercede with the prelate. " It is not," he said, " so much a question of my particular interest, as of the adornment of the city ; " and as he had done before and did many times again under similar circumstances, he declared " on his faith as a Christian that it would be the finest work he had ever produced." Perhaps Rubens made such assurances, when he wished to dispose of his pictures, rather more often than was seemly. This time, in spite of the Archduke's intervention, nothing came of his request, and it was not until ten years later, under the episcopate of Bishop Antonie Triest, that the artist received his due.

The versatility of Rubens's talent rendered him capable of fulfilling many and various tasks, but as his employers were chiefly Churchmen, he painted, for the most part, religious subjects, and had, at first, little opportunity of showing his powers in other directions. At that time Antwerp was passing through a fresh crisis fatal to her prosperity. In the treaty concluded with Holland in 1609, the Archduke neglected to stipulate for the free navigation of the Scheldt ; the effects of his carelessness were disastrous to the town, because the commercial activity of Amsterdam was developed to the detriment of her rival. An English diplomatist, accredited to the United Provinces,

Sir Dudley Carleton, who, as we shall see directly, became closely connected with Rubens, communicated to one of his friends the bad impression produced by a visit to Antwerp in 1616 in these terms :

" But I must tell you the state of this town in a word : *magna civitas, magna solitudo*, for in the whole time we spent there I could never set my eyes on the whole length of a street upon forty persons at once : I never met coach nor saw man on horseback. . . . In many places grass grows in the streets, yet (that which is rare in such solitariness) the buildings are all kept in perfect reparation. Their condition is much worse (which may seem strange) since the truce than it was before ; and the whole country of Brabant was suitable to this town ; *splendida paupertas*, fair and miserable."

In spite of this state of things, the number of painters had vastly increased, and they had therefore to be satisfied with more modest gains. Rubens alone, thanks to his ever-increasing fame, was certain of important commissions. His kindly nature and wise conduct prevented the jealousies that his position might have aroused. Besides, interest counselled his colleagues to keep on good terms with him, for his high position permitted him to render them signal service, and with his habitual kindliness he did all he could for them. His favour with the governors increased daily, and when his wife presented him with a son, a gentleman of the Court, Johan de Silva, was appointed to represent the Archduke as godfather of the child, who was baptized on June 5, 1614, by the name of Albert, at the Church of St. Andrew.[1] Rubens used his influence for the good of artists of talent less well placed than himself. He introduced them to amateurs, who, in consequence of the gradual rise in the prices of his pictures, were unable to buy them. The following passage in a letter written about this time by one of his friends, reveals his method of procedure. " In that," says Balthasar Moretus, " I only imitate our celebrated painter, my compatriot Rubens, who, when he has to deal with an amateur who has little knowledge of art, sends him to a painter whose talent and likewise whose prices are less. As to him, his paintings of superior merit, although more expensive, do not lack purchasers."[2]

[1] His grandmother, Clara de Moy, was his godmother.
[2] Letter to Philip Peralto at Toledo, April 9, 1615.

His kindly humour and his reliability caused Rubens's society to be sought by all. He was elected dean of the Romanist Guild on July 1, 1613, and presented to the Guild on the occasion two panels representing St. Peter and St. Paul, who were his patron saints, and those of the Association. The panels have disappeared; but a replica, repainted by him, now in the Munich Gallery, shows us what the two figures, larger than life-size, and represented in somewhat

ST. JEROME.
(Dresden Gallery.)

theatrical attitudes, were like. Among the Romanists the master found some of his most prominent colleagues, such as Sebastian Vrancx and Abraham Janssens, who later became his neighbours on the Wapper. He lived in friendly intercourse with another talented painter, Martin Pepyn; Isabella Brant stood godmother to his daughter, named Martha, on March 15, 1615.

The works of Rubens were already sought after outside Flanders; they began to spread through Europe, and the most distinguished collectors, nay, monarchs themselves, were eager to purchase them. His fertility and his methodical, studious life alone enabled him to fulfil the commissions given to him. It was probably through his friends in Italy that he received a commission for a *St. Jerome*, which, after belonging to the Modena Gallery, passed into the Dresden Gallery. The picture is signed with his initials, P. P. R.: the handling is broad, personal, although somewhat uniform. The venerable head of the saint, with its white hair and beard, is a

fine type.   But the calm expression and plump form are little in
keeping with the legendary type of a personage whom the Italians
usually represent as leaner and more agitated.   He would certainly
have to undergo a lengthened mortification before he would lessen
his corpulence or subdue the cheerfulness of his old age.   For the
moment he is at his prayers, and contemplates the crucifix in front of
him with fervent adoration.   The lion drowsing at his feet rests his
big head between his paws with magnificent calm.   All the details
are thoughtfully carried out with a careful touch, and the vegetation

JUPITER AND CALISTO.
(Cassel Museum.)

in the foreground, painted leaf by leaf—tufts of plantain, thistle,
violets, and ivy, in the leaves of which all the veins can be seen—is
evidently very carefully copied from nature.

The same conscientiousness, the same somewhat hard execution,
the same brownish vegetation, are to be seen in the picture of
Jupiter and Calisto in the Cassel Museum.   The edge of the
nymph's quiver bears not only the whole of Rubens's signature, but the
date, the last number of which, half rubbed out, is probably a 3 : 1613.
Lying on the grass, which is dotted here and there with clover and
other plants, the young girl looks with suspicious curiosity at the strange

companion who, under the guise of Diana, lovingly caresses her face. A complacency entirely mythological is needed, it is true, to be mistaken in the expression of the virile features, and the artist, in order to explain with all possible care the somewhat strange subject, has not been content to give the lord of Olympus embrowned flesh tints, which contrast with Calisto's brilliant whiteness; he has placed beside him the quivering eagle, the customary witness of such adventures. A little weak in drawing, without great distinction in the forms, the nymph's body, which reclines on a purple drapery, is modelled in the full sunlight; but pearly reflections somewhat moderate what would otherwise be the excessive contrast of the luminous flesh with the dark colours of the landscape.

In the Cassel Museum is another picture signed by the name of Rubens, dated 1614, a *Flight into Egypt*,[1] inspired by a composition of Elsheimer's. In the midst of the darkness which entirely surrounds the fugitives, the cleverly managed light seems to emanate from the divine Child, and to illuminate the Virgin's face with its radiance. The mysterious flight, the poor family lost in a land unknown and full of snares, the nobility of the Virgin's features, the breadth of the method joined to the delicate execution, the mysterious poetry of the landscape, everything concurs to make the beautiful work one of the master's best productions of the period.

There is the same signature, and the same date, on the *Susannah and the Elders* in the Stockholm Museum, a composition to which Rubens more than once returned, as well as on another picture in the Antwerp Museum, *The Shivering Venus*, which shows us in a gloomy light at the entrance of a humid grotto the crouching, shivering goddess, and by her side Cupid seated sadly on his quiver.[2] Both look perished with cold, and the boy seeks to warm himself by drawing towards him a piece of the light drapery that imperfectly protects his mother. By their side a hairy, red-faced satyr, hardened to all inclemencies of weather, laughs at the wretchedness of the two

---

[1] An old copy of this picture with a few slight variations is in the Louvre.

[2] It is the same quiver which we pointed out in *Jupiter and Calisto*, and that we shall see also in the *Sebastian* of the Berlin Gallery, of which we shall speak later.

12

Study for the " Madonna" of the Chiesa Nova.

(GRENOBLE MUSEUM.)

Printed by Draeger, Paris.

shivering creatures, and in derision offers them fruit and ears of corn. The figures, treated with a soft and easy touch, present less harsh and less defined contours than in the former works.

Although not signed by Rubens's name, two other paintings ought also to be referred to this period by reason of the documentary evidence we possess about them. The first was destined for the funeral monument raised by the widow of Jan Moretus to the memory of her husband, who died September 22, 1610. Moretus (in Flemish Moerentorf) was the son-in-law of Christopher Plantin, the founder of the celebrated printing press which bears his name. Every visitor to Antwerp remembers the interesting collection in the building where his press was first set up, a building which the intelligence and zeal of its curator has made unique of its kind.[1] In the picturesque setting of the edifice occupied by the printing establishment, in the courtyard, where a venerable vine covers the walls with its twisting festoons, in the rooms adorned with works of art, in the old shop still furnished with the counter, scales, and account books, in the different workshops where the presses are, in the proof readers' room, in the collection of type, and in the library, we may contemplate one of the most interesting sides of the past of the old city, and its intellectual activity lives again before our eyes. Christopher Plantin, the founder of the house, came originally, as we have stated, from Touraine, where he was born between 1518 and 1525. After a somewhat wandering existence, he settled at Antwerp, at first as a bookbinder and manufacturer of articles in inlaid leather. But he dreamed of a profession more in harmony with his cultured taste, and he became a bookseller. For a brief period he was suspected of heresy, but he soon found favour again with the governors, and besides the printing of liturgical books, for which he obtained the license in 1570, he began to publish fine editions of the books on all subjects that have made his name illustrious. On his death in 1589, he was succeeded by Jan Moretus, one of his sons-in-law.

---

[1] We borrow the following information regarding Rubens's relations with the chiefs of the Plantin Press from the admirable publications of M. Max Rooses: *Christophe Plantin, imprimeur anversois; Titres et portraits gravés d'après Rubens pour l'imprimerie Plantinienne; Catalogue du Musée Plantin*, etc.

His two sons. Jan and Balthasar. then carried on the business; and Balthasar becoming sole chief, continued the traditions of the noble device: *Labore et Constantia*, until his death in 1641. Almost of the same age as Rubens—he was born in 1574—Balthasar was acquainted with him from childhood, and he preserved the most amicable relations with him to the end of his career. Quite early the artist had worked for the Plantin Press, and we know that in 1608 he

PLATE FOR THE PLANTIN PRESS.
Plantin Museum. (Drawing by Rubens, 1633.)

supplied it with the illustrations for his brother's book, *Electorum libri duo*.

The triptych of the funeral monument of Moretus, now in one of the side chapels of the choir of Antwerp Cathedral, was executed in 1611—1612, for the receipt given by Rubens to Balthasar, and preserved in the Plantin Museum, is dated April 27, 1612. The timidity of the handling in the figures of St. John and St. Martin, painted on the shutters, as well as in the oval portrait of Jan Moretus, which dominates the whole, reveals the collaboration of the master's pupils. Although less evident, it is also positively to be recognised in the *Resurrection of Christ*, which occupies the centre panel. The scene is well composed, and the body of Christ is broadly and skilfully modelled, but the pose is trivial, the foreshortening of one of the legs scarcely correct, and in the opaqueness of the shadows, in the exaggerated play of the muscles, and in the gestures of the soldiers who occupy the foreground, we find some of the defects of the Italian period.

A fairly considerable number of other works were also executed

THE FLIGHT INTO EGYPT.
(Cassel Museum.)

by Rubens from 1610 to 1618 for the Plantin Press, notably the drawings, to which we shall return, and in 1616 ten portraits painted for Balthasar Moretus, now exhibited in the Plantin Museum : those of C. Plantin, J. Moretus, Justus Lipsius, Plato, Seneca, Leo X., Lorenzo de' Medici, Pica della Mirandola, Alfonso of Arragon, and Matthias Corvinus. The portraits, of hasty execution, entrusted by Rubens, undoubtedly, to the hand of his pupils,[1] brought him

---

[1] The last of them, those of the Renaissance, scholars and patrons of letters, are copies after engravings from the books of Paolo Giovio — *Vitae illustrium virorum et elogia virorum doctorum* (Bâle, 1575) — that Rubens procured in 1633 by the intermediary of Balthasar Moretus.

in all 144 florins, which is 14 florins 4 stuivers apiece, a small sum
enough in consideration of the reputation Rubens then enjoyed.
It must be confessed, however, that, taking into account the slight
merit of the paintings, Moretus paid as much as they were worth.
The artist, as we see, despised no gain, and for works painted in
leisure moments, or that he caused to be executed in his studio by
the aid of others, he was contented with a small remuneration. We
shall learn later how, instead of touching the sums due to him from
the Plantin Press for these various commissions, he employed them
to pay for the binding and ornamentation of books destined for his
library.

For another patron, who eventually became his friend, Rubens
painted from 1613 to 1615 a triptych for the funeral monument
that Nicolas Rockox erected in his lifetime for his wife and himself, in the Church of the Recollets at Antwerp. Rockox was one
of the most distinguished men of his time ; he was descended from
a middle-class family, who had acquired wealth, and had been ennobled.
In the most difficult circumstances, he nine times filled the office of
chief burgomaster of Antwerp, and he strove as far as he could to
ameliorate the evils caused by war, or to efface the memory of
the quarrels from which the town had so greatly suffered. He
employed his large fortune in doing good, and during periods of famine
he most generously came to his fellow-countrymen's assistance.
A friend of letters, he was also greatly interested in botany, and
devoted to archæology. His collection of busts, cameos and antique
medallions was famous, and it was through his good offices that
Rubens some years later entered into relations with the famous
French scholar, Claude Fabri de Peiresc, who regularly corresponded
with the burgomaster of Antwerp from 1606. Peiresc commissioned Rockox to purchase books and medallions for him in Flanders,
and in return for his trouble sent Rockox plants from the South : al-
thæas, cistuses, laurels, narcissi, and others. In the triptych which is
now in the Antwerp Museum, painted by the master for his friend,
the centre panel represents the *Doubting Thomas*. The half naked
body of Christ is of a supple, flowing handling, resembling that of
The Shivering Venus ; there are the same brilliant flesh tints in the

lights, bluish in the half tints, deeply coloured in the shadows, with extremely bold reflected lights. Although hasty enough, the painting placed over an altar, and seen at a distance, must have been very decorative, and the portraits of Rockox and his wife, which adorn the shutters, while possessing the same breadth, are of a more delicate and precise handling ; that of the husband especially, in which the honest countenance and delicate profile proclaim the man of culture.

The signatures and dates we have just referred to, relatively fairly frequent on the productions of this period, will henceforth be only rarely found in Rubens's works. We must hasten to profit by them, for they provide us with fixed landmarks, and the formal analogies in the execution, or the similarity of types that we observe in them, help us to determine with some exactness the dates of other productions of the same period. Of this number is the *Dying Seneca* in the Munich Gallery. In treating the subject, Rubens, still full of his Italian reminiscences, was able to satisfy both his literary taste, and his strong passion for the antique. The principal figure, indeed, was suggested by the marble statue of an African fisherman discovered in the sixteenth century, which an unscrupulous restorer transformed into the *Dying Seneca*. Rubens doubtless made a drawing of it at the Villa Borghese, where it then was.[1] Seen from in front, with his veins and muscles complacently detailed, the old man's body lacks distinction and style ; the shadows are opaque, and the contours somewhat strongly defined ; but the severe harmony of the whole is in accord with the gravity of the subject, and Rubens alone was capable of expressing with so much accuracy and delicacy, the Stoic serenity that lights up the features of the philosopher while his life ebbs with his blood.

Another picture, likewise inspired by the antique, but of a totally different character, should probably be dated a few years later, about 1615 ; it is the *Romulus and Remus suckled by a She-wolf*, painted in all likelihood for some Italian amateur, for the picture, which is now in the Capitol, has long been in Italy. Rubens gave a free rein to his imagination, and drew from the legend a work full of charm and

---

[1] It passed from that collection to the Louvre at the beginning of the present century.

poetry. Stretched on the ground on a white cloth, the two children,
entirely nude, lie beside the wolf who nourished them. The babes,
with their rosy cheeks, plump flesh, and golden hair, are of a delicious
suppleness and freshness. The artist places them amidst the most
delightful surroundings. In the branches of the fig tree, under a blue
sky dotted with white clouds, a pair of woodpeckers are making love ;
various plants, all distinguishable, reeds, clover, thistles, grow on the
margin of a still pool ; water-lily leaves spread themselves over its
surface, and in its trans-
parent depths swim a
pike and an eel ; on the
bank are different kinds of
shells, a snail, and a small
crab. The details—in-
dicated at little cost by
accurately applying a few
high lights over the me-
dium tones of the objects
-—add to the charm of the
composition, and show the
masterly skill of a brush
that seems to disport itself
in a work at once so
original and so full of
life.

DEATH OF SENECA.

(Munich Gallery.)

There was nothing
to fetter Rubens in his
treatment of legendary subjects ; reminiscences of the Italian masters
whom he had studied certainly filled his mind ; but his brush naturally transformed them into a more picturesque and a completely
Flemish presentment. Such, indeed, is the character of an episode
that often tempted his predecessors, and to which Rubens himself
returned more than once, that of *Perseus and Andromeda*, of which two
versions, both painted about 1615, are in the galleries of St. Petersburg
and Berlin. Although in the first the figure of Andromeda has greater
charm, and the characteristics of Pegasus—the artist represents him as

a piebald, white with chestnut spots[1]—are more graceful and full of life, the Berlin picture seems to us superior. The arrangement is, however, defective, for about the centre, the panel is divided into two nearly equal parts, which are not sufficiently coherent. Andromeda, with her somewhat flabby corpulence, and her short, thick legs, is not a model of academic beauty. But the little Cupids who hover round the young couple are of a delightful invention; one stands on tiptoe, and tries to unfasten the captive's bonds; another holds the

ROMULUS AND REMUS.
(The Capitol.)

bridle of the horse, who neighs joyously; while the remaining two help each other to scale the gentle steed, and to seat themselves on his ample back. And how can we describe the execution? How can we give any idea of the harmony, the soft brilliancy of the colouring? What an assemblage of bright tones, what perfect harmony between the supple, milky flesh tints of Andromeda and the purple of Perseus's cloak, the steely tones of his armour and helmet; between the little

[1] We give the drawing of the horse which belongs to the Albertina collection on p. 188.

firm bodies of the Cupids and their fair hair and pink pearly flesh ;
between the dapple grey coat of the Pegasus and his white tail, mane
and large wings ; the subdued blue of the sky and the green sea, the foam
of which dashes wildly against the rocks.   The handling is everywhere
vigorous, alert, pleasing to the eye, easy and sure, inspired by the
painter's animation and his delight in the work.

With a similar animation and delight Rubens attacked the most
hackneyed subjects, endowed them with the exuberant life that was
in him, and so re-created them.   He did not always succeed at the
first attempt ; but if, in the beginning, he did not discover all the
resources of his subject, he was not discouraged, and never
abandoned the work he had commenced.   Instead of leaving it un-
finished, he completed it as well as he was able, and, if he thought
good, took up the same subject again, and treated it in a fresh
work.   Then, profiting by the knowledge gained in the former one, he
corrected his composition, and gave it the perfection of which it was
capable.   Such is the profit he drew from a large mythological composition formerly in the Count de Schonborn's collection, *Neptune and
Amphitrite*.   Bought in 1881 by the Berlin Museum for the respectable
sum of £10,000, its authenticity excited violent criticism at the time
of the purchase.   If the attribution does Rubens little honour, it
seems to us indisputable ; both the composition and the handling are
in his manner of the period, 1614—1615.   It contains, moreover,
certain figures utilised by him previously, the nymph in the foreground,
for instance, leaning on a crocodile, whose pose and features resemble
those of the woman throwing herself violently backward in the
Transfiguration of the Nancy Museum.   On the left and a little
apart, the painter represents himself, with his refined and delicate
countenance, personifying a river.   And Amphitrite, with her somewhat massive build, presents a type of beauty for which the artist long
had a predilection.   Her body, seen from in front and entirely nude, is
firmly modelled ; in the lower part it is exposed to the full light of the
sun, while the face, neck, and upper part of the chest, bathed in a
clear and transparent penumbra, are painted with marvellous delicacy
and lightness.   Indeed, with the exception of the animals—a lion, a

XIV

Perseus and Andromeda.

tiger, a rhinoceros, a hippopotamus and a crocodile—gathered round the
central group, which by the variety and accuracy of their characteristics testify to the master's powers of observation, the work is
mediocre, and as insignificant as certain analogous compositions of
Giulio Romano and the Bolognese painters. But in painting it, Rubens
saw the excellence to which similar subjects would lend themselves,
and he proved it admirably soon after in two works in which we find
several of the personages of the former picture. The first is the *Erechthonius and the Daughter of Cecrops*, now in the Liechtenstein collection,
where in the features of two of the daughters of Cecrops we recognise
one of the nymphs accompanying Amphitrite, as well as the goddess
herself in an almost identical pose, the upper part of her body likewise
enveloped in a transparent penumbra. Between them, their sister,
a brunette of piquant beauty with an amiable expression, bending over
the infant's cradle, seems to be a portrait, so natural and full of life is
her face. But save for the faces, and the standing figure of the young
nude girl, which are wholly of Rubens's execution, the handling lacks
distinction, and testifies in too great a degree to the co-operation of his
pupils.

In the other picture which is in the Vienna Gallery, each of the
Four Quarters of the Globe is symbolised by one of the great rivers
that water them : the Danube, the Nile, the Ganges, the Amazon.
They rest on their traditional urns, and are attended by nymphs,
who help to distinguish them. Less heavy and commonplace than the
figures of the former picture, they are also more golden in colour, and
if it is to be regretted that here and there over bold contrasts or
tones spoil the general harmony, we are bound, on the other hand,
to admire such happy conjunctions as that of the grey hair of the Nile,
with the red drapery and beautiful body of the young woman placed
just above him. Besides, Rubens had the happy inspiration of rele-
gating the different personages to the upper plane of the picture,
and of filling the lower part with a fanciful episode, as original
as unexpected. In the foreground, a crocodile, half issuing from the
water, and escorted by three little genii, advances threateningly
towards a tigress who, lying at the feet of the Ganges, is quietly

suckling her young. The animal with her bright fur and frowning eyes, with ears bent down, roars, superb in her rage, and shows her terrible fangs to her enemy, while the cubs, disturbed in their repast, but already well satisfied, remain suspended at her teats. The forbidding characteristics of the crocodile, its enormous open mouth, and wrinkled body bristling with quills and scales, form a most unexpected contrast with the joyous carelessness, roguish air, and the freshness of

the smooth, ruddy flesh of the three children engaged in teasing the monster. The artist's inventive faculty enabled him to express here with all the breadth, animation, and magnificent simplicity of his talent, the most dissimilar acceptations of life, and also to place together the most unexpected forms and colours; and thus, by the power of his imagination he recreated subjects to all appearance hackneyed.

He attained the life and movement which is one of the characteristics

STUDY FOR PEGASUS IN THE PERSEUS AND ANDROMEDA OF THE HERMITAGE.
(Albertina Collection.)

of his genius by an intelligent observation of nature ; and he derived the strength of his creations from the manner in which his imaginative power enabled him to interpret, and occasionally even to exaggerate, nature. He had his own method of consulting it, and he easily transformed the studies made from life and nature into pictures. The various animals in the archdukes' collections, or perhaps some itinerant menagerie visiting Antwerp, furnished him with the opportunity of observing the wild beasts, that so often figure in the works of this period,

at close quarters. Like most of the great artists, he was attracted
by the beauty of their forms, their noble characteristics, the regal
majesty of their faces. He carefully stored up valuable notes in his
memory and his portfolios, of which he afterwards made profitable
use. Perhaps the sketch of a *Tigress Suckling her Young*, in the
Academy of Fine Arts at Vienna, is a study from life. In any

NEPTUNE AND AMPHITRITE.
(Berlin Museum.)

case Rubens introduced it in the composition of the *Four Quarters
of the Globe*. With an almost identical pose, the beast has,
however, a slightly different expression, and the master represents
her crushing bunches of grapes under her fore-paws, as if greatly
excited by the intoxicating fumes. In the Albertina collection are, all
on one sheet, about ten remarkably powerful pen and ink sketches of

lions and lionesses in various postures. Most of the sketches (seven
out of the ten) are used in a picture, formerly in the Hamilton
collection, *Daniel in the Lions' Den*, a frigidly correct work
without much character. For the type and expression of Daniel,
Rubens used an admirable study made by him from life, which he
transformed into *St. Sebastian* (Berlin Museum), a large academic
boldly painted figure, which would be very elegant, were it not for
the heaviness of the knee-pans, a fault that too often spoils the
artist's nude figures.

That was not the only way in which Rubens turned his studies of
wild beasts to account. While observing them in their somnolent
state, and condemned to a long and weary captivity, his active
mind imagined them at liberty, displaying their suppleness and
vigour. He imagined the lean, languid bodies in action, in scenes
best calculated to bring out the ferocity of their instincts, and the
impetuosity of their appetites. The *Lions* of the Hermitage, for instance, appear before us transformed by his imagination, with glowing
eyes, threatening jaws, in all the violence of their savage lusts.
Better inspired still, and carrying to the extreme the *crescendo* of life
and movement in which he delighted, Rubens painted the dramatic
Lion Hunt of the Munich Gallery, for which there is a sketch in the
Hermitage. There is nothing more striking than this composition,
where, animated by the same fury, beasts and men mingle in a
desperate struggle. Beset, harassed, wounded by the hunters, the
two lions furiously defend themselves with their teeth and claws against
their aggressors. They, terrified, losing their self-control, strike
the beasts with redoubled blows from their lances and spears.
Wherever we look, we see amid the frightful tumult of rearing
horses, trembling with fear or pain, nothing but bleeding wounds,
torn flesh, threatening faces, distorted by suffering or already
pale with death. But beneath the apparent chaos, we recognise a
firmly balanced mind which foresaw and arranged everything that
might give the work its full significance. On the right, where the
main effort of the picture is placed, very strong values support the
weight of the masses, and concentrate the effect ; skilfully distributed

neutral greys bring out the values of the brighter tones scattered here and there. The low horizon of the landscape allows the uneven silhouette to stand out entirely against the sky, and greatly adds to · the grand impression of the scene.

In treating subjects of this character, Rubens found how thoroughly they suited his temperament. Judging by the number of variants that he painted himself, or caused to be painted in his studio, they must have found favour with the public. Of the picture in the Munich Gallery executed "for His Serene Highness the Duke of Bavaria," we know that the master offered Sir Dudley Carleton "a copy commenced by one of his pupils, but all retouched by his own hand." Afterwards came a *Lion and Lioness Hunt*, now lost, but which we know from Soutman's engraving ; then a *Lion and Tiger Hunt*, in the Dresden Gallery, also painted after a sketch by Rubens, less happy in arrangement, less compact and original ; and leaving aside other works of the kind, to which we shall have to refer again, we may mention the *Crocodile and Hippopotamus Hunt*, in the Augsburg Museum ; this, again, is the work of a pupil ; but here the exotic character and savage power of the two aquatic monsters are more skilfully suggested. Delacroix greatly admired this work. While he found the "aspect of the *Lion Hunt* confused, and regretted that art had not presided over it in a sufficiently great degree to augment the effect of so many inventions of genius by a prudent distribution of the light, or by sacrifices," he preferred the *Hippopotamus Hunt*, "which is more ferocious, and of which he liked the emphasis, and the relaxed, extravagant forms." [1]

One work with Rubens led to another, and the *Last Judgment* supplied animated and tumultuous scenes still more calculated to appeal to him. The subject had attracted northern artists before; mediæval sculptors represented it on the doors of French cathedrals, and painters of the early schools of Cologne and Flanders endeavoured to interpret it on canvas. Besides the picturesque contrast of angels and devils disputing the possession of mortals, the subject afforded an opportunity —so far rarely used—for the introduction of nude figures, whose naïve ugliness is complacently displayed by the artists. When Rubens was

[1] *Journal d'Eugène Delacroix*, March 6, 1847.

at Rome he carefully copied the prophets and sibyls of the Sistine
Chapel, and also some fragments of Michael Angelo's stupendous epic
which covers the large wall.   Rubens now attacked the theme, complicated and vehement in style as in method of presentment, on his
own part, and in so doing gave free play to the lyric range of his ideas
and to the skill of his execution.   The actions and sentiments of the
Hunts become somewhat artificial when compared with the terrors of

ERECHTHONIUS AND THE DAUGHTER OF CECROPS.
(Liechtenstein Collection.)

the human tumult and inexorable fate which the prose of the *Dies Irae*
brings before the mind of the Christian.

At that time a German prince, a great admirer of Rubens's
genius, commissioned from him a somewhat large number of
important works.   Newly converted to Catholicism, Duke Wolfgang
Wilhelm von Zweibrücken-Neuburg, was anxious to show his
neophyte fervour by founding a Jesuit College in his domains,
and by adorning the principal churches of his residency and its
neighbourhood with pictures.   Besides a *Nativity of Christ*, a
Descent of the Holy Ghost, and an allegory of the *Triumph of Religion*
that he successively commissioned from the artist, Rubens painted for

him a *Fall of the Rebel Angels*, and a *Last Judgment* of large dimensions, for which alone he received 3,500 florins. These various works, all now in the Munich Gallery, reveal somewhat too clearly a large amount of collaboration on the part of the master's pupils, and, in spite of their size, scarcely deserve attention. Rubens showed his power better in executing about the same time variants of the two last compositions, a *Fall of the Damned*, and a *Small Last Judgment*, also in the Munich Gallery, which are wholly by his hand. He studied the

THE FOUR QUARTERS OF THE GLOBE.
(Vienna Gallery.)

details of the chief groups of the *Fall of the Damned*, painted about 1615, in a series of bold and rapid sketches in Italian chalk now in the British Museum.

Generally speaking, subjects of such vastness are not suited to painting. They are too complicated in themselves to produce a strong impression. In the tumultuous confusion the spectator does not know what to look at, and he hesitates between the numberless details that demand his attention. Multiplying the groups and episodes

beyond all measure, Rubens failed to give prominence to any.
He tried, it is true, to bring some sort of unity into the chaos, by
joining together in the centre, in a compact mass, the two oblique
lines in which the figures in the *Fall of the Damned* are arranged.
Between the two narrow lines that divide the composition, the repro-
bates, seized, torn and quartered by demons, are presented in the greatest
confusion ; their despairing gestures, their contortions, their struggles
and somersaults form so insignificant and ragged a silhouette, that the
eye finds no place whereon to rest.   But if we take the trouble
to unravel the confused heap of outstretched hands, contracted
arms, and quartered legs, we are struck by the enthusiasm and
marvellous precision of the master who, with the tip of the brush
and his swift facility, gave motion to masses of humanity projected through space, everywhere scattering terror, everywhere
accumulating the horrors of the most terrible tortures.   On all sides
monsters with gaping mouths, sharp claws and fangs accomplish their
sinister work, lighted by the reflections from the fires of hell.   But
despite the accumulation of horrors, Rubens, playing as it were with his
invention, mingled with them an element of the grotesque.   Some of
the monsters cause laughter rather than terror : well in view, well in
the centre among the voluptuous, the violent and the slothful, who
painfully expiate their sins, the artist, as if in involuntary derision, has
placed a couple of fat gluttons ; they spread forth on all sides their
overwhelming masses of flesh, and force the devils who carry them off
to sink beneath the burden.

There is more sobriety, taste, and unity in the *Small Last Judgment*, painted a little later, about 1616—1617.   It is of smaller dimensions, the figures are less numerous and the masses more respected.
By certain wise sacrifices the effect is better concentrated, and, as a
result, the impression is much stronger.   Even in a greater degree than
usual, the simplicity of the work is exquisite.   Commencing with a
little colour lightly rubbed in that allowed full value to the transparent
ground of the panel, Rubens indicates with a graceful stroke of the
brush the figures that he afterwards models in a medium tone with
light touches of colour ; then with a few bold strokes he gives

13

Child Playing the Violin.

(THE LOUVRE.)

Printed by Draeger, Paris.

precision to the contours, or deepens the shadows. The lustre of flesh, the gloss of hair, the suppleness and plenitude of the forms, and the relief of the contours are expressed with decisive accuracy by very clear high lights. In spite of the similarity of the subjects, there is no repetition of the former picture. The master was under no obligation to copy himself, and he always found new combinations in which to express ideas he had treated before.

It seems strange to find a man so gentle and amiable in the ordinary course of life, taking pleasure in horrors, in veritable nightmares. But besides being to the taste of the time, violent subjects suited Rubens's temperament. He delighted in them all his life, gratuitously emphasising their cruelty, and not sparing us any unnecessary or startling brutality. The features he presents to us are more exuberant than select, and with more vigour than taste he enjoyed pushing things to extremes. The same vigorous imagination that led him to show us a hell of monsters and of tortures, inspired him, when, immediately afterwards, he painted a heaven, peopled by smiling, graceful figures as in the *Madonna with Angels*, in the Louvre. He always loved children, and excelled in painting them. In Italy he saw the success obtained by the Amoretti, who, in the pictures of his contemporary, Albani, displayed their frigid, precise prettinesses. But Rubens was too full of the sentiment of life to enjoy such insipidities, and Titian, with his greater naturalness and his picturesque richness, offered nobler examples. With Rubens, charm never bordered on affectation. The picture in the Louvre of the Virgin holding the Infant Jesus and surrounded by cherubs, is a feast for the eyes. With what vivacity, with what enthusiasm the crowd of little ones press round the Madonna to present her with palms or crowns, to seize a fold of her robe, to obtain a glance from her! With what perfect art the light plays among the groups, setting up contrasts between them, putting each of them into its plane, and brings the discreetly applied high lights into relief by subdued half-tones. With an art even superior, the great colorist diversified to infinity the contiguous shades in the flesh-tints, making them more enjoyable by means of the greys and blues of the sky, and giving all poetic significance to the beautiful bevy of innocents who disport themselves in the blue heavens.

In dealing with the pictures of this period we have been often obliged to point out their hardness, stiffness and exaggerations ; but they possess, none the less, maturity, the marked originality of an individual genius which we are bound to admire, a tardy maturity also, for in spite of his precocious talent, when Rubens reached its height, he was approaching forty. Through the experience gained by incessant work, the timidity or crudity of his early compositions gave place to the supreme ease and vigorous simplicity which more and more characterised his genius. But whatever the skill and fertility he now possessed, he never ceased to progress, because he preserved the same love of, and enthusiasm for, his art to the end.

TWO CHILDREN EMBRACING.
Weimar Museum.)

CHAPTER IX

RUBENS'S PUPILS AND COLLABORATORS—METHODICAL DIVISION OF THE WORK
BETWEEN THEM—PURCHASE OF SIR DUDLEY CARLETON'S COLLECTIONS: CORRE-
SPONDENCE ON THE SUBJECT—FRANS SNYDERS—JAN BRUEGHEL—VAN DYCK AND
HIS WORK FOR RUBENS—PAINTINGS FOR THE CHURCH OF THE JESUITS, AND
THE 'HISTORY OF DECIUS MUS'—PORTRAITS PAINTED AT THAT PERIOD BY
VAN DYCK AND BY RUBENS: THE DIFFICULTY OF RIGHTLY ASSIGNING THE
AUTHORSHIP.

PORTRAIT OF VAN DYCK.
Facsimile of an etching by Van Dyck.
(National Library, Paris.)

ALTHOUGH it is not possible to mention all the works of this period, we know how numerous they were. His incessant production, and the great variety of his subjects, testify to the versatility of Rubens's talent, and to the universality of his capacity. But however well ordered his life, however expeditious his execution, he could not have accomplished the commissions entrusted to him unaided. We have already pointed out among his works some of very unequal value, that clearly reveal the hand of collaborators. We

have also seen that very soon after his return to Antwerp, his pupils
were so numerous that he found it impossible to receive all the
young men who sought to work under him, a point on which his early
biographers give us precise information.

Sandrart, who knew Rubens, mentions the numerous pupils
"whom he carefully trained, each according to his capacity, so as to
utilise their collaboration. They often painted animals, the ground,
the sky, water and woods for him. He made a rough draft of the
work himself in a sketch 6 or 9 palms in height; then the composition
was transferred by the pupil to a large canvas, and Rubens painted
or retouched the principal parts." Sandrart adds that through the
influence of the great painter, "the town of Antwerp had become a
wonderful academy, where it was possible to attain the highest perfection in art." Sandrart's testimony is confirmed by that of a Danish
physician, Otto Sperling, who visited Rubens, and also by Bellori
and De Piles. The last writer is most explicit on the subject:
"As he was so much solicited on all sides," says De Piles,
"Rubens had a large number of pictures executed by skilful pupils
from his designs in colour; these he afterwards retouched with fresh
insight, quick intelligence, and a ready hand, and in so doing breathed
his spirit into them, a process which he turned to excellent account. But the difference between the pictures that passed for his,
and those that were actually by his hand, injured his reputation,
because the former were for the most part badly drawn and carelessly
painted." [1]

It would not be fair to criticise a method of procedure permitted by
the custom of that age by the light of modern ideas. Under the
articles of apprenticeship, the pupils' works, until they were admitted to the guild, belonged by right to their teachers, who invariably
utilised them to their own advantage. The custom, moreover, was
not confined to Flanders. Rubens had seen to what an extent it prevailed in Italy, especially at Mantua, where Mantegna and Giulio
Romano could never have accomplished their numerous works without
the aid of their pupils. Everything conspired to make the artist profit

[1] *Abrégé de la Vie des Peintres : P. P. Rubens.* Paris, 1699. P. 393 *et seq.*

by the facilities thus placed at his command. Rubens, always practical, neglected no opportunity of turning his talent to the best possible account, and he never liked to send away amateurs who desired to possess a specimen of his work empty handed. If at times, when they could not adequately remunerate his labour, he sent them to less celebrated colleagues, he more often undertook the smallest commissions himself, on condition that he should only devote to them time proportionate to the remuneration offered. From the point of view of a legitimate care for his reputation, it would doubtless have been better that everything issuing from his studio should have been worthy of his talent, and should have shown the perfection of which he was capable. But in Italy many works unworthy of Raphael bore his name, and in Flanders it was not long before painters undertook all the works demanded of them. Thus it was merely a question of cost, and each of the interested parties was only liable in proportion to what he undertook to perform. From this time forth Rubens rarely signed his pictures—either those wholly by his hand, or those to the execution of which he was almost a stranger—and therefore the merit of the work can alone establish its value.

Under these conditions, Rubens showed the talent for organisation that he invariably brought to the conduct of his life. He excelled in judging character, and upon a slight knowledge of his pupils he promptly discerned their capacity, and decided what was to be gained from their assistance. One was skilful in painting the nude, another in painting animals; others, again, excelled in landscape, architecture, or accessories. According then to his appreciation of their various powers, Rubens organised a methodical division of the work of collaboration, a work which admitted, on their part, of every degree of participation. For the more important canvases, Rubens painted with his own hand, on a panel previously covered with a coat of greyish-white plaster, a clearly-defined sketch; the grouping, the figures, and the smallest details were carefully drawn with the brush in a dark brown tone, something like bitumen. The whole effect was boldly indicated in the same tone. The composition, for which the master had made all the necessary studies beforehand, was then considered fixed in its essential elements

in a sufficiently irrevocable manner.   Having thus determined the
forms of the lights and the shadows, Rubens, knowing which of his
pupils were to transfer it to canvas, indicated in his sketch more or
less summarily the scheme of colour to which they were to conform.
In this way he tested for himself his means of expression, and at the
same time instructed his interpreters and marked out their task.   He
watched over them during the course of the execution, hastening one,
retarding another, directing each by the instruction specially suited to

VENUS AND ADONIS.
(The Uffizi.)

his temperament and skill.   When the work reached the point
previously settled in his mind, according to the importance he attached
to it, or the interest he felt in it, Rubens intervened to carry it on and
complete it.   His mind was calm, "his eyes were fresh," he saw at a
glance, and accurately, the points to be emphasised, the parts to be
placed in light.   Every stroke told.   With a few touches the flesh was
rendered more brilliant, the countenances more expressive ; vigorous
tones and luminous high lights brought out the effect, gave more
prominence to the forms greater brilliancy or harmony to the colour,

more unity or significance to the work. All this was done boldly, with the discernment of an alert intelligence, and the sureness of inimitable skill.

But Rubens had to deal not only with pupils who, in order to become his collaborators, submitted to his will, but with artists who, already regarded as masters, put themselves under him, because they recognised his superiority ; they became his assistants, because they were certain of the material advantage to be derived from an associa-

IXION DECEIVED BY JUNO.
From the Duke of Westminster's collection. (M. S. Bourgeois' collection.)

tion thus freely entered upon, and of the instruction to be gained from his teaching. Rubens left a larger share of initiative to them, and paid greater respect to their individual work. Over both, however, he exercised full and uncontested authority, based as much on the undisputed pre-eminence of his talent as on the amiability of his disposition. Among those who passed through his studio, and they are numerous, there is not one who ever had a grievance against him, or hazarded any recrimination. In the concert of praise there is no discordant tone, but a unanimous desire to please the master.

Interest, gratitude, affection, kept them at his side, for he was full of devotion and attention to them. His sincerity was delightful ; without rebuffing or discouraging them, he discovered what was good in them, even in the least gifted, and took pains to develop it. His pupils were deeply attached to him ; many could not make up their minds to separate from him ; they formed, as it were, part of his family, and to some among them he entrusted the execution of his last wishes.

Thus surrounded and respected, Rubens justified at every point the favour and consideration of which he was the object. His punctuality and accuracy towards the patrons who overwhelmed him with commissions, were unfailing. They knew in advance on what they could count. A fixed tariff provided for every degree of his own participation in the work entrusted to him : so much, if it was all by his own hand ; so much, if he touched up the whole ; so much, if he only worked over the principal parts. No mistake was possible, and he himself explained the matter with perfect clearness in several letters that have been preserved, letters which, as we shall see, also afford us information regarding his habits and character.

By the beginning of 1618 the alterations undertaken in the house purchased by Rubens were almost completed. He arranged commodious apartments for himself and his family, studios for his pupils and for himself, and delighted in adorning the fine dwelling with pictures, marbles, and other valuable works of art. But no matter what may have been the ardour of his desires, he was not the man to go beyond what seemed to him reasonable. His purchases were always in accordance with his means, and without diminishing his property, he proportioned their value to his gains and to the income at his disposal. But at that time an opportunity offered for acquiring an important collection of antiquities formed by the English ambassador, Sir Dudley Carleton. Before his appointment to the Hague, the diplomatist had been accredited for five years to the republic of Venice, and had there purchased the nucleus of the collection to which he continued to add. An intelligent amateur of the arts, and himself

XV

Adam and Eve.

(HAGUE GALLERY.)

a painter,[1] Sir Dudley Carleton was in friendly relations with other English connoisseurs, especially with the Earl of Arundel, and he often made purchases for them through one of his agents, named George Gage. Informed by Gage of Sir Dudley Carleton's intention of disposing of a portion of his collection in exchange for pictures by him, Rubens hastened to write to the ambassador, that having heard his collection much praised, he had long wished to see it; but that he was at the moment prevented from so doing by press of work. If, as Mr. Gage informed him, Sir Dudley Carleton had "the intention of making some exchange of the marbles for pictures by his own hand, as he was exceedingly fond of antiques, he was disposed to accept any reasonable offer." Under those circumstances, it seemed that the best means of coming to an agreement would be to allow the bearer of the letter to view the collection, and take note of its contents, in order that he might give Rubens an exact account; and Rubens, on his part, would send a list of the works then in his studio. Thus the transaction might be speedily concluded. The agent, whom the artist recommended as an honourable man, "enjoying public consideration, and on whose honesty every reliance might be placed," was Frans Pieterssen de Grebber, a native of Haarlem and a distinguished painter of that town. (Letter of March 27, 1618.)[2]

A month after (April 28) Rubens resumed the subject. He was advised by his agent that the matter was progressing favourably; he would not discuss the prices paid by Sir Dudley Carleton for the objects that formed a part of his collection; on that point he relied on his word as a gentleman, and believed that the prices were not exaggerated. As a prudent man he might, however, observe that persons of distinction were often liable to be taken at a disadvantage, because the seller proportioned his demand to the rank of the buyer, a proceeding that he should himself never imitate. "As for me," he added, "Y. E. may rest well assured that I shall fix the

---

[1] The dedication, dated 1620, of an engraving by J. Delff after a portrait of Sir Dudley Carleton by Mierevelt, praises him not only as "an admirer of the art of painting, but as himself practising the art with great distinction."

[2] Sir Dudley Carleton, like Rubens, was familiar with Italian, and they corresponded in that language.

prices of my pictures absolutely, as if it were a question of selling
them for ready money, and I beg you in this to rely on the word of

PORTRAIT OF JEAN CHARLES DE CORDES.
(Brussels Gallery.

an honest man." It happened that he had just then in his studio
a choice of pictures, and some which he had even repurchased for
more than he had received for them, because he wished to retain

possession of them, but all were at His Excellency's service, since
" he preferred brief negotiations, concluded at once according to the

PORTRAIT OF JACQUELINE DE CORDES.
(Brussels Gallery.)

liking of each of the parties. Although he was just now so overwhelmed with commissions both public and private that his time was
filled up for some years to come, yet if, as he hoped, they came to

an agreement, he would not fail when his other tasks were done, to complete those of the paintings on the list that were not quite finished at once, and those that were ready, he would forward directly." There followed a list of twelve pictures, with the price and dimensions of each.

LIST OF THE PICTURES IN MY HOUSE.

Florins.	Description.	Dimensions.
500	A Prometheus bound on Mount Caucasus, with an eagle who gnaws his liver. Original, by my hand, the eagle by Snyders	Height, 6 ft. ; breadth, 12 ft.
600	Daniel amidst many lions, painted from life. Original, entirely by my hand	Height, 8 ft. ; breadth, 12 ft.
600	Leopards painted from life with satyrs and nymphs. Original, by my hand, except a very beautiful landscape done by a very distinguished artist in that style	Height, 9 ft. ; breadth, 11 ft.
500	Leda, with the Swan and a Cupid. Original, by my hand	Height, 7 ft. ; breadth, 10 ft.
500	A Crucifixion. Life size, perhaps the best picture I have ever painted	Height, 12 ft. ; breadth, 6 ft.
1,200	The Last Judgment, begun by one of my pupils, after a picture of very large dimensions that I did for His Most Serene Highness the Prince of Neuburg, who paid me 3.500 florins cash for it : the picture being unfinished, I should retouch it in such a way that it would pass for an original	Height, 13 ft. ; breadth, 9 ft.
500	St. Peter taking from the fish the money to pay the tribute, with other fishermen round him ; painted from life. Original, by my hand . .	Height, 7 ft. ; breadth, 8 ft.
600	A hunt of men on horseback with lions, begun by one of my pupils, after a picture that I did for His Most Serene Highness, the Duke of Bavaria ; wholly retouched by me	Height, 8 ft. ; breadth, 11 ft.
Each 500	The twelve Apostles and Christ, painted by my pupils, after the originals by my hand in the possession of the Duke of Lerma ; they would all be retouched by my hand	Height, 4 ft. ; breadth, 3 ft.
600	A picture of Achilles clothed as a woman, painted by my best pupil, and entirely retouched by me ; a charming work, and full of many beautiful young girls	Height, 9 ft. ; breadth, 10 ft.
300	A St Sebastian, naked, by my hand	Height, 7 ft. ; breadth, 4 ft.
300	A Susannah, painted by one of my pupils, but entirely retouched by my hand	Height, 7 ft. ; breadth, 5 ft.

According to his custom, Rubens does not neglect to extol his pictures, which, to believe him, were "the flower" of his work, although it
must be admitted that their merit was somewhat unequal. Sir Dudley
Carleton hastened to reply, and on May 7, wrote that he agreed to the
prices of some of the pictures offered him, "considering them reasonable for compositions that are neither copies, nor the labours of pupils,
but the work of the master." The dimensions of the *Crucifixion*,
however, seemed to him too large for the room in which it was to
hang; therefore, he relinquished that, preferring to take the *St.
Sebastian*. Not wishing to be outdone by Rubens, Carleton praised
his own collection, "his marbles and other works of art being the
rarest and most costly of the kind possessed by any prince or amateur
this side the Alps. But liable, like all diplomatists, to continual
changes of residence, he found it inconvenient to carry about objects
of so much weight . . . . in fact, to speak the truth, taste is subject
to change, and he now preferred paintings, and especially those by
Master Rubens, to the sculptures of which he was formerly so fond." It
would be best if he could come himself and see the collection at the
Hague, where the ambassador would be happy to entertain him, "in
order not to buy *a pig in a poke*, as people say." If, however, the artist
could not make the journey, in order to shorten the discussion, as Sir
Dudley desired, above all, the pictures that were wholly by Rubens's
hand, that is to say, the *Prometheus*, the *Daniel*, the *Leda*, the *Crucifixion*, the *St. Peter*, and the *St. Sebastian*—and as those pictures only
came to a sum of 3,500 florins, he had proposed to de Grebber to leave
out the *Crucifixion*, and to take in exchange for his collection, half
pictures and half Brussels tapestries; and he wrote to an English
merchant at Antwerp for information about the purchase of tapestries
of the required dimensions.

This did not suit Rubens, and on May 12, he replied that Sir
Dudley was doubtless mistaken concerning the value of certain of the
pictures that he was wrong in regarding as mere copies; in fact, he
had retouched them so largely, that although they were valued at a
much lower price, they would be taken for veritable originals. "The
reason why I wish to make the exchange entirely in pictures is

sufficiently clear," said Rubens, " for, although I have put them down at their exact value, nevertheless they cost me nothing, and as everybody is more inclined to be generous with the fruits of his own garden than with those bought in the market, having this year spent some thousands of florins on building, I do not wish, for a mere caprice, to

ST. SEBASTIAN.
(Berlin Museum.)

exceed the bounds of prudent economy. In fact, I am not a prince, but a man who lives by the work of his hands. If, then, Y. E. desires to have pictures for the whole amount, whether originals or copies well retouched (of which the price is lower), I will treat you generously, and as regards the cost, will refer you to the opinion of any intelligent person." If, however, Sir Dudley persisted in his desire for tapestries, Rubens offered to help him to purchase them, the matter being easy for him on account of the numerous commissions he received for Italy, and his position with the Brussels merchants whom he supplied with cartoons which they executed for Genoese noblemen. He would, in short, procure him tapestries to the value of 2,000 florins, and the 4,000 florins remaining might be employed in the purchase of some other pictures on the list, or of some that he would undertake to paint himself.

Without pledging himself in the matter of the tapestries, Sir Dudley agreed to the transaction so far as the pictures were concerned ; but criticising the artist's declaration that he was no prince, he assured Rubens "that he regarded him as the Prince of Painters and of gentlemen." In order to conclude the business, Rubens paid Sir Dudley the sum of 2,000 florins in ready money; and, to make up the remaining 4,000 florins, besides the *Lion Hunt* and the *Susannah*, he added to the other pictures a *Hagar*, "painted on wood which he thought preferable for pictures of small dimensions," where

PHILOMENEN RECOGNISED BY AN OLD WOMAN.
Sketch by Rubens. (The Louvre : Lacaze Gallery.)
(From a photograph by Braun, Clément et Cie.)

everything was by his hand except the landscape, the execution of which he had, according to his custom, entrusted " to a very skilful artist." The bargain was thus concluded, to the satisfaction of both parties; and, in order to fulfil the desire expressed by Sir Dudley Carleton, Rubens promised to send him his portrait, on condition that Sir Dudley would also bestow on him some personal souvenir. The business, conducted so gallantly on both sides, formed the prelude to lasting relations. To testify his gratitude, Rubens dedicated Vorstermann's plate after the *Descent from the Cross*, to the

diplomatist, and a few years later asked his assistance in obtaining a
license for the sale of his engravings in the United Provinces.

The precise information given in the list of the pictures which
Rubens desired to make over to Sir Dudley Carleton, testifies in a
most certain fashion to the aid the master derived from the pupils or
collaborators who were then working for him.   If, in the works in
which they took a more or less important part, it is generally easy to
recognise what portion they actually executed, it is, on the contrary,
fairly difficult, without the aid of extant documentary information, to
determine in any given case who was the artist's co-operator.   It is
known that Jan Wildens, after his return to Antwerp in 1617, was
employed until Rubens's death in painting the backgrounds of his
pictures.   It was probably to him that the master alluded when he
spoke of "the distinguished artist" who painted the landscape in the
Leopards, and when he repeated his praises in the letter of May 26.
Paul de Vos, although he had been a pupil of David Remeus, sometimes
painted animals for Rubens, who entrusted him later with important
work for the King of Spain.   But his correct and rather frigid talent
was eclipsed by that of his brother-in-law, Frans Snyders, who,
although never a pupil of Rubens, was a frequent and valuable collaborator.   Two years younger than the great artist, Snyders was,
from 1593, the pupil of Pieter Brueghel the younger, before entering
the studio of Hendrick Van Balen.   Admitted to the Guild in 1602,
Snyders travelled in Italy in 1608-9, and after his return to his native
city, married, in 1611, the sister of the painters Cornelis and Paul de
Vos.   His amiable and stedfast disposition gained him the affection
of all his colleagues.   Van Dyck, who soon followed him into Van
Balen's studio, was especially attached to him, and the various portraits
in which he painted Snyder's frank countenance are reckoned among
his best works.   Rubens showed a similar affection for Snyders,
esteeming equally his talent and his character, and before his death,
proved his confidence in him by appointing him one of his executors.
Exclusively devoted to the representation of animals, Snyders raised
the modest branch of painting, to which he gave himself up, to a
height never before attained.   He owed Rubens much, and under his
influence gave greater breadth to his forms, and more brilliance to his

14

Portrait of a Man.

(THE HERMITAGE.)

Printed by Draeger, Paris.

colour, and also acquired the dramatic sense and the feeling for poetry which mark some of his best compositions.

The benefit, however, was reciprocal, and Rubens derived no slight advantage from his collaborator's aid. Through the frankness and bravura of his execution, Snyders, more than any of the others, associated himself intimately with Rubens's manner. The analogies between them are so numerous, and the fusion is so perfect, that it is often difficult to distinguish their individual work : they had the same method of handling the paint, of placing the high lights, of giving the idea of relief, and the expression of life by sureness of touch. Rubens was not forced, as with the others, to go over Snyders' work again ; he was always certain of being thoroughly understood when he reserved for Snyders the execution of domestic or wild animals, of fruits, or of the various accessories which found a place in his works. At the head of the list of pictures offered to Sir Dudley Carleton is a *Prometheus Bound*, in which Snyders painted the vulture gnawing his victim's liver, a fact that proves the collaboration of the two masters to have begun early. It continued long ; and Snyders, on a footing of absolute equality, painted in numerous works of Rubens, hinds or stags fleeing from Diana and her nymphs ; wild boars at bay and the dogs worrying them ; lions or panthers quietly accompanying Silenus, or struggling furiously against the horsemen who attack them. Sometimes among the fish, poultry, joints of meat, game, and other substantial viands, heaped up in Snyders' larders or kitchens, Rubens, in his turn, painted a figure—a housewife, a huntsman, one of his sons with a maid-servant, or even an historical personage, as in *The Recognition of Philopœmen, General of the Achœans*, which is, in fact, only a huge still-life.[1] The sketch in the Lacaze Gallery reveals the ease and taste with which Rubens himself could, in a few hours, arrange and brush in the numerous objects, fruits, vegetables, or game displayed in the composition.

There is perfect unity in the works of Rubens in which Snyders co-operated ; but this is not the case with another of the master's

---

[1] The picture for which the sketch was made was in the Orleans Gallery last century : we do not know who is its present owner.

collaborators, Jan Brueghel, his elder by ten years. When they first
became acquainted, each possessed a strongly marked individuality,
and Rubens could have had no influence on Brueghel.   Even
had Brueghel wished it, he could scarcely have altered his style ; it
was precisely his minute finish that pleased his admirers.   Just
as his father's manner of seeing and expressing reality, showed
strength, vigour, sometimes even brutality, so the son's work was
conscientious and delicate ; fond of detail, he sought to represent the

DECIUS MUS CONSULTS THE AUGURS.
(Liechtenstein Gallery.)

more graceful sides of nature with a somewhat small, but precise and
skilful touch.   Like most of his contemporaries, the artist had, as a
young man, been drawn to Italy, where he lived from 1593 to 1596.
During his residence beyond the Alps, Brueghel formed habits of
collaboration with Rottenhammer and Paul Bril, which he continued
at Antwerp with the painters of interiors, Pieter Neeffs and Steenwijck,
and with the landscape painter, Josse Van Momper.   A practical man,
he had a tariff for the assistance thus rendered ; and we learn from his
account books, that for putting in the figures in Momper's landscapes,
he received forty florins a picture.   Hitherto he had painted figures

in the works of his Antwerp colleagues, but henceforth he painted
flowers, fruits, arms, animals, in the pictures in which he collaborated.

In the fairly regular correspondence between Cardinal Borromeo
and his *protégé*, Brueghel, from October 7, 1610, onwards, we find
the laboured writing, the fantastic orthography, and the involved
style of Brueghel, replaced by very readable letters, and here and there
Latin quotations are introduced among thoughts expressed with greater
accuracy and elegance. On those occasions Rubens held the pen
for his friend, and in the future he often filled the office of "secretary."

THE FUNERAL OF DECIUS MUS.
(Liechtenstein Gallery.)

While rendering a service to Brueghel, Rubens, as a prudent man, did
not forget himself, and when opportunity offered, he furthered his own
affairs, and gradually made a place for himself in the Cardinal's
favour and in his commissions. On September 5, 1621, Brueghel
sent a picture to the prelate, "the best thing and the rarest he had
ever done; in which Rubens, also, displayed the full strength of
his talent, painting in the centre an admirable Madonna. The birds
and other animals were painted from life after models in the possession
of his most serene Highness, the Infant." The picture, well deserving
of praise, is *The Virgin surrounded by a Garland of Flowers*, in the
Louvre. Brueghel is, however, careful not to attract too much

attention to the beautiful wreath in which insects, butterflies, birds, and even a little marmoset, disport themselves among anemones, pinks, lilies, tulips, irises, and many other flowers, all painted with extraordinary finish. He modestly effaces himself in the interest of his illustrious colleague, whose Madonna, occupying the centre of the garland, is the principal subject of the composition, and stands out with marvellous brilliance.

Several notable specimens of the collaboration of the two artists are in the Munich Gallery. Another wreath of small flowers enframes a *Virgin with the Infant Jesus*, while round the wreath a bevy of little angels is grouped in varied attitudes, and a *Diana Asleep* of smaller dimensions, combines extremely delicate handling with very vigorous colour. But the most perfect work of all those in which they collaborated is the *Earthly Paradise*, in the Hague Gallery, a veritable masterpiece. Never has Rubens touched the female form with a more mellow brush, never has he enwrapped it in clearer, more pearly, or more transparent shadows, than in the white figure of his graceful Eve. In this instance the suppleness and finish of his touch harmonise perfectly with that of Brueghel. Brueghel's landscape and his innumerable animals are admirable for their truth of execution. Each artist seems to have been on his mettle, so that they vied with each other in courteous rivalry, and, with the legitimate pride of an equal perfection, they associated their two signatures at the bottom of the precious panel.[1]

Their friendship was unclouded to the end, and at Brueghel's death, Rubens, with three of his friends, Cornelis Schut, Paul van Halmale, and Hendrick van Balen, was appointed guardian of his children, who were under age. It is probable that by virtue of his office Rubens concerned himself with the children's future; at least, on January 13, 1636, he acted as a witness at the marriage of one of his wards, Catherine, with the painter J. B. Borrekens, and he probably helped more directly to marry Anne, the youngest but one of Brueghel's daughters, to David Teniers. In any case, he assisted at that marriage on April 22, 1637, as a witness, and the next year his second wife, Helena Fourment, was godmother to the first child of the union.

[1] In the French text facsimiles of the signatures are given here.

The master's kindness and the amenity of his disposition, combined with a superiority recognised by all, sufficiently account for the ascendancy he exercised over his contemporaries. It was to be felt in a greater degree than by any of the others, by a young painter—after Rubens the most eminent artist of the Flemish school—Van Dyck, who was at that time, and for many years afterwards, his favourite collaborator. It was to him Rubens referred under the designation of "my best pupil" (*il meglior mio discepolo*) as the painter of *Achilles among the Daughters of Lycomedis*, when he offered the picture to Sir Dudley Carleton (April 28, 1618). But, as a matter of fact, Van Dyck was never a pupil of Rubens. A member of a wealthy and important Antwerp family, Van Dyck was scarcely ten years old when, in 1609, he entered the studio of Hendrick van Balen, and on February 11, 1618, he was made free of the guild. With his handsome face and extraordinary precocity, he combined the charm of youth, and talent; attracted, however, by the genius of his celebrated compatriot, and recognising the advantages to be gained from his teaching, he desired to associate himself with him. Roger de Piles informs us that it was arranged through mutual friends that "Rubens should receive Van Dyck into his studio, and that the excellent man, so soon as he recognised Van Dyck's strong leaning towards painting, conceived for him a particular affection, and took great pains to instruct him. Van Dyck's progress was not useless to his master, who, overwhelmed with work, was aided by him to finish several canvases supposed to be wholly by Rubens's own hand."

A few pictures executed by Van Dyck at this period permit us to see what was then his manner of painting. The *Drunken Silenus* in the Dresden Gallery, which bears his monogram, is probably one of his earliest works. While the composition, the attitude of the old man, the red drapery of his companion, and the neutral grey sky against which the figures stand out, clearly show the influence of Rubens, many features peculiar to his collaborator may be found in the picture. Among others we may mention the pallor of the Bacchante who accompanies the two drunkards and her particular type, with the melting eyes and the slight inclination of the head noticeable later in more than one of Van Dyck's portraits. The

method of execution is not less characteristic of the master, notably
the way of laying on the colour and the fused handling that prevailed
in his work at that time. In the *St. Jerome*, also in the Dresden
Gallery,[1] hung fortunately near that of Rubens, the differences
are still more apparent. Although the harmony is forcible, the touch
is less broad, the handling more flowing. and the contrast of warm
and cold tones in the flesh
less boldly opposed.

The *Martyrdom of St.
Peter* in the Brussels Museum passes, with good
reason, for having been
painted before the visit
to Italy under the in-
fluence of the pictures by,
or of the copies from the
Venetian masters that Van
Dyck may have seen in
Rubens's house. It pre-
sents numerous analogies
with the *St. Jerome.* There
is the same intemperate
use of blue in the dis-
tance, the same uniformly
reddish flesh tints, and,
above all, the same way of
working up the colour to
obtain that even surface
upon which the artist
often applied the high lights with more vigour than accuracy.
A certain bravura of intention is evident ; there is nothing that
resembles the learned contrasts, the free handling of the brush,
the play of under-tone, or the gleams of light applied with the
master hand that Rubens then possessed. If the work reveals
the enthusiasm, the ardour of eager youth, it does not manifest the

PORTRAIT OF FRANS SNYDERS.
(Facsimile of an engraving by Van Dyck.)

[1] The same model served for the *St. Jerome* and for the *Silenus.*

perfect sureness, the self-control, of an artist in the full maturity of
his genius.

The same analogies and the same dissimilarities may be found in
the four pictures of the series of *Christ* and the *Apostles* at Dresden,
in the *Samson and Delilah* at Dulwich, in the *Christ Healing the Sick*
at Buckingham Palace, in numerous studies of heads and nude figures,
and in two large canvases in the Madrid Gallery, the *Ecce Homo* and

THE RAISING OF THE CROSS.
(Sketch for the picture in the Church of the Jesuits. Lacaze Gallery.)

the *Kiss of Judas*,[1] which, presented to Rubens by Van Dyck before
his departure for Italy as a testimony of his gratitude, remained in his
house until his death. More marked in works of large size, it is com-
prehensible that the analogies of execution of the two artists led to
confusion between their works, and, solicited as he was by amateurs,
who overwhelmed him with commissions, it can readily be understood

[1] De Piles informs us that Rubens was particularly fond of the last picture, "which
he hung above the fireplace of the principal room of his house."

that Rubens would make use of so valuable and skilful a collaborator.
We believe, with Dr. Bode, that traces of the co-operation are to be
recognised in the *Bacchanal*, and the *Raising of Lazarus* in the Berlin
Gallery, and in the *Supper at the House of Simon* at the Hermitage.

Many important works were commissioned from Rubens at this
time, and we know from documentary evidence that Van Dyck had
a large share in them. A regular contract, entered into in 1620 by
Rubens with the Rev. Father Jacques Tirinus, superior of the Professed
Brethren of the Society of Jesus at Antwerp, furnishes us with formal
testimony. On April 15, 1615, the foundation-stone of a church, built
by the Jesuits from the designs of Father François Aguilon, was laid ;
he was then rector of their college, and Rubens had, in 1613, designed
the frontispiece and plates for his *Treatise on Optics*, published at the
Plantin Press. In 1617 Father Aguilon died, and Father Huyssens
became director of the works. When the building was nearly finished,
the chiefs of the Order applied to Rubens for the decoration of the
church ; and in the contract drawn up on March 29, 1620, it was
arranged that the artist should supply, at the latest before the end of
the year, thirty-nine pictures, each averaging 6 ft. 10·67 in. by 9 ft.
2·23 in. " He undertook to execute the drawings in small with his
own hand, and to have them carried out and completed in large by
Van Dyck and some other of his pupils . . . promising to act honourably and conscientiously in the matter, and to put the finishing touches
with his own hand to whatever might be found defective." He was to
receive a sum of 10,000 florins for the work. Rubens and Van Dyck
would each be further commissioned, "at an advantageous time," to
execute a large painting for one of the four lateral altars. A list
of subjects for the pictures destined for the decoration of the church
was appended to the contract ; each of the episodes borrowed from the
Old Testament had as a pendant the corresponding episode from the
Gospel of which it was regarded as the forerunner or symbolical preparation. We know that on July 18, 1718, a fire caused by lightning
reduced the paintings and the greater part of the building constructed
in the pompous florid style affected by the Society of Jesus, to ashes.
The church is only known to us now by the paintings of Sebastian

XVI

Lion Hunt.

(MUNICH GALLERY.)

Vranex and Antonius Gheringh, in the Galleries of Vienna, Munich, and Madrid, and by an interior view of the building painted by Van Ehrenberg,[1] in which Rubens's pictures are skilfully and accurately reproduced.

To give us an idea of the lost originals, we have only somewhat mediocre copies executed in 1711 by the Dutch painter, J. de Wit, two engravings by Jegher after the *Temptation of Christ*, and the *Coronation of the Virgin*, another by Rubens himself, representing *St. Catherine*, and those of the master's sketches that have survived : the *Ascension* in the Vienna Gallery, *Esther and Ahasuerus*, *St. Cecilia*, *St. Jerome*, and the *Annunciation*, also at Vienna, in the Academy of Fine Arts ; *St. Barbara* in the Dulwich Gallery ; the *Prophet Elijah*, *St. Athanasius*, *St. Basil*, and *St. Augustine* in the Gotha Museum ; *Abraham and Melchisedek*, the *Coronation of the Virgin*, and the *Raising of the Cross* in the Lacaze Gallery at the Louvre. The breadth with which the sketches are treated proves that in executing them with so great a freedom, Rubens felt certain of being understood and adequately interpreted by an artist like Van Dyck. In fact, Rubens gave full rein to his powers, and delighted in multiplying the bold foreshortenings. He showed a perfect understanding of the ceiling compositions of which Flanders, at that period, offered no examples, but which Rubens had studied during his visit to Italy.

Considerable as this work was, another, almost as important, occupied Van Dyck's energies at this period : we refer to the series of large pictures on the *History of Decius Mus*, painted by him after his master's compositions, to be reproduced as tapestries. Bellori tells us regarding them : " Rubens derived no small advantage from Van Dyck's talent as a colourist. Unable himself to accomplish all the commissions entrusted to him, Rubens employed Van Dyck to copy and sketch his compositions in colour on canvas, or to transpose his drawings and sketches into paintings, and thus profited much by his assistance. Van Dyck executed the cartoons and painted the pictures

---

[1] The picture figured in the exhibition of old masters at Nancy in 1875, and belonged at that time to M. de Lescale, of Bar-le-Duc.

for the tapestries of the *History of Decius Mus*, as well as other
cartoons which, by his great talent, he easily brought to a successful
issue."[1]   Notwithstanding Bellori's testimony, it seems to us certain
that the *Decius Mus* cartoons are exclusively the work of Rubens, and
we agree with M. Max Rooses that none of his productions show a
greater individuality.   In any case none give a better idea of Rubens's

PORTRAIT OF A MAN.
(Liechtenstein Gallery.)

conception of the antique.
But we have the positive
affirmation of the master
himself on the point; when
he proposed to Sir Dudley
Carleton to act as his agent
in the purchase of tapes-
tries the latter wished to
acquire, he wrote (May 20,
1618) : "the choice in all
this is a matter of taste.
I will send you the
measurements of my car-
toons for the *History of
Decius Mus*, the Roman
Consul who sacrificed
himself for the triumph
of the Roman people; I
will procure them cor-
rectly from Brussels.
They are all in the hands
of the tapestry-workers."

If, according to his custom, Rubens retouched the pictures
here and there—both the pictures and the tapestries are in the
possession of Prince Liechstenstein — he did so very slightly,
and with full respect for his collaborator's work.   With the exception of certain high lights placed by Rubens on the flesh, and
a few touches calculated to enhance the brilliance of the general

[1] Bellori, *Vite dei Pittori*, I. p. 257.

aspect, Van Dyck is really the author of the pictures, and a careful examination confirms both the traditions and the documents that concern them.[1] The eight canvases of the *Decius Mus* series present a total area of 861 sq. feet, 15·75 sq. inches. If we add to the works already ascribed to Van Dyck, *grisailles* like the *Miraculous Draught of Fishes*,[2] after Rubens's Mechlin picture, and also the

fairly numerous drawings after Rubens's pictures, made for the engravers, we must acknowledge, especially when we remember the short time spent by Van Dyck in the master's studio, that it was a truly prodigious amount of work. The period, in fact, lies between dates that are quite close together, and that can be established with the utmost precision.

PORTRAIT OF A WOMAN.
(Liechtenstein Gallery.)

Van Dyck entered the studio of Rubens shortly after he was admitted to the guild in 1618.. His precocious talent soon made him known : in a letter sent from Antwerp (July 17, 1620) to the Earl of Arundel by one of his agents, the writer spoke of the young man's talent, "which

---

[1] Among the documents it is well to mention the declarations made successively in 1661 and 1682 by two Antwerp artists, G. Coques and J. B. van Eyck (the latter a pupil of Rubens), who, at that time owners of the pictures, certify that they were "composed by Rubens, and finished by Van Dyck." These documents were recently discovered in the Antwerp Archives by M. J. Van den Branden, the well-known scholar.

[2] The sketch, now in the National Gallery, London, was painted by Van Dyck for the engraver Bolswert to work from. [Translator's note.]

began to be almost as much esteemed as that of his master ; but
as he belongs to one of the richest families in the town, it will be
difficult to prevail on him to leave him." The artist, however, was
soon to yield to the solicitations made him ; and on December 25 of the
same year, Toby Matthew, who acted as Sir Dudley Carleton's agent
in his purchase of works of art, wrote to him : " Your L^r. will have
heard how Van Dyck, his famous Allieno, is gone into England, and
that the King has given him a pension of £100 per annum." But
Van Dyck's first visit to London was not of long duration ; for on
February 28 following, a passport, valid for eight months, was
granted him. We do not know how long he was away ; but it is
certain that the artist was again in England shortly after April 8,
1621, and that in November, 1622, he was obliged to return to
Antwerp, whither he was suddenly recalled to assist at his father's
death-bed. We know that after his father's death (December 1,
1622) Van Dyck went to Italy. He had scarcely spent three years in
Rubens's studio, and it would have required his powers of rapid
work, and a prodigious energy, to accomplish the works which we
have noted. The fairly numerous portraits painted by Van Dyck at
this period must be added to the already formidable number.
Considering his precocity, it would have been strange if he had produced nothing in the style in which he was to excel ; nevertheless,
until recent years, his biographers were silent on the subject.
They mentioned as the only works of the kind painted at that early
period, a portrait of a man belonging to M. A. de la Faille, of
Antwerp, and two portraits in Poland : on the back of the latter,
according to Mols,[1] was the following inscription : " Painted by me,
Anthony Van Dyck, in 1618, at the age of nineteen."

With the sagacity that has already enabled Dr. Bode to restore
to Rembrandt the hitherto ignored works of his youth, he has
rendered a fresh service to criticism by calling attention to Van Dyck's
early portraits. But he has, perhaps, allowed himself to swell
the list unjustifiably by withdrawing from Rubens all the portraits
attributed to him at that period, and assigning them to Van Dyck.

---

[1] *Notes sur Rubens*, manuscript in the Royal Library at Brussels.

Whereas in the first of the studies devoted to the subject[1] he thinks these portraits may be reckoned by dozens, in the second[2] he brings the number to over fifty, and this seems to us excessive. The question is one of great difficulty and deserves to be more closely investigated. Although our conclusions differ sensibly from Dr. Bode's, we agree with him that the matter can be most profitably studied in the Dresden Gallery, and in that of Prince Liechtenstein at Vienna, because of the facilities afforded by the two collections for comparison.

In discussing the pictures in the Dresden Gallery, painted by Van Dyck in his youth, we have already noted the characteristics which then distinguished his execution. We find identical characteristics in the portrait of a man aged forty-one, dated 1619, in the Brussels Museum, erroneously attributed to Rubens; in the fine portrait of Isabella Brant (Hermitage) presented to his master by Van Dyck before his departure for Italy; in the half-length of a young man, and in the portrait of a lady with a child, both in the Dresden Gallery (Nos. 1023A and 1023B). All these works are recognised by critics as incontestably by the hand of Van Dyck; the last, on account of the somewhat niggling delicacy of handling, the fused colour, an elegance of drawing that tends to exaggerate slightly the delicacy of the features, the lengthened oval of the faces, and the aristocratic slimness of the hands, appears to us a perfect specimen of his manner at that period. But if we agree with Dr. Bode that it is correct to attribute the woman's portrait to Van Dyck, it is, in our opinion, right to restore to Rubens that of the man putting on his gloves (No. 1023C), hanging by its side in the same gallery, and consequently under the most favourable conditions for comparison. In the first place, we may observe that they ought not to be regarded as pendants. Their dimensions, it is true, are not sensibly different, but as they are similar to those of the two neighbouring portraits, no deduction can be made from that fact. Moreover, while the woman is represented seated in

---

[1] It occurs in Dr. Bode's work on the Berlin Gallery: *Die Gemaelde der koeniglichen Museen.*

[2] It appeared in the *Graphischen Künste*, under the title: *Die Liechstenstein'sche Galerie.* Vienna, 1888 and 1889.

an interior decorated with columns and draperies, with her armorial
bearings painted above her, the man is standing, and is relieved
against a plain unadorned background. Besides, M. Max Rooses has
clearly determined the personality of the female model in establishing
the coat of arms to be that of Clarissa van den Wouwere, while the
type of her so-called husband in no way resembles that of Rubens's
friend, Jan van den Wouwere. A careful study of the execution leads
to the conclusion that the two paintings are not by the same hand.
The characteristics of the male portrait are breadth and force, an
easy nobility of attitude, extreme sureness of touch, a method of
modelling in large planes, and of contrasting the brilliant colours of
the high lights with the bluish-greys of the penumbra. And the bold
summary touches, the ruddy cheeks, the perfectly-formed hand, the
hasty yet intelligent painting of the hair and beard, the vigorous
aspect, and the sense of life that marks the most important features,
offer further evidence. Whether we look at it close by or from a
distance, everything proclaims the name of Rubens, everything agrees
with what we already know of the master; and the method continues
in his later works as by the natural and logical development of his
talent. We shall find a similar breadth and simplicity, those supreme
qualities of maturity, in two other portraits, forming pendants in the
Dresden Gallery (Nos. 960 and 961), which Dr. Bode takes from
Rubens to give to Van Dyck, and also in the portraits of Jean Charles
de Cordes and Jacqueline de Caestre, his wife (Brussels Gallery),
both painted between 1617 and 1618; Jacqueline died in the latter
year. To quote M. Max Rooses,[1] "the careful work, quiet handling,
and sureness of touch, denote a matured talent, a perfect master such
as, in 1618, Rubens was, and Van Dyck was not."

The Liechtenstein Gallery affords still more conclusive proofs that,
in his eagerness to change names, Dr. Bode has allowed himself to be
carried a little too far. In fact, the fine portrait of Jan Vermoelen in
that gallery furnishes an important proof; together with Vermoelen's
escutcheon it bears the inscription: *Ætat. snae* 27, *Anno* 1616. M.
Max Rooses tells us that Vermoelen was born in 1589; thus in 1616

[1] *Œuvre de Rubens*, vol. iv. p. 149.

he would have been twenty-seven years of age. Now, at that time, Van Dyck, who was only seventeen, had not yet entered Rubens's studio, and in any case, whatever his precocity, he would then have been incapable of the robust maturity and bold perfection shown in this fine portrait. Dr. Bode could not, therefore, attribute it to Van Dyck. But if it is by Rubens, four other portraits in the same gallery, which Dr. Bode wishes to withdraw from Rubens, must certainly be restored to him, for they are undoubtedly by the same hand ; firstly, those of a man and his wife aged respectively fifty-seven and fifty-eight, and both bearing the date 1618, the year in which Van Dyck became Rubens's collaborator. Dr. Bode is justified in remarking "that at the first glance we seem to recognise the handling of Rubens"; but we confess that we do not understand the objections of detail that he afterwards makes to the attribution. In the portrait of an old man holding a paper in his hand (No. 70), in that of a man of somewhat grim aspect, his hand resting on the back of a chair (No. 95), the execution is identical with that of the *Jan Vermoelen*; there is a similar boldness and simplicity of posture, the same robust vigour of handling, and the same modelling of the hands. We may also note in passing that the gilded leather chairs which figure in the two last portraits are identical, and probably formed part of the master's furniture.

We are less positive regarding the companion portraits of a young husband and wife in the Liechtenstein Gallery (Nos. 66 and 68). These questions of attribution are very complicated and difficult to decide in the case of pictures in which the master has retouched the pupil's work, and they have thus more or less collaborated. But it seems to us possible, at least in the works that we have just mentioned, to establish the distinctions we have named. To the technical reasons we have advanced, it is well to add equally convincing considerations of a more general kind. In enumerating the important pictures painted by Van Dyck in his youth, we mentioned the enormous amount of work he accomplished in the brief space of time, about three years, during which he acted as Rubens's assistant. To a total already formidable, how is it possible to add

more than fifty portraits, all carefully finished and of large dimensions? From a material point of view alone, it is an evident impossibility. The moral impossibility is not less. The pictures which
are thus attributed to Van Dyck are taken from Rubens at a moment
when, in the full vigour of production, he would, failing them, have
been condemned to a relative inaction against which his habits of
industry and his fertility protest. How, indeed, in full possession of
his fame, could he have refused so many important persons who applied
to him, and have referred them to his young pupil? How is it that
they all agreed to the substitution, and that he did not paint any of
them? In fact, while we deem it just not to withdraw from Rubens the
portraits which, being in his usual manner, mark a logical stage in the
progression of his talent, it would be perverse to attribute them to
Van Dyck, who, if indeed their author, would have scarcely entered
the master's studio before he became at once the superior artist. May
we not rather think that each followed his natural bent, than that de-
viations so unexpected and incomprehensible occurred in the sequence
of their respective works? Rubens's method was already fixed; he
advanced steadily towards brilliance, freshness, and penetrating expression of life, while preserving his masterly qualities of strength and
breadth: Van Dyck's method was as yet uncertain, but he profited
largely by the examples before him, and the imprint of so mighty a
genius was deeply impressed on his supple and facile nature. As
Fromentin rightly says: " Van Dyck would be altogether inexplicable
if we could not see the solar light whence so many beautiful reflections
came to him. If we sought to discover who taught him the new methods,
the free language so unlike the old tongue, we should perceive in him
lights come from afar, and in the end should suspect that a bright star,
now invisible, had been in his neighbourhood." [1] But soon, under a
fresh influence, that of Titian, to whom he felt even more powerfully attracted, Van Dyck's portraits gradually approached the refined
elegance which an older civilisation and a higher culture had produced in Italy. In contrast to the types of robust and somewhat

[1] *Les Maîtres d'Autrefois.* p. 51.

15

Study for the "Procession of Silenus" in the Munich Gallery.

(THE LOUVRE.)

Printed by Draeger, Paris.

stout men of massive build, and of exuberantly healthy women with
plump, highly-coloured flesh, which the natives of Flanders offered
him, and of which Rubens has given us faithful portraits, Van Dyck
was to paint the gentlemen, the elegant Cavaliers, with their picturesque accoutrements, and the great ladies of exquisite distinction
with their beautiful drooping hands and their slightly languid postures,
which are the charm and the ornament of our galleries. The same
differences may be noted in the portraits executed by the two
painters as in their own persons: the one of virile appearance,
with will in his expression, determination in his features; the
other with his handsome countenance, his attractive grace, his
sprightly physiognomy, his soft eyes reflecting a tender heart,
yielding to his enthusiasms and to the attractions of luxury and
pleasure.

In any case, at the beginning of his brilliant career, Van Dyck
derived great advantage from his connection with Rubens. It was,
indeed, by his master's advice that Van Dyck decided on the journey
to Italy, the results of which were so beneficial. In daily intercourse with his master, and with the original works of Titian or
the copies that Rubens had collected, Van Dyck was prepared
for the journey to which all his instincts urged him. The alleged
jealousy, to which it is said that Rubens yielded in persuading his
young friend to quit Antwerp, in order to rid himself of a rival
who began to give him cause for uneasiness, is a pure invention
of eighteenth-century biographers, more eager for apocryphal
anecdotes than respectful of the truth. The whole life of Rubens
is a protest against such an allegation, and vainly do we seek
in it any trace of so base a feeling. The way in which he always
spoke of Van Dyck, the praises that he lavished on him on every
occasion, his desire to bring him into notice, the care he took of his
interests, the testimonies of gratitude that Van Dyck left him on his
departure, all give the lie to such a fable. On the contrary, Rubens
generously deprived himself of the assistance of " his best pupil " when
he decided that he had nothing more to teach him, and in directing
him to Italy he gave a fresh proof of the affection he bore him, and

of the discernment with which he appreciated what would be most
advantageous to his career and progress. He really anticipated his
desires. Scarcely had Van Dyck crossed the Alps than, introduced
by Rubens into the Genoese society in which he had formed such high
connections, he felt at home. It required no long apprenticeship for
him to become acquainted with the refinements of the elegant life led
by beautiful ladies and noble lords : it might have been said that he
was of their race, and had found his true fatherland.

PLATE FROM THE DRAWING BOOK.
(Engraving by P. Pontius. After Rubens.)

CHAPTER X

BIRTH OF NICHOLAS, RUBENS'S SECOND SON (MARCH 23, 1618)—PICTURES IN
WHICH THE MASTER'S CHILDREN FIGURE—NUMBER AND IMPORTANCE OF HIS
WORKS AT THAT EPOCH : 'THE ADORATION OF THE KINGS' AND 'THE MIRACULOUS
DRAUGHT OF FISHES' AT MECHLIN—'THE MIRACLES OF ST. IGNATIUS' AND 'THE
MIRACLES OF ST. FRANCIS XAVIER'—'THE COMMUNION OF ST. FRANCIS'—'THE
"COUP DE LANCE" '—'ST. AMBROSE AND THEODOSIUS'—'BATTLE OF THE
AMAZONS'—'THE BOAR-HUNT'—'"LE CHAPEAU DE PAILLE" '—'PORTRAITS OF
THE EARL AND COUNTESS OF ARUNDEL.'

PORTRAIT OF NICHOLAS RUBENS.

Albertina Collection.

(From a photograph by Braun, Clément et Cie.)

RUBENS'S life flowed on peacefully and happily. He found his pleasure in the affection of his family and in congenial work. Without luxury or ostentation, he maintained a certain domestic state in keeping with the ever-growing importance of his position. Those years were privileged and fruitful, and his productions show a kind of luminous reflection of his domestic happiness. His eldest son, Albert, was nearly four years old, when, on March 23, 1618, another son was born, who was also

baptised in the Church of St. Jacques. His aunt, Maria de
Moy, was his godmother, and a Genoese nobleman, Niccolò
Pallavicini, with whom Rubens was on friendly terms, represented by Andrea Picheneotti, one of his countrymen living at
Antwerp, stood godfather to the child, who received the name of
Nicholas. The growth of his family put charming models at the
great artist's disposal, which he turned to admirable account.
He was always fond of painting children, and even before he had
children of his own, introduced them into his compositions, and made
them the chief subject of several of his pictures. *The Infant Jesus
playing with St. John the Baptist*, in the Vienna Gallery, proves how
charmingly Rubens excelled in rendering their supple bodies, their
naive, awkward gestures, and their vivacious and innocent faces.
The charm of those pleasing pictures sufficiently explains the welcome
given them by the public, and the numerous repetitions or variants
which issued from the master's studio.

The facilities for observation provided him by his own children
whenever Rubens assisted at their games or watched the first
awakening of their emotions, gave increased interest and value
to the works in which he portrayed them. The well-known types
of Albert and Nicholas, and their apparent age in these pictures,
help us to assign an approximate date to the execution of the paintings
in which they figure. Thus we see the Virgin and the Infant Jesus
with the features of Isabella Brant and her eldest son, on one of
the shutters of a triptych painted about 1618 for the funeral monument
of Jan Michielsen, an Antwerp merchant, a monument of which the
pathetic composition, known as *Christ à la Paille*, occupies the central
panel.[1]

A study in the Berlin Museum, very broad and fat in handling,
shows us Rubens's younger son, Nicholas, in profile in a little shirt.
He is a fair child with rosy cheeks and long curly hair, wearing a
pearl and coral necklace round his neck, and holding a string to which
a little green parrot is tied, in his chubby hand. The *Holy Family*,
in the Pitti, known as the *Holy Family with the Cradle*, represents the

---

[1] It is now in the Antwerp Museum.

two brothers, one as the Infant Jesus, the other as St. John, caressing each other while their mother looks on; in the St. Anne and St. Joseph, we recognise the already familiar faces of Isabella's parents. The master again painted his two sons in the *Madonna* of the Munich Gallery which we have already mentioned, and round which "Velvet" Brueghel wove a dainty wreath of flowers with his usual delicacy. Another composition of the same style and of the same period, also at Munich, presents the two children with five others, all naked, carrying a heavy garland of fruits, by the skilful and vigorous brush of Snyders—plums, cherries, pears, figs, with the sour-looking green grapes which the pale Flanders sun has no power to colour. Rubens seemed to find the greatest delight in modelling the supple, plump bodies of the children, who, judging by their roguish, happy expression, are proud of their burden.

Again, in the Cassel Museum, we find the artist's wife and his two sons in a more important composition painted about 1620: *the Virgin and the Infant Jesus receiving the Homage of several Saints*, assuredly one of the finest productions of Rubens at that period. The decorative beauty of the arrangement is allied to a rich and strong harmony. St. Dominic, St. Francis of Assisi, St. Augustine, St. George with his Standard, are grouped in a pleasantly diversified line—a virile quartette—close to the throne on which the Virgin is seated, while King David and the Prodigal Son half kneel at her feet, all crowding round her, united in fervent adoration; Mary Magdalene, reverently inclining her body and modestly covering her bosom with her hands, lifts her suppliant face and her tearful eyes towards the little Jesus. As Herr Eisenmann observes in the Cassel Museum catalogue, it is possible that Van Dyck collaborated in the upper part of the canvas; the more elegant refinement of its types, its more brilliant colouring, and its more liquid execution, reveal those leanings towards the Venetians which haunted the artist with a kind of prescience even before his departure for Italy. But Rubens undoubtedly retouched it in order to render the painting wholly his; he himself painted the Virgin, the two children, and the Mary Magdalene—at that date he alone was capable of executing a piece of work so masterly in design and so brilliant in colouring. Perhaps he rehandled the fine work later, for he kept it until his death, and it figures in his inventory under the somewhat inaccurate designation of the *Seven Repentant Sinners*.

Another picture in the Munich Gallery, painted at the same period, presents some analogy with the last, and better justifies its title : *Christ and the Four Penitents*. It represents King David, St. Peter, the penitent thief, and Mary Magdalene imploring the Redeemer for mercy,

HEAD OF A CHILD.
(Berlin Museum.)

who, with an expression of compassionate affection, shows them the wounds in His hands and side as pledges of His love and of their pardon. Of a more summary yet extremely skilful handling, the work, wholly by the master's hand, has preserved a freshness and brilliance which testifies to the excellence of his methods. The transparency of the penumbra in which the figure of St. Peter is bathed is wonderful, and the greys of the sky co-operate with the browns of the rocks to bring the scene into marvellous relief. Lowly and overwhelmed in her repentance, the beautiful sinner, with her pearly shoulders, her flowing fair hair, and her unconstrained attitude, is one of Rubens's most delightful creations.

Religious pictures, it must be remarked, fill a more and more important place in Rubens's work. But, in episodes taken from the preaching of Christ, or in purely devotional subjects like *Madonnas* or *Holy Families*, he possesses neither the naïve grandeur and the austere seriousness of the early masters, nor the choice forms and the absolute accuracy of the masters of the Renaissance. His types sometimes lack nobility and even beauty, and too many Italian reminiscences enter into his ideal. Too often, also, the figure of Christ is without authority or distinction ; he is a handsome man with long flowing hair, silky beard, pleasant, but somewhat insignificant, features. Rubens's virgins, who resemble the young Flemish matrons, are equally wanting in expression. But when he represents Christ in the more

CHRIST "À LA PAILLE
(Antwerp Museum.)

pathetic situations of His earthly life, submitting to the insults of His executioners, climbing Calvary, or expiring on the cross ; the Virgin presiding at His long torture or supporting His corpse on her knees, then, by the sincerity and sympathetic power of his emotion, he dares to be simple, and profoundly human, and he attains the highest eloquence in the inventions that burst forth spontaneously from his heart, and that he transmits to the canvas in all their vitality. It is in this aspect he appears to us in the *Crucifixion* in the Louvre, with the Virgin, St. John, and Mary Magdalene assembled on Calvary, all instinct with the same reverent sadness and adoration, a picture of a profoundly striking desolation. Even in subjects less dramatic, but which allow of a picturesque setting, his imagination gave his conceptions originality. Of this fact, the important works executed at that period for the town of Mechlin offer the best proof.

Almost at the same time he received two important commissions from that town. The first in date was that of the triptych for the high altar of the church of St. John ; he received it on December 27, 1616, from the parochial administration of the church for the sum of 1800 florins, which was not paid until March 12, 1624. The *Adoration of the Magi*, which occupies the central panel, was, however, delivered on March 27, 1619. It was a subject of which Rubens was fond, and to which he often returned. Not to mention the large picture presented by the town of Antwerp to Don Roderigo Calderon, he had also treated it about 1615 in an analogous composition, now in the Brussels Gallery, painted for the church of the Capuchins of Tournai. Although it shows a marked advance on the Madrid picture, the handling still lacks suppleness. The tonalities here and there are heavy and harsh, especially in the Virgin's costume and the red draperies of one of the Magi. The faces are uniformly vermilion, and the opacity of the blackish shadows betrays the persistence of the unfortunate habits contracted in Italy. Although badly hung, tarnished, and spoiled by restorations, the Mechlin *Adoration* presents a better arranged composition with a broader execution and a more skilful harmony. From a distance, the general aspect is magnificent, full of strength and unity. In examining the picture more closely, we discover many happy combinations of colour : for instance, the gold of the old King's brocade cloak, and the red of the tunic of his companion standing by him [1] ; the Virgin's grey dress, yellow sleeves, and violet cloak. The Virgin herself is charmingly graceful and ingenuous, and the transparent half tint which envelops the persons of the second plane gives additional radiance to the figure of the little Jesus, round whom the white beard of

[1] Again we recognise the types of Rubens's young sons in the two pages who hold the skirts of the tunic.

XVII

The " Coup de Lance."

(ANTWERP MUSEUM.)

the kneeling King near him and the ermine which covers his shoulders form an aureole of soft white light. With his sense of refinement and delicacy, Fromentin could not fail to admire this natural and brilliant painting, controlled by a lofty spirit, executed by an alert and obedient hand, and which, " without a trace of anything emotional or literary," seems made to delight the artist's eye. " Observe," he says, " the manner in which everything lives, moves, breathes, looks, acts, is coloured, fades away, harmonises and contrasts with the setting, dies away in the light tones, establishes and asserts its meaning by vigorous touches. And as to the intermingling of tones, the extreme richness obtained by simple means, the violence of certain tints, the softness of others, the lavish use of red, and yet the freshness of the whole, as to the laws, I say, which govern such efforts, these are things that baffle the mind.": [1]

The commission for another triptych, given to Rubens for the Church of Notre Dame on the other side of the Dyle, by the Mechlin fishermen was not less important. It was destined to adorn the altar dedicated to their corporation, and the account book of the association furnished M. Max Rooses with some curious information regarding it. The work of adapting the altar and panels having been done by a joiner of the town, the corporation applied to Rubens for the paintings, and on October 9, 1617, the master repaired to Mechlin, where the dignitaries of the Society awaited him at the " Helmet " inn. They proceeded together to the church to see the altar and arrange the price ; but as no agreement was come to that day, the members of the council went to Antwerp on February 5, 1618, to confer with the artist. The price was then fixed at 1600 florins. As soon as he received the panels, Rubens began the work, and on August 11 of the next year the delegates of the fishermen were informed that he had finished it. They then went once more to Antwerp to superintend the transport of the pictures, which, thanks to the facilities enjoyed by the corporation, was effected by water.

---

[1] The two small panels of the *Adoration of the Shepherds* and the *Resurrection*, which formed part of the decoration of the altar, and are in the Marseilles Museum, are Rubens's compositions, but somewhat ill painted by one of his pupils.

According to Cornelius Huysmans, the well-known landscape painter, Rubens went to Mechlin to assist at the hanging of the pictures, and touched them up slightly on the spot.

The subject of the *Miraculous Draught of Fishes*, chosen by him for the central panel, and the manner in which he conceived it, testify to the tact with which the master adapted himself to circumstances. Desirous of pleasing simple, uneducated persons, he sought

THE CRUCIFIXION.
(The Louvre.)

to place himself at their point of view and to conform to their tastes. He felt how necessary it was to remain on the common ground of reality with them. So he gave them no subtleties, no abstractions, but a clear idea expressed by vigorous forms and boldly asserted tonalities. The remembrance of Raphael's *Miraculous Draught* possibly haunted his mind, but he immediately transformed it, and gave it a Flemish aspect, such as the elder Brueghel might have imagined, with somewhat coarse characteristics, and bright, full, almost harsh colour. Rubens had often seen the scattered elements of his work in action on the banks of the Scheldt, but he alone was capable of placing them together, of concentrating them in a truthful, vigorous picture. Under a stormy sky, a little brighter towards the right, the fishermen strive to drag the heavily-laden nets, which almost break under the spoils, on to the beach. Amid the confusion, St. Peter, indifferent to the scene, bows reverently before Christ, who, receives his homage with a benevolent air, and reveals his vocation

to him. Although Rubens tried to impress a character of nobility
and authority on the figure of Christ, he did not succeed; it is clumsy
and commonplace. A drawing belonging to the Duchess of Weimar
bears traces of the successive attempts of the artist, who, after seeking
a pose for the figure which should satisfy him in vain, left the
Christ two faces and three hands. In contrast, the figures of the
fishermen, with their determined looks, their tanned and ruddy skin,
their robust build and
well-developed muscles,
were exactly what would
please their Antwerp pro-
totypes. They recognised
themselves in the rough
toilers, inured to all inclemencies of weather,
hardened to all the dan-
gers of their adventurous
life. The execution of
the varied work offers the
incomparable mixture of
boldness and delicacy, of
unconstraint and skill, of
improvisation and method,
of which Rubens pos-
sessed the secret. Once
again we refer our readers

THE MIRACULOUS DRAUGHT OF FISHES,
Study for the Mechlin picture : Weimar Collection.
(From a photograph by Braun, Clément et Cie.)

to Fromentin, to those admirable pages, the best perhaps in his book,
in which, in describing the *Miraculous Draught*,[1] he tries to penetrate the secret of the swift, yet severely logical work, "of the apparent
fever, restrained by profound calculations and assisted by a thoroughly
practised mechanism . . . of the summary colours, which only appear
complicated through the advantageous use the painter makes of them,
and the part he assigns to them . . . . of the calm and wise premedita-
tion which rules the most unexpected effects . . . in fact, all the

[1] *Les Maîtres d'Autrefois*, pp. 58-73.

magic of the great workman, which, with others, turns either to mannerism, affectation, or mediocrity, and which, with Rubens, is the exquisite sensibility of an admirably sane eye, of a marvellously obedient hand, and, above all, of a heart truly alive to everything— joyous, confident, lofty." *Tobias and the Angel* and the *Tribute Money*, painted on the shutters, frame in the central panel, below which the decoration of the altar was finished by three small prédelles. They have like qualities somewhat weakened by the more active intervention of his collaborators. Two of them are in the Nancy Museum ; the handling, although somewhat hasty, is intelligent and bold in method, with bright reds skilfully contrasted with the glaucous tone of the waves, in *Christ Walking on the Water* and *Jonah Falling into the Sea*. In the latter Rubens expressed in a very striking manner the terror of a man suddenly threatened with approaching death.

Many other religious compositions which issued at that time from Rubens's studio deserve less attention, since his pupils took too considerable a part in them. Among them are the *Pentecost* and the *Adoration of the Shepherds* (Munich Gallery), two large companion pictures, the commonplace execution of which helps to emphasise their insignificance. Finished in 1619, the artist received 3000 florins for them, and the Duke of Neuburg, who had commissioned them, was so well satisfied, that his agent at Antwerp, besides the stipulated payment, was charged to make a present to Isabella Brant. Two variants of the *Adoration of the Shepherds* are in the Rouen Museum and the Church of Mary Magdalene at Lille. In the latter, where the Virgin is of the same type as the Madonnas painted in collaboration with Brueghel, the group of cherubs contemplating the infant Jesus is a marvel of brilliance and freshness. The *Pietà* (Brussels Gallery), commissioned by the Duke d'Arenberg, was presented by him in 1620 to the Capuchin Church at Brussels. Save for the angel's robe, the red of which is somewhat discordant, the general effect of the harmony of blacks, greys, violets, browns, neutral blues and reds, is sober and expressive, and attention is naturally drawn to the body of Christ, which stands out in its livid paleness in the centre of the composition.[1]

[1] The St. Francis does not figure in the study for the picture among the drawings at the Louvre.

The *Assumption of the Virgin* (also in the Brussels Gallery), which Rubens painted by order of the Archdukes for the high altar of the Church of the Barefooted Carmelites, is dated by M. Max Rooses 1619-20; it seems to us to be of a somewhat later period, the colour being more brilliant and golden, and the touch freer and surer. The type of the Virgin, an evident reminiscence of Titian's *Assumption*, has no great distinction ; but the group of the Apostles, with their dark green, red, yellow, and blue costumes, finds a pleasing echo in the yellow and dull blue of the dresses of the two young women who gather up the flowers scattered on the shroud. The direction of the principal lines, and the skilful distribution of the colour, invite the spectator's gaze upwards towards the figure of the Virgin, who ascends radiant and glorious, surrounded by cherubs, their pink, pearly bodies standing out brightly against the grey clouds and blue sky. By the contrast of the colouring, which, strong and austere in the lower part of the picture, gradually brightens till, in the upper part, it becomes clear and brilliant, the artist has happily indicated the transports of joyful aspiration which he desired his work to express. The Düssel-dorf Academy and the Vienna Gallery possess slightly modified replicas of the *Assumption*. That at Vienna, executed in 1620 for one of the four lateral altars of the Church of the Jesuits, bears indubitable trace of Van Dyck's co-operation, especially in the heads and garments of the Apostles in the foreground.

These pictures are magnificent decorations, of a somewhat theatrical splendour, calculated to appeal to the crowd and act upon its imagina-tion, and consequently in harmony with the current ideas of the time. The Society of Jesus, which by the predominance it had regained in Flanders, especially favoured such ideas, commissioned Rubens to paint two large pictures (17 feet 6·62 inches by 12 feet 11·51 inches) devoted to the memory of the two greatest saints the Order had produced : *the Miracles of St. Ignatius* and *the Miracles of St. Francis Xavier*. Both were executed during 1619 and 1620, for in signing the agreement concluded with Father Scribanius on March 29, 1620, Rubens spoke of them as already finished, and to be paid for by a sum of 3000 florins on the day the ceilings of the Church of the community

for which they were both destined should be finished. In the
Vienna Gallery, which contains, not only the pictures, but the sketches
made for them by Rubens, the director was happily inspired to place
them all close together. We can thus better appreciate the distance
which separates the master's work from that of his collaborators, despite the fact that on this occasion the most active of them was no less

a person than Van Dyck.
Although   Rubens   re-
touched   nearly   all   the
faces   in   order   to   give
greater precision to the
expression, although here
and there, with his usual
sureness   of   touch,   he
gave more animation to
the general aspect, spread
more life and air among
the figures, and emphasised
the   general   harmony,   it
must   be   recognised   that
spontaneity and the breath
of inspiration are far more
apparent in the sketches ;
the   heavier   tonalities
of the finished   pictures
and their monotonous and
somewhat rigid handling

THE MIRACLES OF ST. IGNATIUS LOYOLA.
(Vienna Gallery.)

betray the brush of the pupil.   Strong in colour and vivacious in
design, the sketches are in fact veritable pictures, and are reckoned
among the best of a man who has produced so many of great excellence.   We recognise the ease and certainty which the clearly
defined conception of his subject combined with a perfect joy in painting
gives to the artist.   But, however great his enthusiasm, he always
restrained himself ; the skill of his hand never degenerated into
virtuosity, but helped him to express his thought more completely.

In the first of the compositions, St. Ignatius, clothed in a white alb, over which is a red and gold chasuble, leans against the altar, his hand placed near the chalice as if to show the source whence he derived his strength. He raises his eyes to Heaven, imploring the divine assistance for the performance of the miracles which consecrate his mission. By his side stand his companions, monks wrapped in long black cloaks, austere, motionless, watchful figures. Below them is the crowd of sick and afflicted persons who have come to seek a cure for cruel sufferings, or to demand that their dear ones may be restored to life. Every variety of physical or moral pain is represented; children dead, or attacked by incurable disease; a woman in the pangs of some extremely violent crisis, with haggard eyes and disordered garments, who struggles, falls, and raves in the midst of bystanders too weak to hold her; in the foreground is

THE MIRACLES OF ST. FRANCIS XAVIER.
(Vienna Gallery.)

an almost naked man struck down by epilepsy, livid, wild, howling, with hands contracted, foaming at the mouth. The sight of these distorted wretches creates a feeling of pain. The relentless accuracy of the spasmodic convulsions that shake their whole being is so striking and so scrupulously truthful, that MM. Charcot and Richer in their curious treatise, *Les Démoniaques dans l'Art*,[1] declare that among the madmen and convulsed persons in the picture all the

[1] Paris, 1887. 4to, pp. 34, 35.

characteristics assigned by the most recent scientific researches to neurosis and hysteria are to be found. Like the elder Brueghel, Rubens was always desirous of exact information, and he evidently studied from nature the effects of the mysterious maladies which, under different names, have afflicted humanity in every age. Deprived of the solid support of reality, the master was less happy in his inventions of monsters and demons, and the eccentric and grotesque forms of the abortions in which he attempted to represent the impure spirits exorcised by the saint are more ridiculous than awe-inspiring. From a picturesque point of view, the scene is admirably composed, and the figures stand out boldly against the clear tones of colonnades and cupolas adorned with sunk panels, with glimpses of blue sky through the openings. The light is broadly distributed, and the brilliance of the discreetly contrasted colours is further relieved by the skilful variety of neutral tones which help to give them their full effect.

The *Miracles of St. Francis* present less unity, and the more crowded composition is less well arranged in the masses, and gaudier in the colouring. Amid the medley of tones, and the slightly broken movement of the lines, there is no point to fix the attention, and the numerous persons clothed in diverse costumes, and vying with each other in gesture, attract the eye in equal measure. There is no repose in the immense canvas, where, without any common action, a multiplicity of episodes and groups are placed together pell-mell, with no sufficient links between them. In the chaos, and the tumult of swarming figures, we recognise some old acquaintances : one of the blind men is a reminiscence of Raphael's *Elymas*, and the dead man returning to life had already been utilised by the artist in the large *Last Judgment* at Munich. However, in spite of its incoherences, the execution of the slight and animated sketch attracts the spectator, and its piquant vivacity keeps him under its spell.

A slightly modified replica of the *Miracles of St. Ignatius* painted at the same period for the Marquis Niccolò Pallavicini, who was godfather to Rubens's second son, is now in the Church of St. Ambrose at Genoa. The composition is more concentrated and less

16

Job Tormented by his Wife and by Demons.

(THE LOUVRE.)

livid, but as if supported by a last impulse of his faith, he raises his
fine effulgent head to Heaven, while, in a glory, angels bring him the
martyr's crown and palm branch. The varied colouring—the purple
and gold of the saint's chasuble, the blue, the light and dark greens
and the reds of the executioners' garments, and the deep blue

of the sky—balance each
other at a distance, and
with the greys of the
architecture, form a
magnificently rich har-
mony. Unfortunately, the
execution, although very
skilful, betrays a pupil's
hand; we could wish in
it rather more ease, and
some of the decisive tones
to be found in the fine
drawing at the Hermitage,
probably made by Rubens
for the use of an engraver,
but never reproduced.
The two inner shutters
complete the remarkable
decoration. The handling
of the left, the *Preaching
of St. Stephen*, seems freer
and more individual. The
saint's inspired counten-
ance, his hands, his cos-
tume, the head of one of

STUDY OF LIONS.
Albertina Collection.
(From a photograph by Braun, Clément et Cie.)

his listeners, and, here and there, energetic hatchings traced with
a firmer and surer brush, testify to the larger participation of the
master. If in the *Burial of St. Stephen* on the right shutter the
too prominent reds and greens attract the eye more than they
should, to the detriment of the chief panel, the composition, never-

theless, shows wonderful boldness and ease. As M. Max Rooses says, only Rubens could have placed one above the other with such ease

THE FALL OF THE DAMNED.
(Munich Gallery.)

in so narrow a space (4 feet 1·6 inches by 13 feet 1·48 inches) these more than life-size figures which comprise women overwhelmed by despair—one of whom reverently kissing the martyr's cope is charmingly

graceful and tender. Below is the corpse piously passed from hand
to hand to be placed in the tomb ready to receive it. The *Annunciation*, painted on the outer shutters, is a pupil's work, parts of which
Rubens retouched, notably the Virgin's head, and those of the fair-
haired cherubs who form the Angel Gabriel's *cortège*. Florid and
brilliant in the *Martyrdom of St. Catherine* and in the *Triptych of
St. Stephen*, the tones are simple and sober in the *Communion
of St. Francis* in the Antwerp Museum, which was commissioned
from Rubens by Jasper Charles for the Church of the Recollets
at Antwerp.[1] The reproduction which accompanies these lines
renders it unnecessary for us to describe the picture, the touching
and pathetic beauty of which Fromentin has so eloquently praised as
the sombre panel "of a severe style, where everything is low in tone,
and where three incidents only show themselves with absolute clearness from a distance : the saint in his livid emaciation, the Host
towards which he bows, and above, at the apex of the tenderly
expressive triangle, a glimpse of the pinks and blues of happy eternity,
a smile of the half-opened heaven." With admiration as legitimate as
it is well-expressed, the painter-writer speaks of the moribund who,
"emaciated by age and a life of holiness, has left his bed of ashes and
has been carried to the altar to die there receiving the Sacrament
. . . . of the group of men so differently affected, self-contained or
sobbing, who form a circle round the wonderful head of the
saint, and the little white crescent, like a lunar disc, which the priest
holds in his pale hand."[2]

The composition is evidently borrowed from Domenichino's *Communion of St. Jerome* ; but we forget that fact in the presence
of the saint's noble figure, of his bent body contracted by suffering,
of the radiant countenance, of the expression illumined by love; in
which is concentrated all that remains of life. As M. Max Rooses
observes, "Rubens forgets his usual methods under stress of profound
emotion, and creates a special style to give an appropriate form to a

---

[1] The family of Van Havre still preserves the receipt for 750 florins, the price of the
work, a receipt written by Rubens with his own hand, May 17, 1619.

[2] *Les Maitres d'Autrefois*, p. 102 *et seq.*

new and intense inspiration." The harmony here is not, as usual, loud and pompous. Except the red and gold of the priest's cope, and the dull red of the dais which leads to the altar, the picture is almost in monochrome, and the heads, which stand out boldly against the scarcely varied browns of the monkish robes, represent every shade of fervour, despair, and admiration. Like the saint to whom he dedicated this masterpiece, it might be said that Rubens, at that moment, took a vow of poverty in reducing the colours on his palette to what was strictly necessary; and that from this voluntary indigence he derived a most eloquent method, a method best suited to the intimacy and pathos of the subject.

If, in describing the picture as one of the most perfect masterpieces of art, Fromentin has not overrated it, he is perhaps a little severe, even a little unjust, towards another picture of the period, the *Coup de Lance* in the Antwerp Museum, which was commissioned from the artist by his friend, the burgomaster Rockox, and formerly adorned the high altar of the Church of the Recollets. He finds it "incoherent, with wide empty spaces, harsh lines, large and somewhat arbitrary sweeps of colour, beautiful in themselves, but having little connection with each other. . . . Finally, an incoherent work, conceived in fragments, of which pieces, taken separately, might give an idea of one of its finest pages." Save for St. John's red cloak, "too ample, and badly supported," we confess that we do not understand Fromentin's strictures, and with good judges we think that, by the splendour of the decorative effect and the vigour of the expression, the *Coup de Lance* holds one of the first places in Rubens's work. The effect of the figures, which stand out boldly on the left against a clear sky, while on the right their brilliance is relieved against dark clouds, is very powerful and full of exquisite modulation. Skill in the distribution of light, which is one of Rubens's habitual superiorities, here reaches a marvellous perfection. In spite of the intricacy of the movement and the arabesque of his intersecting lines, the silhouette is generally simple and bold. But if the picture is unattractive at a distance, its beauty of detail deserves our close attention, especially the poetic figure of Mary Magdalene, who, enveloped by her fair hair, tender, beautiful, attracts us by her despair, and by the ineffable gesture with which she attempts to protect the corpse of Him she bewails from a last profanation. With what propriety and exquisite sense of proportion everything in the admirable work concurs to give it the most touching significance! With what art are the happy contrasts of colour resolved into perfect harmony, powerful, pathetic, in intimate accord with the character of the scene, and with the extreme diversity of sentiments that it was necessary to express!

THE BOAR OF CALYDON.
(Cassel Museum.)

Notwithstanding their large dimensions, the *Communion of St. Francis* (13 feet 9·35 inches by 7 feet 8·51 inches) and the *Coup de Lance* (13 feet 10·92 inches by 10 feet 2·04 inches) are painted on wood. It is certain that Rubens had a marked predilection for a material which has greater resistance than canvas, and that as often as he could he employed panels prepared with plaster, on which his handling was always firmer and more vigorous. It was, however, on canvas that he painted, about this time, another of his masterpieces : *St. Ambrose refusing Theodosius entrance to the Church after the Massacre of Thessalonica*, a work in admirable preservation, now in the Vienna Gallery. It is easy to understand that such a subject would attract a mind like his. If the episode in itself seems of little importance, it shows us in reality the two great forces which share the empire of the world. At the root of the particular incident lies the eternal conflict of the spiritual and temporal power. The composition sets the circumstances and the importance of the struggle in a clear light. On the one side, Theodosius, the head of a vast empire, at the height

PORTRAIT OF CHARLES DE LONGUEVAL.

The Hermitage.

(From a photograph by Braun, Clément et Cie.)

of prosperity, in all the intoxication of his recent victories, crowned with laurel, his purple cloak thrown over his military uniform, advances towards the entrance of the Church, with his train of courtiers ; on the

other, the saint, an old man, a mitre on his head, wearing his episcopal
robes, opposes his passage. Agitated by very different emotions, the
bystanders await the issue of the scene, some astonished, or irritated
by the calm audacity of the old man, others speechless in admiration
of his courage. The contrast of the two groups is striking, and if the
Emperor—bent, supplicating, with a sly, yet, amiable expression of
humility, one of his hands placed on his heart, as if protesting his
devotion—seems to be somewhat too forgetful of his rank, the saint,
on the contrary, with his venerable figure and dignified bearing, is
superb in his calm, inflexible gentleness and authority. Never has the
feebleness of age, combined with the moral force of high conviction,
taken a more august aspect. There are no violent contrasts either in
the light or in the colour ; but under an even light, we have a quiet
scheme of composition, skilfully distributed medium and related tones
relieved by a judicious use of grey : the bluish-grey of a bright deep
sky ; the more sustained grey of the architecture, the steps and the
ground ; the iron grey of the courtiers' armour, and of the camail of
one of the priests ; the greenish-grey of a scrap of horizon seen
between the personages. Thus framed and enhanced, the colours,
sober as they are, have their full value, and besides endowing
St. Ambrose with imposing dignity, the artist employs his most seductive methods of painting to adorn the noble figure. Our attention
is arrested by the ruddy freshness of the saint's face, set off by his long
white beard, and also by the broad folds of the green brocade cope
lavishly adorned with gold ornaments. The scene is eloquent in its
magnificent simplicity. It admirably reveals the   supple   talent
of a master who, attacking the most varied subjects, could give each
the most suitable mode of treatment. In sober, natural and lofty
style, the artist here speaks the true language of history.

Rubens felt that he was made for great works, in which he
could display his fertility, his breadth of conception, and the infinite
resources at his disposal for expressing his ideas. After the brilliant
works that he had already produced, it was with a legitimate feeling
of confidence in himself that on September 13, 1621, he wrote to
William Trumbull, James I.'s diplomatic agent in Flanders, offering

XVIII

Fight of Amazons.

(MUNICH GALLERY.)

him his services : "Such things have more charm and vehemence
in a large than in a small picture. I should like the picture for the
gallery of H. R. H. the Prince of Wales to be of larger proportions,
because the size of the picture gives me more courage to represent
my ideas adequately and with an appearance of reality." And
at the end of the letter in reference to the decoration of
the Great Hall of Whitehall Palace, of which the rebuilding was
already projected, he added : "I confess that I am by natural instinct
more fitted to execute works of large size than little curiosities. Every
one according to his gifts ; my talent is such that my courage has ever
been equal to any enterprise, however vast in size or diversified in
subject."

The genius of Rubens cannot be more accurately characterised
than it is by the painter himself; and every time that he allowed
himself free scope in his large canvases, without leaving too
much to his pupils, the sureness and ease with which he moved
over vast spaces sufficiently justify his statement. But it must
be admitted that his powers are best seen in works of moderate size. His genius is more freely displayed, and more deeply
impressed on his creations. As he can better embrace the whole, he
can better concentrate the effect. His handling is more vigorous and
personal, and emphasising where necessary, he excels in revealing his
thoughts by more significant traits of expression. We could not
instance a better proof than the *Battle of the Amazons* (Munich
Gallery), painted at this same period for one of the principal amateurs
of Antwerp, Cornelis Van der Geest, who, as we have seen, was
profitably employed in 1610 in assuring Rubens the commission for
the *Raising of the Cross.*

The care that the artist brought to his work sufficiently testifies
his desire to satisfy so distinguished a connoisseur. The master's
nephew, Philip Rubens, says in his reminiscences, that the *Battle
of the Amazons* was painted in 1615, while M. Max Rooses places
its execution in 1610 or 1612. Judging by the character and by
the perfection of the execution we believe the picture to be later
by a few years. In a letter to Pieter van Veen (June 19, 1622),

Rubens informed him that Vorsterman had not been able to finish
the engraving he had made of it, although he had been paid for
it three years ago, that is, in 1619, the date which, in agreement
with the Munich Catalogue, we think it right to adopt. Inspired by
Raphael's *Battle of Constantine*, the composition represents the last
of the struggle round the bridge of Thermodon, on which the in-
vincible victors approach, while the intrepid Amazons once more

THE OLD WOMAN WITH THE BRAZIER.
(Dresden Gallery.)

attempt a semblance of
defence. It is a confused
mass of arms raised ready
to strike, of shining
weapons, of horses rearing,
biting and trampling on
each other. The green
water of the river, thick-
ened and reddened by
blood, flows under the
arch; further on is a
gaping deep black hole in
which livid corpses are
heaped up. On the hori-
zon is the silhouette of a
burning city : on the right,
the confused tumult of a
flight beneath a stormy
violently blue sky with
heavy white clouds.

Whirlwinds of dust, flame, and smoke mingle with the storm-clouds.
Everywhere the tumult of the elements is added to the fury of the
combat, and amid the disorder, the most expressive details, always
subordinated to the perfect unity of the scene, are brought out with
all possible perfection of art. The touch, by turns firm and caressing,
is always intelligent, revealing the docility of the incomparable hand,
guided by the active and well ordered mind which uses every means at
its command to help towards the complete expression of its thought.

The facility with which Rubens passed from one subject to another is not less surprising. A picture full of colour and action like the *Battle of the Amazons* followed a quiet monochrome painting like the *Communion of St. Francis*, and both equally prove his power. Extreme diversity, far from exhausting his fertility, seemed a relaxation for him. It stimulated his ardour, and any sign of fatigue in his incessant labour is sought in vain. Each time he renewed his strength,

VENUS IN VULCAN'S FORGE.
(Brussels Gallery.)

and not confining himself to the repetition of conventional forms and harmonies, he invented the most varied combinations. The interest he thus had in proposing to himself such different ends, allowed him to explore the vast domain of his art in all directions. His innumerable creations reveal the joy of production, and the splendid generosity of a great talent.

The proofs of the master's suppleness and fertility at this time are

so abundant that we must restrain ourselves, and choose from
among the large number of works which issued from his studio
those that most frankly show his originality. Painted at the same
period as the *Battle of the Amazons*, the *Boar Hunt* in the Dresden
Gallery offers similar qualities in a totally different style. He had
treated the subject before—but with the too evident collaboration of
his pupils—in a large canvas now in the Marseilles Museum, and
he returned to it in a sketch of smaller dimensions which is one of
his masterpieces. A pen and ink drawing in the Louvre collection,
of an oak struck by lightning, whose vigorous branches cover the
ground with their *débris*, furnished him the opportunity of giving
the scene a more picturesque and unusual aspect. The reproduction
here given of the drawing, side by side with that of the picture, for
the foreground of which it was utilised, shows us how conscientiously
Rubens studied nature, and with what freedom he adapted his
observations to his point of view. The boar, going straight ahead
in the depth of the forest, hunted and harried by the breathless crowd,
has become entangled in the branches of the old tree, a venerable
giant which raises its mutilated trunk on the left. The beast
defends itself furiously against the dogs that worry it, against the
rustics armed with stakes and pitchforks who hem him in on every
side. Making a stand against his enemies, he tosses and tears those
who are within his reach with his tusks. In the epic confusion,
disembowelled bloodhounds lie around him, here and there ; others
rush on him in a mass to overwhelm him. Everywhere there is
disorder and confusion, an uproar of cries, shrieks, broken branches ;
riders spur their steeds, horses rear or splash the water up under their
hoofs ; the grooms, beside themselves, receive the shock of the boar
with haggard eyes ; dogs supported on their hind-legs climb the
branches with the help of their claws, or grouped in close order hurl
themselves furiously on the animal. In the mad tumult Rubens excels
in keeping himself calm. He is never more master of himself than
amid a confusion in which others lose their heads. He fixes his
composition in the least details with a firm and precise stroke. Then,
without effort, as if in glancing over it, he places his brief indications

of colour, applied so accurately that they give a marvellous reality to all he wishes to bring before us. By a few strokes of the brush, the panel, the greyish ground of which is left to show here and there, is peopled, and becomes animated. The landscape, too, is touched in with skilful dexterity, and notwithstanding the expeditious work, the different species of trees may be distinguished with their varied trunks and masses, the clear cut foliage of the oak, the fresh verdure of the broom, the complicated indentation of the ferns, the glossiness of the ivy, and the twisting branches of the brambles. It is as if the vivacious brush had itself gone a hunting in this sketch, which did not probably take more than a day. Side by side with the painter and the prowess he brought to the practice of his art, may be discovered the accomplished cavalier who understood the charm of all noble sports, and who placed on his animated canvas an epitome of all the intoxications of the chase.

Legendary tales with their variety of invention and the freedom of interpretation they permit, attracted Rubens, and at all periods of his life they played a large part in his work. We shall have to return to some of the compositions with which they inspired him at this period, *Dianas Sleeping, Dianas Hunting, Silenuses*, &c. ; for the moment, it is enough to mention some of the more important. *Venus and Adonis* was one of Rubens's favourite subjects, and he treated it several times in pictures now in the Hague Gallery, at the Hermitage, and in the Uffizi. The last example seems to us the best. It contains some of the figures already used by the artist, or to be used afterwards : the Fury who attempts to lead off the handsome hunter, the group of somewhat mincing Graces, who try to keep him near the goddess, and several of the Cupids who play with his dogs. If the handling is in places a little timid and small, the pearly colour and transparent shadows of the flesh reveal the eye and hand of the master.

There is more force and simplicity and even a fuller maturity in *Boreas Carrying off Orithyes* in the Academy of Fine Arts at Vienna. The old man with his long grey beard, his ruddy flesh, his wild expression, is, it must be confessed, somewhat wanting in distinction. But the little genii who gather the snow-flakes as they fall, or throw snow-

balls at each other, are of piquant invention, and the superb form of the
body of the young girl stands out brilliantly against the leaden sky.
The same model probably served for one of the figures in the *Rape of
the Daughters of Leucippus*, of which there is a hasty yet masterly
drawing in the Louvre. There also the milky-white of the young
girls' bodies forms an excessive contrast to the tawny tones of the flesh
of their ravishers. But the silhouette of the group stands out boldly
against the sky, and the
freshness of the captives'
flesh-tints, the firm supple
modelling of their abun-
dant forms, and the soft
charm of the contours are
veritable marvels, the radiant image of which re-
mains profoundly fixed in
the memory.

PORTRAIT OF SUSANNA FOURMENT.
(The Louvre).

The study of the *Old
Woman with the Brasier*
(Dresden Gallery), her
face lighted from below
by the embers on which
the boy by her side blows,
is a fresh proof of the
curiosity which led
Rubens to try his skill at
all the effects Nature had
to offer. In such subjects, very much in vogue at that time, which
the greater number of contemporary painters, especially Honthorst,
treat by means of excessively harsh contrasts, the master shows a
marvellous delicacy of observation. The transparent red of the
hands held against the flame, the scarcely perceptible passing of the
shadows into the lights, and the delicately refined modelling of the
good old dame's face, prove the insight which enabled his great mind
to solve problems that were new to him at the first attempt.

But while others kept exclusively to effects in this style, and made it a necessarily monotonous speciality, Rubens did not let himself be absorbed by it. After this successful attempt, he hastened to return to the diffused light which, while leaving the nature of tonalities unaltered, permitted him to show his individual qualities better. The Dresden

study is, as MM. Hymans and Max Rooses have proved, only the fragment of a mutilated work the other part of which is in the Brussels Museum— *Venus in Vulcan's Forge.* Neither the lighting nor the conception of the two portions harmonise however. The fragments when placed together in the original composition could not have presented much unity. We can therefore understand, although we cannot excuse the act of vandalism committed by a former owner either from excess of prudery, or from a desire of possessing two pictures instead of one. To hide it he had painted, very

STUDY FOR THE DWARF IN THE PORTRAIT OF THE COUNTESS OF ARUNDEL.
(Stockholm Print Room.)

clumsily, the figure of Vulcan which in the Brussels panel takes the place of the *Old Woman with the Brasier.*

Under more normal conditions, the portraits painted by Rubens at this time permitted him once more to steep himself in the immediate study of nature. One of the most celebrated of those portraits is that of a young girl in the National Gallery known as the *Chapeau de Poil.*

Turning her face three-quarters to the spectator, and wearing a felt hat, the wide brim of which throws a clear, transparent shadow over her charming face, she is dressed in a black bodice, with scarlet sleeves, open low enough for her breasts, brought very close together, to be visible; her slim hands are crossed in front of her. Rosy and smiling, she is in the full flower of her youth. It would seem that by scarcely covering his panel with a light rubbing of colour, the artist wished to preserve his purity of colouring and spontaneity of execution in all their freshness. The excessive soberness of the materials employed causes perhaps a slight inconsistency, but the diaphanous painting derives from that very sobriety the indescribable charm of candour and virginal beauty which justifies the reputation of the work. Rubens loved the naive countenance, and multiplied representations of it: it occurs in a sketch in black and red chalk in the Albertina collection, and in several other portraits such as that in the Hermitage, and that in the Louvre, described in the catalogue as a lady of the Van Boonen family.[1] The Louvre copy was painted a few years after that of the National Gallery, and is far from equalling it. The excessively big eyes are not in harmony, and the handling is more than summary. The extreme pleasure which the master took in reproducing the young girl's features is the sole justification for the title of *Rubens's Mistress*, which the National Gallery portrait has also received. In reality the girl, Susanna Fourment, belonged to an important Antwerp family with whom the artist was at that time on fairly intimate terms; she had six sisters, most of whom were married to friends or connections of Rubens, and of whom the youngest, Helena, became the great artist's second wife.

Another portrait, that of the Earl and Countess of Arundel in the Munich Gallery, is in size (8 feet 6·75 inches by 8 feet 8·34 inches) the largest work in this style painted by the master. It is a state picture conceived to give an idea of the elegance and splendour of one of the best known noble English families of the time. Seated under a slightly raised portico, adorned with twisted columns ornamented with

---

[1] The correct name is Boonem; the inventory drawn up after Rubens's death contains seven portraits of the same lady, all painted before the death of Isabella Brant.

17

Study of Cherubs.

(Pen and Ink Drawing.)

(ALBERTINA COLLECTION.)

(From a photograph by Braun, Clément et Cie.)

P. P. Rubens F.

Printed by Draeger. Paris.

bas-reliefs, the countess wears a rather low, black satin dress. One of
her hands hangs down, the other rests on the head of a big white
hound spotted with black. Her fool, dressed in green and yellow
silk, stands on the left; on the right is a dwarf in a vermilion red
costume embroidered with gold, a falcon on his wrist; and a little
behind, also standing, is the earl with his hand resting on the back
of his wife's chair. A large eastern carpet is spread beneath their
feet, and a thick drapery, on which the family arms are embroidered
in relief, floats between the columns. In the distance are a pale grey-
blue sky, and a vast stretch of country in the midst of which rises the
baronial castle. A letter written from Antwerp to the Earl of
Arundel on 17 July, 1620, by one of his agents, informs us that
Rubens, although overwhelmed with work at the moment, had consented
to paint the portrait of the earl whom he regarded "as an evangelist
for the world of art, and a great protector of artists." The next day he
made a sketch of the countess, her dog, her fool, and "her dwarf
Robin,"[1] but when he wished to transpose it on to canvas, he could
not find one sufficiently large. It was therefore necessary to postpone
the painting of the picture until a canvas was mounted. Did the
countess, who left the next day for Brussels, return later to Antwerp
to give Rubens a sitting, or what is more probable, was the artist
contented to paint her from the sketch he had already made? Judging
by the somewhat timid execution of the lady's face, it would seem that
the painter did not have his model before him when he completed the
work. The figure of the count, also somewhat shadowy, was added
afterwards, doubtless during the visit paid by Rubens later to London.
There are, in fact, a study in black and red chalk (in the Count
Duchastel-Dandelot's collection) and two other half-length portraits
(Castle Howard and Warwick Castle) of the Earl of Arundel painted
at that time by the master. However, if the heads in the large canvas
at Munich do not possess the striking individuality which Rubens
generally gives his sitters, the work is marked in the highest degree by
the taste and decorative breadth befitting a picture of the kind. It

---

[1] The sketch has been preserved, and is in the Stockholm Museum; notes in
Rubens's hand indicate the different colours of Robin's costume.

testifies to the author's talent and to his desire of pleasing the distinguished amateur whose fine collections he was later to admire and study with so much pleasure.

The number and importance of these different works prove Rubens's inexhaustible fertility during the period of production that corresponded to the best filled and happiest years of his life. Although painting held by far the largest place therein, he busied himself with many things. His energy was marvellous; but only the extremely methodical fashion in which he mapped out his time made it possible for him to fulfil his complex tasks, to each of which he invariably brought the care for perfection that was a fixed rule with him.

STUDY FOR THE RAPE OF THE DAUGHTERS OF LEUCIPPUS.
(The Louvre.)

THE TEMPTATION OF CHRIST.
(From an engraving by C. Jegher, after Rubens.)

CHAPTER XI

PLATE FROM THE DRAWING-BOOK.
Engraving by P. Pontius. (After Rubens.)

WE have mentioned the legitimate ascendancy which Rubens possessed over his pupils, and the assistance he derived from their collaboration. But it was not only painters who worked under his direction. His influence on the art of engraving in Flanders was so important that it is necessary to dwell on it. There is no better guide for the study of the subject than the excellent work, *La Gravure dans l'école de Rubens*, published in 1879, by M. Henri Hymans, the conclusions of which Herr A. Rosenberg confirms, adding the attraction of fine heliogravures after plates chosen from Rubens's best interpreters, to his individual researches.[1]

From the first the masters of painting perceived the fame and profit to be derived from the reproduction of their works. Many engraved their own pictures, and all who did so showed their creative faculties in this form of art, and employed the methods to which they had recourse for their own advantage. The art of engraving owes its most original and admirable productions to painters like Mantegna, Lucas van Leyden, Schongauer, Albert Dürer, Claude Lorraine, and Rembrandt. Others like Raphael, Titian, and Veronese did not themselves handle the graver or burin, but ensured a faithful reproduction of their pictures by the advice and guidance they gave their interpreters.

Rubens was too intelligent not to perceive how useful skilled engravers would be to his reputation, and too wise not to take advantage of such assistance. He had seen his masters entrust the reproduction of their pictures and of drawings made for illustrated books to publishers of repute. In Van Veen's studio he had met engravers with whom he later entered into relations : Adriaen and Jan Collaert, Egbert van Panderen, K. Mallery, and Gysbert van Veen, Otto's brother. At Mantua he had examples before him still more calculated to impress him. His study of Mantegna's prints had familiarised him with that great artist's vigorous and noble style. The school of engraving founded by Giulio Romano at Mantua, had left its traces there, and the large plates so freely and broadly treated by G. Battista Scultor, by his daughter, Diana, and later by Giorgio Ghisi, could not fail to attract his attention. To satisfy his collector's instincts Rubens had acquired some of the works of his favourite masters, notably Marc Antonio's engravings after Raphael, and the large compositions drawn by Titian on wood for his engravers. His taste was thus gradually formed, and associating at Rome with Italian artists or with those of the foreign colony, such as Elsheimer, he learned their methods, compared their styles, and worked himself for the engravers. We have seen how, at the request of a compatriot, he consented not

[1] *Die Rubensstecher.* 4to. Vienna, 1893.

only to furnish drawings for the completion of a series of engravings dealing with the life of Ignatius Loyola, but also to make corrections on the margins of the very mediocre plates included in the series, in order to minimise their worst faults of drawing. At Rome also, Rubens drew for Jan Moretus the details of costumes and antique objects that Cornelis Galle had engraved for his brother's book, *Philippi Rubenii Electorum libri duo*, published in 1608 at the Plantin Press. On his return to Antwerp, the artist entered into regular relations with the publishing house, and with the engravers employed by it on the frontispieces and illustrations for which Rubens supplied the drawings.

One of his first undertakings of this kind was the illustration of a *Treatise on Optics* in six books, published in 1613, by Father François Aguilon. Rubens designed not only the vignettes at the beginning of each of the six books, but also the frontispiece, a curious fantastic composition engraved by Th. Galle, brother-in-law of B. Moretus, of which M. Hymans doubts the authenticity. It is certainly in poor taste, and absurdities abound in the details; for instance, the Genius of Optics, his sceptre surmounted with an eye, enthroned beside a peacock whose tail is set with eyes, and a bust of Mercury, on a term, holding an Argus head with innumerable eyes.

As a rule, an architectural motive of a more or less fantastic style —pediment, temple or altar—forms the framework of the design in these frontispieces: in the centre is an oval or a rectangular space for the title of the book. Framed by the rigid lines of the architecture, allegorical figures and suitable attributes symbolise the character of the work, and sum up its contents. Although a large number of the publications of the Plantin Press were connected with religion, their list includes a great variety of subjects. Among those for which Rubens designed the frontispieces, along with purely devotional or apologetic works like the *History of the Church*, the *Commentaries of the Bible*, the *Works of St. Dionysius the Areopagite*, the *Divine Lily*, and the *Chain of the Sixty-five Fathers of the Greek Church*, we find others such as the *Medallions of the Roman Emperors*, the *Annals of Brabant*, the *Customs of Guelders*, the *Account of the Siege of Breda*,

by Father Hermann Hugo, the *Siege of Dôle and its happy deliverance*,
a *Treatise on Forestry*, etc.　Regardless of the diversity of subjects,
Rubens accepted all the commissions offered him.　But he did not
like to be hurried.　"When I want a frontispiece," wrote Moretus,
"I tell him six months in advance, so that he may have plenty of time.
But he only works at them on holidays : if he gives up working days

STUDY FOR THE FALL OF THE DAMNED.
Munich Gallery. (Drawing in the National Gallery.)

to them, he demands 100
florins for each drawing."
It took the author of the
*Embassy of the Chevalier
de Marselaer to Philip IV*.
three years to obtain the
frontispiece—one of the
last Rubens designed—for
that work.　Rubens himself
provided a commentary [1]
—a very necessary pre-
caution—on the fantastic
images he put into the
composition.　"Above,"
he said, "surveying and
protecting everything,
watches the eye of Divine
Providence, the arbiter
and master of embassies.
Lower rules Politics, or
Art, the squarely-formed
pedestal indicates the
stability of her reign, and

like Cybele she carries towers on her head. . . . ."　And so the
laborious and fine-drawn explanation runs its course, filling two pages.
Thus nothing—and we could produce innumerable instances—is
wanting to the allegories, veritable rebuses, whose pretension and
puerility verge on the ridiculous.　Here and there, however, the

[1] It is written in Rubens's own hand on a proof belonging to the Brussels Library.

banality is relieved by a happy idea, or a few simpler or more
spontaneous figures. Occasionally Rubens returns to them to utilise
them in his pictures : but the contrary is generally the case, for
abundant and scarcely disguised reminiscences of former works are
unscrupulously intercalated in these compositions.

It is strange that a man whose way of life proved his firm and
clear good sense, whose
correspondence, conversa-
tion, and criticisms of
literature show an abso-
lute hatred of bombast
and fustian, should have
complacently abandoned
himself to such a display
of affectation. Although
we cannot entirely ex-
onerate him, it must be
remembered that such
subtleties were altogether
in the taste of the time.
Men of letters and preach-
ers, especially among the
Jesuits, set the example
in their writings and sermons, and in most cases
Rubens conformed to the
programme sketched out
for him. Such is the
case with the frontispiece

STUDY FOR THE FALL OF THE DAMNED.
Munich Gallery. (Drawing in the National Gallery.)

to the *Latin Poetry, Epigrams and Poems* of the Jesuit Fathers
Bauhusius, Cabillavius, and Malapertics. Father Bauhusius expressed to the publisher his great desire to have, according to
the general custom, at the beginning of the volume, some of
those designs which, as he said himself, "are a recreation for the
reader, a bait for the purchaser, and without much increasing the

cost, an ornament to the book." He asked Moretus to secure the co-operation of Rubens who, with "his divine spirit," would know better than any other artist what was most suitable. Returning to the subject later on, Bauhusius himself proposed to put "the Muses, Mnemosyne, Apollo, all Parnassus," in the frontispiece. At first Moretus turned a deaf ear ; his engravers were too busy just then, and the excellence of the typography and the reputation of the authors would sufficiently recommend the work to the public. Nineteen years later, however, Moretus yielded to Bauhusius's desire, and Rubens, who was commissioned to design the frontispiece, adopted the programme set down for him with slight modifications. "Authorised by numerous examples," he wrote to Moretus, when sending him the original drawing, "I have replaced Mercury by a Muse ; I do not know if the idea will please you, but for myself I rejoice in, nay, I almost congratulate myself on my invention. Observe that in order to distinguish her from Apollo, I have put a feather on the Muse's head." It was not only in 17th century France that affectation, and subtleties of wit prevailed.

With his facile, fertile talent, his cultured mind, and excellent memory, Rubens easily translated the ideas suggested to him by authors for their frontispieces into picturesque images. He met warm encouragement to persevere from his closest connections, and among his immediate surroundings, and doubtless often found a zealous collaborator in his friend Gevaert. In the numerous laudatory or funeral inscriptions, of which the registrar of Antwerp made a sort of specialty, we find abuse of antithesis, bombastic parallels, hazardous puns and alliterations, all the fashionable rhetoric of the age, to which Rubens himself paid a large tribute. It was certainly not because he needed to spend much thought over these commissions that he demanded such long delays from Moretus, but because he did not wish to be distracted from the execution of works more worthy of him, works to which he desired to devote himself entirely. Amid the innumerable tasks that occupied his time, he desired to preserve intact the necessary liberty of mind for the accomplishment of work the perfection of which he had more at heart. He probably attached

XIX

The "Chapeau de Poil."

Printed by Chassepot Paris (France)

no great importance to the almost improvised drawings done at his
convenience, in which he let his pen or pencil run freely over the
paper. If he occasionally defended the arrangement, or discussed the
details with those interested, he did so, in all probability, that he might
not have to refer to the matter again. More often, however, he
received nothing but praise: he was the recipient of inexhaustible
eulogies on his ingenuity, his learning, the aptness of his allusions,
the wealth and originality of his ideas, and the force and charm of
his manner of expressing them. If the unchastened exuberance of
the works horrifies us now, we must not forget that they responded
to the taste of their age, and justified the superiority of the artist
in the eyes of all. They pleased not only men of letters and
connoisseurs, but also the publisher; the unbroken and always
excellent relations which Rubens preserved with the Plantin Press
during the whole of his life, and the continual occasions on which
Moretus demanded his active co-operation, clearly show the value
attached to it.

With the exception of a few that bear the names of Jan Collaert,
Jacobus de Bie, and Pontius, nearly all these frontispieces were
engraved by members of the family of Galle, Theodor, and the two
Cornelis, father and son. Rubens had long had relations with them.
On his return to Antwerp, Cornelis Galle, the elder, executed a large
plate after the picture, *Judith and Holophernes*, which Rubens, as we
have seen, dedicated to Jan van den Wouwere in fulfilment of the
promise made him at Verona. With this plate, known as the *Large
Judith*, begins the series of proofs which Rubens corrected himself;
the Print Room of the National Library, at Paris, possesses about a
hundred of them. Until then he had rarely retouched the engravings
executed after the drawings which he supplied to the Plantin Press;
the account books of the firm only note retouchings for the figures in
Aiguilon's *Treatise*, and Justus Lipsius's *Seneca*. But he was more
solicitous about the reproductions of his paintings, and he exacted
complete obedience and all possible perfection from the artists who
undertook them. Remarkable as the work of Cornelis Galle was—
he showed in the *Large Judith* great superiority to his preceding work

in boldness of touch and fidelity of translation—Rubens did not fail
to correct the proofs of the plate submitted to him with the greatest
care. He strengthened the angels' wings with broad strokes of the
pen, deepened the shadows in the modelling of the forms opposed to
the light, and by the help of a little body-colour gave more brilliance
to the parts he considered too dark.

Although, in the dedication to Wouwerius, the master presented
him with the Judith as the first of the plates engraved after his
pictures, others had, in fact, preceded it. But he was dissatisfied with
the interpreters he found at Antwerp; they seemed to him to be
animated by a mercantile spirit rather than by a desire of perfection.
He, therefore, applied to the Dutch engravers, who appeared to be
doing more conscientious work. The greater number of them had
studied in the school of Goltzius, and thoroughly understood all the
processes of their art, though, following their master's example, their
practices too often bordered on virtuosity. But when restrained
and directed by Rubens, W. Swanenburch in the *Pilgrims of
Emmaüs*, J. Matham in *Samson and Delilah*, and notably Jan
Muller in the *Portraits of the Archduke Albert and the Princess
Isabella*, show the most reverent fidelity to the originals. They
are, however, isolated attempts from which Rubens derived no great
advantage.

The first engraver with whom the master entered into regular
relations was Pieter Soutman, also a Dutchman. He was born in 1580
at Haarlem, and settled at Antwerp, where, in 1619, he already had a
pupil inscribed on the lists of the Guild of St. Luke. Perhaps he
had been in Rubens's studio, but in any case, as a painter, he was
well qualified to understand the master's meaning, and to reproduce his
work exactly. A marked originality distinguishes his plates from those
of his contemporaries. Without making a display of his talent, he
attempted to reproduce the values of the colour of the pictures he
engraved, and he rendered the effect with a very broad method.
Like Rubens, he preferred compositions full of contests and movement, such as *Hunts*, the *Fall of the Damned*, the *Miraculous Draught*,
Sennacherib thrown from his Horse, and the *Rape of Proserpina*. In

the *Large Wolf-Hunt*, in which the free execution suggests an etching while preserving the bold general effect, he correctly expressed the characteristics of each of the animals, and if he did not reproduce the character of the execution, he gave the episodes the animation and life with which the great painter had endowed them. Rubens's relations with Soutman were most affectionate, and he entrusted him with the reproduction of some of the drawings which he made in Italy after masterpieces such as Leonardo's *Last Supper*, a *Venus* by Titian, &c. Formed in his school, several of Soutman's

THE BOAR HUNT. (SCHOOL OF RUBENS.)
(Munich Gallery.)

pupils, C. Visscher, and J. Snyderhoef, for example, worthily carried on his traditions, and engraved a considerable number of Rubens's pictures.

But Rubens found a more pliable and faithful interpreter in another Dutchman, one who, in his best works, completely came up to his standard.[1] Lucas Vorsterman, born in 1595 at Bommel, in Guelders,

[1] M. Henri Hymans's remarkable monograph on Vorsterman (Brussels, 1893) forms a valuable complement to his fine study, *La Gravure dans l'école de Rubens*. We have largely availed ourselves of these excellent works.

was probably a pupil of Goltzius, and early became skilled in his art.
Perhaps his fervent Catholicism made it difficult for him to remain in
his own country ; perhaps Antwerp attracted him as offering greater
resources for the development of his talent and the placing of his
works.   However this may be, we know that on August 28, 1620, he
received the rights of citizenship there, in order to practise the
art of engraving, and trade in prints, and he was admitted to
the Guild the same year.   The previous year, on April 9, 1619, he
had married a young girl, sister of a copper-plate printer, Antonie
Franckx, through whose press several of the best of his plates after
Rubens passed ;   on January 17, 1620, the great painter stood
godfather to his first child, a son, who received the names of Paul
Emilius.   Whatever Vorsterman's professional knowledge may have been
previously, he produced no notable engraving until he worked under
Rubens's direction.   Contact with the master produced a complete
transformation in his talent.   He had never handled a brush, but he
possessed the instincts of a colourist, and used them in his own art,
gaining thereby the surname of "painter-colourist."   Sandrart tells
us that, versed in the difficulties of his work, "his earlier method
was a style much in vogue at the time, and was founded on a beautiful
arrangement of the stroke, so that each regular and prolonged sweep
corresponded to another. . . .   On the advice of Rubens, he adopted
the method of the painters .   . essaying especially to preserve a just
proportion between the lights, the half-tones, the shadows, and the
reflections."

He could not have attained such a result all at once, and doubtless
as a means to that end, and to break him in, Rubens made him
execute a few preparatory plates.   It was for this reason, probably,
that Rubens advised him to engrave several pictures after the
elder Brueghel, whose bold, original handling was best suited for the
special practice he needed : such as the *Peasants' Brawl*, which
Rubens had copied, and the *Yawning Man*, which was in his
possession.   But from that time, with only rare exceptions, Vorsterman
devoted himself exclusively to the reproduction of Rubens's pictures.
A letter from Rubens to Pieter van Veen, chief magistrate of the

Hague, dated June 22, 1621,[1] supplies us with information regarding the earliest of those engravings. First in order is a *St. Francis receiving the Stigmata*, after the mediocre picture painted by the master in 1617 (Cologne Museum), with the too evident assistance of his pupils. Rubens describes the engraving as a first attempt, and as somewhat rough in treatment. The dry and slightly hard execution is monotonous, but if the contrasts are excessive, the perfect exactness and accuracy of the drawing testify to the interpreter's conscientiousness. There is less tension, and the passage from black to white is better managed in *Lot's Flight*, which was executed, Rubens says, " at the time when his connection with the engraver first began." Progress is increasingly noticeable in the plates he afterwards mentions as engraved from his compositions, the *Return of the Holy Family from Egypt ;* the *Virgin Embracing the Infant Jesus,* " which he considered a good work " ; a *Susanna and the Elders,* which he ranks "among the best plates," and the *Fall of Lucifer,* which he mentions as " fairly successful." Vorsterman preserved the same conscientious fidelity to his originals in those works, while showing more freedom and breadth. His burin reproduced the manner, and even the touch of Rubens more successfully, and the skilful gradation of the tones, and the supple sweep of the graver, give the plates a more animated and harmonious effect.

The almost incredible rapidity with which the plates followed each other testify to Vorsterman's enthusiasm for his task. Rubens understood the advantage to be derived from so able an interpreter. Naturally desirous of spreading his works abroad, he recognised the material profit that might be gained from the enterprise, and neglected nothing that might ensure its success. From this period onward he personally superintended the execution and the sale of the prints, and spared neither time nor pains to obtain all possible perfection from his interpreter. It was first necessary to supply the latter with exact reproductions of the pictures to be engraved. Some of them were difficult to reproduce on account of their size ; others had to be sent at once to the churches and public buildings for which they were commissioned.

[1] It is in the archives of Antwerp.

In such cases carefully executed drawings would supplement the originals, and be of the greatest assistance to the engraver. But such drawings required great skill, and overwhelmed with work as he was, the painter had not time to make them all himself. Fortunately there was at that time among his assistants an artist on whose talents he could occasionally rely, and so he entrusted the task to Van Dyck.

PORTRAIT OF L. VORSTERMAN.

(Facsimile of an Engraving by Van Dyck.)

Bellori's testimony on this point is conclusive.[1] " Rubens," he says, " was fortunate in finding in Van Dyck an artist who could reproduce his compositions at will in drawings destined to be engraved." While confirming this statement, Mariette declares that " the fine prints of Rubens's works engraved in his life-time were not from his pictures, but from carefully finished drawings or *grisailles*, which he knew how to paint in black and white oil colour so as to preserve the effect of the chiaroscuro required in engraving, which gets all its excellence from the contrast of black and white. I have seen," he adds, " a large number of pieces prepared by Rubens to be engraved, and I possess some which were in M. Crozat's collection, and which Jabach bought at the sale of Rubens's prints after his death. Bellori, in his Life of Van Dyck, stated that Rubens often employed this pupil to prepare such drawings and *grisailles*, and I am inclined

[1] Bellori, *Vite dei pittori, scultori ed architetti moderni.* Pisa, 1821. Vol. i. p. 257.

to believe it, for his delicate and facile brush was exactly fitted for such work." [1]

It is, however, certain that when Rubens had the leisure he executed some of the drawings himself, and we may content ourselves with noting a *Holy Family* in pen and ink and wash (British Museum), which was engraved by Michael Lasne ; the *Crucifixion*, in Italian chalk and body-colour, engraved by Pontius (Boymans Museum) ; the central

panel of the *Miraculous Draught*, a pen and ink drawing and wash (Weimar Museum), engraved by Scheltius à Bolswert ; and the *Stoning of St. Stephen*, a very fine drawing, washed with Indian ink (in the Hermitage collection), of which we have already spoken. The drawings alluded to by Mariette are certainly not by Rubens. The greater number are in the Louvre, where copies of seven out of the nine pictures mentioned in the letter to Van Veen as engraved by Vorsterman are to be found ; the copies are ex-cellent, and carefully made for the engraver, and Rubens doubtless retouched them here and there, but he would never have tied himself down to finish them with such exactness. Moreover, it is easy to recognise the elegant workmanship of which, at that time, only Van Dyck among all Rubens's collaborators would have been capable.

A BUST OF SENECA.

(Facsimile of an Engraving by Rubens.)

By the aid of such models, Vorsterman was sure of interpreting the originals even more faithfully than if he had had them before his eyes. When the plate was finished, or while it was in course of execution, the proofs were submitted to the painter, who tested the quality of the work and retouched it where necessary. It is most instructive to study the corrections on the trial proofs in the Louvre Print Room. They furnish a fresh proof of the master's unerring eye, and of the accuracy of his corrections. As a rule, his changes bear on the general effect, for that was the end he had specially in view. It should be noted that it was not an easy task in the case of Rubens, for if the local values are exactly observed in his works, the chiaroscuro plays a subordinate part, and the effect is obtained by a judicious distribution of colour, rather than by contrasts of light and shadow. It would therefore seem that the interpretation of the artist's works would present very great difficulties to the interpreter, since he had to reproduce gradations of colour rather than differences of tone. But the discipline imposed by Rubens on his engravers, combined with their skill, made the realisation of these delicate transpositions possible. Vorsterman's skill in this respect was very great, and always tended to a more complete fidelity of reproduction ; as he was an excellent draughtsman, it was only on rare occasions that Rubens had to correct a faulty line. If he sometimes reproved the engraver, he did not hesitate to correct himself. Finding the scene in the plate of the *Supper at the House of Simon* badly arranged, he suppressed a portion of his work on the left which seemed to him useless, and on the right of the engraving added a strip of equal width to complete the figure of a negress, and sketch in broadly at her feet a dog of which only the head was seen before. But, as a rule, he turned his attention to the masses, to the general coherence and aspect, to making the contrasts bolder or less marked, to everything that might add expression, air, life, and variety to the work. With these reservations, he left his interpreters a large measure of liberty, and, never over-zealous about trifling details, his corrections bear the stamp of the acute and thoughtful mind that so vastly aided his great experience.

18

Landscape with Figures and Animals.

(THE LOUVRE.)

But to make the corrections effective, it was necessary that Rubens should know how far the changes indicated by him were possible, and that he should therefore possess accurate and practical knowledge the technical part of the engraver's art. We are here confronted by a question that has been much discussed, and answered by the most competent critics in very opposite ways. Did Rubens practise the art of engraving himself? Mariette, and those who follow him, declare that he did, and certain plates, three in particular, seem to justify the assertion. The *Old Woman with a Candle* is a copy of the master's picture[1] (now in the possession of Lord Feversham), and the type, the attitude, the lighting of the old woman, are almost identical with those in the *Old Woman with the Brasier* in the Dresden Gallery. At the bottom of a proof before the letter which is in the Print Room of the National Library, Paris, and is reproduced here, Rubens wrote with his own hand :

" *Quis vetet apposito lumen de lumine tolli ;*
Mille licet capiunt ; deperit indè nihil."

It is said that the engraving was begun by Rubens, and finished by P. Pontius : the signature *P. P. Rubens invenit et excudit* added beneath the inscription and the notification of the license of sale, and like these, in the master's hand, authorise the attribution, which is confirmed, in our opinion, by the simplicity and breadth of the handling. The handling presents evident analogies with that of another plate also thought to be by Rubens, the *St. Catherine in the Clouds*. Careful comparison reveals an exact similarity in the method of treating the draperies, in the masterly modelling of the figure—especially notable in the *Old Woman with a Candle*—a modelling obtained by a process of regular hatchings, a broad and simple process, but exercised with a comprehension of form and effect that is not found with a similar degree of delicacy and sureness in any of Rubens's inter-preters.[2] We find the same analogies, the same simplicity and

[1] It appears in the inventory drawn up after his death under the number 45 : *Portrait of an Old Woman with a Boy ; A Night Piece.*

[2] The engraving of *St. Catherine*, an exact copy of the principal figure in one of the panels of the ceiling of the Jesuits' Church, was retouched by Vorsterman.

boldness, in the trial proof of an etching of a so-called bust of *Seneca*
in the British Museum, which, in our opinion, is also by Rubens.
Besides the fact that the bust belonged to Rubens, the bold, sure, and
broad execution of the plate shows, over and above a desire for
technical excellence, the spontaneity of an original work.   The plate, like
the *St. Catherine*, was retouched by Vorsterman, and is signed by him.
Rubens probably attached little importance to such attempts, which he
made chiefly with a view to acquiring knowledge of the engraver's art.
During his visit to Rome, and indeed at all times, he had kept himself
informed of its processes without any idea of practising it himself;
testimony to this fact is contained in the letter to Pieter van Veen,
from which we have already quoted.   " I am glad," he wrote, " to hear
that you have found a way of engraving on copper by drawing on a
white ground ; that was Adam Elsheimer's method : for an aquafortis
engraving, he first covered the copper with a sort of white paste, and
then cut through it with the graver down to the copper, and this being
of a reddish colour, he seemed to be drawing on white paper with red
chalk.   I cannot remember the ingredients of the white paste, although
Elsheimer kindly explained its composition to me."   In the margin,
Rubens added, " but I expect you have a better receipt for the purpose yourself."   It is clear—the date of the letter, June, 1622, almost
the same as that at which the *Old Woman* was engraved, should be
noted—that Rubens, always eager for knowledge, sought to profit by
every invention that might facilitate or improve the work of his
engravers.   His own knowledge of their craft enabled him to give
them the practical advice most likely to obtain from them the results
he desired.

Rubens was careful to make arrangements which ensured him against
loss, after all the expenses and labour incurred in the work.   Engravers
had long complained of the piracies of their work, and of their
inability to obtain redress from those who not only defrauded
them, but compromised their name by imputing unworthy copies to
them.   Lucas Van Leyden and Albert Dürer, among others, were
thus deprived of their rights in their original prints, and often laid their
grievances before the authorities.   If, in answer to their petitions, they

obtained a grant of special privileges, they were given at the same time no powers of proceeding against the delinquents; but it must be confessed that, considering the state of Europe, it would have been difficult to carry out measures for maintaining ill-defined rights in countries that were constantly at war one with another. Considering all he did in the matter, Rubens may justly be regarded as the first to insist on a recognition of the rights of artistic property, and his name deserves to be mentioned in connection with the legislation which, in

THE HOLY FAMILY RESTING IN EGYPT.
Facsimile of an Engraving by C. Jegher retouched by Rubens.
(National Library, Paris.)

our own day, has attempted to settle the question by regulations that have been the subject of lengthy and delicate controversies. In seeking his own advantage, he was the first to bring new ideas to the notice of the authorities. He used the celebrity due to his talent, and his relations with numerous great men of the day, to further so legitimate a cause; neither did he hesitate throughout his life, to engage in lengthy proceedings and obstinate struggles, when it

was a question of defending his rights, or punishing his despoilers.
He did not fear trouble, and returned to the charge as often as
necessary; his tact and knowledge of the world enabled him to
formulate his claims clearly, and to interest all who could further
his cause. If he considered himself injured, he claimed redress
with great vivacity, applied to every one whose interest it would
be useful to gain, bestirred himself in all directions, was never
discouraged by a rebuff, and in the end obtained justice.

The campaign began in 1619. He desired a formal and definite
grant of privileges in all countries where his engravings were likely to
sell. He commenced by establishing his position in Flanders, and on
January 29, 1619, the Archdukes granted "their painter" the privileges
he desired. France followed suit on July 3. Gevaert obtained the
intervention of the celebrated French scholar, Fabri de Peiresc, and,
thanks to him, letters patent of Louis XIII. state that since Rubens
"was invited by his friends to have drawings of the finest paintings
by his hand, engraved and printed on copper, a thing that cannot be
done without much expense and trouble," it was necessary to protect
him from possible forgeries. The United Provinces of Holland remained; in view of their proximity, and of the prevailing taste of the
inhabitants for fine prints, it was needful to take careful precautions
here. But in consequence of the incessant hostilities and strained re-
ations between the two countries, the matter was a very difficult one.
Four letters from Rubens to Pieter van Veen, earlier in date than
the one from which we have quoted, were recently discovered at Ghent,
and they enlighten us as to the different phases of the negotiation.
As Pensionary of the Hague, the brother of Rubens's old master
was in a position to show him the best course to pursue with the
States-General. On January 4, 1619, Rubens asked him what
means it would be best to take, and what protection the privileges
he demanded would give him. As it was some time since he had
had any communication with Van Veen, he tactfully began by
apologising for his long silence; so close to the beginning of a new
year he did not wish his letter to be confused "with the mutual
greetings common between casual acquaintances at that season. . . .

He was not a man to feed on the incense of vain compliments, and he believed that all wise men agreed with him on this point." But he wanted to know what steps he ought to take to secure that certain plates he had had engraved in Flanders should not be copied in the "United Provinces," and what rights the privilege he intended to solicit would assure him. He would regulate his proceedings according to the advice of one whose wisdom he well knew. Van Veen gave the required advice, and offered his assistance. Rubens wrote again on January 23, that "he was of those who abused courtesy by accepting everything that was offered him." He was not, however, able to supply proofs of all the engravings that the privilege demanded should cover, "but no difficulties would arise on that score, because the subjects were free from ambiguity or mystical meanings, and in no way touched affairs of state ; that could be easily proved from the list of the engravings." . . . Then he added, and the words are significant, "in order to ensure a greater fidelity in the reproduction of the original on the part of the engraver, I prefer to see the work done under my own eyes by a conscientious young man, rather than to rely on the caprice of a more celebrated artist." He promised to reimburse Van Veen for any expenses he might incur, and thanked him for the trouble he was taking. A list of eighteen engravings follows, for which he desires the licence: some must have been executed later, for they bear the names of Pontius, Bolswert, Witdoeck, and Marinus, engravers not employed by Rubens until long after. There is even an engraving in the list that was never executed, that of a picture of *Hero and Leander*, now lost, which formed part of Rembrandt's collection, and was celebrated in the verse of Vondel and Jan Vos.

The negotiations however, were protracted, and on May 17, 1619, the States of Holland refused Rubens's demands. But he did not regard himself as beaten, and determined to avail himself of the intervention of Sir Dudley Carleton, the English Ambassador to the United Provinces, with whom he had preserved affectionate relations. With his assistance, plates engraved after Rubens's pictures, among others, Soutman's *Wolf Hunt* and *Miraculous Draught*, were presented to several members of the Assembly in order to dispose them favourably to the matter. Among the difficulties that had been raised, difficulties that caused the rejection of his demand, was an objection to Rubens as an alien residing beyond the boundaries of the United Provinces. The artist expressed the most lively astonishment, and remarked that such an argument had never been urged by Princes or Republics, for "they invariably considered it just to provide that their subjects should do no wrong or injury to any person by encroaching on the labours of others. Besides, all potentates, however distrustful in greater matters, are usually of one accord in encouraging and protecting virtue, science, and art, or, at least, they ought to be." Sir Dudley Carleton, with his well proved wisdom, must decide if a fresh application would have any chance of success. If not, Rubens, preferring not to be importunate, would refrain from further proceedings, in spite of his great interest in the matter.[1]

Through the diplomatist's intervention, the States-General agreed on February 24, 1620, to grant, instead of the privileges demanded for a space of ten years, a prohibitive act the effect of which was limited to seven years. The decision was communicated to Rubens by Carleton. Rubens, however, thanked Van Veen for his good offices, declaring himself willing to acknowledge the kindness of the intermediaries to whom he had been obliged to have recourse, while taking care at the same time to distinguish those whose assistance had been actually efficacious.

In order to gain the sympathy of persons who might prove useful, Rubens, directly the completed engravings were published, presented them, with dedications, to influential and well-known men, to intelligent amateurs, or personal friends. He dedicated the *Nativity of Christ* to Pieter van Veen, and the *Descent from the Cross* to Sir Dudley Carleton, "*pictoriæ artis amatori*," as a mark of gratitude for the services they had rendered him. Other plates were dedicated to the Archduke Albert, to Duke Maximilian of Bavaria, to Pequius, Chancellor of Brabant, to Juan Velasco, secretary to Ambrogio Spinola, to

[1] Letter of May 28, 1619.

Jan Brant, the artist's father-in-law, and to L. Beyerlinck, dean of Antwerp Cathedral ; to Adrienne Perez, the wife of his friend, Rockox, he dedicated a small *Holy Family*, and to the brothers Louis and Roger Clarisse, both Franciscans, the *St. Francis Receiving the Stigmata*. The plate of *Susannah and the Elders*, "that rare example of chastity," was dedicated to one of the most distinguished young ladies of aristocratic Dutch society, Anna Roemer Vischer, "the celebrated

THE CART IN THE MUD.

(Facsimile of an Engraving by Schelius & Bolswert after Rubens's picture in The Hermitage.)

star of Batavia, skilled in the practice of many arts, and possessing in poetry a fame beyond her sex."

There was as yet no question of obtaining the privileges demanded by Rubens in Spain or England. He was, therefore, able for the moment to avail himself largely of the assistance of the conscientious engraver who made such rapid and remarkable progress under his guidance. Vorsterman had now familiarised himself with the master's manner, and his quick comprehension of Rubens's directions enabled him to carry them out satisfactorily. His enthusiasm and energy were unbounded, and in 1620 Rubens published nine prints engraved by him after his pictures. Five others followed in 1621 : the *Adoration of the Magi* filled two large sheets, and the six sheets forming the *Battle of the Amazons* were almost completed. Bellori tells us that Van Dyck made a very careful drawing for it, and Mariette, who saw it, said that Rubens's retouchings "would have made it a priceless work had he gone over the whole of the drawing in the same way." It seemed as if these harmonious relations would secure the uninterrupted production of a long series of excellent works. Unfortunately, the connection was not of long duration. In a letter to Pieter van Veen, dated April 30, 1622, Rubens thanks him for some fresh service he had rendered him, and apologises for his inability to present him with some more plates. He continued, " For a couple of years things have been at a standstill in consequence of the caprices of my engraver ; he has fallen into such a state of *exaltation*[1] that nothing can be obtained from him. He declares that it is his talent alone that gives value to the prints. I reply with absolute truth that the drawings are more carefully executed and finished than the prints, and as the drawings are in my possession, I can show them to the whole world." [2] In the letter of June 22, from which we have already quoted, Rubens returned to the subject. He was desirous of presenting Van Veen with the plates he did not yet possess, "and regretted that he had so few, but in consequence of his engraver's aberrations (*disviamento*) nothing had been done for some years." Besides the plates in the list he had given, "was a *Battle of the Amazons* on six sheets, which only required a few days' work, but, although Vorsterman had been paid for it three years previously, he could not prevail on him to give it up . . . and there was no sign that it would soon be finished."

What brought about this state of affairs ? Was Rubens too exigent with his engraver? Such is Mariette's opinion ; in mentioning

---

[1] The letter is as usual in Italian, but the word *abbasia* used here does not exist in the language.

[2] He refers to the drawings made by Van Dyck after the original pictures, and which Rubens gave Vorsterman to work from.

XX

Christ and the Repentant Sinners.

the *Fall of the Rebel Angels*, and praising "the great skill with which the lights and shadows were distributed," he says that " Rubens takes great pains to direct his engraver, who applies himself so closely to his work that his intellect is considerably impaired."[1] Or was Rubens not properly mindful of Vorsterman's vanity and susceptibility, to which the sentence in the letter of April 30, quoted above, bears witness ? It should, however, be remembered that the master usually treated his pupils with the greatest consideration, and that his affectionate sympathy with them was one of the causes of his influence. In this case his interests were so in harmony with his disposition that he would surely have tried to gain the affection of an artist so useful to him, an artist whose talent he largely helped to develop. But Vorsterman was, it must be confessed, of a restless humour. The admirable portrait of Vorsterman Van Dyck has left us in the etching for which Mr. J. P. Heseltine has the original drawing, shows us a handsome head, with refined features and a charming abandon, but with an expression of restlessness. In another portrait, painted by Van Dyck, and engraved by Vorsterman's son, the face is thinner, and the expression sad. The sadness is more marked still in J. Lievens' portrait of the artist, where the eyes are haggard, and the hair dishevelled, while the lines in the forehead cause an expression of suffering and wildness. Vorsterman's humour, in fact, grew more and more sombre, and the mania of persecution from which he suffered led to momentary acts of veritable madness. He evidently considered himself exploited by Rubens, and desired to regain his liberty. Rubens showed great patience in face of tendencies that had been growing gradually worse during three years. But things at last took an almost tragic turn, and though this seems to have disturbed the artist very little, it greatly troubled his friends. A first petition addressed to the Magistracy of Antwerp "by certain persons having the public weal and order at heart," demanded protection for their illustrious fellow-citizen, who "ran great risk of

---

[1] *Abecedario VI.*, p. 93. Rubens dedicated the engraving of the *Battle of the Amazons* to the Countess of Arundel.

his life by the attacks of a certain insolent person who, in the opinion of many, was not quite right in his mind." Rockox, who was then at the head of the Magistracy, did not respond to the petition, either because he did not apprehend any serious danger for his friend, or because Rubens himself intervened. But on a fresh petition, the Infanta Isabella, on April 29, 1622, moved "by the danger which had latterly threatened her 'pensioner' through the attacks of a malevolent enemy who was said to have sworn his death," prayed her *ames* to take precautions that "no hurt or injury might be done to her painter."

News of those events reached Paris, for on August 26, Peiresc wrote to Rubens that "a rumour had just gone abroad that he had been nearly murdered by his engraver"; but that he was greatly surprised at the report since in the letter received from Rubens on the 18th, no mention was made of the matter. It was probably only a passing madness, but however little Rubens may have been disturbed by it, he could not continue his connection with Vorsterman. The latter remained at Antwerp for some time after the rupture, and then, thinking to live down the affair better in England, he spent several years in London. Before the end of 1630 he was back at Antwerp, and inscribed two of his pupils, J. Witdoeck and Marin Robin, better known as Marinus, both of whom engraved Rubens's pictures, on the lists of the Guild of St. Luke. But although he worked very hard until an advanced age, Vorsterman died in poverty, probably in 1675.

Rubens must have felt the loss of such a collaborator very acutely. But he soon found in one of Vorsterman's pupils a worthy representative of his talent. In Van Dyck's portrait of him, Paul du Pont, or Pontius —for so he signed his works—has the appearance of an accomplished young cavalier with an attractive, open countenance. He early acquired a skill which might easily have degenerated into virtuosity, and was certainly marked out to take Vorsterman's place with Rubens. As the master no longer had Van Dyck to provide the engravers with reproductions of his works, he prepared the drawings for them himself, notably that for the plate of the *Assumption of the Virgin,* which was finished by Pontius in 1624. He has more charm though less vigour than Vorsterman, and his plate of *St. Roch* after the fine picture in the Church of Alost equals that of the *St. Lawrence* by his master. But Rubens did not long enjoy the collaboration of Pontius ; the prolonged visits paid by the painter-diplomatist successively to Spain and England, did not allow him to superintend

THE CORONATION OF THE VIRGIN.
(Facsimile of an Engraving by C. Jegher after Rubens.)

the reproductions of his pictures, as he always preferred to do. The engraver then turned to Van Dyck, with whom he had greater affinity, and who benefited in a higher degree than Rubens by the trouble the latter had taken to educate his interpreter.[1] The engravings, the *Virgin appearing to the Blessed Herman Joseph,* and *Christ taken down*

---

[1] Pontius, however, engraved several of Rubens's pictures painted in the last years of his life, notably the *Virgin Surrounded by Saints* in the Rubens chapel of the church of St. Jacques at Antwerp.

from the Cross, both after Van Dyck, are veritable masterpieces equally remarkable for their accuracy and their ease of execution.

The two brothers, Boetius and Scheltius à Bolswert,[1] soon co-operated with Rubens yet more actively. They were Dutch by birth, and first worked at Utrecht in the school of Bloemart ; after a brief residence at Amsterdam they settled at Antwerp. They were united by a perfect community of ideas, and profited by Rubens's advice with equal docility and success ; after carefully observing their works for some time, he recognised that he might fully rely on their conscientious interpretation of the pictures entrusted to them. He retouched only a very small number of their engravings, which were not invariably exact as to details, but which reproduced the general effect of the picture with admirable success. Marked by great breadth and freedom they perfectly suggest the animation and the decorative brilliance of colour of the original paintings. The accuracy of the chiaroscuro is obtained without effort by discreet and skilfully managed contrasts. The deepest shadows in the plates preserve their transparence and velvety richness. The elder of the two Bolswerts, Boetius, who died prematurely in 1634, produced much less than his brother ; but the *Judgment of Solomon*, the *Raising of Lazarus*, the *Coup de Lance*, and the *Last Supper* are reckoned among the best engravings after Rubens. Boetius deserves a place beside Vorsterman for the number and diversity of the subjects he attempted, and for his broad, supple handling. The *Adoration of the Magi*, the two *Holy Families*, the *Conversion of St. Paul*, and the *Lion Hunt* are models of boldness and fidelity. The plate of the *Miraculous Draught* is perhaps still more remarkable. As M. Hymans correctly observes, Rubens rendered it even more imposing than the painting, by making the silhouette of the composition stand out against a more extended horizon of sky and water, doubtless in imitation of Raphael's treatment of the same subject. Scheltius à Bolswert's sense of the picturesque marked him out as the engraver of Rubens's

---

[1] Scheltius is an abbreviation of Chilpéric, and the name of Bolswert assumed by the two brothers is that of the small town in Friesland where they were born.

19

*Study for the " **Holy Family with the Parrot** " in the Antwerp Museum.*

(THE LOUVRE.)

landscapes, and in these plates he showed an entire comprehension of the harmony and diversity of the aspects of external nature. His skies, simple in workmanship, are full of depth, and the skilfully cut lines from foreground to horizon give the impression of the varied elements Rubens introduced into his pictures, indicating them by a sure and vigorous touch as if sporting with his material. The most delicate and evanescent effects, sunbeams filtering through the clouds, or the morning mists rising gently from the water, are accurately rendered, without excessive detail, by a hand at once light and firm.

Many other masters might also be mentioned; Pieter van Jode, for instance, J. Witdoeck for his *Raising of the Cross,* and Marinus who, despite the multiplicity of episode in the *Miracles of St. Ignatius,* and the *Miracles of St. Francis Xavier,* succeeded in preserving the unity of effect, while confining himself to medium values. But although skilled engravers continued to reproduce Rubens's compositions with great talent from 1630 to 1648, the master's control no longer made itself felt in so efficacious a manner. The most brilliant interpretation of his works by engraving belongs to the ten years preceding. But when the school formed under his direction had begun to decline, a new method of reproduction, emanating directly from him, more strikingly characterised his genius. We mean the drawings made on wood by Rubens, and engraved by Christoffel Jegher under his direction and at his expense. These were not indeed, a novelty. Titian, in plates engraved by delle Greche and Boldrini, the *Passage of the Red Sea,* the *Conversion of St. Paul,* and the *Six Saints,* for example, had already demonstrated the power of expression obtainable from a simple outline drawn by a master who determines to reveal his art by elementary means. We learn from Vasari that the painter of Cadore drew the picture of the *Six Saints* on wood himself for others to engrave. Rubens probably saw these notable works of his favourite master's at the shop of Andrea Andreani, a printseller of Mantua; Andreani either copied the prints himself, or had them copied by engravers in his employ, whose works he often appropriated and signed with his name. He had an inventive mind, and reproduced the original drawings in the Gonzaga collection in *camaïeu*, among others those of Raphael, Barroccio, and Parmigiano. A print published by him after Giovanni da Bologna's group, the *Rape of the Sabines*, is remarkable for boldness of effect and handling. But Rubens must have been more particularly interested by his series of plates after Mantegna's *Triumph of Julius Cæsar*. He himself copied a portion of

THE CHÂTEAU OF STEEN

Facsimile of an Engraving by Scheltius à Bolswert. (Vienna Gallery.)

this splendid series of paintings of which Andreani dedicated the engravings to Duke Vincenzo Gonzaga in 1599. Andreani informs us in the dedication placed below Mantegna's medallion at the beginning of the series, that the original pictures "were then in the courtyard of the Palace of St. Sebastian, where they attracted a crowd of admirers," and that he had endeavoured to reproduce their general effect "by means of shadows obtained by a new process" invented by him to give his engravings more relief. The series, executed from the drawings of a Mantuan painter, Bernardo

Malpizzi, reproduce Mantegna's noble, manly figures with the utmost fidelity. The white paper ground, covered here and there with a light wash of bistre, forms the lights, and co-operates with the lines of the engraving to produce a bold rendering of the modelling.

Rubens's eager desire for knowledge doubtless led him to study the conditions of this method, and he himself attempted similar *camaïeux* for several of Jegher's engravings. But it was a process he soon

THE GARDEN OF LOVE (FRAGMENT).
(Facsimile of an Engraving by C. Jegher after Rubens.)

abandoned, wisely preferring wood-engraving; he derived from this self-imposed sobriety greater vigour and style. Thus in the fulness of his maturity, the fine wood-engravings in which Jegher so scrupulously respected the outlines traced by his master, reveal the best results of Rubens's experience, the very substance of his talent. Jegher's engravings are, as M. Duplessis rightly observes, "facsimiles of Rubens." But he neglected nothing that could lend his drawing, all the conciseness and eloquence of which he was capable.

In some of the engravings executed earlier after his pictures

Rubens seems to have foreshadowed this style of work, notably in
Vorsterman's *Pan with Tigers*, a piece of rather soft and summary
execution, and in C. Galle's *Venus suckling Cupids*, where the workmanship is firmer and more delicate. But he aimed at a still greater
simplicity, and as the problem interested him, he preferred to attack it
vigorously. The proofs in the National Library, at Paris, testify to
the trouble he took. He had two proofs pulled successively for the
Holy Family resting in Egypt—judging from the lightness with which the
landscape is treated, it was perhaps engraved on lead—and retouched
them with extreme care, suppressing everything unnecessary. He
made the silhouettes stand out so as to give added animation and style,
he determined the different planes with greater accuracy, and specified as
exactly as possible the nature of the objects. He strove, as if for a
wager, to render the most trifling details by the aid of summary
methods ; he placed a thistle in flower, water-lilies, a bird, a frog in
the *Infant Jesus with St. John* ; a squirrel climbing a branch of the
tree, a serpent coiled in the foreground, butterflies, a lizard, &c., in the
Temptation of Christ. In such familiar details he followed the traditions
of the early masters. But he alone, with rare ability, was able to
preserve the charm and fulness of life in such summary notes. The
more restricted his resources, the more it became necessary to
make the best use of them, to force them to contribute to the
required end. For such a purpose nothing was unimportant, nothing
was left to chance ; neither the relative thickness of the strokes, their
direction, the difference of the workmanship, the rhythm of the lines,
the general aspect of the silhouettes, nor the accentuation of the effect.
Confined within the narrowest bounds, the master showed an ease and
freedom of manner which testifies to the clearness of his mind, and to
the versatility with which he could adapt himself to the most varied
tasks.

The commencement of these attempts should be placed about 1630.
Born on August 24, 1596, at Antwerp, Jegher began to work for the
Plantin Press in 1625 ; but at first he engraved current works
of little artistic value. He was admitted to the guild of St. Luke
in 1627—1628, under the qualification of " a graver of figures on

20

Study of Trees for the " Boar-Hunt " in the Dresden Gallery.

(THE LOUVRE.)

Printed by Draeger, Paris.

wood"; he then proceeded to work under Rubens's direction, and in
1635 the great painter stood godfather to his last child.   The plates
engraved by Jegher bear the signature *P. P. Rubens delineavit et
excudit*, and the special notification *cum privilegiis*, a fact that proves
the importance attached to them by Rubens.   There are nine plates :
the *Temptation of Christ*, and the *Coronation of the Virgin*, after the
paintings on the ceiling of the Church of the Jesuits ; the *Holy Family
resting in Egypt* ; the *Infant Jesus and St. John* ; *Hercules triumphing
over Discord*, after one of the paintings for the great hall of Whitehall
Palace ; the *Chaste Susannah* ; *Silenus* ; the two sheets of the *Garden
of Love* ; and the *Portrait of a Man*, in *camaïeu*.   M. Hymans thinks
that he recognises in the last a reminiscence of a head by Titian,
but we take it to be only a reproduction of a bust of the Duke of
Tuscany as Rubens painted him in the Medici Gallery portrait.

If neither his talent, nor the time he devoted to them is reckoned,
the low cost price of the prints allowed the artist to sell them for a
very small sum.   The books of the Plantin Press have the following
entry under his name on April 12, 1636, for pulling the plates : " Item,
debtor for the printing of 2,000 wood-cuts, with paper, &c., Fl.72 3st."
Conceived and executed in this way, the plates realised admirably the
frequently discussed programme of the popular picture-trade as it
ought to be.   Simple enough to be understood by all, they appealed
to the unlearned as well as to artists, who of course recognised the rare
talent that lay beneath their apparent simplicity.   In art, as in literature,
only the greatest minds are capable of interesting all sorts and conditions of men.   Those works, taking the place of the childish insipidities and banalities usually offered to the masses, which neither
tend to raise the level of their taste nor of their intelligence, formed
a progressive education for the general public, while at the same time
they satisfied those hardest to please.   Their clearness, and the
intentional simplifications made by a man of genius, caused them to be
understood by the least cultured, who thus had perfect works of art
within their reach.   It is satisfactory to find Rubens here consistent
with himself, to see his great mind put its mark on small things which
others would have thought beneath their attention, and to find that he

rightly understood the advantages that might be derived from the
humblest means of expression. Far from despising such means, he
rejoiced in them, transformed them, and made manifest the wonderful
resources they afforded his genius. He imposed his will on his interpreters; severe with himself, he had a right to be exigent with others,
and he set them an example of untiring labour and continual effort
towards perfection. By raising them to his level, he not only
ensured the progress of their talent, but spread the knowledge of
his works over the earth and made the glory of his name to resound
for ages.

HEAD OF AN OLD MAN.
(Facsimile of a drawing in the Louvre.)

END OF VOL. I.